Acclaim for Thomas Berger's
THE RETURN OF |

"In the fictional person of Jack Crabb — the one-hundred-eleven-year-old narrator of *Little Big Man* and now, thirty-five years later, its sequel, *The Return of Little Big Man* — Thomas Berger has created the ideal historical witness to the 19th-century American West."
— Verlyn Klinkenborg,
New York Times Book Review

"Having another chance to hear Crabb spin his tales is a gift indeed."
— William McKeen, *Orlando Sentinel*

"Berger sets the record straight by stretching the truth. Crabb's action-packed, picaresque misadventures are 'accurate' make-believe, blending scrupulous research with partisan imagination. . . . It's not merely local color that makes *The Return of Little Big Man* a highbrow page-turner, though there's lots of that. . . . More enthralling is Berger's playfully serious revisionist history."
— Peter Szatmary, *Houston Chronicle*

"Thoughtful, funny, drenched in irony, and rich in history. Jack Crabb springs from the tradition of David Copperfield."
— Colin McEnroe, *Hartford Courant*

"Berger shows what the historical novel can do in sure hands."
— Nathan Ward, *San Francisco Chronicle*

"If our American history textbooks had been half as interesting as the twisted Old West tales in this fact-based novel, we might've spent more time studying and less time drawing rude pictures in the margins."
— Kevin Giordano, *Maxim*

THE RETURN OF
LITTLE BIG MAN

Also by Thomas Berger

THE RETURN OF
LITTLE BIG MAN

by Thomas Berger

LITTLE, BROWN AND COMPANY

Boston   New York   London

To
ROGER DONALD

Originally published in hardcover by Little, Brown and Company, 1999
First Back Bay paperback edition, 2000

Library of Congress Cataloging-in-Publication Data

Berger, Thomas
The return of little big man / by Thomas Berger.
p. cm.
ISBN 0-316-09844-2 (hc) / 0-316-09117-0 (pb)
I. Title.
PS3552.E719R48 1999
813'.54 — dc21 98-26862

Printed in the United States of America

Contents

| vii |

Prologue

MY NAME IS JACK CRABB, AND IN THE MIDDLE OF THE last century I come West with my people in a covered wagon, at age ten went off with and was reared by Cheyenne Indians, given the name of Little Big Man, learned to speak their language, ride, hunt, steal ponies, and make war, and, in part of my mind, to think like them, and in my teen years was captured by the U.S. Cavalry and went on to have many adventures and personal acquaintanceship with notables of the day and place like General George A. Custer, James B. "Wild Bill" Hickok, Wyatt Earp, and many others, surviving Custer's fight at the Little Bighorn River, which the Indians called the Greasy Grass.

Now I already give a detailed account of these and other episodes of my early life to a fellow name of Ralph Fielding Snell, who come to the old folks' home back a few months, or years — when you're old as me such distinctions don't matter much; I happen to have just turned 112. Yeah, I don't believe it either, but I'm the one that's got to live with the fact.

Snell brought along his recording machine and asked me to talk into it everything I could recall from the old days. My reason for agreeing with this was, pure and simple, I expected to make a buck or two on it, having been on my uppers, so to say, for the previous several decades, owing to the grievous lack of opportunities for a person of my years to make money.

I took a figure out of the air, because when you don't have any funds it is hard to calculate *on the basis of* — which by the way is a mode of thinking that Indians don't use and don't understand whereas whites can't do without it. The sum I come up with for giving my story to this fellow was fifty thousand dollars, which depending on your station in life, and the age, might be a tidy amount or mere pocket change if you was Snell's Dad, according to his son anyway, who claimed to be a victim of the old man's stinginess but apparently never considered trying to earn a penny on his own — until he begun to get big ideas of how much *we*, me and him, would make once *our* story went on the market if only for what happened at Custer's Last Stand as told by the only white survivor, somebody there wasn't ever supposed to be.

"Why, fifty *big ones*" — as he said, pursing his lips in that way people have when using a slang expression they ordinarily don't but hope will make you think they got your best interests at heart — "why, Jack, we might make as much as that for one personal appearance! Uniqueness, Jack, always commands the highest price, and not just in this country of ours but as a principle of Western civilization. A premium is always put on one of a kind, and you, my friend, are that."

My mistake was in saying one word to him before we made a firm financial arrangement, either in my preferred form of cash on the barrel-head or at least a written agreement which covered the expected earnings from such use as he would make of the account of my adventures. I went on and on, yapping into the recording machine and in turn hearing his talk of ever bigger rewards, until by God I even finished the entire Little Bighorn fight, and suddenly I was struck by the feeling that the son of a bitch intended to squeeze me dry of every incident in my entire long life before beginning his book or books, newspaper or magazine versions, movies, lecture series, and the rest of the plans he had for "us," or paying me one red cent.

Now, I had taken Snell as somebody with the character of a chicken feather, but he turned out to be amazingly willful when I finally told him I wouldn't do no more talking. He begged, he howled, he moaned, he once even wept real tears, and when none of that worked, he turned ugly, which in his case meant bringing up the matter of lawsuits, because according to him though neither of us ever signed anything written on paper, what I had spoke onto the tapes constituted a so-called oral contract recognized by any court in the land. Now, starting as a little kid I survived every peril life had to offer, but I tell you there's one kind of menace that paralyzes me with fear. I mean a lawyer. I would say more, but one might get hold of this tape and sue me for my comment and of course win, because the lawyers who invented the system made sure of one fact above all: *the judges too would be lawyers*.

You might think Snell had me by the short ones at this point, but I have hung on through the years by means of more than dumb luck. I'm naturally devious, so much so that had I been born and bred in other circumstances I would probably have become . . . a lawyer. In no time at all, I come up with the perfect scheme to get Snell out of my life: my death.

I mean, a fake one. In the first place, he always figured, at my age, my days was close-numbered, which is why he worked me so hard, trying to get everything down on the tapes before I croaked. All I would have to do to pull off such a stunt is get the people that run the home to back it up, and that was easier than you might think, for the reason that Snell had been able to spend so much time with me, in defiance of the ordinary rules all such institutions have against the inmates doing anything but eat, sleep, dump, and die long before they're old as me, was that Snell was supposed to persuade his Dad, this influential man, to find more funds for the place. I know for a fact that that hadn't yet happened, and from what Snell made known to me about his father's opinion of his pursuits, I was pretty sure it would never occur.

I made my case to the fellow in charge of the section where they kept me, man name of Teague, who was by profession a doctor specializing in mental matters, what I prefer to call by the old term, alienist, because they tend to find things normal that are actually weird, and vice versa, and probably that is the reason why they are so easy to lie to.

"Boy," says I, and if you think he ever took offense at being so addressed you would be wrong because, after money, Teague's great concern in life was age, and not in the sense of the inmates in the old-folks' home but rather his own, given his interest in the young girl volunteers who helped out at the home after school, he being in his late forties, with a spoiled daughter gone off to college and a wife sneering at him with little mean eyes from a picture mounted on his desk. "Boy," I says, "you just listen to me for once. I been trying to tell my story around here for years, and nobody including you believed me, then this fellow Snell shows up and does. That's what's important about him. What's crap is that he's ever going to do anything for me or you. You just get hold of his Daddy and ask if he ever heard of you or your enterprise. And if the son promises to give you a cut out of what he does to market my life, ask him to sign a paper to that effect."

In fact Teague after years of scoffing had give me more respect when Snell begun to come regularly to interview me, so he didn't reject out of hand what I said now. Also, he tended to put a lot more weight in talk of profit than he ever did to the mental affairs that was supposedly his chief stock in trade.

I went on. "Whereas you give me a little help with a certain matter, and I'll be glad to cut you in on the money I intend to make on that story of mine."

Teague's specialty was to appear to be cogitating on what he was told, though I believe that was seldom actually the case, him thinking instead of his own concerns, but this time he showed some real interest, pointy little chin twitching and some vitality coming into his usually ditch-water eyes.

"Jack," says he, dit-dit-dahing on his desktop with a silver pen, "it might astonish you to know I'm not necessarily in disagreement with you, in at least a general, exploratory sort of way. As it happens, becoming somewhat impatient as the months went by, I finally took the trouble to try to get in touch directly with Mr. Armbruster C. Snell, father to our own man, and have been spectacularly unsuccessful. The nearest I could get, by phone or letter, was to a secretary who finally, after some bad-taste banter and outright rudeness, offered to send me an application for a grant from the so-called Snell Foundation, which I might say, after long experience in fund-raising, I had never otherwise heard of, and having since received the application and the accompanying brochure, I understand why. Many of the projects supported seem to be in studies that really don't sound scientifically legitimate: research, by continent, in the effects of cold water on the scrotum, for example. 'The Role of Urolagnia in Social Change.' The masturbatory practices of zoo-born Old World monkeys as compared with those of teenage boys in southeastern Iowa." Teague stopped for a derisive sniff. "In any event, my own application was rejected by return mail."

"Then you get what I'm talking about."

"What I get," said he, pointing his pen at me, "is that we have nothing to expect from the Snells, but that you are projecting for your own unaided efforts some profit, which, if it appears, you may be willing to share with us. What I haven't heard is what you ask of me in return for this theoretical reward."

Notice that, like Snell, he was big on "we's" and "us's" when talking of what advantage might come to him, but used "me" and "I" with regard to his own responsibilities.

I explained my plan, which was this: next time one of the other old coots in the place went under, and if he didn't have no living relatives to show up, why Teague could just tell Snell it was me, and clue in a nurse or two to refer to the stiff in the closed coffin as Old Jack. He'd never have to look at Ralph Fielding Snell again. Meanwhile, I'd steal and hide the recording machine Snell left behind between sessions, and soon as he was out of the picture I'd start in on my recollections again and sell them and give Teague his cut.

It didn't take that alienist long to agree. I don't think he believed any part of the idea except it would get rid of Snell, who made him bitter when he thought of what he had done for the man, which of course was only letting him talk to me, but the doctor belongs to a profession that specializes in doing nothing about anything, taking credit for any success and disclaiming all failure, so this was right up his alley.

So the fake funeral was held, or rather I should say the real services for a young geezer of only ninety-four, who had been a real person, if not historical like me, but had outlived or been lost sight of by everybody he had been related to. Therefore the only people at the services was other old folks from the home, most of them so senile they never knowed or cared who it was for, but it was something to do: waiting your turn to die is real boring.

I stayed holed up in the room where they had the TV set and having no wish to peep in on my own funeral, even if it was phony (because at 112 how much longer can it be till the real one?), or laughed at a Western movie on the tube.

According to Dr. Teague, Snell came to the services and never questioned they was for me, and afterwards he went away and was never seen again though he did call on the telephone from time to time asking if his recording machine turned up. I'm just sorry I told him the earliest part of my story, for there was a lot of interesting stuff in it and I'm too old to go through the whole works again here, with everything else I got to tell. So if you want to hear what really happened at the so-called Battle of the Little Bighorn, go find Snell.*

Where I'm starting in here is not long after that fight, and just after the death of Old Lodge Skins, the Cheyenne chief who was like a father to me.

---

*EDITOR'S NOTE: *The late Ralph Fielding Snell published the reminiscences of Jack Crabb's early life under the title* Little Big Man, *in 1964.*

THE RETURN OF
LITTLE BIG MAN

1

Deadwood

OLD LODGE SKINS WAS THE FINEST MAN I EVER KNEW, and though I spent years apart from him, I guess it was always in the back of my mind that he would live forever, so that any time I needed to, I could go back and find him and get him to set me straight about things of the spirit, which I have found apply to all people whatever their material ways.

He killed plenty of his fellow men and scalped them to boot, and took torture, given or received, in stride, but he had what in my experience up to then, and in fact since, was unique: a firm grasp of a lot of fundamentals, and he always knew where his center was, a knowledge which has eluded me for much of my existence.

I was still in the Indian garb my Cheyenne friends had give me so I wouldn't be slaughtered on the Greasy Grass battleground, and I had stayed for a spell with Old Lodge Skins's little band in the Bighorn foothills. Some of the rest of the big encampment which Custer had rashly attacked went north with Sitting Bull after the fight was over, up to Grandmother's Land, which is what they called Canada, after Queen Victoria, whose image they saw on some medallions presented them in years past by the Canadians.

I had had my own grievance against Custer, whose attack on the Cheyenne camp on the Washita, years earlier, had resulted in the loss of my Indian wife and child, and thought for a while I'd kill him if I could, but I never got the chance, and now that somebody had done it with no help from me, I both lacked a feeling of satisfaction and a sense of purpose as to what I'd do with the rest of my life.

I also had my hide to think of. Now that Old Lodge Skins wasn't there
to vouch for me, some of the other Indians, too young to remember my
years with the Cheyenne, might get to wondering why I was hiding out
amongst them, wearing a breechcloth and leggings, having been too polite for such wonderment while he was alive. Not only do Indians have
natural good manners, but they reverence their elders. I was worried now
that if I went back to camp and told of the old chief's death, some of the
more excitable individuals might believe I rubbed him out and wanted
to take over his power, all ten cents' worth of his material possessions,
and his wives, the latest of whom was quite young and, despite his advanced age, showing a swollen belly.

But I'd have a better chance there than looking for the U.S. Army
dressed as a Cheyenne, and I didn't have no access to a change of
wardrobe at the moment, unless I wanted to ask a warrior to loan me
some of the clothes he stripped off the corpses of the Seventh Cavalry.
Any white soldiers I encountered in the region would want to know
what I was doing there, however I was dressed, and given their state of
mind after the Custer defeat, I would of had a hard time convincing
them, having lost, at least temporarily, my gift for verbal invention.

Indeed the events of recent days had taken the heart out of me. I
hadn't rejoiced at the sight of two hundred dead of my own kind, and
there was plenty red men too who had died at the Little Bighorn, having
been no enemies of mine. Now Old Lodge Skins was gone. I tell you I
could have sat down and cried like a white person, or sung Indian songs
of grief and mourning, or maybe both, but I did neither. That part of the
world was far too perilous to let sentiment affect your provisions for
safety. What I had to do was get out of there pronto, my expressions of
bereavement done in silence, in the heart.

I figured if I could get unharmed down to the new settlements in the
Black Hills, I could rejoin white society in a inconspicuous fashion, for
people was crowding into that part of Dakota Territory on another of
them gold rushes that happened periodically in the West. I had myself
participated in that earlier one at Cherry Creek, Colorado, and after a
lot of panning, got less gold dust than paid for the equipment, but then
made the real discovery: namely, that almost all the money made from
gold strikes is by them that sell miners their supplies, liquor, and women,
at inflated prices.

I managed, traveling on foot and mostly by night, after about a month to get down to the mining town of Deadwood in Dakota Territory, undamaged except for being three-quarters starved because food is hard to come by in the dark without the eyes of a catamount, and I had to eat wild turnips and unripe plums and bullberries still green and hard, along with a lot of bark and weeds. I had no weapon but a real poor knife I had begged off my recent red comrades who despite their big victory was poor as ever, a kind of standard Indian situation.

I was still wearing the skin shirt, which I might of gotten away with, but not so with the breechcloth and leggings. Nor did I have sufficient money for the buying of replacements, and the people of them days, in that part of the world, generally wore the same clothes for months at a time, even when sleeping the night, having no extras, so it wouldn't be easy to swipe anything.

Deadwood at this time was more or less one long ditch of, depending on the weather, mud or dust, lined on both sides by saloons. They had spared from the axe one or two tall pines like what the Indians used for lodgepoles — another reason the Black Hills was precious land, the plains being treeless — a few stores, a number of harlotries, and a bathhouse.

I took the lay of the land in the wee hours of the morning, by which time the streets was deserted and even the soiled doves had turned down the lamps in their rooms, else I might of tried to get past the madam (who was always a hard case) and talk one of the girls into extending me a little loan. I've had some experience of ladies of pleasure and while they won't give sexual favors for free, because that's a professional matter, they are otherwise at least as generous to needy men as are respectable women, maybe more so, having even more reason to look down on the male sex, encountering few customers who are either sober or have bathed in the previous year.

Then I heard a groan coming from inside the bed of a wagon in the street out front of one of the saloons, not so much parked as abandoned, at an angle and without a horse. There was enough moon by which, if I stood on tiptoe and looked over the side, to see some fellow flopped there, either drunk or dying, in them days both being pretty routine in a gold town.

I asks, "Partner, what ails you?"

In response I got a stream of indecent abuse, so apparently he did not require medical treatment. "All right, then, you son of a bitch. I'll fight you," I says. I didn't mean it. It was just a test and earned me some more abuse, but this time it was too slurred even to identify the words.

I boosted myself up into the wagon and proceeded to strip off the drunk's outer clothes, a wool shirt and a pair of pants that stank worse than anything I ever smelled until his filthy long underwear met the air. I drug these garments back up into the high woods back of the town, where I had hid, and soaked them the rest of the night in a cold mountain stream. Next morning they still stank though not as much, and somewhat less as the sun heated up and begun to steam them dry. If they shrunk some as well, all to the good, for I wasn't so large as him I stole them from. I buried my Indian attire and went down into town again, now dressed at least as good as most of the other people on the main or in fact the only drag in Deadwood.

I hadn't ate real food in ever so long, and being that drunk had enormous feet, I hadn't taken his boots but continued to wear them Cheyenne moccasins that might be questioned by the inevitable people who like to make trouble, especially when the liquor's flowing. I was in grievous need of funds, now I was amidst whites once more. In an Indian camp I could of walked right in and got my needs met free of charge, no questions asked, except "Where are you going?" and "What do you want?" which, however they were answered, entitled you to the basics. This was true even of an enemy band: if you could get in before you was killed, they had to be hospitable to you, for being a guest outweighed any other identity. It was owing to such practices that they proved at a disadvantage when dealing with people of a superior civilization.

The wagon where the drunk had been was still in its old position, half blocking the road, but not one person had troubled to move it out of the way, driving their own conveyances through the narrow space left at one side, which meant one-way traffic and a lot of cursing and probably a fight sooner or later, so I put my back into it and rocked the wagon out of the ruts and pushed it to the side of the roadway. I probably wouldn't of been so public-spirited had I not known some qualms about swiping the owner's clothes, for I never been a thief except when I had no other choice. I did this even though he wasn't nowhere in sight.

But then I heard a groan and climbed up and looked into the wagon box, and there he was, in his long underwear (even filthier by day than in moonlight), squinting in the sun under a dirty hand raised as shade. I had left his boots alongside him after determining they wouldn't fit me, and he grabbed them now and pulled them over his filthy socks. He licked his lips and rubbed the cactus patch of his beard. He hadn't yet noticed having no outer clothing.

Then he discerned me and made a sickly grin. "I beg your pardon, sir," says he. "I didn't know it was your wagon. I wasn't trying to steal it, I swear. If I pissed in it, I swear I will clean it up so you'll never know. Same for puking or shitting, though if the last-named, it is likely it's still in my pants." Only now did he notice what he was wearing or rather what he was not, his grin turning more shamefaced, and he felt around under him, like his clothes might be bunched up there.

I didn't feel right, but not so much as to return his shirt and pants, which obviously he didn't recognize. "Tell you what I'm willing to do," I says. "I'll go back to your camp and bring you some articles of clothing."

"I wouldn't think of putting you out further," says he, crawling to one side and throwing a long leg over. The trapdoor in his long johns lacked a button or two and, flapping, afforded the sight of his hairy arse. He dropped to the roadway on hands and knees and stayed that way awhile, groaning and blaspheming. "God damn the people who can sell rotgut of that quality. I could never of gotten away with it when I was in the business myself."

"Let me help you, partner," I says. "You go over and sit on that stump, and I'll go fetch some clothes if you'll tell me where."

He complained again about his entrails, and then he says, "Way it is, I don't have no clothes but them I was wearing last time I looked but have mislaid since." With difficulty he got to his feet by a process you might call climbing up himself.

As his face went past me I peered at him with new interest. His cheeks was smeared with dirt and his eyes was bloodshot. When he grinned all his front teeth was missing. I knew that nose and chin. "Your name wouldn't be Bill Crabb, would it?"

Now you might think he'd be surprised, but instead he says with all the confidence in the world, "The very man. My reputation has preceded me. You have me at a disadvantage, sir. Are you an officer of the law?"

"I'm your brother Jack," says I.

Without a change of expression, he leans over and vomits on the toes of his boots. He straightens up, wiping his lips on the sleeves of the long johns. "You was saying?"

"I'm Jack. Your brother. Long-lost."

It's a real feat to acquire a haughty expression when you're in his state, but I swear he did as much. "Hmm," says he, squinting down that long nose he got from our Pa, whereas mine is snub like our Ma's. "Anybody can claim anything."

"Meaning it's so great to be related to you somebody would lie about it?" I asks, which would of been insulting to anyone of respect, which could never be said of my brother Bill. "Last time I saw you was years ago down on the buffalo range, where you was selling whiskey dosed with rattlesnake heads. I believe it was a gent named Wyatt Earp saved your hide before the buffalo hunters could string you up."

"What I recall about Earp was it was me who taught him to shoot a sixgun." Bill had a real annoying chuckle, which started like a hacking cough and ended in a shrill *hee-haw*. "Shoulda seen him in them days, held a gun like a girl. Didn't know where the trigger was. And he was yella to the core. Nothin' I could do about that."

"What I want to know is, do you recognize me at all?"

Bill stared awhile, twisting his lips. "I'll say this, I can hardly swally, I'm so dry. My memory works better after a drink or three." He purses his lips and looks real smug. "After five or six I'll recall anything I'm told to."

I was standing apart from him, on account of the stench, and luckily so when he had begun to puke. "I doubt anybody but me would claim kinship with you, Bill. There can't be much profit in it." I was sorry I said it as soon as it was out: why assert a connection with a man so you can insult him? But no matter what you said to Bill, he would use it for himself, without doing himself any real good. Funny how that works. Nobody thinks anything of you, so you tell them what they ought to think, and the result is they think even worse. I run into plenty more of that sort in life, but my brother was a notorious example.

Standing there now on the main street of Deadwood in his underwear, from which his behind was showing, he cocks his chin real superior like and says, "You might wanta get your dirty little paws on my claim. It happens to be the richest hereabout. If I wanted to work that hard, I could take out a bucket of dust every day, nuggets the size of peach stones."

"Bill," I says, "I'm dead broke and without prospects myself," realizing however that a give-and-take with him would always be useless. "But we're family, and I'll give you a hand soon as I'm able, which better be soon, for I haven't ate in a while. Now, where are you holing up?"

He takes me down an alleyway between the saloons and around back to where there's a big overturned, rotting hogshead which he called home. There was some burlap sacks inside and a piece of originally red blanket, on top of which laid a yellow dog who bared his teeth at me until Bill told it I was O.K. The animal then come out and smelled my moccasins, no doubt picking up the scent of Indian dogs, for its tail went rigid for an instant, but finally it wagged its tail and went back into the barrel and laid down in the middle, so that when my brother crawled in he had to push it aside. But I guess its idea was to stay as close to him as possible. Dogs make good friends for the likes of Bill, for they don't have a critical faculty and also like stuff that stinks.

"You just stay here awhile," I says, stating the obvious, "and I'm going to see how the Crabbs can come up in the world," stating what might seem laughable at that moment. Bill was somewhat older than me though, I figured, still under forty. I doubt he would ever recognize me as the little kid who went off with the Cheyenne, but when you're in his condition what do you care who your well-wishers are? I had seen Bill a couple times in the years between, selling whiskey to the Indians who hung around some fort and then again in that incident involving Wyatt Earp some time after, but to be fair, he hadn't never recognized me and I sure didn't ask him to.

So leaving my brother where he was, sleeping with his dog — to tell you the truth, it looked real snug in there — I went out to the main street, wearing his clothes, still slightly damp from their overnight soaking. I felt more hopeful than I had in some time, being reunited with Bill, who in better circumstances I would no doubt have avoided any association with. But I decided now to straighten him out, make some money somehow, and acquire a place for us to live. Deadwood seemed as good as any, for it was all new, such as it was, where everybody was starting out more or less from the same level. What I had to do was figure out a profession for myself. Looking along that street, all that immediately come to mind was something connected with whiskey, gambling, and whores. There was plenty room for legitimate business establishments, but to set up a shop you had to be grubstaked to lay in your stock, and credit is mighty hard to come by in a gold-strike area. At the moment I didn't look much better than Bill had when wearing the same clothing, too big on me besides, and I had not washed a lot on the route down here. I hadn't shaved in ever so long, either, but the way my whiskers growed I still looked more dirty than bearded to the quick glance I give my visage now and again when kneeling to drink in a stream slow-moving enough to reflect an image.

I ain't mentioned that as of midmorning the street was crowded with men and vehicles. I hadn't paid much attention to them while attending to my brother, and if anybody was offended by or even noticed him dressed in his underwear with his arse showing, they didn't indicate such. That kind of place is made up entirely of greedy people who can only see a dollar and for most of them even that is only a dream. Fact is, most people who run to gold strikes was losers.

Now, while I'm standing there on the board sidewalk in front of an establishment bearing a crude handpainted sign, "The Congress," which was more likely to be another saloon rather than a legislative chamber, though glass windows was rare in Deadwood, so I couldn't see inside, who should step out through the door but a frock-coated tall figure who was right familiar to me.

Under the broad-brimmed sombrero, he looked considerably older than when I had last seen him just the previous early spring in Cheyenne, Wyoming Territory. His hair was still shoulder-length, but it had gone wispy at the ends, as was his drooping mustache, and his once clear gray-blue eyes was red-rimmed and kinda watery. His face was real pale. That long hooked nose of his had got pointier.

"Wild Bill Hickok," I says. "So you got here too." Now that I seen him, I recalled we had talked of prospecting for gold in Deadwood.

The keen nostrils at the end of that long nose was twitching, and he backs away. "Is that stink coming from you, hoss? Have you shat in your clothes?"

I was more than embarrassed. "I'm down on my luck, Bill," I says, "wearing borrowed clothing and ain't ate in some time. I don't know if you heard yet, Custer and most of the Seventh was rubbed out by the hostiles up in Montana. I happened to be there but got away with my life due to a Cheyenne I knowed. . . ."

Hickok had backed away a few more paces as I spoke. He was shaking his head, his long tresses brushing the shoulders of his swallowtail. "Hoss," he says, breaking in, "I never shot anyone for telling tall stories of that nature, which I've done myself to greenhorns, but I've knocked him down. If a handout is what you need, then you oughta ask and not try to make a fool of me." He sweeps away the coat with his left hand and plucks a silver dollar from the lower pocket in his fancy vest. Bill was famous for his sartorial tastes, as well as his personal cleanliness. "I will stake you to a bath, shave, and a trim."

I didn't persist with my story but right away says, "Thank you kindly. I wonder if you would mind if I get something to eat with some of the money?"

Wild Bill slowly blinks those sore-looking eyes and goes again into the vest pocket with two left fingers and finds me another dollar. This one felt funny, and I looked and saw it was knicked at one edge, but I guess it was still good, and I thanked him again.

"After a plate of bread and beans, you'll have enough left to pick up a shirt and pants where they sell used clothes, down the street. Then burn what you're wearing now."

He turns and moves away, though not with the assured stride of old. Also he stayed on the walk, instead of the middle of the street, which he had once been famous for using so he could scan the area for possible bushwhackers and also keep a certain distance between him and them who might fire on him from ambush. But one thing I was sure about: namely, that when he played poker he still sat with his back to a wall.

I had no reason not to act on his suggestion, having some pride in my appearance when I could afford as much, and I returned to my brother's barrel-home so clean-washed and -shaved I bet I'd have to identify myself to him all over again. I was wearing a pair of canvas pants in reasonably good condition and almost clean along with a flannel shirt that was wore through at the elbows but had no discernible odor. These with the other goods heaped in the tent of the old-clothes dealer had been sold by gold-rushers who had run out of funds, either because they never panned any dust or lost it all gambling. Imagine what the original owners had got for a pants and shirt that cost me seventy cents altogether. That dealer throwed in a beat-up old hat with so greasy a sweatband I tore it away.

I had enough left for coffee and two orders of beans and bread, the second of which I made sandwiches from and brung them back for my brother Bill. Even so, believe me when I say prices was greatly inflated at Deadwood, as at all gold towns.

When I got to the hogshead, no Bill was in evidence, his yellow dog being there all alone and lonely. It never snarled at me this time, knowing me now, but sank its head real low and whimpered.

The one order given me by Wild Bill I had not obeyed was to burn the pants and shirt I took off, for they belonged to my brother and was balled under my arm at the moment.

"Dammit," I says now to the dog, "where has he gone in his underwear?" The answer I got was another whine. After the kindly face and big brown eyes, what was most noticeable on this animal was his prominent ribs, all of which you could count at a distance. "I'm going to look for him. While you're waiting, eat yourself one of these bean sandwiches." Now that was a real sacrifice, for it had been all I could do to save some food for Bill, being still famished myself, but I took this here dog as part of my family responsibility, and he was likely to be more reliable than my brother.

He swallowed that sandwich in one and a half bites, living for the instant as a dog does, and in expectation of more, but I put the other sandwich in the pocket of my pants, which as always was too roomy for me, cinched at the waist with a length of rope and folded up at the cuffs, and went out along the street, trying each of the saloons, of which already at that time there must of been two dozen or more within a mile and a half. As time went on, somebody told me at a later day, the number rose to seventy-six. Some of them I looked into had a bar consisting of a wooden plank supported by a barrel at either end, a bottle or two, and tin cups you'd never see washed out between drinkers if you watched all day. They didn't have no windows usually, so was lighted by oil lamps at high noon in blazing sunshine outdoors. The bartender might not have a towel or apron — fact is, he was often dressed like his customers, even to the hat — but he was never without a prominent shotgun, leaning close to hand. This was used mostly as a pointer to indicate the door when the level of bad feeling amongst the drunks sounded like it would take another form than mere verbal abuse. But since only two or three people per week was shot to death in Deadwood at this time, it was not considered necessary yet to hire an officer of the law.

I didn't have no more money and therefore could not afford a drink, which in some of these places was as much as a dollar per shot, being at that price presumably something on the order of real whiskey, whereas the cut-rate joints, at fifty cents per, no doubt served up the kind of concoction of tobacco juice, gunpowder, pepper, and snake venom which my brother Bill had sold as liquor in his heyday.

I hadn't looked in more than three or four places when through the open door of the next one in line come the hurtling figure of somebody wearing only a suit of filthy underwear, followed by the sole of a big boot. My brother had enough momentum to take him on across the walk and down the couple feet to the dust of the street, which in that spot was actually a mess of mud, probably because a horse had staled there.

Now I tell you Bill was the sort of person who if you owned a place of business you wouldn't want as a customer, for stench and appearance aside, he likely wouldn't have no money and would be there only to beg, borrow, or steal. But he was my brother, and that you can't let your kin be treated badly by others is a self-evident truth. So after I had pulled Bill out of the muck, propped him up against the wheel of a parked wagon, and put his clothes in his lap, I told him for godsakes stay put for a spell, and I went into that saloon to deal with the son of a bitch who had, if for understandable reasons, insulted my family.

But this was the darkest place I had been yet, and for a while I couldn't make out anybody but a table full of poker players back a ways, under the light of a hanging lamp, and one of them was Wild Bill Hickok.

For a number of reasons I did not want to disturb Wild Bill, who took his poker real serious, so I postponed dealing with the matter of honor and returned outside, where I expected I would not find my brother, but in fact Bill was still slumped where I left him. I got him to his feet and into the shirt and pants, and maintaining as little physical contact with him as I could, steered him back home through the wheeled and pedestrian traffic, and more than once he lurched towards oncoming wagons but was snatched back at the last minute and was kicked once by a horse and again by a cursing man who however was belted with both a pistol and an unscabbarded butcher knife, so my protests would of been foolish.

I got Bill back to his barrel and tried to feed him the bean sandwich, but he got stubborn like a drunk will and clamped his jaws together so tight I would have needed a crowbar to pry them open. I ended up giving half the sandwich to the yellow dog and ate the rest myself. With the Indian knife I sliced some extra material from the tails of my too-long shirt and trouser bottoms, and used it for bonds to fasten Bill's ankles together and also his wrists, so he couldn't untie the former, and telling him to sleep it off went back to the saloon known as the No. 10, which before long was the most famous in Deadwood.

Wild Bill was just leaving the poker game as I arrived, and was asking them standing at the bar if anyone wanted to take his seat, and one fellow went over and pulled the stool up to the table. He had a sandy mustache and there was something wrong with his eyes too, which in his case was slightly crossed.

"You're greatly improved, hoss," Wild Bill says to me, inspecting me at close quarters. "You was the worst I seen until that drunk staggered in here in his underwear a while ago and Harry kicked him out the door." He indicated the bartender with a nod, and he rubs his sore eyes with the back of his left hand. He buys me a shot of whiskey, which I drank real slow, as I had not tasted any for ever so long. Even so I felt its vapors hit my brain shortly after the first sip.

Wild Bill introduced me to the bartender, man name of Harry Sam Young, and told me he knew him too from back in Kansas.

"This town's full of friends," he went on. "California Joe, Colorado Charley Utter, White-Eye Jack Anderson, they're all here. But the real news is I recently got married." He got a refill from Harry Young. I was still working on my first. "Which reminds me." He looks around like he's worried somebody's listening in, and decides maybe they might yet, and asks me to step aside for a confidential matter.

Coming into the bright sunlight from a semidarkness smelling of lamp oil, liquor, and sweat was probably more the cause of my swimming vision than even the fiery hooch (which in case you never knew it is an Indian word, though not Cheyenne).

Wild Bill's own eyes was squeezed into sightless slits, and it's funny that what I thought of was how helpless he would be if someone was to shoot him at such a moment.

He takes me by the elbow of my shirt and bends down and in a subdued voice he says, "Hoss, I seem to recall being in your company once in a certain kind of establishment, or am I wrong?"

"That's right, Bill, you and me went to a whorehouse."

He flinches and says, "Keep your voice down, willya?"

I had not been shouting, but I did as asked, and went on. "That was right after you shot Strawhan's brother, which was the damnedest thing I ever witnessed. Not only did he have the drop on you, he was about to shoot you in the back. You seen him in the mirror. My God, you was fast."

He showed a thin smile, lifting his head and opening his eyes away from the sun. "I'm not that good any more, hoss. I don't say I'm bad, but I don't see as well as I used to. They still get me to shoot coins on edge, but nowadays it's dollars, not the dimes of the old days."

I reflected that one of the dollars he give me had that nick in it. "I saw you put ten loads into the O in the sign across Market Square in K.C., a hundred yards away."

Wild Bill continues his distant smile. "The Odd Fellows' sign," says he. "I couldn't do that nowadays. I'm taking something for my eyes. It makes me pale, and maybe it is doing something to my well-being. . . . But here's what I wanted to tell you, hoss: If you remember that sporting house, well, I'd as soon you forgot about it insofar as I am personally involved."

Now Wild Bill Hickok wasn't the sort of man from who you would deny a favor requiring as little effort as this, so I hastened to reassure him.

"I got nothing against sporting women," he goes on. "Some of them been real good friends of mine. Fact is, the wagon train we brought up here from Cheyenne stopped at Laramie and loaded on Dirty Emma, Sizzling Kate, and others who have set up shop down the street here, should you have a natural need." Now his smile became something you might of seen on a preacher. "Now I'm married I have changed my ways." He looked real high-minded, lofty eyebrows, pious mouth under the drooping mustache. "Agnes," says he, "owned her own show, she and her previous husband, one of the noted clowns of the time until some little bastard shot him through the heart on account of not getting in free one day."

Wild Bill had told me about Aggie on a previous occasion, so I was able to say, "I do believe she is a celebrated equestrienne," using the word as he originally did, and he was right pleased now.

"That's right, hoss, also a tightrope walker, but them days is behind her now. You might of heard of Adah Isaacs Mencken, who is renowned for a theatrical presentation called *Mazeppa*, where she is tied buck naked to a horse that runs around the stage. Well, those who saw both of them in the part gave their preference to Agnes, and she never rode naked, I'll tell you that: she always wore tights that looked that way." He frowns. "I don't even like that, for I know there were sons of bitches who *thought* she was naked." He clears his throat. "Well, like I say, that's a thing of the past. No wife of James B. Hickok, Wild Bill, is ever going out to work. I want her home in our little nest, sweet Agnes of mine."

He had taken to calling himself by the whole two names together, like it was some legal matter of correct identification, and maybe it was, for

Wild Bills were all over the West in that era, at least one of them a white man who claimed to have joined the Cheyenne at an early age — no, not me, but obviously some goddam liar.

"I'd be proud to meet her, Bill. Has she come along with you to Deadwood? Or is she back in Cheyenne?"

Wild Bill snorted. "Neither, hoss. She's a fine lady. I wouldn't let her set foot in a hog wallow like this. I just come here to make money. She's back in what they call the Queen City, Cincinnati, Ohio, waiting for my return."

I figured she must be a real beauty to tame him like this, but not to compare with Mrs. Elizabeth Custer, who I seen only once, but long enough so that she become my ideal of femininity. Now of course she would be a widow, which you might consider a rotten way for me to think at this early time, but in fact I couldn't imagine the likes of Libbie Custer looking in my direction and even seeing I was there.

"Say," Wild Bill says now, "come on back to my wagon and I'll show you her picture."

We walked not far along Deadwood Canyon to what was still then the outskirts of town and found there, amongst a goodly number of tents that constituted the residential district, a covered wagon that was a bit smaller than the vehicle in which me and my family come West years earlier. I believe this one was from the Army.

Bill climbs up inside and comes back out with a photo, which he hands down. "Now tell me if that isn't the finest-looking woman you ever seen."

Wild Bill was not the kind of man I would have disagreed with even if he wasn't lovesick, so I was as complimentary as I could be, but as it happened I admit I found his Agnes to be remarkably plain in appearance, at least as she was represented by the camera, which is not to say I doubted what he said about her talent.

"What you might wonder is why a person of her high type would be interested in me," he says with what I took as real modesty for a man many ladies had had a crush on, including my own crazy sister Caroline, but then I never knew any dead shot on either side of the law that did not attract more women than anybody peaceful. "I'm trying my hand at something more dignified than what I done previously, and also more profitable. You can't put aside much on a lawman's eighty-to-a-hundred per month, and you can always get shot for your trouble."

He brought a bottle with him when he clumb down from the wagon, and we sat on a couple wooden boxes, former Army ammunition crates. He took a big gulp himself and then passed the bottle to me.

That whiskey was nowhere near the quality of that which Harry Sam Young had poured for us at No. 10, but Wild Bill didn't seem to notice. I could hardly get it down or keep it there.

"I ever tell you about my time as a showman?" Wild Bill asks.

"Wasn't you at Niagara Falls with a herd of buffalo?"

"That's right," he says and takes another slug from the bottle. "But later I traveled around the East for a time, performing in a stage play with Bill Cody, but I forgot my lines half the time even though they was the same night after night and I was playing myself, so it didn't call for much acting on the face of it. But the fact is, hoss, the hardest thing I ever tried to do was to be a make-believe Wild Bill Hickok. It got to be too much for me to be the real myself pretending to be the fake Wild Bill, speaking words written by some little fellow that never been west of Chicago, and shooting blank rounds, which foul up a barrel real awful. I got to drinking too much and having some fun to pass the time, like using live ammunition and firing too close to the toes of them real actors, and they whined to Cody, who asked me to tone it down. But I couldn't take it for long, even though the pay was real good, the best I ever made. I ain't got Bill Cody's way with horseshit. Nothing against Bill, God bless him, he always dealt straight with me, but he's got a natural talent for showmanship. I don't, that's for sure." He swallowed more of that awful whiskey and was just offering me the bottle when somebody spoke nearby.

"This is what you been doing?" asked a peevish voice. It come from a fellow not much bigger than me but all duded up in fringed buckskin and wearing a pearl-handled pistol in a fancy holster held by a tooled belt with an enormous silver buckle. His hair was long and fair, as were his mustache and pointy little beard. "Sitting here with him and that bottle?"

"Simmer down, Charley," Wild Bill said in a mild tone. "Me and him are old friends from Kansas. Shake hands with — "

But as this dandy turned up his nose at the idea of meeting me, the shaking did not take place.

"My pardner Colorado Charley Utter," Bill said, when the other went into a tent that was pitched nearby. Most of the other Deadwood tents was torn and tattered, but the canvas of this one looked brand-new and was taut-stretched and well pegged. "We got plans for an express service between here and Cheyenne."

I had never seen Wild Bill so bluffed by anybody else. The next instant, out comes Charley Utter from his tent, saying, "Goddammit, Bill, you been sleepin' in my blankets again? They're all messed up."

Wild Bill smirks and shrugs. "I'm real sorry, pardner. They're nicer than that scratchy old Army blanket of mine."

"I want you to stay out of there," Utter says.

In the old days Wild Bill would have laughed in the face of a little fellow like that, as he had laughed at me first time I flared up at him. But now the once fearsome gunfighter only repeated his apology. When Utter went back into the tent, where he could be heard fussing with his property, Bill says to me, "He's a good friend and has got a real head for running businesses. My own specialty is the ideas: I don't always have the knack for the practical details." He tilts his head back till the rear of the brim of his big hat, touching him between the shoulders, stops him, at which he removes the sombrero so as to align his throat with the verticaled bottle, and he drains the remaining liquid in the latter down the former. Now that he is momentarily bare-headed for the first time since I become reacquainted with him, I see his hair is thinning in front, and I got a right funny feeling, for Custer too was losing some hair on top, which is why the Indians claimed they never scalped him. Never knowing baldness themselves, redskins see it as still another strange and distasteful thing about whites, whereas they find cutting off an enemy's crowning glory and hanging it on their belt perfectly normal and even admirable, and when I lived as a Cheyenne I admit so did I.

Having emptied the bottle, Wild Bill tossed it over his shoulder into the area between his wagon and Charley Utter's tent, and no sooner than he did so, out come Colorado Charley, who picked it up and brought it back to hand to Wild Bill without a word.

"Oh," Wild Bill says. "Sorry about that."

"If you're back here this time of day," says Utter, "you already lost the money you was advanced."

Hickok replaced his hat. "You wouldn't believe the hands I had, Charley."

Charley hooked his thumbs in that fancy gunbelt. He *hmmphed* and said, "It's like that every single day, ain't it?"

Wild Bill got to his feet real slowly. He didn't seem to be drunk though he had undoubtedly been drinking for hours before he topped it off with the remainder of that bottle. But he could still apparently hold his liquor as of old.

He tossed the empty bottle up into the wagon and clumb up to follow it. "I'm going to catch forty winks, so I'm rested for tonight's game." Then, on hands and knees, he looked down at me. "Hoss, if you ain't got a place to stay, why there's lots of room here, and I got an extra blanket if you don't mind the smell of horse."

"Right nice of you, Bill," says I. When he had crawled back into the interior, I told Colorado Charley I wouldn't do it if *he* objected, for I wasn't in no position to make enemies at this time.

"Hell, that's between he and you," Charley said in a kinder tone than he had used theretofore. "I noticed you ain't a drinker."

He had been watching Wild Bill from his tent. "Never to excess," I said, which was true except when it wasn't.

"You don't look like you've had the best luck lately."

"Thank you for noticing," I says, but then decided it sounded too sarcastic, so added: "That ain't the half of it."

"Well, spare me the facts," Charley says hastily. "I got an offer for you. There are them in Deadwood who like it fine without law, and maybe I agree with them up to a point, but some think Wild Bill come up here to be marshal, like he was in Abilene, and will clean up the town. They're wrong about that, but I hear they might be gunning for him. Nobody's going to come at him straight on, I tell you that. He might of lost some of his powers, but he's still better than anybody hereabouts." Charley fingered his fair mustache and goatee. I found it amazing that he looked as clean and shiny as he did in that place. "What worries me is he might get absentminded while playing cards." He glanced with concern up at the wagon and spoke in a lowered, confidential-type voice. "Also lately he's been feeling real low. He told me the other day he thinks his days is numbered."

"He ain't the Wild Bill I once knowed," I told him. "I'll swear to that. But maybe he'll change if he begins to win at poker."

Colorado Charley screwed his face up. "He told me he wrote a letter to the same effect to that new wife of his. Now, ain't that some weddin' present!" He had raised his voice some to say this, and he glanced up at the wagon again as he lowered it. "Now, what I want to offer you . . . your name is — ?" I told him, and he continued. "I'll pay you to keep an eye on him. I'll give you a dollar a day, which seems to me mighty generous considering all you got to do is watch his back."

I can't be condemned for trying to sweeten the deal. "Bodyguarding Wild Bill Hickok ought to pay a little better than that."

"Did I say bodyguard? Bill don't need none, and from the looks of you, you couldn't do much anyway, and I ain't going to supply you with no firearms. What I'm talking about is just keeping an eye on him — and just when he's playing cards. Rest of the time I'm with him, or California Joe Milner or his other friends. You see something funny going on behind his back, you give a holler. He'll do the rest himself. He can still use a gun better 'n anybody who'd go up against him: he can see that good."

I didn't like his insults, but a dollar a day would keep me and my brother going till something better turned up, so I accepted his offer but did ask why he trusted me. How'd he know I wasn't one of them who wanted Wild Bill rubbed out?

"You'd of made your move by now," says Colorado Charley.

He wasn't necessarily right about that, but not wanting him to mistrust me after all, I didn't say anything more on the subject, but I did promise to show up that evening at the No. 10 Saloon and watch Wild Bill's back, then walk him home and collect my dollar.

I went back into town now and found my brother sleeping in his hogshead, tied up the way I left him, and that dog pranced out, expecting me now to bring him food on every visit. Seeing I didn't have none for him, he goes back to curl up alongside Bill. I could have used a nap myself, having been up most of the night on my reconnoiter of Deadwood by moonlight and the trip to and from the hills, but I could not of stood the smell inside the barrel even if there would have been room for me, so I sat outside with my back against the staves, and napped off and on, but I was too spooked by my recent experiences to sleep soundly with my brother's peace of mind.

2
Aces and Eights

GOT TO NO. 10 BEFORE WILD BILL SHOWED UP, BUT
the poker game was already in progress. I explained to Harry the bartender I was working for Colorado Charley Utter, but he said I
couldn't sit there unless I was drinking, so I waited outside till Wild
Bill showed up, which he did before long, looking none the worse for all
the liquor he had drunk earlier.

"Charley says you're working for us now," says he.

"You know about that?"

"I'm not too proud to have somebody watching my back. Way I've
lasted up till now is not because I'm faster or shoot straighter than every
one of them I've gone up against. It's because I never lie to myself. I
never lied much to others, but I would do so if my life depended on it,
like everybody else. But not to myself."

"All I can do is holler," I told him. "I ain't got no gun."

"Just as well, hoss," said Wild Bill. "You might shoot yourself in your
manly parts."

This gibe irked me some, for it was him, back in Kansas City, who
taught me to use a pistol well. "Your pal Harry Sam Young won't let me
hang around without spending money, and Charley won't be paying me
till later."

"I'll speak to Harry," Wild Bill said. "Now, about Charley, such money
as he advances me for cards ain't his own but from the funds of our partnership. I threw my savings into the pot, which he manages better than
I ever could, but I'm not on his charity."

This information made me feel better about him. "I ain't forgot I owe you two dollars, Bill."

"You'll pay me when you can," says he and saunters through the door into No. 10 looking more like the old Wild Bill than I seen him for a while. One of the fellows at the card table wanted to vacate his stool immediately though I don't think the hand was finished, so influential a presence was Wild Bill Hickok, but the latter grandly waved him down and stepped over to the bar, where Harry had already poured him one.

Wild Bill swallowed the whiskey, then throwed a thumb towards me and says, "This little fellow is working for me 'n' Charley. Put him on my tab, but don't serve him so much he can't see." He laughed at that statement.

As it happened, all I swallowed that evening was some of the coffee which Harry, like all bartenders I ever met, drank instead of what he sold. Unfortunately they didn't serve no food there, and I guess Harry had already ate his supper, so there wasn't anything I could mooch. I just stayed there, watching Wild Bill's back for hours while they played hand after hand, with the usual curses, grunts, and other such noises made by the participants that don't mean nothing whatever to anyone not in the game.

But what was special, I gathered, was that Wild Bill was winning for a change. After a while, one of the original players, being busted, had to drop out, and the same short fellow with the sandy mustache and slightly crossed eyes who had took Wild Bill's place the day before come over from where he had been watching the game to claim the vacated stool, as he had taken Wild Bill's place that afternoon. But now Wild Bill stayed in the game, winning hand after hand, his luck still holding, and before long this man too was cleaned out, and he pushed away from the table, looking more sad than mad.

"Damn," says he, head down, "I ain't got enough left to get a bite to eat."

Wild Bill stood up too. "Look here, Jack, I done well tonight after a long run of bad luck. I'd be proud to stake you to your supper." He picked up some of the piled coins in front of him and proffered them to this Jack McCall, as Harry Young told me he was called.

McCall took the money, nodding, still not looking at Wild Bill, and left the premises.

To the other players Wild Bill said he was turning in, being not as youthful as he once was, but tomorrow would give them all their chance to get even.

We walked back to the wagon. It was still early enough on the mid-summer evening to see our way without a lantern.

"You must of give me good luck, hoss," said Wild Bill. "I always square my debts, so you're getting a dollar bonus for tonight, and I'm also canceling what you owe me."

"That's mighty generous of you, Bill."

"Well, I want to do it while I can, for luck that's good today won't necessarily hold on forever, or even tomorrow." He was taking such long strides, tall as he was, I had to make two for every one of his. "Custer's luck," he says. "He was famous for it, till it went bad."

I considered trying again to tell him a first-person account of the Little Bighorn fight, but decided against taking the chance as yet, for I needed this job.

"I believe you was acquainted with him."

"And liked him," said Wild Bill. "I had to shoot a couple of his men when four or five of them jumped me once in Hays, and I had a difference of opinion one time with his brother Tom, but the General was always mighty nice to me. Couple years back, he complimented me in the written word, or so I was told. His lady is a fine woman, and now a widow at a tender age, poor little gal."

"Beautiful," I says with feeling. "I saw her once."

"Well," Bill says with that new sanctimoniousness of his, "you might be right about that, hoss, but I am married to the most beautiful lady in the world myself."

I figure his eyesight must be even worse than I thought, on the basis of that photograph of his Aggie, but naturally did not say anything, and we had by now arrived at the camp, where I was looking forward to getting my wages from Colorado Charley.

But when I peeked into the door of his tent, the interior of which was arranged neat as a hotel room in a city, with a cot and square-folded blankets, a leather-strapped trunk, and a nice hide rug on the ground, no Charley was in evidence.

When I informed Wild Bill, who was still standing there, breathing the evening air with apparent satisfaction before mounting the wagon, he said, "He's probably down to the bathhouse. He missed his bath this morning, being too busy at the time. He takes one every day whether he needs it or not. He's famous for that habit."

"I thought the same was true of yourself, Bill."

"Not to that extreme," says he, and by now it was getting too dark to accurately judge by his expression if he was joking. He goes into the pocket of the frock coat where he had put his winnings and withdraws two dollars and drops them clinking into my now outthrust hand. "There you go, hoss. After you drink it all up, if you want to come back and bunk in the wagon, kindly don't kick me when you climb in. You'll find that extra blanket in back."

I went back to town to find the place, a kind of lean-to open on three sides, where a burly woman, one of the few females in Deadwood at the time not working as a harlot, cooked up beans and the stone-heavy loaves she called bread, in which you was likely to find not just hairs but whole strands as well as other substances not so easily identified.

I was still real hungry. "Ain't you got no meat?" I asked the cook.

"Had some couple days back but et it myself," says she, shifting the wad in her jaw and spreading the feet beneath her so she could spit between them. I reckon the unusual flavor her beans had was from spattered tobacco juice. I've ate a lot worse than that when famished, which like the Cheyenne who raised me I so often was as a young man. "It wasn't no goddam good, so you didn't miss nothing. And you could not of afforded it nowhow."

I've got a policy of seldom passing up an insult when I'm in a position to answer, so I says, "You think you run the grand dining room of the Palace Hotel?"

She spits again, this time right near me, and grins with her teeth brown in the light from the lantern that hung from a nail in a support pole. "I got a well-to-do sweetheart. He's made a big strike lately."

No matter how dubious you get about the likelihood of anybody finding significant amounts of gold on his own, there's something magic about the very sound of the word that causes the coldest heart to pound, probably because if you find some of that substance you don't have to go to no further work to make it salable. Everything else that brings in a profit requires more work than separating gold dust from sand by shaking a pan. So for a minute there, picking up my order of bread and beans, I considered staking a claim of my own next day.

But then this large woman wipes her hands on her stained apron and says, " 'Course, he's never told me the truth about anything else, so maybe he never paid five dollars for that beefsteak but bought it off some Indin for a drink of whiskey. It tasted like real old bear."

Back at the barrel all was as before. My brother Bill was sleeping so quiet, in the same position as earlier, that I thought maybe he had up and died, and there wasn't enough light in there to see if he was breathing, but when I poked his foot with mine he sighed and uttered an indecent word. The dog of course had been all over me right away and once again got more than his share of the grub I carried.

I left my brother in as good a situation as he was likely to find at the moment and went back to get a night's rest in Wild Bill's wagon, which was real cozy in the rear where I slept. Wild Bill seemed asleep when I stepped past him, and I thought if I could so easily gain access to the wagon, so could an assassin, but Colorado Charley had not hired me to guard him twenty-four hours a day, without a weapon, and I was real tuckered out by then.

I had a good sleep that night, waking up at dawn to look over and see Wild Bill's blanket already empty. By time I got up and out and took a leak, careful to keep well away from Charley Utter's tent, and returned, I see Wild Bill's tall figure oncoming at a brisk pace up the gulch.

"You're up and at 'em," I says when he gets there.

"Generally at first light," says he, "I trot down for a wake-me-up."

"Get your coffee from that big gal who cooks beans?"

"Whiskey's what I mean, hoss. Coffee'd put me back to sleep."

Colorado Charley come out of his tent at this point, looking bandbox-fresh as always, and according to Wild Bill went off to arrange a competition in which their pony express went up against a rival outfit to see who could run the Cheyenne newspaper up to Deadwood the fastest.

I throwed some water on my face from the rainbarrel Wild Bill pointed out, and having got his schedule said I'd see him around noon at No. 10 and went into town.

I never knowed what I'd find whenever I returned to my brother's location, but this time I was pleasantly surprised to see him standing erect and sniffing the air, looking healthy and cold sober.

"Well sir, Jack, what have you been up to?" says he, with a gap-toothed grin amidst the mess of whiskers that constituted his lower face.

"You remember me."

"From recent days," says he. "That wagon-train story of yours is another matter."

"I got me a job," I says. "It don't pay much but will feed us till something better comes along. I know some people starting up an express between here and Cheyenne and Laramie. If it pans out, they'll probably be hiring."

Bill raises his chin in a superior way and says, "I was going to offer you a partnership in my claim. Due to circumstances beyond my control I lost my pan and shovel and the wood I had bought for a sluicebox, and all, and if you could help me with — "

"Goddammit, Bill, I'm trying to be serious. You ain't got no hopes for gold. Just forget about that."

"It's why I'm here at all, Jack," he says loftily.

"You're laying around drunk for days on end."

"That's just in my off time," says he. "I'm usually out working my claim."

I tell you, it hadn't been that long since I found my brother and already I was real sick of him. I glanced around and asked, "Where's your dog?"

"How do I know?" says Bill. "I never asked him to join up with me. He goes off when he feels like it. Maybe he's giving it to some coyote girlfriend."

"I got enough money to take you for a bath and breakfast."

Bill wrinkles his nose under its layer of grime. "What I could use is a little — "

"Yeah, but what you're getting is a bath and some beans and coffee."

When we reached the bathhouse, where you sat in a tin tub while some fellow poured hot water on you from a bucket he dipped out of a big pot over a wood fire, and then after you soaped yourself, rinsed you with another, I forced Bill to take the dousings with all his clothes on.

"Jeezuz," he whined afterwards, when we went outside. "I'll catch my death all wet like this."

It was a warm morning in August, as I pointed out, and he'd be dry in no time. "Come on, a cup of coffee will warm you up."

I took him to the husky woman's open-air kitchen, where she says, "Hey there, Billy, I wondered where you was lately."

"You already know one another?" I asks, looking at each.

"Hell," says she. "He's the one I was telling you about."

"He's your boyfriend?"

"You tell him, Billy," she asks my brother, but he just keeps looking miserable from being wet.

"He's my brother," I said sourly. "Feed him some coffee and beans."

Bill now spoke up. "Nell, if you could sweeten my cup with a little bitters, I'd think kindly of you."

Bitters is what some in those days called whiskey, probably because it sounded like medicine and could be pronounced before ladies and children.

"Don't you do it, Nell," I broke in. "I just got him washed, and I'm taking him to get shaved."

She slams down a tin plate of beans on the board counter stretched between barrels, but so neatly none of it slopped over. "I don't want him shaved," said she. "I think he's real handsome with his whiskers, like President General Grant."

"You're mighty pushy."

She glared at me with little blue eyes set in a big red face. "He might be your brother — if so, he's got all the looks in the family — but he happens to be my intended."

"I'll be damned."

"I won't stand for cursing in my establishment," says she. "Any more of it, and I'll wipe the floor with you."

"You ain't got a floor," I says, real annoyed. "And earlier on, you had quite a foul mouth yourself."

We was eye-to-eye for a while, and she turns her head and spits a long brown stream just past the coffeepot, and she says, turning back, in a nicer voice, "You're a spunky little runt, ain't you? But I guess I just got a soft spot in my heart for the Crabb boys."

I didn't want a row with her, so making up suited my purpose. "All right then," I says. "I'm going to leave my brother in your capable hands, Nell, for I have an appointment. I don't think he should drink any more right now, is all. I think he should eat them beans."

I tried to pay her, but Nell said, "How'd it look if I charged for his grub?" To Bill she says, "I was saving that steak for you, Billy, but it was going bad, so I et it."

"Goddammit," says he, and of course she don't chide him for the language. "That was a prime piece of beef: I stole it at Jake Shroudy's when he went out to look at somebody getting shot in the street."

She winks at me, over the head he lowered to the beans, and says sweetly, "Tenderest I ever tasted, dearie, only a little high."

I took my leave of them two lovebirds and went down to No. 10, which was crowded at midday as always, by which I mean a dozen or so persons, for it wasn't spacious. A game was in progress with three players, one of them occupying Wild Bill's favored place, that which had a view of the front and back doors and only wall behind it. Carl Mann, part owner of the joint with a man named Jerry Lewis, was one of the men at the table, and a gent called Captain W. R. Massie, who like old Sam Clemens had been a Mississippi riverman, was another.

I went back outside and leaned against the raw boards of the wall. As I said, I found it a real relief to know my brother had a girlfriend, even if I was baffled as to what she saw in him, her with a successful business, and him not even washing unless I made him, but I was disinclined to examine the teeth of a gift horse. I begun to think now that if Bill had Nell to look after him, then I might be in the clear to go ahead and find a deal for myself. If I performed in the current part-time employment to Colorado Charley's satisfaction, then maybe he would promote me to something better in his express operation. My luck had turned up on running into Wild Bill Hickok.

Who I now saw coming along the street, looking real tall and stately in his sparkling clean-looking linen (which he must not have worn to bed in the wagon), Prince Albert coat, and wide sombrero, walking the confident way he had in the old days when he was the most feared man on the frontier, with eyes like an eagle.

But he never recognized me now till he almost reached the door of No. 10.

"Hoss," says he, blinking, like I appeared out of nowhere. "I been looking for you. Step over here for a spell." He moves to the corner of the building. When I gets there he says, "I ask you to do me a favor."

"Anything at all, Bill."

He reaches into an inside pocket of the tailcoat, where I remember he often carried a hideout gun useful if there was trouble when seated at the poker table and it was awkward to draw a weapon from the belt, but what his fist come out with now was not a pistol but a roll of paper money, which was not awful popular with men of the West at that time, especially card players, who preferred coin, which you could bite to see if it was silver or lead.

Glancing around to see if we was being observed, he slips me the roll in his closed hand, saying, "Put this away before anybody sees it."

So I did as asked, without counting, though I pointed out that having no armament I could hardly give it effective protection.

"Nobody'd think looking at you that you was carrying that kind of money, hoss," says he.

"I'll do a better job of protecting your cash than *you* can?"

He stares down at the rough wood boards underneath us, an uncharacteristic thing for him, for there was nothing significant to see at our feet. "I got this feeling my days are numbered. I can't shake it off." He raised his head and looked at the high and cloudless sky on that August day in Dakota Territory, which reminded me some of the one in June over the Greasy Grass, and he said, "If your number's up, you've got to go." He shrugs. "Now that wad I been keeping aside. Even Charley Utter don't know about it. If I get mine any time soon, as I think I might, I ask you to take enough from this roll for the train fare to Cincinnati, Ohio, and back, and whatever other expenses you run up — don't be stingy, nor lose your head neither — and carry the rest of it, by hand, to my bride, Mrs. James Butler Hickok, with the compliments of her late loving husband, so-called Wild Bill. Now can you make me that promise, hoss?"

"Why sure I can, Bill," says I, though not taking it seriously. I shoved the bankroll into my pants pocket, where it would be safely anchored by that Indian knife, the blade of which I kept wrapped in a piece of leather so it wouldn't cut me. I didn't have no belt in which to carry the latter, just that piece of rope. "I guess you better give me her address."

"It's back at the wagon," said he, "but you wouldn't have no trouble in locating her in any event. She's famous." He frowned and stroked his handlebar mustache. "You sure you can do this for me? That's a long trip, but you oughta see more of the country before you cash in your chips. Maybe you won't like it back East: I didn't much myself, but I'm right glad I saw it when me and Cody traveled with that show. You're an American, you ought to see where most of them live, which is real close together."

His voice had taken on such a melancholy tone that to change the subject to something lighter, I says, "Ever notice how most everybody you meet west of St. Louie turns out to be named either Bill or Jack?"

This had the desired effect. Wild Bill brooded on the matter for a moment, and then he threw back his head and uttered a big guffaw. "You're a comical little fellow, and that's a fact, hoss." Which seemed to amuse him even more, so he was feeling good when he strode into No. 10, as usual attracting the attention of all present. Nobody paid me any mind, bringing up the rear.

I glanced over the little crowd again, but still couldn't see nobody who looked like a threat to anybody's life but their own, if they kept drinking like that. Several wasn't even carrying visible weaponry, which didn't mean they didn't have any hid-out, but if so it would take longer to bring it into play, by which time even a somewhat impaired Wild Bill could have emptied five cylinders into their vital areas.

All of them except one or two soon turned to the bar, backs to the game. Speaking of backs, Wild Bill sat down on the empty stool that presented his own spine to the world at large. It was a man name of Charley Rich who had Bill's habitual seat on the wall side. Wild Bill thought it only a temporary arrangement, for he says, "Let's swap places, Charley. You got mine."

Rich snickers and says, "There's nobody in Deadwood man enough to take you on, even from behind. You know that, Bill."

So Wild Bill had sat down, but he asks again a little while later, and Rich just shrugged, examining the hand he had been dealt, while Captain Bill Massie says with goodnatured impatience, "Come on, Bill, I wanna win back what you took off me last night." The other player was Carl Mann, as before, and he too had no interest in the subject.

So Wild Bill begins to play without further complaint, maybe because he was counting on me to do my job behind him. I say this with the guilt that has bothered me ever since, whenever I think of this episode, and not till this moment have I found the nerve to tell of my role, or lack of it, in what happened that August 2nd, 1876, in the No. 10 Saloon. When I recounted the first part of my life to that R. F. Snell, I lied and said I never again saw Wild Bill Hickok after running into him earlier in the year at Cheyenne. I done that because I was ashamed to tell the truth, even three-quarters of a century later. But here it is now, blame me if you will.

Wild Bill proceeded to lose hand after hand this evening, and Captain Massie did win back his losses and more, to the point at which Wild Bill was out of the ready money, and he twists on the stool and calls me over to him, I expecting to be asked for the return of his roll or some of it anyway, but what he wants is for me to get fifteen dollars' worth of pocket checks from Harry Sam Young at the bar.

So I tell Harry, and he says all right, he would bring them himself, and while he was doing that, the door opens and in comes that cockeyed fellow Jack McCall who Wild Bill had staked to supper the night before. Now, McCall was nothing to look at except if you wanted the perfect picture of a loser, so as he slinks along the bar I don't pay no further attention to him, he being if not a close pal of Wild Bill's then an acquaintance anyhow, who Wild Bill furthermore had lately befriended.

What I was doing instead was keeping an eye beyond McCall on the rear door, through which a bowlegged, red-mustached fellow had lately entered, showing a horse tied up right outside, a fact that bothered me a little, as if it was for a quick getaway. But that man proved to be no trouble, just drinking whiskey at the bar.

My attention was claimed by Wild Bill saying, with some spirit, to the river captain Massie, "You broke me on that hand!"

And right at that point Jack McCall, now directly behind Wild Bill's stool, cursed loudly and brought up a pistol so close the muzzle all but touched him, and he shot Wild Bill through the back of the head, just under the brim of the sombrero, which flew off in the short forward pitch of the body, after which Bill went over backwards off the stool and crashed onto the floor like a felled tree.

Still cursing at his fallen victim, Jack McCall next turned his smoking gun on everybody else at hand, shouting, "Come on, you sons of bitches, and get yours!" He keeps pulling the trigger, but his weapon proved defective after that one cowardly shot that dropped the greatest of all gunfighters and never fires again, so he drops it, and at that I run at him, but he's quick out the back door, and by the time I get there he's mounted that horse right outside and starts to ride away, but the cinch was loose and he don't get far before the saddle slips off the horse, him sprawling with it.

I'm almost on him at that point, but stumbled on something hard in them soft-soled Indian moccasins, laming me briefly, and he gains ground. We was out on the main street now, and the people rushing out of No. 10 had joined the chase, yelling, "Wild Bill's shot!" "He kilt Wild Bill, get the little bastard," and the like, with McCall still out well ahead of us, but then he does a fool thing for himself, ducks into one of the stores there, which turns out to be Jake Shroudy's butcher shop (where my brother stole that steak he give Nell), and I run in and corner the yellow skunk cowering behind a bloody side of beef hanging from a hook in the ceiling, and though he is if on the small side still bigger than me, but I pull him out and draw my knife to cut out his gizzard, but the others who now arrived stopped me, presumably in the name of the law which did not exist in Deadwood at that time.

If you're wondering why revenge seemed to mean more to me than Wild Bill's health, why I chased McCall instead of checking to see if my friend was still alive and could of been helped, all I can say is I seen enough violent deaths by that time in my life to recognize one that took place within a few feet of me. You get shot through the head point-blank with a lead slug the weight of them used in those days, you was a goner beyond all doubt.

And it could be seen as my fault. I knew Colorado Charley would sure see it that way. The least I could do was catch the killer. After I done that but was prevented from doing him in on the spot, I sadly returned to No. 10. The others took McCall someplace where they held him, there being no jail.

They had already locked the saloon up, waiting for the doctor to come, and I had to talk Harry Young, the state he was in, into letting me enter. First other person I seen was Captain Bill Massie, with his forearm wrapped in a bloody kerchief. The bullet that killed Wild Bill had passed through his brain to strike Massie, across the table, in the wrist.

Wild Bill's body lay on its side, his knees bent in the position they had assumed when he had sat down to play poker. From the flow around him, it looked like he had already lost every drop of blood that ever circulated through his tall person. His fingers too was bent as they had been when he held his last hand, but the cards had stayed on the table: the aces of spades and clubs and two black eights, ever afterward known as the Dead Man's Hand.

Finally in hurried the aproned barber whose shop I had visited the day before on the money Wild Bill give me. He turned out to be the local doctor as well, which was not necessarily as bad as it sounds, for haircutters learned how to staunch wounds, apply bandages, etc., and Doc Peirce acted like he knew his way around a corpse.

Colorado Charley Utter made his appearance not long after. It took him a while to get around to me, and I could of avoided him that night if I had tried, but like I say I did believe I was at fault, so after they carried Wild Bill out to prepare him for burial, probably at Doc Peirce's barbershop, I went up to Utter, who was talking to Carl Mann, and I says, "All right, Charley, shoot me if you want."

"I heard what happened," says he. "You couldn't have done much about it, with him sitting where he was. There's nothing can be done about somebody who decides his number's up." He nods in his decisive way and goes back to a practical discussion of funeral arrangements with Mann. That's the kind of fellow Charley was and why he was a good businessman. And next day he gave Wild Bill a good send-off, out there at their camp.

The coffin had been quickly pounded together from some pine boards of the type used as siding on the Deadwood shops, but it was made presentable by covering the outside with black cloth and the interior was lined with white. Wild Bill himself looked nice, his long hair all cleaned of blood and brushed out, the big mustache with a more agreeable curve in death than the melancholy droop it had lately acquired in life. You could hardly see the wound the slug had made on exiting through the cheek, like only a little scratch. Doc Peirce was also an accomplished undertaker, having much practice locally. He had even, so somebody said, changed Wild Bill's underwear for clean, though that sounds like Colorado Charley's idea. And Wild Bill Hickok did not go into the afterlife unarmed: his Sharps rifle lay alongside the body. As to his famous ivory-handled sixguns, somebody must have walked away with them between his death and now, for they wasn't buried with him or ever seen again.

There was quite a crowd out at the funeral, including my brother Bill and Nell his big girlfriend, and I'll say this for her: she kept him sober so he acted with proper respect for the occasion, though without alcohol in his veins he had begun to look real pale and weak.

Once Wild Bill had been lowered into his mountainside grave, the assembled throng rushed back in a mob to the town saloons and had I not been quick on my feet I'd of been trampled down. Within a few seconds nobody was left but Charley Utter and, standing back a ways in respect, me. Charley had found a rock and was using it to hammer a flat board into the earth at one of its short ends. When he finished, I went close enough to where I could read what was cut or really scratched into the wood with a knifepoint. I can't quote it verbatim after all these years, but

I do recall that after giving Wild Bill's age and day of death at the hands of Jack McCall, Charley Utter had wrote, "Goodbye Pard Till We Meet in the Happy Hunting Ground."

I was right affected by the sentiment. Them two really was good friends, unlike me and Wild Bill, who I knew for a number of years but would have to admit not closely for all that. In fact I was privately critical of him for a large part, maybe mostly because of envy, even though all in all he done me a number of favors. It was different with Custer, who I never much liked but who I realized, seeing him die, had been more than what I thought he was when I hated him most. I doubt I ever could of been Custer's friend in the best of times — and to be fair to the man, what would he have seen in me? But it might of been different with Wild Bill. Fact is, nearest I ever come to having any friends was amongst the Cheyenne, and there race came into play sooner or later, even with Old Lodge Skins, who was more of a father than a friend anyhow. I just wasn't an Indian, but I sure hadn't done well amongst whites.

Charley had been alone with his thoughts, but when he turned to head back to his camp, he noticed me. Now, in distinction to the way he acted in the No. 10 Saloon just after Wild Bill was murdered, he narrows his eyes to mean slits, and he says, with real bad feeling, a hand on the butt of the gun in the holster at his hip, "If I ever see you again, I'll kill you."

"What?" I was not prepared for this.

"You heard me."

"You said you wasn't blaming me," I reminded him.

"I wasn't standing by his grave at the time," said Charley Utter. "God damn you."

"All right," I told him. "I got it coming, I admit, and you have a right to hold me responsible. I do myself. I'm leaving Deadwood directly anyway, to keep the promise I made to Wild Bill not an hour before he died: to travel to Cincinnati and see his wife. I wanted to ask you: I seen you cut that lock of hair from Bill's head before the coffin was nailed shut, and Doc Peirce said it was for Mrs. Agnes. I know you don't think much of me, but would you trust me to take it to her?"

Charley drew his pistol. "By God, I think I'll kill you anyway. You rotten little son of a bitch, to stand there and lie through your teeth on a sad occasion like this." His eyes was bulging with fury, and I judged it would not be long before he couldn't restrain his trigger finger, so I didn't try to make the point that he ought to first shoot Jack McCall, but went away as ordered and kept going without looking back, taking the shortest route out of town. I expected my brother and Nell was in one of the saloons. Well, I didn't have time to say goodbye.

It was on the trail just outside Deadwood, now become a crude road by reason of the deep ruts resulting from all the gold-rush traffic, I heard some barking behind me and turned and seen that yellow dog formerly partnered with my brother Bill but who was now taking up with me. I was glad to have his company, though I could not right away meet his expectation I was a sure source of grub, for I never had any myself at that point, facing the long hike to Fort Laramie, the nearest white place. In fact I had little more means than I had arrived in Deadwood with a couple of days before, except that roll of money I was supposed to take across the continent to Mrs. Hickok.

. . . Well, as it turned out, I didn't have that either. I searched my person four or five times, but I no longer was in possession of the nest egg Wild Bill had put aside for his widow. I must of lost it on that chase of Jack McCall, maybe when I pulled out my knife. Or maybe someone picked my pocket at some point, could even have been at the funeral, for in them days there was a lot of rotten people around when you wasn't on the lookout for them, but maybe that's always the case in any age.

So that was the real end of Wild Bill Hickok, who unfortunately won't be coming back again in my story. He was the third of the influential people in my life who had died in hardly more than a month, and the only one with regard to which I felt guilty. How much was in that roll I never knew, never having counted it, but I intended to take some amount of money to the bereaved Mrs. Agnes soon as I earned enough, living up to that promise.

In the days to come I heard about what happened to Jack McCall, who was tried right away for the cold-blooded murder committed before the eyes of a dozen witnesses, but was found not guilty by a jury of Deadwood miners, a number of who even cheered him on announcing their verdict, and despite all the threats by Wild Bill's friends, the murderer left town with his skin intact.

But before long it was determined that the first trial had been illegal, due to Deadwood's own illegality as a town, being part of an Indian reservation! Which was real ironic, for none of the Americans would of been there, including General Custer, had the treaty forbidding them from the area not been broken when gold was discovered in the Black Hills on land guaranteed to belong to the Sioux unto eternity.

Anyway, a few weeks later Jack McCall was rearrested and retried in Yankton, and they hanged the bastard. Nobody ever knew for sure why he did the deed, and his own explanation was a barefaced lie: he never had a brother for Wild Bill to kill. Probably he was hired by people who was afraid Wild Bill Hickok would bring law to unlawful Deadwood — there's another example of how reality can be at odds with what's supposed to be.

I'll tell you what I had in mind now, with no serious means for bringing it about at this time: looking up Mrs. Elizabeth Custer and consoling her. I say that with all respect.

3

Bat Masterson

L IKE ALL MY INTENTIONS REGARDING THE CUSTERS—
like that time I intended to assassinate General George A. — this
one had to be delayed in execution, me being at the moment on the
trail to Fort Laramie, owning nothing but the clothes on my back,
unarmed except for that Indian knife, and with no better prospects than
I had on reaching Deadwood. The last time I seen her, Mrs. Libbie
Custer was up at Fort Abraham Lincoln, Montana Territory, from which
her husband had marched away never to be seen again amongst the living. It was not the time to head up there, through hundreds of miles of
country where the war between the hostiles and the U.S. Army sure had
not ended with the Indian victory at the Greasy Grass, and the Fifth
Cavalry was in fact going north along more or less the same route I was
traveling going south, as I found when I finally reached Laramie, but it
was easy to miss even a large collection of people or animals in the wide
open spaces of that day, unmarked by the billboards and Burma-Shave
signs that come later along with foot-long hotdogs and soft ice cream
squirted out of a machine.

Such delicacies come to mind on account of I was in the same need of
finding food again as I had been before arriving at Deadwood, or sure
would of been were it not for my new supplier, namely that dog what had
left the company of my brother Bill for mine, which was so far nameless.
My main experience with this type of animal had been when amongst
the Cheyenne, who carry a lot of dogs with them at all times but generally don't make pets so don't give them names. They put dogs to work,
hauling smaller travois, and on occasion, usually a celebratory feast of

some kind, knock a puppy in the head, singe off its hair, boil it up, and eat it. From the redskin point of view this is practical, not cruel, and my own position on the matter was as usual divided: when amongst Indians I ate dog if it was offered, yet when with whites I would never of thought of doing so.

But what about now, when I was real hungry soon enough after leaving town, with no weapons with which to acquire meat and no place to buy, beg, borrow, or steal even a plate of beans? Unless you been in a similar situation you don't know what it's like to have to personally catch or gather every morsel of food you swallow. Sure, you can locate a springy bough and make a bow of it with your shoelace, find some flint and chip a point from it then tie it to a straight twig, and with such an arrow drop an elk or antelope, and your problem's gone. I estimate to accomplish this wouldn't take no longer than a month or two. Or you spear a mess of fish — if there happens to be fish in the streams you come across. Incidentally, the Cheyenne was one of the few Plains tribes that would catch and eat fish, dating from the ancient days when they lived in the lake country, before the coming of the horse. But fish like game was not always to be found.

However, as it turned out with that dog, I didn't have nothing to complain of, as I first realized when, not far along the trail, he run off on his own and, not long after I figured I'd seen the last of him, he returns with his teeth sunk in the nape of a limp jackrabbit of a sufficient size, when roasted over the little fire I started (real little because you never knew who it might attract), to feed us both. He thereby proved, and confirmed it further as we proceeded, that he was a real partner, catching our red meat all the way to Laramie, jackrabbits, prairie dogs, and the like, being partial to that with hair on it, which is to say he just backed up, barking, at rattlesnakes, which was left to me to kill with knife and forked stick, but he weren't shy about eating the result, which when cooked is real palatable, but if you ever offer any to a white woman you better say it's chicken. Anyhow, seeing the kind of association we had established, I gave him the name of Pard.

At Fort Laramie the talk was all about the aforementioned Fifth Cavalry, which in July had departed from there to get the Cheyenne what had illegally bolted from the nearby Red Cloud agency to try to join the hostiles up in the Little Bighorn region. At a place called War Bonnet Creek, William F. Cody, so-called Buffalo Bill, who returned briefly from what had become his full-time career of showmanship in the East to serve as Army scout, supposedly had a personal fight with a Cheyenne called Yellow Hand. There was many accounts of this incident from the first, beginning with them that claimed to be eyewitnesses, with the most lavish coming from Cody himself, which had him in a hand-to-hand with knives, concluding with lifting Yellow Hand's bloody hair and crying, "The first scalp for Custer!" This is naturally the one given in dime novels and the later moving-picture shows. I got to know Cody right well in future years, but wasn't at this event, for which I heard he wore one of his theatrical costumes, a black-and-red velvet Mexican suit with silver buttons and lace, and a enormous big-brimmed hat of the kind favored south of the border, so I can't comment except to say there was a lot of people, including Yellow Hand's own sister, who said Buffalo Bill never did it. I mention this because it was typical of everything that ever happened in the West that became famous. You don't know what the truth was unless you was there — like me, on so many well-known occasions, and I never claim anything I can't vouch for, like the Cody–Yellow Hand combat. It is especially hard to determine what was or was not true about Bill Cody, one of the greatest masters of the art of throwing buffalo chips who ever lived, in a time when there was a lot of competition.

I know there's some of you saying, "Of which you, old boy, might be the last living example." If so, just listen to what I tell you, and then check it against the facts if you can.

My trouble, most of my life, was nobody would listen. You recall Wild Bill wouldn't let me tell him about being with Custer at the Greasy Grass. Well, this continued. Occupied at Deadwood with my brother Bill and then Hickok's last days on earth, I hadn't encountered talk about the destruction of most of the Seventh Cavalry by the Sioux and Cheyenne but at Laramie that was still the main topic, and of course there wasn't nobody representing the redskin side of the argument, least of all the tame Indians what was called Hang-Around-the-Forts because there was a lot of them still doing that, begging for whiskey, et cetera. This was definitely not the place to reveal my intimate experience of the fighting Cheyenne, but I could and did try to tell a few folks I knowed Custer well, starting out at that, with an intention of going on, but everyone was sick of the many impostors already circulating, hardly two months since the event, claiming to have survived the Little Bighorn battle. Anyway, all anybody wanted to talk about was how there wasn't any longer no excuse for not just wiping out every rotten dirty Indian in the country. We tried to get along with them, and look what happened! The men who expressed this feeling strongest was, as always, them so drunk they could hardly stand up, let alone take on the savages.

Me and Pard didn't linger long at Laramie. For one, the dog couldn't do much hunting at or around the fort, owing to the commotion there, and I still never had no money, having, properly, not been paid by Colorado Charley for bodyguarding Wild Bill the day he was murdered. I was once again in my familiar need of a profitable occupation, and I thought the pickings might be better down at the town of Cheyenne, which had been a growing place on my visit of the previous spring and was surely even more so by now, for that's how it went in them days and those parts.

When me and Pard got there, indeed I saw a city of some fifteen thousand souls, with all manner of shops, eateries, dance halls, variety theaters, gambling places, sporting houses, everything men really like but little of what's supposed to be good for them. The latter was sure to come, given the natural progression in human affairs, usually due to the arrival of respectable women, like mothers and schoolteachers and churchgoers, them who believe life ought to be more than the mere pleasuring of the lowest appetites which uninstructed men think is just fine. But this has even been true of the more than a few harlots I have known: they was always saving up some kind of nest egg for when they left the profession and settled down with a fine decent man and raised a family, and what's more, some of them actually done as much.

In some ways I was not much better prepared for civilization than an Indian, with the difference that I was white and therefore, if ever the target of hatred or contempt on the part of the civilized, it was only personal and not general. Also, I had a term or two in decent society, beginning when I was the adopted son of the Reverend and Mrs. Pendrake, which also represented the only period of formal book-learning I ever endured. Then there was the time I was in the trading business with Bolt & Ramirez in Denver and thought I had settled down with a Swedish-immigrant wife named Olga, but she and our boy, little Gus, was captured by the Indians, who I myself rejoined from time to time, by fate and not by choice, for I could recognize there wasn't no future in barbarism however attractive it might at times seem.

Looking at the main street of Cheyenne, I realized that I had to find me a more profitable kind of life than heretofore. I was real tired of being hungry, broke, and dirty and not having a shelter against the elements, which was unruly in my part of the world that summer, with storms of rain and hail.

"Pard," I says to my canine pal, who had got chilled and soaked along with me, "we got to find a way to get in on this prosperity." He was a good listener but being a dog was not equipped to understand as I did that any number of them frequenting these pleasure palaces was likely to be no more prosperous than me, but simply able to put up a better front.

While I was standing there, thinking, being careful to keep out of the way of more affluent-looking passersby, what does Pard do but approach a dandified sort of fellow with derby hat, stickpin, and gold-headed walking stick. Now Pard was right friendly, but I was afraid a man dressed like that might get the wrong impression when approached by a mutt, maybe take a swipe at him with that stick, so I moves up to defend my pal if so.

But this fellow, who wore the standard droopy mustache of the day, just smiled down at the dog, then at me.

He says, "He looks like he could use a good feed."

"I expect he could," says I. "Him and me just come in off the trail from Laramie, and there ain't much game around."

"Lots of people have gone that way for gold," says he. "That was the reason I came here, but before I could get outfitted to haul up to Deadwood, a lot of them started to come back. They say all the good claims are gone and the vein is already running thin."

"That's where I come from myself," I told him. I was trying to decide whether to say much further when he up and asks me if I happened to be at Deadwood when Wild Bill Hickok was shot.

I decided on caution. "I might of been."

He grins under his black mustache. "What kind of answer is that? Either you were or were not."

Now speaking well as he did, and being so nicely dressed, he was a far cry from the usual type I run into. In fact he struck me as probably hailing from back East, like one of them writers what came West looking for colorful topics to write about for the cake-eaters in the big cities. He didn't look like no sissy, being of a husky build though of the middle height, and talking in a straightforward manly way. But I decided he was likely a tenderfoot in matters pertaining to the frontier and therefore just the right person to tell my story to, and not just about Wild Bill but also Custer and all. I starts in, but he says his whistle could use some wetting and he'd be glad to buy me one as well.

Pard was already lowering his head and long nose, giving me a dirty look from the tops of his eyes, because by now he could foresee things in that canine way. "Sorry," I told him, "saloons and gambling halls are just for them with two feet, probably to their detriment. You're lucky to get to stay outdoors. Just wait here for me. If you spot somebody with a drawn gun, you run away and hide."

"You're fond of him," said my new acquaintance.

"Friends of any breed come in handy out here where your back is often to the wall," I says self-importantly as we enter a big fancy establishment I wouldn't of had the nerve to try alone, shabby as I was at present, and I sure wouldn't have got in now, I figured, had the big mean-looking, Colt's-wearing fellow posted at the door not recognized my companion, nodding at him respectfully, from which I gathered my benefactor was wont to spend a lot of money on the premises.

Now this place was enormous, being a complex under one roof of full-sized theater, hotel, gambling hall, and a bar all full of polished brass and mirrors and big shiny hanging lamps, where we bellied up and my friend tells the bartender to leave the bottle.

He proceeds to throw down three fingers in one swallow, and I wondered if he knew what he was doing, for I had been told once that liquor has more effect in the high air of the West than at Eastern sea levels. I was myself more sparing, having so little food in my belly. I didn't rightly care if *he* got drunk, though, for he might then listen with more credulity.

But the one who got plastered, and soon enough on an empty stomach, was me, not him. By my second shot I was feeling it, and with the third all that glass and glitter lost its clear edges and I felt more and more like I was trying to see things with my head immersed in a stream.

But the other fellow just kept drinking without no visible effect, at least to my impaired vision. This situation however did not stop me from not only telling the truth about Wild Bill's last days but embellishing it quite a bit. Why would I do this when the facts was remarkable enough as they stood? Well, remember what a poor job I done as bodyguard: I wouldn't want to boast about that. But why *boast* about anything? Because that's what Westerners always done when in the presence of them from the East. It was expected of you, you felt you owed it to the landscape, but the real reason was you could get away with it to some tenderfoot who traveled by parlor car and never ate a meal except by knife and fork. And also I was drunk.

I don't remember after all these years and, at the time, all that whiskey, exactly what I said, but it is likely I come out the hero of the event even though failing to stop Jack McCall from shooting Wild Bill in the back. Maybe my gun misfired — though I never had one at the time. But at least there was a grain of truth within it, unlike a good many first-person accounts around in them days, and it seemed to go over with my friend, who poured me regular refills at the rate of about half the frequency with which he poured for himself while remaining cold sober.

"I never had the good fortune," he said at one point, "to personally meet Wild Bill, and I am sorry I now won't ever have the chance."

"Well sir," says I, "I can tell you anything you'd like to hear. And not only concerning Bill Hickok. I've knowed them all, General Custer and his lovely wife" — it was true I had some personal association of the General though only seeing Mrs. Libbie once — "and old Kit Carson" — just barely factual, for on my sole face-to-face with him, he slammed his front door in my face when I asked him for a handout. But then I made a big mistake, I picked up my brother Bill's line on another famous gunfighter. "I expect the fellow still alive that I know best is Wyatt Earp, whose name might be recognizable. Fact is, I taught him most of what he knows about shooting."

I had met Earp briefly once, down on the buffalo range, and he coldcocked me with the barrel of his pistol for a fancied insult. He had went on to make a name for himself as peace officer in the Kansas cattle camps like Ellsworth and Wichita. He never came up this way to my knowledge, so I felt safe with my claim.

"Is that so?" my drinking pal asks, his blue eyes twinkling in what I took for admiration. He put his glass down for a second while checking in the back-of-bar mirror on his appearance and then changing slightly the angle of the derby hat, his gold-headed stick secured under his arm. "I've met Mr. Earp myself. I always wondered how he got to be the fine shot he is."

I should have stopped at that point, but the liquor had taken away all my good sense, so I goes on. "Met him, did you? Well sir, if that ever happens again, you just ask him who learned him how to handle a sixgun."

I grins foolishly. "Of course, he might not be man enough to admit it, with the rep he's acquired since."

"I'll be glad to," says my friend. "I'm thinking of heading back to Dodge one of these days soon. I've decided not to waste my time going up to Deadwood."

"That where old Wyatt is now?" I asks. Well, I wouldn't be going anywhere near.

"And what name should I mention?"

"Jack Crabb is what they call me," I says. "And what, sir, may I ask, is yourn?" Exchanging names was a polite matter amongst whites, and I always enjoyed the gentility of it, but with Indians it's actually rude to ask a man his name: it might end up being used for bad medicine that would destroy its owner, so you do better to ask a third person. I should of done that in this case.

"W. B. Masterson," says he, giving me a salute with the gold top of his cane. "I'm pleased to make your acquaintance, Mr. Crabb."

"Just call me Jack."

"All right, Jack, I'm usually 'Bat' to those I drink with."

"You're *Bat Masterson?*"

"At your service," he says, with another lift of the stick.

"I'm a fool, Mr. Masterson. I want you to know I admitted that before you kilt me."

He has a good laugh at that. "I'm not going to kill you, Jack. I wouldn't have the nerve to draw on the man who taught Wyatt Earp to shoot."

Drunk as I had been, I was immediately all but sober. "Aw, that was a joke, Mr. Masterson. I figured you'd see through it." I took a real deep breath to flush out some of the alcohol fumes, and decided to stick to the facts. "I run into Mr. Earp oncet on the buffalo range, but I never rightly knowed him for a friend. I *was* telling the God's honest truth about Wild Bill, though, being there when he died, but I was also acquainted with him some years prior, back in Kansas City, and he really did give me shooting lessons which I never forgot."

I don't know if Bat believed that or not, but since it had actually happened I was able to get his respectful interest once I talked with authority on the more technical aspects of the shooting and the weapons used, for he like Wild Bill and every other gunfighter I had experience of was fascinated with the tools of their trade, and no wonder, seeing how you could get killed if you wasn't. Wild Bill's trouble came when he lost the fine edge of that obsession and got occupied with making money to afford being married.

Bat was rightly renowned for his prowess with weapons, but now is as good a time as any to tell you what ain't generally known, and I didn't myself know it then, at the bar of the McDaniels Variety: it's possible that Bat *never killed another person in a gunfight*, his life long. I have said before that what mattered in the Old West, and maybe everywhere else as well, is the impression others have of a person. Bat was an outstanding shot with any kind of firearm, and he was a forceful man who never, with or without a lawman's badge, backed down from anyone, and though, as you have seen, on the quiet, gentlemanly side and not even real tall, he had a commanding presence, but he didn't kill no three dozen men, like the legend has it nor, having captured several Mexican outlaws, cut off and brung their heads back in a sack for the reward. As a peace officer he rarely fired a gun. He didn't have to: he was Bat Masterson. Am I saying that name done it all? Well, you must admit it was a good one, though maybe not as obvious as Wild Bill. Like the latter, it wasn't the real name of its owner, which was not the "William Barclay" he used, either. The famous gunfighter, who had few gunfights, was born as Bartholomew Masterson. Nor did I ever see him employ that gold-headed cane to bat persons in the head. He used it rather for the limp he had got after being wounded in a quarrel over a harlot's favors, and that ruckus is where his reputation started, his opponent being an Army sergeant named King, at a dance hall down in the Texas Panhandle, but a lot of shooting was going on by a lot of people on either side, and there was no real telling who shot who, but it ended up with King dead and Bat with a bullet which might of made him a woman had it struck a bit lower down on his pelvis. This had happened only half a year earlier, so he was still limping a little.

Of all the celebrated figures I met in the white world of the day, I guess I respected Bat Masterson the most because not only didn't he ever boast about himself, which was also true of Wild Bill and a few others, but unlike them he never even took it serious when anybody else did it for him, and that's a man of balance. For example if Bat was asked by some arse-kisser journalist if it was true he had killed x-number of persons, he might inquire whether the count was supposed to include Mexicans and Indians, and give no further answer. Also he was real smart and, something that appealed to me on account of I felt I was too, a master at self-preservation without compromising his principles. The fact that he rarely drawed a gun and never took many lives if any, while standing up to any challenge, made him all the more outstanding.

You might well ask, though, what he saw to make me a suitable pal of his for a while, and I'd have to say he found me amusing, as others had done for one reason or another, sometimes maybe only because I was shorter than them but had a lively temper, a combination often seen as hilarious because of the apparent harmlessness of the undersized individual, but I'd say that Bat also seemed to have a regard for me. I don't claim he always believed I was telling the truth, after that big mistake I made at the outset, but I think he came to accept at least some of what I told him about Wild Bill, having the details as I did, and he sure learned in time to come, when my command of their language proved handy, that I had had an association with the Cheyenne Indians.

Anyway, here at the McDaniels Variety, we eventually went into the eatery part, where I further sobered up on a big beefsteak with fixin's, a lot of coffee, and a couple hunks of pie, all on Bat of course. When he seen me leave a considerable piece of the meat he asked if it was too tough or what? and I said I owed it to my dog for all the meat he provided me on the trail.

"I approve of a man who pays his debts," Bat says, "and I do a lot of wagering. That's what I've been doing since I landed at Cheyenne, bucking the tiger, and I've won a bit. Let's buy your dog a steak all his own." And he sends a waiter to fetch one, after I told the fellow to leave off the onions and all else that was not flesh and in fact not even bother to cook it.

When the steak arrived, me and Bat took it outside on its platter to find Pard, who was still waiting where I left him but not in peace, as there was three or four men who had come along from one of the saloons feeling their liquor, and seeing the animal decided to have some fun, barking at him and sending big kicks his way with heavy boots that would of done damage had he not been so deft at dodging.

Now I had that Indian skinning knife in my grasp and would have used it forthwith, were it not that Bat says calmly to the biggest of these worthies, who was a good head taller than him and maybe forty pounds heavier, "I wouldn't do that."

"Oh, you wooden, woodjew?" snarls this big bastard, sending still another kick Pard's way, with boots large enough to shoe both my feet at once. "Tell me why you wooden, afore I give you a good kicking for yourself."

But one of his companions, after a stare and a sobering gulp, jabs him with an elbow and says, "He wouldn't on account of he's Bat Masterson."

"Oh, sweet Jesus," the big fellow whines immediately. "I beg your pardon, Mr. Masterson. I can't hold my liquor nohow. I am a foolish son of a bitch, as anyone can tell you, but I mean well."

Bat says, "Nice to have met you," and he pays no further attention to this bunch, who slinks off, hats in hands, sniveling apologies.

Neither was Pard fazed by this experience. He had the smell of meat in his nose and no doubt would of lighted into the meal with gusto even while being kicked. As it was, with no hindrance, he more or less inhaled that big steak except for the bone, which he proceeded to crunch like it was pastry.

Bat went back inside to the Gold Room, which was the gambling hall in the McDaniels Variety, and played faro, what they called bucking the tiger, and won so much he was glad to stake me to some decent clothing, till I could get gainful employment, and even offered to pay for a room, but none of the hotels would admit a dog, so I got a tent on more borrowed money, and me and Pard went out a ways beyond city limits and camped beside a little stream.

After another day or so and finally a session at the faro table where he lost a little, Bat, who was as smart at gambling as he was elsewhere, figured his streak was running out and saw it as the moment to return to Dodge City. Now I knowed that town some years back and would probably have disliked it even if I had not been shot in the back there by someone whose identity I never learned, it being a nasty place in a hard time, with too many cowboys even then, when there was still lots of buffalo hunters to take them on.

"What's so great about that town?" I asked my friend. "It's all cattle nowadays, ain't it? I'm a buffalo man myself and can't stand a cowboy even when he's sober."

"Times change, Jack." Bat wiped both sides of his mustache with a kerchief he took from up one sleeve, then put it away, after which he took another swallow from his glass. "I went for buffalo myself, but they're mostly gone now, and anyway you want to make a place suitable for women and children, churches and schools. You can't have buffalo occupying all that space." He laughs. "Any more than you can have the main businesses in any town be gambling, drinking, and whoring. He swallows more whiskey and says, "That's another reason why I want to get back to Dodge: I prefer the women there."

Now that made *me* laugh. "Let me get this straight, Bat. Your own pleasures are the ones that ought to be done away with, but before that happens, you'll enjoy them to the hilt?"

"You're right on the mark, Jack old boy," says he. "Maybe you will want to come along. I'm thinking of going into business there, setting up an establishment like this McDaniels. You might not like those cowboys who come roaring into Dodge, but they get paid off at the end of their drive, and their money's as good as anyone's — and easier to take."

I didn't have no other offers at the moment, that was for sure, and I wanted to repay Bat what I owed him, which by now was a tidy sum of fifteen to twenty dollars.

"I might also run for sheriff of Ford County," Bat added. "That is Wyatt's idea for me, but I don't know if I'm not too young."

I figured him to be at least my age if not older, but when I asked him now he says he's twenty-two.

"I got a few years on you then," says I. "But don't tell me I'm older than Wyatt Earp."

"I'll have to," says Bat. "I believe he's twenty-eight."

I mention this only to point out that some fellows growed up faster than others in them days when so much armament was around, but I happened to have had as much as if not more action in my first three decades than these youngsters, yet thought of both as my seniors, which might of been owing purely to my size. Even I, until I got to be eighty or so, tended to assume I was younger than everybody bigger than me. Which might be one of the reasons I have lived so long.

So my next port of call turned out to be Dodge City. Now I had to make a painful decision as to Pard. I didn't think Dodge was the right kind of place for him, being he had growed up in the high country. Around these parts he didn't need to rely on me for his grub. But I doubted if there on the flat plains of Kansas he could of found any small game that had not been scared away by the thousands of pounding hooves of cattle drove up from Texas, and seeing him in the field some damn cowboy was likely to shoot him as a coyote, for he greatly favored that creature in form and color, especially when going through the grass. Then I admit I wouldn't want to keep living in a tent if I could afford better in a town, and Pard wasn't the sort of pet what would be tolerated on civilized premises. I was used to his smell by now, but you couldn't ask that of others, and of course he had took a dump or pissed anyplace he pleased his life long.

I ain't real proud of the way I deceived him when it came time to leave, but though he was real smart for an animal, I could never be sure just what he understood or didn't at any given point, so what I stuck to was what I knowed was within his mental grasp, namely matters of food. On getting up that morning I told him we was clean out of anything to feed on, to demonstrate which I poked around the tent and then throwed up my empty hands, seeing which he made a movement of his long nose that could of been taken as a nod, and off he loped towards the nearby wooded foothills.

I myself headed the other direction, to join Bat Masterson for the trip to Dodge. However long it would take Pard to gather that I wouldn't be coming back, he wouldn't starve, and that was the main concern in a life like his. I was grateful to him for his companionship, but after all he was just a dog, meaning he was hungry all the time but randy only in season. He couldn't talk or laugh or use tools or have a faith or creed, which meant he only killed to eat. I was fond of Pard and would miss him, but as I couldn't have explained that to his face, I sneaked off as I did. Reason I struck the tent, folded it up, and sold it in town was not only for the money but because I didn't want Pard guarding it for the rest of his life.

4

Dodge

MOST OF WHAT YOU EVER HEARD ABOUT DODGE CITY took place along a couple of blocks of Front Street, which run parallel to the Santa Fe tracks: the Alhambra Saloon, another of them combination barroom-gambling-hall-eateries, this one owned by Pete Beatty and "Dog" Kelley, formerly called "Hound," both names coming from the greyhounds he raised; the Dodge House hotel; the famous Wright and Beverly general store; the Long Branch and Alamo and Lady Gay saloons, and the Opera House. This was the fancy side of the tracks. On the south or wrong side was the lowdown part, consisting of rougher kinds of saloons and gambling joints, cheaper hotels, and of course whorehouses, one of the more famous of which, from the colored glass in its doorway, giving its name to the type everywhere else, namely, the Red Light.

Now in the late '70s the cowboys had the town to themselves or would of had not the local businessmen decided that though they desired the money of them Texans just in off the trail and thirsty and in need of entertainment, they wanted it to be handed over peaceably and not accompanied by the lethal exuberance of earlier times, so the lawmen hired or elected included at one time or another many of the noted names with the exception of Wild Bill Hickok: Bat Masterson and his brothers Ed and Jim, Charlie Bassett, Bill Tilghman, Mysterious Dave Mather (supposed to be a descendant of some preacher named Cotton who burned witches back in Massachusetts in the old days), and to be sure, Wyatt Earp, though the last-named while getting most of the subsequent attention of history was probably the least of the bunch, never killing a soul while he was in Dodge and never holding a higher job than assistant town marshal, but his accomplishments was usually greatly exaggerated by them who wrote about him on the basis of his own claims.

Now Bat was good as his word, and when him and Ben Springer opened up their Lone Star Dancehall, they give me a barkeep's job, and I wore a striped shirt with sleeve garters and sprouted a handlebar mustache, which come out slighter redder than my naturally ginger hair. The Lone Star, as could be told from the name, was designed to attract the cowboys that come up from the state of that designation. Not every single man who herded cattle for a living was a native Texan — and amongst them you could find Mexicans, Indians, breeds, and even some colored fellows what had been born slaves — but it was a convenient handle for all concerned, and sometimes them who had originated someplace else was more sentimental about the Alamo, Sam Houston, and suchlike than those with a natural right to be so, especially if they was drunk, which of course is more or less the only way you seen them if you worked in a place like the Lone Star. They also tended, ten years after the fact, to be still displeased by the outcome of the War Between the States, and as usual not all of them with such strong feelings had even been involved in it.

Bat had gotten some ideas from the McDaniels in Cheyenne, and the Lone Star was one of the more ambitious of the establishments south of the tracks, offering a big dance floor, all kinds of gambling games, a stage for variety shows, an orchestra stand decorated with bunting, and quite a number of girls who might dance on the stage, showing their garters, or with the customers on the floor, and/or entertain privately in their rooms on the second story. Though whoring was not a requirement for a female who worked there, you might say it was a recommendation and the only way to make a decent income. But what I mean to say is, there wasn't no compulsion or white slavery.

There was those who disapproved of the selling of flesh as a degradation of the fair sex. Aside from preachers, it was a rare man who held this opinion unless it come to his own daughter, sister, wife, or mother. Out West in the time of which I speak, there was the usual distinction between good girls and bad, but if you didn't consort with a soiled dove you might never have no women at all, there being not that many of the respectable type. So Wild Bill Hickok, Bat Masterson, and most of the others had intimate associations of more than a night at a time with sporting women, and the same was true of Wyatt Earp.

Working at the Lone Star, I come to know the girls on the premises well enough, and not all was what if you enjoyed full sight you could call pretty, but all seemed to know how to appeal to a man, and this was sometimes most true of them who was the least attractive in feature or form, like Cockeyed Kitty, Iron-Jaw Tillie, and Liz Big Bottom, for a turn at any of who there might be a waiting line. I expect they could make a fellow live up to a better idea than he normally had of himself, and you can't ask more of a woman than that.

I was making a nice income tending bar at the Lone Star, where in addition to the wage, a cowboy who had won at faro or chuck-a-luck might ask you to drink on him, and you'd swallow from a glass of cold coffee but credit yourself for what he was paying for whiskey, and there'd be some who would tip generously if you would listen to how they was a-going to skin alive the next greaser they encountered because one cheated them on the sale of a horse, or how no Yankee lived who could put a head on John Wesley Hardin, a famous Texas gunfighter of the day, though I do believe he were in prison down in Texas at this time, so he never had the chance to lock horns with Bat or Wyatt, though there was a claim by Hardin's admirers that once in Abilene, years before, he had got the drop on none other than Wild Bill "Heycox," as they called him. If so, that was the first I heard of such, but I'm not saying it couldn't of happened, not having been at that scene, which was the only way you could test the truth of anything you heard by way of gunfighting. You'd hardly get it from some whiskeyed cowboy with his talk of "John Wesley," like he was his best friend.

Back to the Lone Star girls, I guess the ones most popular was them that would make a fellow like this think maybe, for as long as he were in bed with them, he *was* J. W. Hardin or maybe his cousin Manning Clements, another with a big rep as a troublemaker.

There was some girls pretty enough to make you wonder why they was doing that, until you considered how good the money was and then the alternative, marrying some sodbuster like their Pa and between childbearing and all the heavy-labor chores, dying young, or staying in a city tenement (for some was Irish from Boston and New York, come West for new opportunities), ditto as to disadvantages as well as breathing bad air. The Lone Star, under Bat Masterson's ownership, was not the kind of place where a man no matter how much he spent could abuse or mistreat a member of the fair sex just because he was hiring her favors. I was on good terms with all the girls, and even had a couple I felt especially friendly towards, one because she was so young-looking and the other on account of she seemed so old and tired (though as it turned out, the little one had turned thirty and the other was only two years older and eventually had put by enough money to open her own brothel down the road), and to either of them two I might direct a cowboy who had not yet spent his roll at the bar or in a game of monte or poker. These women seemed more like sisters to me than persons towards who I felt lustful, so for a while there I was amidst all that carnality, being a teetotaller in flesh as well as in alcohol, for pouring all that whiskey, I couldn't stand the smell when it came to drinking any myself. I reckon I was cleanest of all indulgences there for a while as I ever been my life long, a-working in a den of same, drinking only coffee and with enough money to eat good beef and pay for a nice lodging, I instead lived at a leaky-roof shack of ten rooms, in the red-light district, calling itself a hotel, and unless I could grab a free meal at the Lone Star, I ate hog-and-hominy, as if I was near down and out. I was saving my money for better things.

I decided if I was ever going to make anything of myself, it was more than time, else I'd continue to wander around the country from one plight to the next, as I'd been doing all my life up to that point, with nothing to show for it, meanwhile civilization was settling in. At ten years younger than me, Bat Masterson was half owner of a thriving business. He also run for sheriff of Ford County in the fall of '77 against Larry Deger, who had been town marshal, a real mean three-hundred-pounder who had arrested him once when Bat sided with some little fellow Deger was beating up in the street. Here was another example of how Bat handled himself the smart way, instead of what a hotter-headed man might of done: the revenge he got on Deger was not shooting him but whipping his fat arse in an election.

These was the years when Dodge was the cattle capital of the West, with the drive of '78 setting a record at better than a quarter million longhorns, drove up from the Texas range by fifteen hundred men. Crowds like that could mean trouble, not only as to the unruly cowpunchers, but the money they brung to town was alluring to real criminals. Having said which I should add that with a lot of miscreants of them days the situation was real complicated. A fellow might be a thief and even a murderer at one point, but then at another, and by different people, be thought a credit to the community. For example there was a man named Dave Rudabaugh, who had a rep as a desperado and robbed some trains, for which Bat and a posse tracked him down. Rudabaugh escaped punishment by informing on the other members of his gang, after which he swore he was going straight, and he removed to Las Vegas, New Mexico, where he up and become a policeman! But then he turned bad again a little later and lived a life of crime till, down in Old Mexico, an outraged mob cut off his head and mounted it atop a pole in the town square.

Bat was sheriff of the whole of Ford County, which included Dodge, but the primary job of keeping peace in the town itself was that of head marshal, formerly fatso Deger, but just as Bat had beat him for sheriff, Bat's brother Ed got the marshal's post when Deger was fired, and as his younger brother Jim was an assistant marshal, law enforcement was pretty much dominated by the Masterson family when Dodge was at its height, and not Wyatt Earp, the way you might of heard.

When he worked as only another assistant marshal, Wyatt was best known for beating up disorderly cowboys, either with his fists or by bending the barrel of his Colt's over their head (like he done to me that time on the buffalo range). But no doubt that was better than killing.

Another thing I want to set the record straight on: given all the commotion that could be caused by big crowds of rowdies under conditions like those, during Bat Masterson's time in and around Dodge, only seven homicides occurred. Them showdown gunfights happening every few minutes in movie versions of the frontier begun with the make-believe of Eastern scribblers like Ned Buntline, a confidence man, and in fact the tradition has continued ever since by more or less the same type. But you take people like Wyatt Earp, they ain't going to object when they're made heroes in print, and a Bill Cody will know how to build a profitable business on it.

Having said as much, I should make it clear that every once in a while there was real bloodshed and somebody got hurt, and now and again they died, but never as the result of a fair and equal draw. Take my word for it, when what's at stake is one life or another, fair and equal don't play no part.

Now I'm going to tell you about two of the violent deaths that took place in Dodge during my time there in the late '70s, for they affected me most personally. Once I become an employee of Bat's, and especially after he got to be sheriff, I didn't hang around with him as much as I done in Cheyenne, for he had better things to do, and for a time I saw more of his brother Ed, who was a year older than him and real easygoing. As assistant town marshal and then chief, Ed was one of them genial policemen who smile at passing kids and stop to chew the fat with the storekeepers on their beat. Everybody liked Ed, but that would be better in a place run for the sake of decent women and children, like Dodge City not so many years later, when temperance came and the saloons was turned into soda fountains, if you can believe it, about 1885.

In the Dodge of '78 it was preferable to be respected over being liked — and for that matter, over being feared, because if a man is scared of another he might get drunk enough to take him on, and someone will get hurt. Whereas if you was held in high respect, like Bat, nobody knew what you was capable of; you had imagination going for you, and a normal man's fantasy except for sex is mostly about force: who's got it and who ain't.

There was a few rules regarding public conduct in Dodge. No horses allowed on the sidewalks, and none could be rid onto the premises of a business, namely into a saloon; firearms could not be carried by anybody not a peace officer or on Army duty, unless they was entering town, when all was obliged to check their weapons at the first place of call, saloon, shop, hotel, et cetera, or after picking up their guns on the way out of town. The public discharge of firearms was prohibited except on the Fourth of July, Christmas, New Year's Day, and the eves thereof. Public intoxication was taken seriously only if a man in that condition tried to reclaim his weapons or committed an offense against order and decency, like taking a leak in one of the whiskey barrels full of water kept at intervals along the wood sidewalk in case of fire.

If you was to break one of these ordinances after calling Ed Masterson's attention to it, he would surely do something, but unlike some peace officers, he never went about looking for an excuse to make an arrest. Ed was a live-and-let type of fellow, in a place that was kill-or-be. He ended up shedding more blood, of his own and others', than did his brother Bat, who nevertheless is the famous one, while Ed has been forgot, and you will see, the same was true with Virgil Earp and his brother Wyatt.

Ed Masterson dropped in frequently to the Lone Star, both on his marshal rounds and off-time, and I got to know him well enough, by which I mean we talked about the usual subjects men cared for, the old days of buffalo hunting, the latest gold or silver strikes, horses, firearms, whiskey, and women.

As to the last-named, you might gather from my previous remarks that every single female to be found in Dodge was a harlot. Now with regard to Deadwood, that wouldn't of been far wrong, but there was others in Dodge City. It's just that in my situation it was not usual to run across the trail of schoolteachers and churchwomen, who didn't patronize saloons. Respectable females of that time was not supposed to like strong drink or know much about sex even after having ten kids. And a man wasn't supposed to enjoy himself with them: for that there was whores.

Now on the particular afternoon in question, a fellow name of Bob Shaw stood in the Lone Star, accusing one Texas Dick Moore of taking forty dollars off him by some dishonest means, and what made this a troublesome matter was that Shaw was not only in the state of drunkenness in which the rest of the world is also guilty for his grievance, but he was also brandishing the pistol which by law he should of checked on entering the premises. Under the bar I kept a club and a double-barreled shotgun, but I didn't want to kill or even maim him badly. On the other hand I also didn't like the idea of clubbing him enough to make him madder but not enough to knock him out. So I quietly asks a man named Frank, further along the bar, to go fetch Marshal Masterson to come before this thing got out of hand.

Meanwhile I pushed a bottle in Shaw's direction, telling him to drink on the house, for free whiskey will sometimes calm a man down temporarily. But the offer only riled Shaw further, and he waved the muzzle of his pistol from Texas Dick over my way, advising me in abusive language to horn out unless I wanted my own case of lead poisoning.

I was delicately fingering my way along the underbar towards the scattergun, without moving that part of my person that could be seen by Shaw, when Ed Masterson arrived.

In his nice way Ed asks Shaw to just hand over the weapon.

"I aim to kill thish sson of a bish," Shaw says, meaning to my relief Texas Dick, on who he again directed his gun, "and if you try to sstop me, I'll kill you, you sson of a bish."

At this, Ed draws his own pistol, steps up and hits Shaw in the head with the barrel. I had knowed what I was doing when I decided against trying to club the bastard: just as I feared, Shaw had too thick a skull to be dented, and the blow served only to increase his grudge. He turns and shoots Ed almost point-blank, right under the shoulder blade, putting Ed's whole right arm out of action, to say the least. That shot might of killed anybody not a Masterson. But as he falls bleeding to the floor Ed coolly swaps hands with his Colt's, and with the left he puts two rounds into Shaw, arm and leg, dropping the man, though not before Texas Dick takes a slug near the crotch, and Frank, what had fetched the marshal and stayed outside, a-peeping in the door, catches Shaw's last wild shot in the left arm.

If you ever heard two .45s discharge multiply at the same time under a roof, you know the reverberations ring inside your head for some minutes thereafter, and with the black powder then in use, there was so much smoke it could of been from a roaring fire, and I admit I was stunned for a minute, not reacting as quick as I did after Wild Bill's murder, but in fact Ed didn't need no help, being still in control of the room. Laying there in his own blood, he continued to cover the likewise fallen Shaw, who had not been killed, as well as a few of Shaw's nearby friends, who might otherwise have been seeking revenge.

To show you further what kind of man Ed Masterson was, after only a couple weeks off, he did the rest of his recuperating back on duty.

Not long after this Ed was appointed chief town marshal. Dodge City entered the years that gave it its subsequent fame, as I have said, but for me what made the place so special was the entertainment and I don't mean the low order available elsewhere, but the high-class type come from back East, headed by the great Eddie Foy, famous the country over, who could sing and dance better than anyone else alive and was so funny with his costumes and antics your belly would ache from laughing so much. The hall he performed in was called the Comique, which naturally was pronounced to rhyme with "stew" by the ignorant louts (like myself at that time) who packed the place. This was my first exposure to what come to be known as show business, and it made a permanent impression on me, and in time I'll be telling you of my own career in another form of it.

But let me get back now to Ed Masterson, who returned to marshal's duty long before the wound he got from Bob Shaw had healed, and he was just as friendly and easygoing as ever though having been almost killed. Unlike his brother Bat, Ed often managed to get hurt while keeping the peace. Even in court this could happen, like the time one Jim Martin was charged with stealing a horse and at his trial got mad and beat up the city attorney, broke a lot of courtroom furniture, and cut Ed's nose before being coldcocked with the barrel of the marshal's .45.

The Lady Gay was another of the popular saloons of the time, right near the Lone Star, and in fact was where the political meeting was held that had nominated Bat for sheriff the year before. On their rounds, Ed and Nat Haywood, an assistant marshal, come into the Lady Gay one night in April of '78, where a half a dozen hands from the same outfit was swallowing a lot of drink and making normal noise, which for cowboys tended to be louder than that made by a convention of preachers, but nothing wrong with that, though it wore you out some having to hear it all night, and in fact I stepped outside the nearby Lone Star, to get a little relief as well as a breath of fresh air free of tobacco smoke, whiskey fumes, and sweat.

In a minute I saw Ed Masterson come out of the Lady Gay, and I stepped over to him.

"Say, Ed," says I, "I been working on a business idea for a time, and saving my money towards it, too, but I ain't got quite enough yet to go it on my own."

Ed favored Bat in appearance, with the same dark hair and mustache, but his features was a little finer, and there was always a look in his eye that could be called somewhat sad.

"What I got in mind," I went on, "is opening a place of my own, with the usual games of chance, drinks, eats, women naturally, but the main attraction will be the entertainment. I swear that's the coming thing, but you got to get real talent to put it over, which means you got to bring it in from quite a ways, from back East or San Francisco." Ed was listening carefully, as was his manner. "Now what I thought I'd mention to you is if you might want to go in with me on this here idea, for I require at least one partner."

He smiled slowly. "It's Bat you ought to talk to. He's the one with the head for business."

What I hadn't said was I already talked to Bat, who didn't care for the idea, maybe because he already had the Lone Star and regarded my place as competition, or he didn't think I could handle it. I have to admit Bat still thought of me as a kind of character.

"Bat's got plans of his own," I says. "Look, just keep it in mind is all I'm asking. And I wouldn't expect a big investment from you personally, but your good name and fine rep in this town would help out in getting a loan from the bank."

At this point Nat Haywood walks briskly out of the Lady Gay and he tells Ed, "Walker didn't check the gun. He give it back to Jack Wagner."

Ed shook his head, but he wasn't all that disturbed. "One of Alf Walker's hands was wearing a loaded shoulder holster," he told me. "I took the gun away from him and gave it to Alf to check. He ought to know better." He and Nat headed back into the Lady, and I returned inside to my own job behind the bar.

A few minutes later somebody yelled something through the Lone Star door, but the noise near me was such I couldn't hear what was shouted and didn't take no alarm from it, for yells was routine in the saloons of Dodge and unless they employed the term "Fire" did not attract much attention. But next this person or another runs in with enough commotion that the crowd quieted a little, and I could hear, "— so close his clothes was burnin'!"

"Who?" I yells back.

"The marshal, goddammit. Ed Masterson! He's dyin'."

I dropped the bottle I had been lifting, and it broke when it hit the floor, drenching my boots with whiskey. I run out of the Lone Star, ramming my way through the drinkers, and reached the street, where there was another crowd, everybody talking about the fight inside the Lady Gay and giving different versions thereof.

"Where is he?" I yells. "Where is Ed?"

"He walked away," somebody says. "He crossed the tracks!"

I felt some better. That a dying man could of walked two hundred yards across the plaza was unlikely. He was heading for the marshal's office. "Why did they say he was a goner?" I asked nobody in particular.

A tall cowboy shifted the wad in his jaw and says, "If'n he ain't, no man ever was. He's got a hole in him big enough to put your fist through. Ed tried to take Jack Wagner's gun, but Jack shoved it right against him and pulled the trigger. The blast set Ed's coat on fire."

"Yet he walked away?"

"Sure did," said another man. "I don't know how he stayed on his feet. First he gut-shot Wagner, and when Alf Walker tried to horn in, Ed put a round into his lung and two in the arm."

Another voice says, "I seen Ed go into Hoover's."

Which was another of the well-known Dodge saloons not in the red-light district. I run over there, across the tracks, and entered the place.

Ed Masterson was laying on the floor. There was still some wisps of smoke coming from his coat. The bartender, George Hinkel, was crouching beside him.

I bent down. I says, "Ed . . ."

He looks at me with them sad dark eyes. "I'm done for, Jack" was all he said, and then he passed out, never to come to life again.

Jack Wagner soon died too. But Alf Walker, the trail boss, managed in time to survive his wounds. Nat Haywood's excuse for being of no help to Ed Masterson was that Walker kept a gun on him. Some said Nat had just proved yellow and run out, but in things of that nature you don't know the truth unless you was on the spot and maybe not even then. In any event Nat left town right away, which meant there was two openings in the police department. A well-known figure of the time, Charlie Bassett, replaced Ed Masterson as chief marshal of Dodge City. As for Nat Haywood's assistant marshal job, it went to a fellow name of Wyatt Earp, and that was the highest rank Wyatt ever held as peace officer at Dodge, irregardless of all subsequent lies told by him, his arse-kissers, or both.

You might wonder about Bat Masterson's reaction to his brother's murder? Lots of lies has been told about that too. Bat sure grieved for Ed, but he didn't go berserk with rage and gun down a lot of people. He didn't shoot nobody over this matter. When Alf Walker got well enough to travel, he was allowed to go home to Texas in peace. Whether or not he held a gun on Nat Haywood couldn't be proved, as Nat had run off and most of the witnesses worked for Alf, and so he weren't charged with any crime. Jack Wagner had paid with his own life for what he had done, so the book was closed on the sorry event. Bat was the duly elected sheriff of Ford County and as such had to uphold the law. Still, it might be considered funny that one of the most feared gunfighters of his time would not of been vengeful, but as I have said, Bat Masterson was a man of reason. Besides, he always thought his brother run too many foolish risks. If Bat himself had took a gun off Jack Wagner, Wagner wouldn't of dared to put it back on. Wyatt Earp would of coldcocked Wagner at the outset, and Wild Bill would of killed him right away and got it over with.

So obviously my thought of getting Ed to go in with me on my business idea was at an end, and anyway before long Bat's old partner Ben Springer opened the Comique, which I swear was a lot like what I had had in mind, and not long thereafter Ham Bell's similar enterprise, the Varieties, started up in competition, luring away the Comique's Dora Hand, reputed to be the most beautiful woman west of the Mississippi, who supposedly come from a high-class Boston family and sung opera before the crowned heads of Europe, and it might well of been true a dozen men got killed for competing for her favors, for women like her was uncommon in the cattle camps.

Now maybe I was not being strictly literal when I might of given the idea a while back that I abstained from all traffic with the opposite sex at this phase of my life: what I meant was I didn't do so any more than was necessary for my health. That warrior society amongst the Cheyenne called the Contraries was undoubtedly right in not losing any power to sexual activities when preparing to go to war, but though living in a fairly violent part of the world, I myself was notably a man of peace while living in Dodge City. I carried a hidden derringer, so as not to be totally helpless if I encountered someone too drunk or crazy to handle with talk, but went otherwise unarmed, relying on all them famous local gunfighters to do their job. Let me say this: a sense of ethics kept me from being a customer where I worked, so I never had any but a professional association with my female fellow workers at the Lone Star, except for what you might call a brotherly sort of affection for the two girls I mentioned whose troubles I listened to.

What I had never had in my adult life thus far was what you could call a real romance. I mean, I had white and Indian wives, and while I was real fond of them, being married was a kind of practical matter, making sense for a home and family, which I had had in both white and Cheyenne worlds, and it was events, and not me nor my wives, what brought them marriages to an end. I had loved but had not been *in love* in the way them men who got killed over Dora Hand had apparently been to have gone that far. I wasn't itching to die similarly, but thought when I first heard her sing I might be missing something, and I commenced to get a big crush on her. Now this had happened before, when

I was a boy, with my white foster-mother Mrs. Pendrake and then again, and ongoing, was what I had for Mrs. Libbie Custer, but in both cases unrealistic and in the latter, notably remote. Dora Hand was here and now, and I was grown up and well employed, being at this point head bartender of the Lone Star, which meant I could give myself time off so as to frequently attend her performances.

Now I sure wasn't alone in my admiration for the lady. Not a wildflower remained on the prairie for miles around Dodge, all having been plucked out and sent backstage for Dora, and for a time the fancy boxed candies from back East was all sold out in the stores, along with yew-de-cologne or whatever it's called, lace hankies and other fineries, though nothing naughty like satin garters, for what was maybe Dora's greatest distinction was her regular Sunday presence at services in the little church on the respectable north side, where her sweet singing of hymns was admired by the other ladies of the congregation, the wives of the better element of merchants, who did not resent her, as they would of others for being young and beautiful, on account of she was showfolk, then and now a special category.

There wasn't nobody in Dodge City did not admire Miss Dora Hand, and most men, included yours truly, downright adored her. She was an ideal specimen of the fair sex, the sort of lady who makes the average fellow think he has got a high odor even after taking his annual bath (which was true of some of them cowboys), and I knowed men who claimed to change their underwear for the first time in months just to go watch her sing, and even buy a pair of socks.

There was never no one more awkward around a lady than the rough kind of fellow of that place and time, who would sooner shoot it out with a murderous enemy of his own sex than try and talk to a decent female, though according to the sporting women at the Lone Star, pretty much the same was true of them with harlots, except in the latter case they was not apologetic. Did I want to deal with smut, I could pass on some of the stories told me by them girls, who got a mostly unflattering impression of men, but it never discouraged them from eternally looking for a good one, not always without success: anyway, they usually got married sooner or later and insofar as any men ever admitted to marrying a former working woman, he invariably swore they made the best wives.

I don't say I had the oily tongue of a lounge lizard or big-city masher, but my childhood experience of living under the same roof as Mrs. Pendrake and being read poetry to by her give me a definite advantage over most of the other men in Dodge. I was also smarter than most, and willing to make a greater sacrifice. I went pretty far: namely, I begun to go to church of a Sunday, something I hadn't done since being obliged to listen to the Reverend Pendrake's endless sermons as a boy, the only compensation for which was sitting next to Mrs. P. and inhaling her flowered scent.

It took me a few Sundays before, using not dissimilar skills to those I had learned from the Cheyenne in hunting game, I could devise a way of getting next to Miss Hand in her pew, for being she was a celebrity, as many women as men wanted to be near her, but eventually one Sunday I managed to get on her immediate left, though to do so I had to jostle several of the regular churchgoers, incurring an un-Christian enmity.

I waited until the second of the hymns was finished before, in the brief interval we was sitting back down, to apologize for my own croaking rendition.

"Oh," Miss Hand said prettily, from under her big bonnet, turning her sparkling eyes on me, "all voices are sweet to the ear of the Lord."

"Praise God," I says. I don't want you to think I spoke sacrilegiously, for just because I seldom found myself in a church don't mean I was an unbeliever any time in my life. We all have a Maker, who will take us back one day, and him who has never had a home in life will be assured one Over There.

Having said as much, however, I wouldn't have been in that pew or anywhere else in church had Miss Dora Hand been elsewhere. And I didn't much listen to the sermon even so, for religious lingo never appealed to me. I had heard too much of it from my Pa and the Rev. Pendrake. The Catholics have a lot of sense, using Latin which nobody understands and therefore seems more like a language God would speak rather than even the loftiest old-fashioned English.

What I was doing instead was thinking of other ways to get acquainted with Miss Hand without arousing her suspicion that my motives wasn't pure. I come up with an approach I considered perfect. I acted like I didn't know she was famous. This immediately distinguished me from everybody else she had met in Dodge. I went even further: I pretended to disapprove of professional entertainment of all kinds.

"Oh," says she, with a beautiful little pout of her soft pink lower lip, "you are very stern, sir, I must say."

We was walking out together after the service. I had managed to fend off the others who tried to get to her, thus earning more dark looks. I was misguided to believe my conspicuous large donation when the collection plate was passed would make up for the bad feeling I had aroused: there are times when I had been too cynical about money. For example, Miss Hand, who probably earned more at this time than the richest merchants in Dodge, did not come to church for mercenary reasons.

Anyhow, I says to her now, pursing my lips in the sissified manner of the holier-than-thou, "Better to err on the side of righteousness than on the side of laxity." This was on the order of something I hope I recalled correctly from the Reverend Pendrake's spiel.

"It is true that the arts," says she, lowering them feathery eyelashes, "or should I say the performers thereof, have acquired a reputation for immorality, one that may not always be undeserved. But there are those of us who do what we can to redress the balance."

"Do I rightly gather from your comments," I says, surprising myself with the genteel elevation of speech, "that you have some connection, distant no doubt, with entertainment?"

"I'm afraid I must confess I do," Miss Hand replied. She proceeded to raise her little parasol against the glaring Kansas sun without halting or losing a step, in the way persons like her do on the stage while singing. "I do so hope you won't be shocked to hear as much."

"Already I have began to reconsider," says I, and we exchanged introductions. "It might well be," I went on, "mine has been a limited life, confined to them, uh, those who purchase the Good Book."

"Do you sell Bibles, Mr. Crabb?"

Suddenly, there on the church path, I was conscience-struck and reluctant to lie further, so I says, in truth, "I am a parson's son."

Some old biddy, waddling up behind, could no longer tolerate my monopolizing of Dora Hand, and she gets her hefty figure, all gussied up in her Sunday best, in between, and she says, "Dora, will we see you at the Ladies' Aid?"

Miss Hand smiles graciously. "Of course you will, Martha. Have I ever missed?"

She allowed me to walk her home, which turned out to be not far away, in a little house tucked away behind the Western Hotel.

"Miss Hand," I says, "I am so pleased to of had this real pleasant conversation. I wonder if I go too far in hoping we might talk again, after next Sunday's service. I would like ever so much to know more about your career as an artist."

Her smile was quite different from what she had shown to the church lady. It might be called a smirk, except I couldn't see any malice in it. "Meanwhile, Mr. Crabb, will I continue to see you every night in the front row at the Varieties?"

I laughs and stamps my foot, being both embarrassed and thrilled. "How do you like that! You mean from up there, back of them footlights, you can see people in the audience?"

"I'd have to be blind to miss you, Jack, with the commotion you make after every number."

"Miss Hand, I'm overwhelmed. Let me just say I wasn't lying about being a preacher's son, but I don't sell Bibles. I'm chief bartender over at the Lone Star, which by your lights must be a pretty lowdown place. But I really will go to church again if I could just talk to you afterwards."

"Jack," says she, and she actually grazed my sleeve with her slender fingers gloved in dove-gray. "I don't think we should make a deal about going to church. But naturally I will always be happy to see you there."

You couldn't call it a real social engagement, but it was good enough at that point, and I tell you I waited all week for that upcoming Sunday service, which was a unique anticipation for me, who used to dread the same thing when living with the Reverend Pendrake even more than I hated school.

But the unhappy fact is that I never set eyes on a living Dora Hand again.

I didn't go to the Varieties all week long, owing to the embarrassment I still felt on her catching me in that misrepresentation. I really intended, in whatever connection me and her would have in the future, no matter how slight on her part, that it should bring out the best in me. I resolved to listen to the sermon next Sunday and not show off with how much I put in the collection plate, also not to be rude to other people in the congregation. That might of been just the beginning of my transformation into a better person, or so anyway I thought at the time.

Now I got to take what might seem a detour but will prove otherwise. Amongst the Texas troublemakers who come to the Kansas cattle camps of the time was one Jim Kennedy, and excuse the language but there ain't a fitting name for him but rotten young son of a bitch. He hung around with the plain cowboys, but his Pa, Mifflin K., was partner of

Richard King of the King Ranch, the biggest such in the world, then and now, with more acreage than some little countries. Being rich, young, and good-looking, Kennedy did pretty much what he wanted, and if anybody objected he would shoot them when they was unarmed or, preferably, with their back turned to him. He had done this elsewhere, but when he showed up in Dodge wearing a gun in defiance of the law, I got to commend Wyatt Earp for once: Wyatt pistol-whipped and then arrested the cocky bastard, and a month later Marshal Charlie Bassett arrested him again, for disorderly conduct.

This kind of treatment seemed real unfair to Kennedy, who had gone through life thus far without opposition to his wishes, and he protested bitterly to the mayor, the aforementioned Dog Kelley, who was also proprietor of the Alhambra Saloon in the busiest block of Front Street. Dog had no respect for Kennedy, who made his hands call him Spike, like he was a hard case instead of being as yellow as they come, and told him next time he got out of line in Dodge the peace officers wouldn't take it so easy on him.

Kennedy was too cowardly to stand up to anybody he thought his match, but he went at the older and slight-built Dog with his fists, and the result was Dog whipped his arse so bad he could hardly limp out of town, swearing to get even.

Suffering from some ailment having nothing to do with this minor event, the mayor went over to the Army hospital at nearby Fort Dodge for a time, and while he was there he let two featured performers of the fair sex borrow his little cottage, and they was Miss Fanny Garretson of the Comique and Miss Dora Hand, and that was where I had walked home the latter after church, to bring the subject back on track.

At about four in the morning of the following Friday, them living in the Western Hotel, unless too drunk to come to life, was wakened by four blasts of gunfire in the street behind. Wyatt Earp and Bat's younger brother Jim Masterson was on police patrol duty, and they rushed to the scene.

The door to Dog Kelley's little house was shot full of holes. Just inside, Wyatt and Jim found Fanny Garretson on the floor in her nightgown, shaking and weeping. In Dog Kelley's bed was Dora Hand, killed with a shot to her soft bosom.

Some night owl up at that hour, hearing the gunfire, seen Jim Kennedy riding hell-bent out of town. It had been him all right, out to kill Mayor Kelley, shooting through the door in the middle of the night, never knowing Dog was not in residence but the girls was there instead.

I won't go into my feelings on getting this terrible news next morning, except to say all impulses I had towards improving myself in a moral way was forgot with the death of this lovely, godfearing, churchgoing young lady. All I cared about was shedding Kennedy's blood, but in that aim I had a lot of competition. The entire male population of Dodge was pleading with Bat to include them in the posse he was organizing, but as he already had Wyatt Earp, Charlie Bassett, and Bill Tilghman, he was resisting the pleas of lesser men.

To mine he says, with the usual slight smile he showed me even at a moment like this, "Sorry, Jack, this is a job for professional lawmen."

"You can deputize me!"

"Look, Jack," Bat says, "I don't want to hurt your feelings, but whatever you did before I met you, since you've been in Dodge you've only poured whiskey. Do you even own a weapon? Or a horse, for that matter? Kennedy's hands are going to want to help him. A couple dozen of them are in town, and somebody said they are saddling up."

"I don't care if all of Texas tries to save that skunk," I says, breathing fire. "This ain't the Alamo. The lady he killed was a personal friend of mine."

Bat squints with his right eye. "Well, Jack, a lot of fellows can say that."

I just hoped he never meant she was common. I wouldn't of taken that from Bat Masterson himself. "Goddammit, Bat," I says, "I got to go after him."

Bat stopped smiling. "Jack," says he, "you're not going."

What should I of done then? To this day I regret not having borrowed or stole a horse (though you could get hanged for the latter) and gone after Kennedy and killed him, preferably in a fashion not so merciful as a shot to the head. For what happened was Bat and that posse of famous gunfighters did track the bastard down and captured him, with no worse damage to Kennedy than a shot that smashed his armbone. They brought him back for a hearing before a judge, who proceeded to let him go for lack of evidence!

You will remember Jack McCall, what murdered Wild Bill in cold blood, was let go by his first jury, and Walker, who gave Wagner the gun used to kill Ed Masterson, was likewise allowed to go free. So if you think justice was better served in the Old West than in your own time, whatever it is or will be, you are wrong.

Jim Kennedy's rich dad come up and hauled him back safe to Texas, where he was protected by an army of cowboys, and he lived to shoot more people in the back till finally his number come up and somebody, unfortunately not me, rubbed out the no-good son of a bitch.

Dora Hand's funeral was the biggest in the history of Dodge.

By now I had had enough of the place, for sure, and was fixing to move on again, though I didn't know to where — I had accumulated a little nest egg, which by rights I should of took to Mrs. Agnes Lake Thatcher Hickok, in Cincinnati, to replace that lost roll Bill had give me, but I wasn't yet ready to do that, think worse of me if you will — when Bat Masterson did give me a special job, which led to a change of direction once again, this time taking me back to the Indians.

5
Human Beings in the Hoosegow

OW I HAVEN'T MENTIONED THE CHEYENNE FOR A while — I mean, in the sense of what they had been up to since the big fight at the Greasy Grass — but that don't mean they disappeared from the face of the earth, like many whites wanted to hear. Them and their Sioux and Arapaho friends all separated into many different bands following the Custer battle and scattered all over Montana and Dakota territories. The hostiles was not done fighting, and at one point they even come close to Deadwood at Slim Buttes, but the three generals they called respectively Three Stars (Crook), Bear Coat (Miles), and Bad Hand (Mackenzie) run them all to ground — except Sitting Bull, who ended up in Grandmother's land (Canada) — within a year, and even the great Ogallala Crazy Horse surrendered and come into the agency, where before long he lost his life in a scuffle the explanation of which depended on not only what race you belonged to, but which faction thereof. I was not on hand for it, so have nothing to say except that the incident involved either his best friend or worst Judas, one Little Big Man. Which was not me, this person being another Ogallala and his name, though translating the same as mine, was Sioux in its original form, as mine was Cheyenne. I think I have said this before, but people don't always listen, and get it wrong. If the distinction is hard to grasp, think of how when I went to Europe with Cody's show (of which more to come) a French lady said "Little Big Man" as *Pertygrandum*, or thereabouts, and in Germany some mustachioed and bemedaled prince told me in his language it was, more or less, *Klynergrossman*. Same name, different lingos.

Dull Knife, what some have called the greatest of the Cheyenne chiefs, finally surrendered in the spring of '77 and immediately come to regret doing so, for him and his band was thereupon compelled, though they was Northern Cheyenne, to join their cousins of the Southern branch of the people, on a reservation down in Indian Territory, which later become the state of Oklahoma, but was known by the likes of me as the Nations, after the other tribes that lived there, many of which had been run out to the region from their natural homelands in the Southeast years earlier, the Cherokees and the rest.

When you consider how the Government treated Indians, which was rarely better than absolutely rotten, you sometimes make out the glint of a bright idea, like *Why wouldn't these folk welcome being collected together into one big happy family of Cheyenne?* There might also of been a thought that the association would make them less warlike, the southerners having been subdued for some time.

Whatever the reasons why they had to go down there, Dull Knife's people found the place intolerable. The game was long gone, and anyway they was not supposed to hunt but rather to be issued Government food, which as usual proved scant on account of the corruption familiar since time immemorial with them that have access to public funds. And the terrain and climate, to which Indians, being on such close terms with nature, was very sensitive, were all wrong in these hot and humid lowlands, whereas their lifelong home had been near the Bighorn Mountains and the Black Hills. The northern Cheyenne took sick with fevers and chills from maladies they had never previously heard of. Not to mention the mortal illness resulting from the heart being broke over and over again.

So after a year they up and left the reservation and headed north, a move that was strictly illegal, so the troops went after them, and there followed that long journey in which about three hundred Cheyenne, only sixty-seventy of them warriors, fought off the U.S. Army's continued efforts to stop them over many weeks and many hundreds of miles.

I had lost all track of the people to which I had been closer than to my natural-born race, for the years I spent with the Indians was the ones where a person absorbs much of what will get him through life, and my existence with Old Lodge Skins's band was more concentrated than any subsequently with whites, including my time with my wife and child, which lasted only a couple of years and besides, as I have said, Olga was

Swedish and though she probably spoke better English than me, I believe she thought in her native tongue, of which I never learned a word, except a drinking toast that says *Skoal* to all the pretty girls.

In fact I tried not to reflect on the Indian situation, which after Custer was rubbed out was all losses for the red side: there wasn't nothing I could do about it. Since telling Wild Bill Hickok that I had survived at the Little Bighorn and not being believed, I had not mentioned that fact to a soul, for I realized if anybody did believe me he'd then have to deal with me getting my life saved by one of the Indians who was slaughtering every other white man in sight, the kind of thing difficult to explain to the folks of that time.

But then, all of a sudden, the matter was at hand. In the middle of September in '78, them northward-moving renegade Cheyenne was within twenty miles of Dodge City, raiding little settlements and ranches, and they killed a mail carrier out from Dodge, who had the bad luck to cross their trail. So there was enough panic locally to distract all concerned from the usual drinking, gambling, and whoring, and since hardly any troops was at the nearby fort, reinforcements was summoned and meanwhile civilian volunteers assembled to save the capital of civilization from the savages.

I didn't join this bunch. The killing of Dora Hand was still eating at me. If Bat had let me go along on the pursuit of Jim Kennedy, the latter wouldn't of stayed alive. So Kennedy escaped all punishment and returned to Texas, but the Cheyenne was to be kept from returning to a home what had been taken from them. I couldn't see the justice in it, so I stayed behind the bar, pouring whiskey for the many others who stayed behind, because when I say the vices was put aside totally for defense of the city, I was speaking loosely. When it come to drinking, there were some who would keep doing it while they was getting scalped alive.

The emergency was over before long with the Indians moving on north and that seemed the end of the matter locally, until the following February when Bat, looking in at the Lone Star, tells me the Governor of Kansas has ordered him to Fort Leavenworth to pick up a half-dozen Cheyenne prisoners from the Army, to bring back for a trial by the civil authorities of Ford County, on the crimes they had committed while in the vicinity of Dodge.

The news hit me hard. Them Indians was likely to get lynched if brung back to this place as common criminals.

"Who you taking along?" I asked him, and he names several deputies including his brother Jim and Charlie Bassett. "Any of you speak the language?"

"I don't," Bat says.

"You could use an interpreter."

He put on his familiar smirk. "Yourself?"

"Goddammit, Bat," I says. "Take me serious for once. I really can speak Cheyenne." I rattled off a stream of it.

He smiled more broadly and threw down a shot of whiskey, then re-settled his derby. "Now, Jack, since I don't speak it myself, how in hell would I know if what you just said was Cheyenne?"

"I'm going to lie to Bat Masterson?"

I'll mention again that Bat's head was a lot less swelled than others of the time, but flattery sometimes worked even with him. "Well," he says, "I can't pay you extra. Just expenses."

I accepted the deal, even though I'd be losing my Lone Star pay as well, for them was the days before paid vacations and sick time off, but I had that nest egg I have spoke of and wasn't doing this with monetary gain in mind.

So me and Bat and the four deputies traveled to Fort Leavenworth, where the Army turned over the Cheyenne prisoners to us, seven of them, in their blankets, dusky countenances totally blank despite the unpleasantness of their situation. They was all handcuffed and in leg irons as well. It was from this sort of lack of display of emotion that whites saw redskins as having no feelings that wasn't prompted by blood-lust. But the truth was rather that Indians wouldn't give their enemies the satisfaction of showing that the latter had hurt them.

We all returned to Dodge on the Santa Fe, taking up half a car for our party, and as the Cheyenne wasn't causing any trouble, the lawmen spent most of their time keeping away the white civilians on the rest of the train and then, at the many stops, fending off the unruly mobs that had formed at a number of the stations with an idea of dragging the now helpless warriors out and hanging them. Speaking from the experience of now more than a century, I can tell you that the type of man who most thirsts for revenge is likely to be one who has himself never suffered any damage from the person who is the object of his vengeance: it might be he feels insulted by the very lack of menace to him by them who have done dirty to others he don't even know.

Now Bat Masterson was at his best in situations where he could assert personal authority without a show of even suggested force, and without no bluster so much as raising his voice beyond the volume necessary while standing in the doorway of the car to address a crowd on the platform. This worked at most towns, but at Lawrence the mob got sufficiently pushy for Bat to have to knock down the man nearest him, which however turned out to be the town marshal, and Bat found himself under arrest. But finally we reached Topeka, where a thousand people was waiting, along with a closed wagon to convey the prisoners to the jail for overnight, which was done through a lot of milling and yelling, but the Indians was protected by our bunch from Dodge and local deputies of Shawnee County.

Since there wasn't no practical need as yet — they went where they was pointed — I had not addressed a word to the Cheyenne, despite what Bat might make of my silence, and the reason was none of them would believe me if I started talking to them in their own language. So far as they could see, I belonged to the enemy that held them prisoner. It wouldn't make no sense by their lights that I would have friendly feelings towards them. If such was the case, then why didn't I let them loose? I had a real problem, and while the lawmen was holding off the mobs, I was trying to figure a way to deal with it.

It called for real delicacy. I sure couldn't show any moral weakness. I decided therefore to start with the one whose name translated as Wild Hog. With Dull Knife he had been a principal chief of them who headed north from the Nations. We was told he had tried to stab himself to death while at Fort Leavenworth and was still not healed, though nobody asked him now to unwrap his blanket for a look. Suicide amongst the Cheyenne was unusual in normal times, though on this subject Bat said he had been with the other buffalo hunters in '74 at Adobe Walls when they was attacked by Quanah Parker's band of Comanche, Kiowa, Arapaho, and Southern Cheyenne, and a young warrior of the last-named, called Stone Teeth, blew out his brains after being badly wounded by two rounds from a Sharps Big 50 buffalo rifle.

Maybe the fact that Wild Hog failed in the attempt to end his own life suggested he hadn't his heart in it, for as a fighting warrior he would sure know how to kill with an edged weapon. Anyway, the Indian prisoners at the Shawnee County jail wasn't given any implements with which to cut the tough-looking meat they was served, and I didn't try to talk with the Hog while he was gnawing at his grub, which like all the others he put away with good appetite, so I guess he intended for the moment anyhow to stay amongst the living.

For the convenience of their captors, all seven Cheyenne was kept in one large cell of the kind for the temporary holding of drunks, and they was all sitting on the floor, not even talking to one another, at least not when under observation, which was most of the time, owing to that worry about suicide.

I wanted to take along a present but was pretty restricted in what was available. The old favorites of flour, coffee, and other foods needing to be cooked would be of no use to them now, and they wasn't allowed to smoke, owing to the possibility of fire, so tobacco wouldn't do.

What I settled on was sugar, Indians having a notable sweet tooth. I bought me a loaf of it at a shop in town when Bat and us went in to feed, and when we come back I asked the county jailors to give me a while with the captives, which they did, so long as I disarmed myself first of any weapons.

None of the Cheyenne paid me any mind when I entered the cell, all of them continuing to stare ahead, each cocooned in a dirty blanket. They wore no feathers or other ornamentation, and none of them looked young. People of a different race from your own, whatever you are, tend to resemble one another, as everyone knows and resents when it applies to his own type, but then when you live amongst the others they become immediately as distinguishable as anybody you ever knowed — only to get blurred again after you move out. I say this because it was true of me as well. When we picked up these men at Leavenworth, I had not recognized any of them, which despite my intimate association with the Cheyenne was not unusual, for mostly Old Lodge Skins's band roamed around on its own, for reasons I give earlier, and were not that close to any other, except for a few special occasions such as at Black Kettle's village on the Washita and then again at the Greasy Grass, attacked by Custer both times. And in a big gathering of thousands you wouldn't get to know a lot of individuals any more than you would if visiting St. Louis or Chicago.

But now when I come into that jail cell and looked down at Wild Hog, I suddenly saw what I had not seen earlier: I thought I could recognize him as one of the boys I had been raised with as a child. We had played together with kid-sized bows and arrows and little toy horses made of wood or clay, and with others we had sat around Old Lodge Skins as he told us the educational stories of great Cheyenne exploits of the past, like the one concerning Little Man, from whose name my own was taken after I had done well in a horse-raiding expedition against the Crow. But two things puzzled me, the first of which was if I knowed him as a young kid, where had he been since then? For I rejoined the band a couple times later on, was with them at the Washita, yet could not recall seeing Wild Hog. Not to mention if we was boys together, how come he now looked so old, whereas I thought of myself as still quite youthful. I put in that last so you can get a laugh out of it. I was considered fairly old for the time myself, being well into the second half of my thirties, with only a year or so left if I was to be as imprudent as Wild Bill and play cards with my back to the door.

I'll tell you about dealing with Indians: in some things it's best to be as direct as possible, like if you're hungry or cold or have to make water or any natural thing, you just say so. Courtesy does not demand otherwise. But with certain matters, for example time, you don't just talk freely about it even with family members and intimates, for that can be rude. In trying to figure out why this is true I come up with the idea that time belongs to everybody and everything, and nobody and nothing can lay claim to any part of it exclusively, so if you talk about the past as though there was just one version of it that everybody agrees on, you might be seen as stealing the spirit of others, something which the Cheyenne always had a taboo against. You could shoot a man and while he lay dying rip off his scalp, but if you felt sorry for him under them conditions, you was trying to steal his spirit as well, and that was out of order.

So whether or not Wild Hog was the grown version of the boy I had knowed, I sure didn't make the suggestion to him. Instead I squatted down and unwrapped the sugarloaf from the piece of paper around it and presented it to him. I didn't say it was for everybody, for that too would of been discourteous. Indians instinctively shared everything they ever got, with the exception of whiskey.

He took the gift, but did not look at either it or me.

I addressed him in Cheyenne. "I will speak for you whenever you want to say something to the Americans."

He flickered his glittering black eyes at me. "Can you tell me why we are here?"

Nobody had even let them know why they was arrested. "The

Kansans," I says, "are going to put you on trial for murder and taking women against their will." Wild Hog shrugged inside his red blanket and said nothing, but some of the others muttered. "You don't have to admit doing these things," I told him, "whether or not you did them. You cannot be forced to speak against your own interest."

"That makes no sense," says he.

I tried to explain though I wasn't no lawyer. "The Americans got that from what happened on the island of the Grandmother, where most of them came from at first. The reason why you cannot talk against yourself is that your enemies might make you do that by torture." I could see I wasn't getting nowhere: a Cheyenne had nothing against torture, which seemed only normal to him. "Just take my word for it. It does not matter whether you committed the crimes or not. *They* must prove you did. *You* don't even have to say anything."

He frowned, the lines cobwebbing his leathery face. "I have not said anything, nor have these others, but here we are."

"The *saying something* doesn't have to do with being arrested. It has to do with only the trial, where you go before a judge, one man who is the chief of the affair and maybe also a jury, which is a kind of council of several people who listen to the accusations against you and decide if you're guilty or not. They might decide you are not guilty, and then you cannot be punished."

Wild Hog was still holding the pale loaf of sugar in his brown hand. He shook his head. "You speak the language of the Human Beings very clearly, so the difficulty cannot be in how you are saying it. All my life I have been unable to understand the Americans. I tell you I have come to prefer those who are just bad, because you can predict that everything they tell you is a lie, and unless you kill them first they will take everything from you including your life. But the others are a problem. Why capture a man when later some other people sitting in a council can decide there was no reason to take away his liberty in the first place?"

"Have a taste of that sugar," I says to distract him from inquiring further as to what I couldn't answer. But this was a mistake.

"It is no gift if you tell me what to do with it. Then it still belongs to you."

"I was only trying to be polite," I says, "as Old Lodge Skins always taught us." I thought I saw a little glint in his eye, but he made no direct response. Let me explain that what I'm putting into English here is not word-for-word from Cheyenne, where you'd not actually say "polite" but rather more like "the way things ought to be" or "how you ought to act," but it was true enough that the Cheyenne was courteous people and brung up their children that way, so long as you understand that don't mean lifting your little finger when sipping from a teacup or patting your lips with a napkin, and there's nothing against belching when you eat, but unlike some white folks I have known you don't exchange abuse when breaking bread with others and you don't insult a visitor in your tepee.

I went on. "White ways might never make sense to you, but you are in their power now, so you have to do the best you can. Here's another matter you might not understand: by law they have to provide a man who will speak for you. He is called an *attorney*. This is another example of what you might think is crazy. Why would the same people who accuse you of doing wrong help you to deny it? There's a reason, and maybe sometime the Human Beings, especially the young people, can learn about this in school."

"I hope not," says Hog with a stubborn expression only an Indian has the facial bones to make seem like it's carved in rock. "Already they are learning too little about a man's proper duties: hunting and fighting."

"Things have changed since you and I were boys," I told him. "Pretty soon there won't be any game at all, just tame cattle, and as for the fighting, you can see that's a thing of the past too, because you cannot possibly win in the end."

"You can die fighting," Wild Hog says, "as a man is supposed to."

"But I notice *you* did not." I put it straight to him. Mind you, I don't make no secret of my regard for the Cheyenne, but I always try to be honest about serious matters. It goes without saying that winning don't necessarily make you one hundred percent morally in the right, but neither does losing. On the other hand, putting a man in his place don't give much satisfaction when he's a helpless prisoner, wrapped up in a blanket, sitting on the floor of a jail built where within living memory his kind rode free, so I quickly added, "I think you did not die because if you did there would be nobody to look after the women and children, and what kind of world would it be with no Human Beings in it?"

For the first time he looked at me as if I was a person worth being looked at with any interest at all.

"Suddenly you speak perfect truth," said he, but quizzically. "Then you go back to being white again. You have been doing that sort of thing all your life."

"*Damn*," I says in English, in my shock. "*You do know me?*" Then caught myself and repeated it in Cheyenne, without the "damn," which they don't have.

"I have seen you since we were children together," Wild Hog tells me. "It is easy to notice a person with red hair and skin so pale except for the blue spots." Meaning my freckles, which was more pronounced as a kid. "Nevertheless, despite your appearance, when we were boys I naturally assumed you were a Human Being."

As I said, I don't recall seeing him again after he was a child, for I could swear he was not with Old Lodge Skins's band as a grown-up. I won't go through what it took to get his story out of him, with the Indian aversion to history as known to whites, as well as the discourtesy of questions that are too nosy, but I finally was able to gather he had been in that big camp on the Washita and seen me at a distance without coming up to talk. I never did find out why his father pulled out of the band when Hog was still a boy, and didn't ask in case it was for some delicate reason like a quarrel with Old Lodge Skins concerning a woman, maybe his own Ma.

"I remember you too," I says, "but only as a child. You were a better rider than I." I was a keener shot with a bow, but I didn't add that. "I wish you had spoken with me when you saw me later on."

"Why?" he asks, suddenly colder than before, though he hadn't really warmed up much.

"It's good to keep in touch with friends."

"You're not my friend," said Wild Hog. "Else you would either be dead or sitting here with me in jail. You are a white man, and you have been one all along. As soon as you got big enough to run away from the Human Beings, you did so."

"Then why did I come back and marry a woman of the Human Beings and have a child by her and live with the band of Old Lodge Skins and be at the camp on the Washita when the soldiers attacked it?"

"Don't expect me to answer such questions," said Hog, but his frown indicated I had got to him. Indians did a lot of thinking, contrary to what you might suppose from the kind of life they lived, if thinking is the right word for an activity that includes more than reason and might even turn on a dream.

"The truth is I am of course white of skin, was born of a white mother and father, and lived amongst whites a lot and am doing so now. But I've also lived and fought as a Human Being."

"You should make up your mind what you are," Wild Hog says, at last placing the sugarloaf on the floor beside him. "You can't be both, and I cannot accept as friend a person of the people who have acted so badly towards us."

"That's because you cannot see beyond what you can touch," I told him, meaning he was deficient in spirit. This is a very serious point to make with an Indian, and he knew it. "The Human Beings killed my father, and not in a real fight but because they went crazy after drinking whiskey. What worse thing can be done to a child than to kill his father? Yet I lived amongst them of my own will as both boy and grown-up."

I could see this argument had its effect, but he was a proud man in a degrading situation, and the fact remained that I was of those who had power over him, so I didn't look for an apology or warm gesture, and dropped the subject to make the point I aimed to.

"I want to help you, whether you trust me or not. White man's law has a lot to do with words. The better you understand them, the more power you have to protect yourself. The people who make the laws know that and often therefore write them so they can be understood by nobody but themselves." But now I was getting into an area that would be incomprehensible to him. The Cheyenne lacked altogether in this feature of a higher civilization by which deceit became an essential part of dealing with your fellow man and the only way you could hold your own was to be as shifty as them you was competing with, namely everybody else.

"That *attorney* I mentioned earlier. They have to provide you with one, but he will not be likely to speak your language, and the interpreter they will furnish — because they are supposed to do that too — might do a bad job. You probably know of the trouble Frank Grouard caused for Crazy Horse?"

"Crazy Horse," Wild Hog said loftily, "though an Ogallala, had a wife who was a Human Being."

Well, I figured he knowed well enough what I was talking about, for Indians without a postal service, telegraph, or a semaphore system — don't believe them movie smoke signals by which complicated messages was supposed to be sent — always was aware of what pertained to them, I can't explain how. All I know is with Old Lodge Skins it was through dreams. In any event, I was referring to a mistake made by Grouard, a breed who scouted for the Army, when translating remarks of Crazy Horse to a white officer, which led to Crazy Horse's death, only with Grouard it was accidental on purpose, for he were a mean man.

"I hope I have made myself clear," I says. "I am going to do what I can for you. I'll listen to everything said by the Americans and tell you about it. I'll also see that you get a good lawyer. If the authorities want to give you a bad one, I'll pay for another myself."

I was feeling noble in promising as much, not on account of the money but rather with the idea that in view of the local crimes them Cheyenne was accused of, on top of the Custer massacre of recent memory, a white fellow who didn't want to string them up might run a risk of having the same done to himself.

Wild Hog brung me down a peg. "Do for yourself what you need to, but do not think that you are doing anything for us."

Well, as it happened the one place where there wasn't no mob when we got there was Dodge, where people had better things to distract them, namely, whiskey, gambling, and whores, and nobody paid any attention to my visits to the Ford County jail to see the Indians while they awaited their trial, though in case they did, in a nasty way, I armed myself with a Peacemaker stuck in my holsterless belt, but run into assistant town marshal Earp while going along Front Street.

He glares at the weapon and then at me. "You know better than that."

I took too long to figure out what he meant, which was the law against carrying a gun inside city limits, and so once again, as he had years before on the buffalo range, he hit me over the head with the barrel of his pistol. But having dodged a little, I wasn't knocked out this time, only bruised.

"God damn you, Wyatt," I says, for we knowed each other by now.

"God damn you, Jack," says he, and takes me to the magistrate, where I was fined five dollars for the offense and another five for resisting arrest, of which each one got a cut.

Another unpleasant incident happened at about this time. I got me a bad ache in one of my teeth so finally had to go to a dentist, something I'd rather be scalped than do, but the doctor turned out to be real good at his job, not exactly painless but he did give me a big slug of whiskey before taking two or three of his own, and turning from his work to cough a lot, proceeded to yank out the bad tooth without giving me more than one sharp twinge.

After this he poured me another drink, along with another for himself, and him and me shot the breeze for a bit, since no other patients was waiting, and the killing of Miss Dora Hand come into discussion.

This dentist, amidst more fits of a hacking cough, commented on how big her funeral was, and then he smiles and says, "I guess everybody who ever had her showed up."

Owing to that law, I had left my gun at the Lone Star, but I told him I was going to get it and come back and kill him.

Now, running along the street, I encounter none other than Bat Masterson, and I know it was foolish to appeal to him, but I was all worked up at the time. I hadn't been able to do nothing to protect Miss Hand from the likes of Jim Kennedy, but by God I could avenge the polluting of her name by some foulmouthed dentist.

"Bat," I says, out of breath owing to the state of my feelings plus the running, "I need to borrow your gun pronto."

Naturally he asks me why.

"I ain't going to let it happen!" I says. "That woman was a saint. I won't let a coughing, drinking, no-good son of a bitch besmirch her name." He gets more details out of me, while I get madder. "Miss Dora Hand," I says. "Just because she were a performing artist on a public stage! That dear lady spent every Sunday in church. I'm going to kill him."

Bat pulls on his big mustache, and says carefully, "Now you listen to me, Jack. I'm not going to lend you a gun, and if you get one elsewhere you'll have to face me first. If you look at that dentist's shingle you will see the name John Holliday. I don't know where you've been living if you haven't heard of Doc Holliday, but then — and hold on, now! — you don't even seem to know that the late Miss Hand was not only a fine singer and a regular churchgoer but also did other things in her life. You can't just put her in one category. For example her real name wasn't even Dora Hand but Fanny Keenan."

As he talked I went from murderous anger into, well, I don't quite know what state of mind, call it confusion. I wasn't ready to face up to the fact then that I had been so besotted first by that heavenly voice and sweet look she had onstage and by what she appeared to be when in church, but maybe that was not the whole of her existence. So you can call me at that point anyway a bartender who for a change didn't know as much as his customers, me who always had quite a high idea of my common sense.

I hung my head. "I've heard of Doc Holliday as a killer," I says. "I guess I missed the news he was in Dodge, and I never knowed he was a dentist and consumptive as well."

Bat sniffed. "I don't like him, but he's kept his nose clean since coming to my county, and he's a good friend of Wyatt's."

So far as friendships went, there was me and Bat's, which probably saved my life in this case, Holliday being as skilled in taking life with either pistol or blade as he was at pulling teeth, and Bat's with Wyatt Earp, and Wyatt's with Holliday. Earp and me didn't take to each other, nor me and Holliday, who incidentally I never saw again in Dodge but encountered later in Tombstone, as will be told, at which time he had no memory of me whatever. You might think a man suddenly runs out of your office saying he'd be back to shoot you would be memorable, but no doubt such incidents was routine in the life of Doc Holliday, who spent most of his time gambling and killing people and not dentisting.

Well I tell you along about now I had a bellyful of Dodge and might of been ready to go back to the tribe if the Cheyenne would let me, but the ones in the Ford County jail give me no encouragement. I had kept my word to Wild Hog and hired a lawyer to represent the prisoners, and he was slick enough to get the proceedings moved from Dodge City to Lawrence on account of the possible local prejudice, though as I have said I couldn't see that nobody in Dodge much cared, while Lawrence was precisely where the biggest mob had assembled the first time and might of lynched the Indians had Bat not taken charge. So maybe this was a bad idea? Not at all. If you know anything about the law, the technique is to keep moving. Not for nothing do lawyers call what they do making "motions." By the time the Cheyenne was taken back to Lawrence, the townsfolk there had forgot all about that issue and had rushed off to the next fad, so this time we — the Indians, Bat and me and the deputies — went there without commotion. After a few more months of jail for his clients, and expense for me, that counselor got the case dismissed for lack of evidence.

Eventually them Cheyenne, along with the others who survived the long journey north from the Nations, got that reservation on the

Tongue, not far from where they helped rub out Custer, so you might say they won another victory and at the usual excessive cost.

Wild Hog, Old Crow, Big Head, and the others never turned more friendly to me over the months I traveled periodically to Lawrence to see them, and I never expected them to. I tried not to think about redskins beyond this specific instance, for how farmers and wanderers could share the same acreage without conflict was beyond my mental capacity, as was what would happen to the loser of this dispute, who would not be the one that fastened himself to one place, built a house, and planted crops. Even though a few such individuals might get massacred, plenty more was coming from over the water to replace them, to the permanent disadvantage of Lo, to use a sarcastic name of the day, which come from

> Lo, the poor Indian! whose untutored mind
> Sees God in clouds, or hears him in the wind;
> His soul proud Science never taught to stray
> Far as the solar walk or milky way;

quoted from Mr. Alexander Pope, whose verse I used to read as a boy with my foster-mother Mrs. Pendrake. Some newspaper writers also would call Sitting Bull "Slightly Recumbent Gentleman Cow." In addition to losing most of their homeland, Indians got made fun of a lot, which was nasty but didn't bother them as much as you might think, for not being able to read they didn't know about most of it, and besides they had quite a high idea of themselves, which wasn't destroyed by them being overpowered and outnumbered.

On the other hand, along about now some of them was beginning to see their children would do well to learn how to hold their own in a world run by whites, at least to read and write and do sums, so they wouldn't be cheated so easy by traders, government officials, and other dishonest Americans, and though it went against every principle of being a warrior, get some acquaintance with the vocations by which white people managed to eat regular and keep warm and dry: plowing and seeding fields, raising livestock, digging wells, erecting buildings permanently anchored to the earth, instead of starving when game was scarce, thirsting in a drought, and freezing every winter.

There was two kinds of white people who wanted to help the Indian. One for practical reasons, for unless you had the stomach just to kill them all, what should be done with them? The second type was usually religious and saw red men, as well as black and the yellow Chinese what built the western railroads, as fellow creations of God and thus brothers under the skin, which meant they all should be treated kindly and helped to become white in behavior. Now, lest you think this theory hadn't nothing going for it but arrogance, you might reflect that whites had the accomplishments to dominate all these folks the world over, whether for good or ill, so the decision was theirs to make by the law of life, and was it not preferable that some of them tried to bring a little decency to the process? If you ever seen the work of somebody without a conscience, then you know what I mean.

This is by way of introducing the next phase of my life. It happened through that church that Miss Dora Hand had went to. I found myself in attendance there after her untimely death, which had an effect on me out of proportion to my slight acquaintance with her — and even so, I had finally to accept that my impression of the lady had been somewhat in error. But the idea underneath it, of grace and goodness and gentility as embodied in a female person, was not discredited. I had gone through that before, with Mrs. Pendrake, and though my illusions was dashed there too, and with a lot more shock, young as I was then, I have a right stubborn personality when it comes to certain convictions.

So I went to church of a Sunday morning, not to meet women, but to be in an atmosphere in which their influence was predominant without them being whores like the girls, all friends of mine, who worked at the Lone Star. Of course there was men in that church as well, but they seemed to be of two kinds, either sissies for whom it was what a saloon was to a cowboy, or merchants who was drug to the services by their wives and, though knowing it was for their own eternal good, was bored stiff by the particulars, and in fact the preacher was mighty dull, lacking in the colorful rant of my Pa on the one hand and the Reverend Pendrake's lofty oratory, taken from Scripture, on the other.

After several Sundays the lady churchgoers begun to view me more kindly than when Miss Hand was alive, and a couple of them come up to me after one service and says they was right proud to welcome me to their congregation and hoped to see me at their lawn fete Saturday next, weather permitting, with lemonade and homemade layer cake, the proceeds going to the Indian mission school run by their parent church body, which I don't intend to name, for it may still be around today and

I don't want to hurt the feelings of any of its followers by what I say here, which is the truth but by no means all negative.

Come the following Saturday afternoon, I went as invited, and I must say I was greatly pleased to be in an atmosphere of ladies in brighter clothes than they wore in church, some real comely and all fine-mannered, making them little gestures of finger and angles of head with pursed lips and squinty eyes shown by people of the better sort as opposed to the gaping mouths, nose-pickings, and arse-scratchings I was accustomed to seeing.

One of them from the previous Sunday comes up and introduces herself as Mrs. Homer Epps. She was quite a sizable person, made even a bit wider by her fancy dress, and taller than me by a couple hands.

"Mr. Epps," says she, "is president of the Merchants National." Which was a local bank.

I give her my name, and as she seemed to be waiting for a statement of my own calling, I told her I had to apologize when in present company, but I was in the entertainment line.

She shows a tolerant smile involving all but maybe one of her chins. "No apology needed, Mr. Crabb. I am aware that you were professionally associated with our dear departed Dora Hand. When we saw you first, I'm afraid we worried that you represented another faith and had come here to lure her away from us. But now I realize your connection was only professional."

You never know what impression you're making on others. Here I had been concerned I'd be taken as what I was, a bartender in a dance hall–bordello, while a bunch of church ladies was worried I might be from a rival church.

"It was personal as well, Miz Epps," I said sanctimoniously but not untruthfully. "Miss Hand and I shared spiritual interests."

More ladies joined us, and Mrs. Epps introduced me to them all. I didn't see any men whatever for a while except for the preacher, who had staked out the refreshment table, along with what had to be his scrawny wife and three or four shabbily dressed kids, and all was stuffing themselves with cake, which unlike Mrs. Epps and some of the other women they looked like they could badly use, being all built real close to the bone. Preaching on the frontier wasn't usually the way to prosperity.

Everybody who spoke to me regretted the loss of Miss Hand and hoped I would nevertheless continue to come to services. One woman, a sharp-nosed, birdy-eyed little person in a shiny green dress, named Mrs. John Teasdale, allowed as how though no Dora Hand she was thought by all to be a soprano singer good enough to go on a stage.

"Yes, ma'am," I says.

"Well then," says she, "perhaps you could recommend me to Mr. Bell at the Varieties or Mr. Springer at the Comique." And she cocks her head to one side, more like a sparrow than ever, and simpers.

I hate to disappoint anyone with high hopes, having had a few of my own, so I said let me look into those matters, which was good enough for her at this point. For all I knowed she could of been the world's best singer, but now I had put my crush on Dora Hand into balance, I realized no female who was altogether respectable, like Mrs. Teasdale surely was, could be a professional performer in that time and place. A girl either went onto the stage or she stayed home and was somebody's wife, mother, or old-maid daughter, and speaking of the last-named, a tall, slender young lady come up to us at that point. She was real pale-complected, fair hair parted in the middle and pulled back so hard her facial skin seemed under tension, bony of cheek and nose, and with deep dark-blue eyes. Unlike the other women she did not wear a hat, and her dress was plain and modest as could be.

"This is my eldest," says Mrs. Teasdale, now assuming the sort of smirk that is intended to ally the person addressed with the speaker and against the other individual present, even though in this case she had just met me and the other was her own flesh. "Amanda," she goes on, "is the serious one. . . . Amanda, this is Mr. Crabb. He is involved in professional entertainment."

The girl's manner was of a kind with her plain clothing. She says straightforwardly in a strong though not loud voice, "You speak Cheyenne."

"Yes, Miss," I says. "I sure do. But could you just look at me and know that?" I intended this remark to be light, but she answered it as soberly as she said everything.

"I was told you translated for the Cheyenne prisoners held at the Ford County jail," said she. "I'll tell you why I am interested."

Her mother broke in here. "Let's hope Mr. Crabb finds it interesting." And again she gives me the special look. "I warned you, Mr. Crabb, she's the serious one. She would even like women to have the vote."

Amanda ignored her, being one of them offspring utterly unlike the parent who would be expected to be their model. She stared at me with them deep eyes that looked larger than they were on account of the paleness of her skin and the delicate but prominent bone structure of her face. "We need a Cheyenne translator at school."

"There are Cheyenne students in public school in Dodge?" I asked in amazement.

"Of course not," she said, wincing irritably. "The mission school. The one for which funds are being raised today."

"Well, Mr. Crabb," said Mrs. Teasdale, "I must tell my friends about your promise to manage my career as a singer. Don't let Amanda bore you too much with her savages." She tittered. "She means no harm."

When her mother had went away Amanda made a smirk of her own, which was a good deal more forceful than her Ma's, and said, "Actually, I mean a lot of harm, Mr. Crabb. Let me ask this. Does being fluent in the Cheyenne language bring with it a concern for the welfare of the Indian?"

"Let me tell you how I come to speak it," I began.

But this stern young woman, who was only in her early twenties, stops me right there. "That's irrelevant," says she. "What I want to know is whether you would like to do something to elevate the Indian from the miserable condition in which we find him today — a position, I hasten to say, into which we white people bear the most responsibility for putting him." This point she accompanied with a gesture of her long white index finger, the nail of which was trimmed back to the flesh.

I was not offended, but I didn't intend to let this girl push me around, either. "What I have got to say is to the point, Miss. I was raised mostly by the Cheyenne, and I am right fond of them and wish them the very best in life and am just sorry I ain't got the power to give them back all their home grounds."

She frowned and nodded. "You're wasting time, Mr. Crabb. What is needed is not sniveling about the past, which is dead and gone. The Indian must face the present and future. He can no longer be a hunter and warrior. But he is capable as any other person of any race. That his ways are now obsolete should not reflect adversely on him. He can learn new ones. For all, reading and writing, doing sums. How to plant and harvest crops, for the men. For the women, the domestic sciences as practiced by the civilized race, which it cannot be emphasized enough is nevertheless not morally superior."

She said this in her usual flat, apparently calm fashion but I begun to sense a real strong emotion underneath.

"Well, Miss, let's just say I'll be proud to help out if I can. If you want me to do some translating, like I done between Wild Hog's bunch and the legal authorities, I'll be happy to do it, and there won't be no charge."

She had still been staring at me with them big indigo eyes, but now she blinked in what I took for a slight softening of manner, and she says, "We certainly wouldn't expect you to work for nothing. We will provide quarters and food and a stipend of . . ." She proceeded to name so low a figure I can't even recall what it was, these many years after, but it didn't seem to matter, for I repeated that I wouldn't charge anything, having adequate income from my present situation.

The fine flanges of her pale nose flared slightly as if she smelled something unpleasant. "You'll have to give up tending bar," said she, revealing she knowed more about me than her Ma did. "Ours is a boarding school, in ———," naming a place some distance away, which I won't identify for reasons that will be self-evident.

Now I could of ended the discussion at that point, unless I really wanted to forsake a profitable job pouring whiskey for cowboys who bought more the drunker they got, and go to a religious boarding school for Indians at wages that was less than the colored fellow, an ex-slave, got for mopping out the Lone Star. It wouldn't be long before I built up another nest egg and started thinking again of opening that place of my own. Why, I might go on to become another Dog Kelley, the businessman-mayor, and get married to a young future Mrs. Epps or Mrs. Teasdale, and have an offspring like Amanda, who somewhere within her severity was not only a young girl but, I recognized, a basically handsome one who however could use some fattening up as well as a realization of what was eating *her.*

But I have said I was sick of the side of Dodge I knowed and was coming to see that hanging around that church was not a successful alternative, having little in common with the folks there, with the exception of this Amanda insofar as she was involved with Indians. I was also aware of her femininity, probably more than she herself was at this time. I've had a remarkable partiality to the ladies all my life, as is no secret by now to the reader of this life story of mine. Young white women can be vex-some, owing to an abundance of expectation, but I consider myself fortunate to have knowed them when I did, which was long ago, for when a man gets past ninety the only females around him tend to be nurses.

Anyway, I ended up taking the job offered by Amanda, and thus begun my involvement, such as it was, in educating Indians to be white people.

6
Schooling the Red Man

NEVER SAID GOODBYE TO BAT MASTERSON, FOR HE HAD
previously left Dodge himself, without a goodbye to me, to go to
Leadville in Colorado Territory, where they had lately struck silver.
As when he headed for the Deadwood gold strike, getting only as far
as the town of Cheyenne, his primary interest was gambling and not
prospecting. I was not unusual for the time in wandering throughout the
West. Everybody done it — everybody that is who didn't settle down on
some land and make a go of ranching or farming and raise children, so I
expect I ought to say everybody who didn't do nothing much to civilize
the place, everybody, that is, you'll pardon the coarse saying, with a wild
hair in his arse. This sure included Wyatt Earp, who also left Dodge, in
his case to go to Tombstone in Arizona, where he was soon followed by
the painless but lethal and consumptive dentist Doc Holliday.

To get to the mission school, me and Amanda traveled by railroad, finally getting off at a town where we was met by an old colored fellow
driving a wagon. Amanda lost no time in climbing up to sit right beside
him, which got her stares from the other people on the platform and
from the windows of the train as it pulled away, for a white woman didn't
properly place herself on an equal level with a man of a darker race, and
that included Mexicans.

She had not sat next to me on the train, placing a number of bundles
on the seat alongside her, and having paid for a bath at the barbershop I
hoped it wasn't because of my odor, but we could not of conversed anyhow. In them cars the noise of the steam engine was deafening, and you
had to keep an eye open for the glowing cinders that blowed in through

the windows along with those that was not burning, just dirty. I was filthy by the time we got off, but oddly enough, especially given her pale skin and gold hair, Amanda still looked spotless.

We finally reached the school after jolting some miles in that wagon with me riding not up on the seat with the driver and Amanda, not having been invited to do so, but in the bed of the wagon with the luggage and lots of sacked supplies the driver had picked up in town. The school consisted of one big whitewashed three-story building and several smaller structures, all appearing fairly new, and some distance off, a weatherbeaten barn with a few head of livestock visible and beyond them fields of tawny grain rippling in the breeze. Between the buildings would of been the usual dust of that part of the world, but rain had fell overnight and instead it was the comparably usual mud.

The wagon crawled slowly up to the big building and came to a sticky stop. Amanda steps down into the mud and sweeps her white hand towards the grounds. "It's still raw," she said. "One of the projects the boys are working on is getting a lawn to grow from seed, but as you know that takes a long time and Indians are impatient."

I agreed, though knowing nothing about domestic grasses, and added, "When it comes to plants they pick what grows by itself."

Amanda was frowning, an expression she wore a lot. "We have our work cut out for us." She nodded her smooth steep forehead at the building before us. "This is the dormitory: boys' side to the left, girls' to the right."

As I found out later, there were two distinct entrances and though it was a single structure, a partition divided the interior. From one side you couldn't get to the other without going outside to the other door, either in front or back.

Amanda told me now I would be shown to my personal quarters later, but it was suppertime at the moment and though we was already quite late we shouldn't be no later, and she hikes off in the mud, besliming her shoes and the lower hem of her dress, so I had to do so too, regardless of a fairly new set of boots, and we reached the one-story building that turned out to house the dining hall and kitchen.

Not a soul but us had been seen till now, but there the whole school was at long tables inside the big bare-board room, all the swarthy-faced, black-haired young Indians, which given my experience was not in itself an unusual sight were it not that I had never seen so many members of that race arranged in alignment, seated on chairs and not the ground. But there was an even more unusual feature: they was all dressed alike, according to sex, the girls in blue-figured gingham dresses, the boys in blue-gray uniforms like soldiers', with short tunics buttoning to the neck and navy stripes up the pants. In addition, all of them, boys and girls, had their hair cut short.

As if this wasn't enough, there didn't seem to be no talking amongst them, and Indians was not naturally a quiet folk when with their own kind, all the less so when eating, which they did fairly enthusiastically. Given the relative rarity that they could count on having enough food, they tended to chew and swallow wolf- or bear-style when nourishment was before them. But these lads and girls looked more like they was in a class than at a meal, with rigid spines against the chair backs and no expressions of face.

At the head of each of the tables, which was either for all boys or all girls, was a white person of the staff, and at one side of the hall, at right angles to the others, was a shorter table at which sat a whiskered, bald gent in, I'd say, his late fifties. He didn't grow no hair on his scalp but had a bushy gray beard which concealed whatever kind of collar and tie he wore. He showed a stern look when no other was called for, so on first meeting up with him you might of thought he would necessarily be disagreeable, but he could be real pleasant, as now when Amanda Teasdale brung me to him, and he stood up smiling politely while she apologized for being late to supper but says she is happy to be able to deliver the sum of money collected by her church in Dodge, where she also found that translator of the Cheyenne language they had been looking for.

"Major," she says, surprising me for he wasn't in no uniform and I took him for a preacher, "this is Jack Crabb."

He works my hand like a pump handle, but just twice. "Mr. Crabb," says he. "We are pleased to see you here. Won't you sit down?" He did so himself. When me and Amanda did the same, I noticed there wasn't no plate nor eating tools before him as yet, which relieved me some, for I was right hungry by then. "It might seem paradoxical to you at the outset," he goes on, "when I say that the purpose of your fluency in Cheyenne for us is to discourage the students from speaking that language." He smiled as if what he meant was self-evident.

"Major," says I, "I was wondering if you could make sense of that for me."

He raised his still dark eyebrows in apparent wonderment, but said, in a paternal way, "It's simple when explained — as I always told my boys in the Tenth Cavalry." His eyes twinkled. "They were Negroes." He makes a solemn gesture with his beard. "Our purpose here being to exterminate the wretched savage" — he waited a little, smiling ever broader, to let the provocation of that comment settle in — "*and replace him with a fine man*, we must begin with the fundamentals, of which language is primary, I hope you agree." He never waited till I answered, which was just as well, for I didn't have no idea whatever of where he was aiming. "What seems paradoxical is that to teach a man to quit his old language and adopt a new one, he must first be addressed in his original tongue, else he will never grasp the idea." The Major blinked his eyes. "I know: we tried that. But we are learning. Hence you are here."

There still hadn't been a sound throughout the dining hall that I heard and nobody was showing up with food. I had caught a faint smell on entering, but that had diminished. As I figured the meal might be waiting on this conversation, I was quick to respond in a way you do when a point's been well made. "Kee-rect."

"Mr. Crabb," said the Major, "having served as an Army officer for a number of years before becoming a minister of the Gospel, I am accustomed to being addressed as 'sir.' As all my other staff observe this practice, it would be awkward if you did not. This is not a military institution, true. But you *are* my subordinate."

Actually he said this in a real nice way. I don't want to give the impression that the Major was a bad fellow, though you might call him a fool.

"I don't mind, sir," I says. "And I take it you prefer to be called Major over Reverend."

He waves a finger at me. "You are quite right, Mr. Crabb! It is simply explained: were I only a parson, with a Sunday sermon to deliver each week and visits to the sick and infirm in between, 'Reverend' would of course be more appropriate. But directing this school has more in common with an Army command. Also, in the realm of language 'Major' has more dynamic connotations than does the other term."

Now Amanda was sitting right next to me, taking all this in and, despite her opinionated nature judging from her attitude towards me, she is saying nothing. Partly to needle her, and partly because it seemed polite, I included her in what I said next. "Sir, I was wondering if we might get a bite to eat. Me and Miss Teasdale just had a railroad ride all day without any food." Amanda wasn't the kind of woman who provides or even thinks about meals, and the train, which, in them days before din- ing cars, used to stop at a town and let the passengers off to feed at meal- times, hadn't done so on this trip, having to make up for a delay up the line.

"Aha," the Major says, as if at a revelation, "but you see we finished our meal a few minutes ago." He swept his coat back and went into a vest pocket and brung out a big silver turnip of a watch, which he studied. "Six and a half, to be exact. The tables were then cleared. Were it not for your appearance, the benediction would have been offered by now and the students would have filed out. I'm afraid you must wait for tomor- row's breakfast, Mr. Crabb. We dine here precisely on time and do no eating between meals. If this seems stern, there is a reason. The Indian is a shiftless soul in his natural state, knowing no order, no direction, no principles. He lives as the wind blows — namely, at random — eating when he has food, abstaining when he has none, like an animal and not a human being. But he is *not* an animal, Mr. Crabb. He is a man, and as precious in the eyes of God as any other. To despise him is sinful. To help him realize himself as God's creation is our duty as Christians."

I should say right here that the Major was real sincere in his beliefs, and his interest in the red man was honestly based on his religious faith. He weren't putting contributions to the school into his own pocket, he never had carnal connections with the female students or them on the staff like at some other institutions of the kind (nor was he a *heemaneh*), and he didn't show any ambition to move on to a higher post in either education in general or his church in particular.

But I didn't take kindly to the idea of going without food all day and all night, in the support of opinions not my own, and I might of quit then and there had I not been in country unfamiliar to me, without weapons or transport.

The Major now gets to his feet, followed by the rest of the assem- blage — damn if it were not a strange sight to see Indians do anything in unison! — and gives a loud, clear, but real boring prayer that went on forever, after which the students line up in military order, table by table. Now Indians was normally quite curious about what went on around them: you got to be if you're living off the land. But these young people didn't pay no attention to one another or their surroundings, and from their expressions or lack thereof, they didn't seem preoccupied by anything else either. They seemed in a kind of spell, which in fact was not in itself an unusual state for a redskin, who in the sun dance for example would get into a trance in which he didn't feel it when he tied thongs to his chest skin that subsequently got ripped out.

Each group or troop was led by the white person who had sat at the head of their table, and now I noticed most of the latter was women, even if their unit was boys. The Major had managed a miracle if he could put Indian males under such a spell they could be marched around by a female of any race.

Then without another word, the Major strode out in his brisk stride, followed by the rest of the school, marching in a column of twos. I hoped I had not made a bad mistake by coming here, for I was sure out of my element, even, from the look of them, the Indians.

I says to Amanda, "All right, where am I going to get something to eat?"

Though being of the type of person who always has to get ahead of you, she would respond to genuine indignation. "I'll take you to the kitchen," she says without additional comment, and does so, at the other end of the building.

Now what had happened before we showed up, as I found on getting into the schedule next day, was that the students on marching in to eat went directly through a mess line at the end of the kitchen, took their trays to the dining-room tables, and after eating, which was timed for seventeen minutes, they marched back again, in units, to leave the trays off in that area of the kitchen where some big tubs was for washing up, went back into the dining room, and sat down again until the Major was ready to stand them up for the prayer.

Me and Amanda now passed them steaming tubs, where a number of young Indian girls was washing the trays and utensils while others was doing the drying with empty flour sacks, and went back to the big brick oven built into the far wall, where a substantial-sized woman of the colored race, hair covered with a blue bandanna, was about to heft one of the big wood paddles used by bakers, loaded with loaves of risen dough, and fill the racks above the glowing hearth, which was so hot you could feel it on your face from ten foot away.

When she sees us coming the woman scowls and says, "I got to git this braid a-bakin'."

I says, using a familiar turn of speech in them days, "Auntie, I'm real hungry. I was wondering if —"

"I ain't you aunt, little man," says she, real peevish, pronouncing it "awnt," like she was English, "and I'll thank you not to call me out of my name." She's still holding the laden paddle, which took more strength than I would of had, but then she were a head taller than me and twice as wide.

"Yes, ma'am," I says quickly. "I didn't mean no disrespect. I'll use your proper name when I know it."

Amanda give me a dirty look. "It's Mrs. Stevenson."

"I apologize, Mrs. Stevenson. I'm a coarse man, been living with no-counts and lowlifes."

The big cook studies me briefly, then she says, "Give you some nice hot braid if you kin wait."

"Why, that will be just fine, Mrs. Stevenson."

"You don't have to say the name ever' time," she tells me and finally shoves that paddleful of loaves into the oven.

As it happened I never learned her first name even though I met her husband on various occasions, for he too called her Mrs. Stevenson. The Major had hired her for the job on account of her husband had formerly served under him in the Tenth Cavalry. The Stevensons lived not far from the school in a town that, like the enlisted men of the Tenth, was all Negro. There was more than one of these towns, the best known of which was called Nicodemus, which had been created by freed slaves what had come north to make a life for themselves and figured they were likely to do it better if they made common cause. Hezekiah Stevenson was one of the more prosperous citizens with his Army pension, a nice little grain-and-feed business, and he was also the local postmaster.

This husband of hers was about the only person Mrs. Stevenson admired. Most everybody else she considered a fool, but she had a soft spot in her heart for me because I greatly favored the food she would of cooked for them all had anybody else, beginning with the Major, cared for it, but they did not, especially them students, all of who just had a taste for what was simply boiled till it fell apart, and that included even the fresh vegetables they growed in the school garden, for that's the only way the Indians of them days knowed how to cook, so that's what their children liked. Though Indians might at times eat flesh that was utterly raw, like the liver cut out of a game animal at the time he was brought down, the only alternative was boiling for hours, with maybe some fried dough, which they had learned to make from the whites and consisted of just a hunk of flour-and-water paste in a greased skillet.

Fact is, I was fond of the fried dough and boiled flesh I ate with the Cheyenne, but being born hungry I liked most of what else was handed me to chew on, my life long, though you'd never know it to look at me, for no matter how much I ate I never gained a pound. I guess I was a challenge to Mrs. Stevenson, whose husband and five kids was also heavyweights. What I would do is take only a small amount on my tray at mealtimes, at which I was obliged as a staff member, one of the few males around, to sit at the head of a boys' table. Then after I marched my bunch out, I would go back to the kitchen and get something special that Mrs. S. had cooked up for herself but was happy to share with me, the cheese biscuits, country ham with redeye gravy, roast chicken, spoonbread, spicy greens, also all kinds of creamed vegetables made with the products from the little dairy herd maintained by the school.

Mrs. Stevenson was helped out in the kitchen by them Indian student girls, as part of their studies in what was called domestic science, and I guess she was supposed to teach them to cook the white way (which in her case was actually black, but then the Indian name for Negro was Black White Man), but according to what she told me, she gave up the attempt after a while on account of they was hopeless at it, being too stupid to learn anything of civilization. Mrs. Stevenson was a fine person who treated me like a mother, but she had in her a good deal of what nowadays in the 1950s they call racial prejudice, but in the 1870s was just the way most people not themselves Indian, and not having had a special experience with them like me, looked at the red man and woman. And of course her husband as a veteran of the U.S. Cavalry was unlikely to be an Indian-lover, especially after the Custer fight.

Now, where I was quartered was in a private room on the top floor of the boys' side of the big building Amanda showed me first, at the end of a big dormitory full of metal-framed cots, at the foot of each of which was a little trunk of the type the Army called foot lockers, and back of each cot, against the wall, was a rack for hanging clothes.

My own room was better than the one in that hotel I had lived in during my time in Dodge City, with a cot like the ones used by the boys and an upended wood crate for a washstand, with bowl and pitcher that was, like the mirror over it, uncracked though the thunder mug under the cot was not, and a beat-up chest of drawers.

Amanda was prohibited from stepping into the male side of the building, so I had been taken there by one of the teachers, a man named Charlevoix, ending in an x, which I would of pronounced had I first seen it written, but having only heard it instead, I believed he was named Charlie Vaw, and I politely called him Mr. Vaw a couple times till he put me straight as to the French origin of the name. He claimed descent from one of the French trapper-explorers who had been throughout much of the West before any English set foot in the region and usually got on well with the natives, even taking wives amongst the tribes they encountered, and he allowed as how he might of had a great-grandma who was of the red race, and maybe so, but he himself come from back East and never knew a word of any Indian language and had fairish hair and light-colored eyes, so I don't know. He come West for his health, having weak lungs or the like.

Charlevoix told me that while I had a climb to my top-floor room, it would be made up for by having fewer boys to manage than he had on the floor below.

"Oh," says I, thinking he had mistook me, "I ain't no teacher. I was hired as an interpreter."

"That's right," says he. "At least you will be able to talk to them and understand what they say in return."

It took more explanation for me to finally get the idea that I was expected to control the boys lodged on my floor, see they obeyed the school rules as to personal appearance and conduct, which included keeping the place neat and clean, and didn't make noise or act disorderly such as young male persons of any race take their greatest pleasure in doing, especially in the years just before they officially become men.

I tell you I hadn't been at this school for more than a couple hours when I was ready to leave for the second time. I never had no experience keeping big kids in order, my own white child having been carried off by the Indians when he was two, and the baby I had with my Cheyenne wife Sunshine disappeared, with his Ma, after the Washita battle.

The place was empty at the moment, for after supper the students had to return to the schoolrooms for a study period in which they did homework, them boys what didn't have evening farm chores and the girls who was not occupied in the kitchen or other housekeeping duties like laundering and ironing the school linens in the washhouse. The way the Major operated the place, it was supposed to be self-sustaining, using student labor, for there was never sufficient funds to pay anybody except the staff, and in fact none of us ever got paid in full and on time. I don't think the Major himself took any wage.

"It's a relief to have another man on hand," Charlevoix told me. "There haven't been enough of us to put anybody on the top floor, and without supervision the boys have had things their own way up here." He raised his thin eyebrows and snickered sadly. "They're probably not going to be pleased when they see you. But as I say, at least you can speak their language. They're Cheyennes. None of the rest of us know theirs or in fact any other Indian languages." He shrugged in exasperation. "But the Major doesn't want the teachers to speak anything but English anyway. How else can the students learn English unless they are forced to use it? He had a point, but these boys haven't learned a word, so far as I can see, and we can't even find out what's wrong. Aren't we teaching the right way? Perhaps you'll be able to find out."

I said I was thinking for the second time that I might of made a mistake in accepting this job without finding out more about it, but what he said appealed to my pride. It hadn't been often in my life up to that time that anybody treated me as though I might know something of value to them, and here it looked like maybe I could help out both sides. Also I admit I wouldn't of minded accomplishing something that might impress Amanda.

So I put the contents of my carpet bag into the chest of drawers, and Charlevoix pulled out his watch, and saying it was about time for the boys to return, he went downstairs.

He was right, for everything around here happened on schedule, which was more remarkable for Indians than it would of been for white students, for the notion of time as measured by a little machine carried in your pocket was altogether foreign to them. I never met an Indian who could understand how 5:00 P.M., say, could be the same in winter when the sky was dark as in the bright late afternoon of summer.

So up the stairs, taking two at a time, come running the young fellows what bunked on the top floor. They was no longer in the stunned condition in which they had sat at the dining-room tables, but was laughing and hooting and chattering like persons their age of any race, added to which these boys had been stifled all day by that routine that meant nothing to them except that they was compelled to follow it, and now at last they could let go until tomorrow morning.

Well, I sympathized with them, but I had a job to do, so when I had judged by ear that all of them had arrived, I stepped out of the doorway of my room and, waiting a second or two till the din died down, announced my presence.

Notwithstanding that I spoke in Cheyenne, they all immediately seemed to fall back into the suppertime trance, and this was rather comical in that already most had stripped off their uniforms and was all but bare-arsed naked, down to the breechcloths they wore instead of the underwear I later found out that they was issued but never took out of the foot lockers, not having any idea of what it was for.

"Can it be," I asks, "that the Human Beings when amongst white men forget their native speech, which is the finest language of all, because it is spoken by the bravest of all men?"

The lads now peered at me, and the tallest amongst them says, "We speak our language all the time to one another." He had the kind of slanty eyes and high-boned bronze face that should of been framed with long hair, but here he stood in his leather breechcloth, his head shorn as close as a white man's who worked in a city bank, an odd combination.

Now he had broke the ice, the others come out of the coma but let him do the talking, as them grown-up Cheyenne had let Wild Hog speak for them back in Dodge. This was courtesy. Indians was less likely than any other race I come across to follow their leaders in lockstep, being by nature of an anarchistic temperament, but they was also the politest and most respectful.

"I am relieved to hear that," I told him, "for I was worried you had been deprived of speech by some trickster." Now, in Cheyenne that last word, *Veho*, is the same term used for "white man."

This lad, whose name I might as well use here though I never learned it till later, was Wolf Coming Out, he scowls in thought and says, "But you are yourself white. Are you therefore a trickster? And if you are, maybe you are trying to trick us by using that name and getting it out of the way before we can accuse you of being one."

"You might not have learned much else since you've been here," says I, grinning, "but maybe you have begun to think like a white man."

"I really hope not," he says, "else I could understand why you would try to make friends by insulting me first, and I don't want to understand that. Nor do I want to know how and why you speak the language so well, because I can see no other reason than to use it to deceive us."

He was working himself up, and he was, at sixteen or seventeen, a head taller than me. For that matter, in this group of boys, from twelve to his age, I was amongst the shorter and outnumbered worse even than the Seventh Cavalry at the Greasy Grass. But I had me a weapon, and I proceeded to use it.

Pulling up my pants leg and uncovering the top of the boot I wore under it, I drawed that knife I still carried from my last days with Old Lodge Skins's band.

Wolf backed up a step when I did so, then with typical Indian bravado quickly took two steps forward to show how brave he was, though unarmed.

"Here," I says, holding out the weapon by the tip of the blade, rawhide-wrapped handle towards him. "Here's a present for you."

For a short while he looked at the knife and then he stared at me. It was just that old skinning knife, but pretty obviously no white man had made it. "Why are you doing this?" asked Wolf.

I must say that question annoyed me, and my answer was, "You are a young boy who doesn't know how to act," which was to say, he had bad manners, a reflection on them who had brought him up, and it was a comment of some force.

But Wolf Coming Out chose to ignore that point, saying, "We are not allowed to own a knife or any other weapon at this place. You must know that if you are one of them."

I couldn't encourage the breaking of rules, at least not a sensible one like that. "I just came here, and I didn't know of the rule," I says, "but I guess it's a good one, for the Human Being boys might want to cut the Pawnees or other old enemies, and also the reverse."

"We don't fight with one another here," Wolf told me, "because we all are in the same trouble." The other boys murmured their agreement, but all of them was less tense now I had shown I wasn't going to attack them with the knife.

"You mean stuck in school."

"What I mean is being told what to do by white people."

"But since the whites run every school I ever heard of," I pointed out, "and Indians have none as yet, you might think about enduring this one until you learn enough to leave it and set up a school run by Indians, particularly the Human Beings, who everybody knows are the smartest." I let this sink in and then I says, "I was given this knife by Buffalo Calf Woman, wife to Old Lodge Skins, when I was last with his band just after the Greasy Grass fight. I was born white but I was reared amongst the Human Beings. I took this job so that you will have someone on your side who can speak your language. But I don't blame you for being suspicious." I stepped over to the entrance to my room and drove the blade of the knife into the door frame deep enough to maintain it at an upthrust angle. "This knife is yours. It's against the rules for you to carry it, so we'll leave it stuck here, where you can see it at all times. I hereby name it the Medicine Knife. Its protection extends to all of us."

Used as what you might call a talisman like that, the knife worked out better than it would of as just a simple present for him. Indians liked stuff of that kind which could be seen materially but had significance that was felt, as do we all when it comes to flags, crucifixes, and, for some, money.

I'm not saying them Cheyenne lads instantly accepted me as a blood brother, but beginning at that point they was not unfriendly and by degrees they come to trust me in large part though I was still an adult, plus I was obviously one of the staff at a place they never wanted to be despite any good reason for so being, the chief amongst which was that their parents wanted them to be there. They was not put in school by force. And when you think their fathers was formerly hostile savages, many of who had fought the U.S. Cavalry, illiterate, counting on their fingers, then you have to admit it was a remarkable thing for them to send their sons and daughters to acquire the white man's learning.

Now, as I say, I hadn't knowed till the Major told me that my job was supposed to be temporary and consisted of using the Cheyenne language to get the boys to learn English, so the more success I had, the shorter time I'd be working there. This by the way was typical of the Major's procedure and might of surprised me in a military man, had I not had enough acquaintance with Army officers to know that if you looked to them for practical sense you'd do better with even a cowboy. You don't tell a man that the better a job he does, the sooner he will lose it, unless maybe he's a doctor.

But I did see the point that them young Indians ought to learn as much English as they could if they was going to prosper or even survive in the coming years now the Plains tribes had no immediate means of keeping body and soul together except on the basis of learning white ways, and you'd never do that talking only in Cheyenne.

What I didn't get was why that couldn't be accomplished without forsaking their own tongue altogether, which is what the Major wanted, and all the teachers agreed with him including Amanda. Various other tribes was represented at the school, Pawnee, Kiowa, Comanche, Omaha, and all had made reasonable progress in English. Only the Cheyenne boys was the holdouts, and they considered themselves to be defending the tribal honor in so doing. There wasn't no Cheyenne girls there, so they felt alone, except now for me, and what I had to do was complicated: encourage them to learn English while being on their side when it come to retaining their own language. But I did have a peculiar advantage over everybody, for I was the only person there who could speak both tongues, and in translating to each side I could say whatever I wanted to as the opinion of the other.

Not that I was the first to discover that power, but I was surely one of the few who ever used it not solely for the benefit of the whites. The translators employed by the Government at the treaty conferences usually told both parties what each wanted to hear, regardless of what either actually said, but it was the Indians who invariably lost, for it was their land that was at issue, and also it was the Government paying the interpreters' wages. Now, the school was paying mine, what little I was getting, but I didn't come there for the money.

The way it worked was like this. Oh, first I should say I was in charge of the Cheyenne boys a good deal of the day, seeing they was up and washed and dressed on time to be marched to the dining hall for breakfast (they was supposed to make their beds too, but unless it was Saturday morning, when the Major come to make an Army-type inspection, I let that go as a task not worth the remarkable effort), sitting at the head of the table and seeing they acted all right during the meal, then to one of the buildings of classrooms where my boys had one all their own so as not to interfere with the other students, who had learned English. This meant they was never in the authorized company of girls, by the way, which the older lads considered a deprivation, about which subject more to come.

Now the first morning, before the instruction begun, the Major come in and addressed the class. After each sentence or so he stopped and let me give a translation.

"What a relief it is," he says, standing there with his erect military posture and gray beard, smiling genially, "to be able to speak to you boys with an assurance that you will be able fully to understand what I'm saying."

Now just remember my version, here in English, was in Cheyenne to them young fellows. "Here me when I speak. I am the leader here and am called Gold Leaf." Which referred to the badge of rank a major wears when in uniform.

The Major went on. "I can at last explain to you what our purpose is here at school." He raised his arms in a kind of general embrace of a multitude. "It is only to help you. Keep that always in mind, and whenever you are asked to do a certain thing that you may not like, or to keep from doing something you want to do, you must obey, for what we ask will always be for your own good."

He stopped, and I translated as follows. "It is right that you show me the respect young people should have for their elders, for in doing so you also show respect for your parents, who sent you here."

The Major resumed. "Mr. Crabb will translate anything you do not understand, but you must immediately begin to use any English words and phrases you think you know, even if you make mistakes. That is the only way to learn."

My translation: "This is Little Big Man. He spent his boyhood with the Human Beings and has always kept them in his heart. He will help you understand white people and their ways, so far as that is possible. If you try you will learn their language quickly, for as Human Beings you are very smart and you will want to show how much better you speak English than the students from other tribes. To do less would be to bring shame to your families."

The Major listened smiling when I spoke, and after I finished this time he nodded his beard reflectively and said, "It is interesting that some ideas take much longer to express in Cheyenne than in English, and vice versa." He turned back to the boys. "You are a fine-looking group of young men, and I'm sure you will do well here. When you are eventually ready to return to your tribe, it will be as educated Christian gentlemen, and you will make them proud."

This I rendered almost literally, including the Christian part, for Indians generally had no objection to anything religious.

"Now," the Major said, "if you have any questions, I'll be happy to answer them." He told me, "You have lifted a burden from us all, Mr. Crabb. Not being able to communicate is a great inconvenience."

I passed on the matter of questions to the boys and added that if they asked any, the asker should politely get to his feet.

The one who did was not unexpected. "This here," I says to the Major, "is Wolf Coming Out."

The Major rolls his eyes and says, "That's another of our responsibilities: to replace those quaint names with real ones. There's a lot these poor fellows have to overcome. You should have seen them when they arrived, in leggings and dirty blankets."

What I wondered is what Wolf's Pa, himself named for some animal, would make of his son coming home in a monkey suit, with his hair cut off, and named Horace Cooper or, as I heard they done at some of these schools, after the famous, like Thomas Jefferson.

"You are heard," I says to Wolf now.

His question to the Major was: "How is it you have so much hair on your face but none on the top of your head, where it belongs?"

What I passed on, however, was: "We thank you for this opportunity, and we are eager to learn as much as we can. We do hope, though, that you and those of the staff are patient with us. It isn't easy to make such a great change in one's life all at once."

The Major was beaming benevolently at Wolf. "The boy speaks well," he told me. "If they can be taught discipline, how fine an all-Indian regiment would be. Best riders in the world, and it's an old cavalryman who's saying that, mind you. I served with the Tenth Horse, you know. Negroes. Very fine fellows."

I told Wolf, "It's me speaking now. I don't blame you for being an ignorant young person, but that was a rude question, and I did not translate it for Gold Leaf. However, since I believe you were not intentionally being impolite, I will answer it in a general way. Some think white men often lose their hair as they age because of wearing hats all their lives, but others say it's because they cut their hair short. I think it represents the way the Everywhere Spirit wants it, as with the hair that grows on white men's faces but not on Indians'."

Still standing there in his neat uniform, with close-cropped head, Wolf says, "I know that at the Greasy Grass a Human Being scalped the beard of one of the soldiers."

"That was Wooden Leg," says I. He cut off one of the muttonchops of

Custer's dead adjutant, W. W. Cooke. "But it's not a good idea to talk of that around here."

"Why not?" asked Wolf. "Nobody but the other Human Beings can understand the language, and they don't mind." And the other boys laughed on hearing this type of Indian joke.

He was getting too fresh, and I told him so and to sit down. Which he did.

The Major innocently joined in the mirth. He said, "They're a happy-go-lucky lot when you get to know them, I see. I can't wait until I can speak to them directly — no offense to you, Mr. Crabb, your help is essential. But surely, nothing beyond the most primitive concepts can be expressed in Indian. Yet we know all peoples are equal before the Lord. The red man is as capable as any other if introduced to the power of the word, beginning with the Word of God as it is recorded in the Gospels."

Of course, I wouldn't of translated this comment to them boys, who come from a tribe whose menfolk was known for orating, usually for hours at a time. And if the Major was referring to the Bible, I believe it dated from the Hebrews, who was unlikely to have wrote it in English. I don't know if I ever mentioned that my old Pa, who made himself a preacher, believed the Indian race might be that lost tribe of Israel as he claimed it said in the Book of Mormon, which however he never read, being illiterate even in his own language. But then it's always been my experience, in well over a century now, that words can be held to mean anything.

7

Amanda

I AIN'T GOING TO TAKE YOU DAY BY DAY THROUGH THE
time I was at that school and done interpreting of the kind of which I
just give you an example which can stand for the rest. I'll say right
now them Cheyenne boys never did learn English or they learned
more than they let on to, but the point remains if they was ever addressed in the simplest terms of it they did not respond, nor did any of
them ever speak a word of English in my hearing. I used to wonder what
might happen if they was tested by somebody saying, in English, that the
people hoping to get the beef at dinner would have to ask for it by name,
for all them boys cared for by way of food was meat, which was the
scarcest item on the school menu, being furnished by the Government
for reservations and schools like this, which meant a lot of the supply
vanished mysteriously before it ever got there.

Or for that matter, what would they do if you yelled "Fire"? But of
course I never tried these tests, for I was mostly sympathetic with the
boys, which even then I realized was the kind of sentimentality that actually works to the detriment of them in whose favor you think you are
acting. Oh, I would give them hell on this matter, saying, "What good
are you doing yourself, or your people, going to school, if you don't learn
anything?"

The answer I'd get, from Wolf Coming Out or Walks Last or Goes in
Sweat (whose names incidentally the Major changed respectively to
Patrick Henry, John Hancock, and Anthony Wayne, though nobody but
him used them, and he couldn't tell one boy from another), the answer

I'd get would be, "But we *are* learning what the white man teaches, for you are explaining it to us."

And then I'd feel worse than ever, because I wasn't really passing on what the teachers said in history and geography, and the least part of the arithmetic lessons was the words. As to English, the kind of young woman who gives the impression of being already old, kind of dried up before her time, was the teacher, Miss Dorothea Hupple by name. The way she taught seemed reasonable enough, and I guess she had some success with the other students, particularly the girls, who didn't mind being taught by a woman.

She begun by pointing to various parts of her own person and giving the English for each, hair, ear, eye, nose, and so on. After hearing the word, the class was supposed to repeat it. But what they done at first was to say every word in Cheyenne, and even I was taken in by that at first, assuming they would go on to the English, which I would chime in, seconding Dorothea, but they never did. When I finally told them to knock it off or they'd get no meat for a week, Walks Last reminded me that nobody including the staff had got any in five days (neither had Mrs. Stevenson, who was thinking of quitting), and Wolf wanted me to tell the *Veho* woman to point to an intimate part of her anatomy and give the English name for it. "Or don't white women have any?" he asks.

Now I had to conceal all this when I spoke to Dorothea because though them boys made me plenty mad at times, I felt more for them than I did for the whites, because of my upbringing but also because I could remember being in school when I was with the Pendrakes. I hated school. The difference was that not being an Indian I knowed I was wrong, which never made me like it better but was more forward-looking in the long run, a real difficult concept for the red man even though they might give lip service to it. They kept thinking they could stay completely Indian despite all the evidence to the contrary. That was what was both great and hopeless about them.

Now if Amanda had been the English teacher this sort of thing wouldn't of gone on for long — I mean, I don't know if the boys would of learned any more, but I would of had to explain what was going on with them, what they was really saying in Cheyenne, and so on, but Dorothea Hupple, see, had taken a shine to me. She was one of them spinsters come West to find a husband, where, respectable females being scarce, the prospects seemed good. But stuck in this school she didn't enjoy such advantages, for not only was the other woman teachers in the same boat, but of the men there the Major was a widower too distracted by all his ideas to see a woman if he looked at her; John Bullock, who taught all the boys, including mine, the basic techniques of farming, plowing, seeding, reaping, and so on, was himself a farmer and lived with wife and kids, several of which were old enough to help him, on the land adjoining the school fields; Klaus Kappelhaus, the instructor in arithmetic, happened to be a German recently come from the Old Country, and though I guess he spoke English grammatically his accent was so strong few could understand him and his harsh voice scared Dorothea; and finally I suspected Charlevoix of being a *heemaneh*, the way he gave some of the lads the once-over in the bathhouse, though when I asked my boys, not mentioning him by name, if anybody tried to interfere with them, they said no, for if so they would of give him a good beating unless he put on a dress, after which he would be treated well, which is the Cheyenne tradition.

Anyway, Dorothea as I say took a fancy to me and therefore never made any fuss about the lack of progress of my boys at English and always accepted my lame excuses for them and my sanitized translations.

I was myself interested in Amanda Teasdale though not in the mooning way I felt towards Dora Hand. Amanda was not a teacher proper, unless substituting for someone under the weather, but rather the second-in-command to the Major in overseeing the school, and insofar as he let her manage things they would be well done until he got his hands on them again, for though his head was in the clouds a lot, he couldn't tolerate a female having too much authority, in which he was like most white men and every male Indian I ever knowed, for example my boys, who thought even poor Dorothea Hupple showed the white woman's tendency to be too bossy. Not that I myself was a radical in this respect, I tell you frankly, though I have never liked being lorded over by anyone of any sex or race, but I have never much resented a person whoever they might be that does or knows something better than myself. An opportunist like me couldn't afford to be otherwise.

Amanda for example was an educated individual who had not only gotten all the way through regular school but then had went to a woman's college in addition, so there wasn't much in the way of learning that must of escaped her — in my opinion, but not in hers, for one of the notable things all that education done for her was make her dissatisfied.

She claimed women wasn't taught the important subjects like Greek and Latin and the kind of mathematics called calculus but rather how to draw and play the piano and read stories. As the last-named sounded preferable to me, I wondered why she would of wanted instead to learn dead lingos and how to calculate beyond the commonsense sums good enough for most folks, but I knew that if I made that point it would only be a further example of how ignorant I was, so I didn't.

I got to know Amanda some during the time I was at that school, for she too seemed to like to talk to a man, with the difference that she was not looking for one to marry. In fact, after I got to know her better, she allowed as how she was against wifing, for herself anyhow, on account of it was a worse form of white slavery than them women who worked at the Lone Star, for they at least got paid and also could quit any time.

This was a new one on me, I had to admit, but I never argued the matter with her, for what did I know over someone who went to college? I did have experience of harlots, however, and could of told her the whole thing got complicated by the fact that, as I have said, them which I had knowed generally looked forward to getting married sometime and the ones that did seemed happier than respectable women in the same situation, make of that what you would. My own theory was that in their working life they got to know the worst weaknesses of men, which left only the good side to find in marriage. As for the husbands, well, they hadn't no reason to sneak around the corner looking for a whore.

It was generally of a Saturday afternoon that I saw Amanda, for that was the only off time you got at school, though I never had much to do at certain times during the week, when the boys got their instruction in farming from John Bullock, who was a man of few words and taught by demonstrating how to use a plow, how to bale hay, and the rest of it, and my boys, according to John, was all right at it when they wanted to be, but sometimes they'd fall into some kind of Cheyenne mood which I had seen many a time when I lived with the tribe, though when they was amongst their own people this tended to happen on an individual basis and not in bunches at once. It was like they went someplace else in spirit while their body remained where it was. When they was in that state, nothing could be done with them.

But back to Amanda. It didn't look to me like there was much to do for pleasure out there on them flat treeless plains that was turning into rich farmland when cultivated by men like John Bullock, and the nearest white town was no more than a whistle-stop and was too long a hike unless there had been something to do beyond watching the infrequent trains come and go, which is what the people who lived there did, but Amanda had found by walking about five miles out into the country you could reach a little stream, which had a nice bend in it shaded by cottonwoods.

She had been going there by herself, which was another of the things she done that was unusual for young ladies of the day but not as dangerous as it might of been at one time, now that wild Indians no longer roamed the region. I didn't pretend I come along to protect her, which I might have done with another kind of girl even so, but Amanda disliked the idea she ever needed a man's help for anything. I hadn't run into that sort of female before, for she wasn't no Calamity Jane type, dressing and acting manly, cussing, spitting, and chewing, and working as a mule skinner. For a hike in the country she even wore her everyday long dress and high-button shoes.

When I invited myself along for the first time I was surprised she agreed, never having shown the slightest interest in me after hiring me for the job, but I guess she was struck by the novelty of it, and low as I was on the totem pole I wasn't in no position to compromise her authority.

On the first walk we had cleared Bullock's acreage without her saying a word, and I therefore didn't think I ought to, but it finally occurred to me that maybe she was being polite and just waiting for me to begin. Being with respectable women made me real nervous.

I finally says, "Mr. Bullock's crop looks good," meaning the nice stand of wheat we had just got beyond. It was all buffalo grass from there to the horizon, level as a body of water. "Makes me feel my years. I come this way as a boy, on the wagons. You wouldn't then have thought you'd ever see farms here."

Amanda nodded but said nothing. I should mention we was walking side by side at her pace, which was right brisk, and while in this part there wasn't no actual road yet, there was a trail what had been made maybe for centuries by buffalo and other animals now gone, so the plains wasn't ever exactly trackless even to white men.

"In them days," I went on, "you might encounter a herd of buffalo that filled the world, or you might not see any at all for weeks, and most of the time you'd never run into an Indian, but then all of a sudden there would come a little band, always seemingly from noplace, though you could see in all directions for miles."

She nods again, like she's not really listening, and then says, "Tell me: are your boys making progress in English?"

"They're coming along," I says. "Probably doing as well as can be expected." If your expectations was nil, as I didn't add.

"Why are they so difficult? We are not their enemies." She asked this earnestly, not with annoyance.

"It's got to do with their manhood. They can't prove it in war any more, and they can't even hunt while they're here."

"I don't like to find fault with Indians," Amanda says, "but we must show them that shedding blood should have nothing to do with being a man."

This of course was said by someone who was not of the male sex. If she had created men they would have been nicer than the ones turned out by God.

"That'll take a bit of doing," I says.

"But it must and will be done." Amanda spoke firmly, compressing her pale lips.

Walking along at her pace under a bright sun built up quite a lot of heat in a person, and I was sweating, though you'd never know it was hot looking at Amanda, who wasn't carrying a parasol like ladies did in town or even wearing a hat. Maybe that wealth of gold hair afforded protection, for the skin of her forehead stayed uncolored. She made quite a contrast when standing next to Mrs. Stevenson, and the latter once beamed at her in my presence and said, "Honey, I guess they couldn't make 'em any whiter 'n you." I don't mean she looked unhealthy by any means. I found her real attractive, and the longer I knowed her, all the more so. Which don't mean I had any ideas of doing anything with regard to her except taking these walks, for after several of them she didn't pay no more personal attention to me than she ever had, and I never made a practice of making an advance upon a lady without getting some suggestion she would not find it repulsive.

Amanda seemed to accept my company easily enough, but I had the feeling that if I hadn't showed up some Saturday when she was setting out, she never would of looked around to see if I was on my way. As yet I had an unusual association with this girl, unlike any other I had experienced, but I believed this was due to her living a privileged life in a family that was rich and high class by my standards, whereas consider my own situation. There wasn't no reason why she should be interested in me unless she wanted to hear some of my colorful history, but she never showed any curiosity as to how I become fluent in the Cheyenne language. As to my participation in battles and being an intimate of gunfighters, well, I have spoke of her disapproval of bloodletting, so there wasn't much of my experience I could have related for her pleasure. Or so I thought anyway, disregarding my association with harlots, which was not all that extensive given the place and time. But even had it been otherwise, Amanda Teasdale would not of been the person I would normally have discussed the subject with. In them days a man didn't speak about sexual matters with a female person, certainly not a respectable one like a wife, if you had such, or a sweetheart, but not even much with the kind of woman you could buy though you might well use a reasonable amount of foul language in her company. What I mean is, at the risk of being indelicate here, a man would get to the business without talking about it unless there was some dickering as to the fee. Oh, maybe sometimes, with the better type of service, he might get asked if he had a preference. But I sure doubt if any customer of any calico queen of that day was ever questioned as to what he was doing there.

So I'll admit I was amazed and also shocked when, on one of them walks, Amanda says, in a matter-of-fact way, "Why would a man go to a prostitute?"

Resorting to humor to conceal my embarrassment, I says, "Well, if you don't want them to shed blood, then that's all that's left to do."

I should mention that Amanda had never shown no sense of humor whatsoever and did not develop one now. In fact she didn't give any indication she heard my answer, but rather went ahead and give one herself. "Is the urge to dominate women so strong that he will even pay someone to feed it?"

I wasn't certain what that meant, but given my own joking response, I expect I owed her some tolerance. "Well," I says, "if you really are puzzled about the matter, it ain't, isn't, hard to explain. When a cowboy comes in off the trail, he wants to have some pleasure on the money he earned by the weeks of hard work, so he gets drunk, gambles, and buys some time with a woman. He would no doubt prefer a free example of the last-named, but is not likely to know any decent females in the town to which he has drove the herd, and he's not going to be there long enough to meet a nice girl in some respectable way, and if he did she's not going to do what he wants until they get married." All of this sounded so self-evident to any grown person I couldn't believe I was explaining it.

Amanda had been listening this time, and when I finished she says, "My father is not a cowboy."

Once again she had me at a disadvantage. I thought I must of misheard. Young women didn't speak of their father and sex at the same time. As I say, they didn't speak of the latter at all, especially to someone they hardly knowed. But now we was in sight of the cottonwood grove at the bend of that creek, and you might need some experience of the plains to know how welcome a sight a tree is after miles of horizontal country, across which the winds blow incessantly, taking me back to memories of my early boyhood with the covered wagon. I was also looking forward to a drink of water.

"We're here already," I says.

But Amanda stuck to her point. "He has bullied my mother all her adult life, he bullies my sisters and of course the women who work for him at the bank. Yet all of that is not enough."

I guess I had heard her rightly but that didn't mean I wanted to know more of what I considered a distasteful topic. "Look here, Amanda," I says. "I think I'm the wrong person to be talking to."

"But you worked at that place."

"The Lone Star?" I shook my head. "I doubt he goes there. He'd stick out amongst that bunch." I said that to make her feel better. All kinds come in there to drink or watch the girls dancing, some dressed like merchants and bankers. Not everybody went upstairs with a working woman, but if he did, there was a discreet back stairs to get to by the same route you used to reach the outside urinal. Anyway, I didn't know her Pa.

"I have *followed* him," she said decisively. "And he has stomach trouble and doesn't drink."

I was really uncomfortable. "I oughtn't be listening to this," I says. "You'd do better to speak to that preacher in Dodge."

"Why?" Amanda asked. "Is he a customer there too?"

"The preacher?"

"He's a man, isn't he?"

"Some of us is stuck with that designation," says I, with a smile, though I begun to think her strange. "And there's nothing we can do about it."

"I refuse to believe that." She pushed her lower jaw forward. "No man has to act like an animal."

"Then, begging your pardon, you ain't met some of them I have," I told her. "Talk about meanness, no animal comes close."

We had now reached the creekside, under the trees, and I was eager to wet my whistle from the stream, which didn't have much of a current and in fact was just a few yards wide at this season in its regular channel but would be deeper at the bend and also, in the shade of the cottonwoods, cooler than in the shallow reaches or under the full sunlight. Not that a warm drink was not better than none when you was parched. Sources of water could be few and far between when you traveled across the plains.

"I don't believe it is natural to have no self-control," Amanda says. "It is self-indulgence, and men are encouraged in it."

She might have been correct for all I knowed, but it never made much difference to me by what theory a man was bad — and when I say bad I mean murdering and robbing and so on, not that he overindulged in women or whiskey — but only what I had to do to defend my own interests against him, which included them of those close to me, and by golly if I didn't get a chance to do so sooner than expected.

The way I would of gotten a drink for myself was just to squat down and take handfuls from the stream, but that seemed too crude in front of a lady, as would taking a hatful, which incidentally was a good way to cool off, by wearing it after you had drunk the contents, letting what water remained run down your face and neck. You see how coarse a man I was at the time, but the thing was, I was ever trying to better myself.

Now, while I was pondering on this matter, with Amanda going on about what was wrong with men, I heard a horse coming about a quarter mile off. I would of heard it long before that had the wind been blowing to instead of away from me. It was walking with a gait that told me it was real tired from having previously been rode hard. Movie horses are rid at full gallop mile after mile, but real ones can't do that. Also they can't gulp a lot of water (which unless stopped they will do and kill themselves) until they cool down some, so this one was being restrained by his rider from dashing up to the creek, which he could smell. I hadn't had a mount of my own for a time, but a few years behind a saloon bar didn't affect my hearing and knowledge of horses, in both of which I had been trained by the Cheyenne.

When the hoof sounds got within a hundred yards I assumed Amanda could hear them as well as me, so I did not state the obvious, but I did want to take a drink of water before a blown horse shoved his lathered face in the creek.

"Pardon," I told her, squatting down on the bank, "but I'm real thirsty, and they'll be here in a minute."

She frowned like she didn't know what I was talking about. I scooped up a handful of water and slurped it, something I had done hundreds of times, when I hadn't just stuck my mouth in and drank like a beast, but never before did I notice what a hoggish sound it made. At least I wiped my mouth on the bandanna I carried up one coat sleeve as a kerchief and not with the back of my hand.

By now the rider was just entering the trees, but Amanda still didn't notice till I said, "We got a visitor."

She finally turns around. The man was tall in the stirrups and riding a big bay, which as I expected looked worn out by recent exertion and was straining to reach the water.

"How do," he says politely, even touching the broad brim of his hat, which was pulled so far down I couldn't see but two glittering eyes and the big mustache many including me wore at this time.

We returned his greeting, Amanda even adding a pretty smile I was not familiar with, she being habitually down in the mouth. Two unholstered pistols was stuck in this fellow's waistband, and the butt of a rifle extended up from the scabbard hung from the saddle ahead of his right knee. Judging from the size of its handle, the knife in his right boot was considerable.

Whilst I was giving him the once-over, he was doing the same to me and could see I had no visible weapons. Fact is, I didn't have any hidden, either. The hideout derringer I had carried in Dodge I had sold to one of the other bartenders. Needing such money as I could collect before leaving town, in view of the low wages the school offered, I had also sold my Colt's to a cowboy. And my Indian knife was stuck in the doorjamb back there at the dormitory. I was dressed in my good clothes, black suit and string tie and all, for that's what you wore when walking out with a girl even on a dusty trail, leisure attire being as yet unknown.

Now you might ask why the matter of weapons would come up at all when some fellow just stopped to water his horse from a stream that was free for all to use at will. I'll tell you. This man had come from a westerly direction, and it was early afternoon, with the sun high above and behind him, so he wouldn't be looking at it, yet that hat brim of his was pulled down so far you couldn't see much of his visage, and in fact I noticed him giving it a further tug when entering under the trees, the kind of thing you'd do when you didn't want your face to be clearly noticed. You might say, well maybe that was just his personal style, to which my answer would be, sure, but he was carrying four visible weapons while I had none, and with a woman to look after. For having run his eyes over me to see what I was carrying, he put them on Amanda and went real slow all across her person, and on her he was not looking for weapons.

This kind of thing with a woman in the company of another man was normally a deliberate provoking of the latter if he was armed. In this case he was dismissing me as if I wasn't there, weaponless as I was.

Amanda, for all her gassing about men in the general sense, never seen what was dangerous in this specimen, but kept smiling at him. She never knowed that might seem immodest to a man of this kind, and her not wearing a sunbonnet made it more so.

He finally let his straining horse get to the creek and drink, at an angle where he could keep us in view without turning too far in the saddle.

"I think I'll just give you a ride, sweetheart," he says, grinning with a set of yellowed teeth stained in streaked brown. "Wouldjoo like that?"

Now there was no mistaking his meaning, but I'll be damned if Amanda did not keep smiling at him prettily as ever. "No, thank you," says she. "This walk is the only exercise I get all week, and I look forward to it." I wasn't too pleased she didn't include me in her remarks, though I wasn't being any help to her so far.

The man on the horse got nastier, saying, "Don't you sass me, little bitch. When I say I'm gonna do somethin', I goddam do it." And then he curses further, which I can't abide in front of a lady. But he is armed to the teeth and on top of a horse.

I never been one to squander myself at hopeless odds, and I don't know what I would of done had Amanda not been there — though if she had not, this particular problem would not of come up. The fact remained that Amanda *was* there, and this bastard had insulted her and would surely do worse when he felt like it.

So I says, maybe foolishly, but I couldn't come up with anything better at that moment, I says, hitching up my sleeves, "Git down here and fight like a man."

He snorts and utters more filth. "Where's the *man* to fight me?" He makes that kind of laugh that is noise only and no facial expression, and pulls one of them pistols from his waistband but don't point it yet, just holds it in his clenched hand resting on top of the saddle horn.

Before I could try something else, whatever that might of been, Amanda goes up to the horse, using a funny kind of walk I never seen on her before, fact is, not on any woman, for a saloon girl's type of approach was a good deal less smooth. However, I soon realized she was giving him a come-on, damned if she were not.

"Don't be so impatient," she tells him in a slow, low voice I had never heard before either, going with that slinky walk. "I haven't said no."

I couldn't know then if she had give up on me and was doing this to save herself from an even worser fate or was playing for time while I tried a tactic more effective than I had done yet, but at that moment I never thought of either possibility or aught else but rage that this fine girl was lowering herself before a low-down skunk like that.

So I rushed him, and he lifted his gun and shot me . . . well, shot at me and would of been dead on the line of my heart had Amanda not grabbed that bowie from out of his boot and stuck the blade through the boot and into the calf of his right leg just as he was squeezing the trigger, throwing off his aim so the slug missed my heart by just enough to go between my ribs and my left arm, tearing my one and only coat but sparing my flesh.

The horse shied and reared, like it had been the one hurt, and swung around, knocking Amanda to the ground. The villain had that rifle and still another pistol, and I was unarmed as ever, and would pretty surely have been drilled by him at that point, for his finger was about to squeeze the trigger again when, with a war cry I knew of old, a naked brown figure, coming from no place, vaulted on to the horse's back just behind him, grabbing his chin and raising it, and then cut his throat from ear to ear.

Spewing blood out the slashed neck, the body lost its hat and toppled off the horse and onto the ground, not too far from where Amanda was just rising from her fall, and she gets spattered with gore.

The loinclothed savage leaps down quick, kneels, and run his knife around the skull of the corpse, whose bleary right eye was yet open and whose left boot was still twitching, rips off the scalp with that sound you don't forget if you ever heard it, and holds it aloft, dripping, and again makes that Cheyenne cry, which will send a chill up your back. It is Wolf Coming Out. And now his pals appear, Goes in Sweat and Walks Last. I should have been embarrassed not to of gotten no sense of their presence back of the trees, had I not been earlier so occupied with my predicament. But I sure did not think *I* had done well. First Amanda saved my bacon and then this Indian boy.

Speaking of Amanda, she were stretched out on the ground again. I reckon she fainted when that bleeding body flopped down near her, either then or when young Wolf ripped its scalp off.

I knelt down and was starting to clean off the blood on her with my wetted bandanna when she came to, saw what I was doing, and indignantly pushed me away as if I was taking advantage to illicitly paw her person. Then she sees them boys in their breechcloths listening to Wolf's boasts about his deed, which is standard Indian procedure on a victory, and though she can't understand the heathen words, she gets their sentiment, and she all but faints again.

I help Amanda to her feet, without a protest this time. In fact, she's holding tight on to my arm. But once she's standing she shakes me off, takes a look at the body, which is still leaking blood at the throat and shows a raw red patch where a head of hair used to be, and she lights with fury into Wolf Coming Out.

"You *killed* him!" she screeches. "You wicked, wicked boy, you have *killed* a man."

What I told him in Cheyenne was, "You have done well. The woman is very pleased you saved her from being mistreated by a bad person."

Amanda kept screaming for a while, but after another look at the corpse, she ran behind the biggest cottonwood and, I judge, heaved.

Wolf shows me his weapon, the bright blood on which he is reluctant to clean off. "You were right," he says, "this knife has powerful medicine. To celebrate this great victory I present you with the scalp of your enemy." And he hands me that slimy object, a shock of hair so dirty I had rather hold it by the gory base.

It was a real generous gesture, for which I thanked him, saying I would add it to my medicine bundle, a private and usually secret collection of talismans an Indian keeps as a defense against bad spirits, this to explain ahead of time why he wouldn't be seeing it again, whereas what I purposed to do, and in fact did a little later, was sneak it back onto the corpse's skull while still moist enough to stick, so as to avoid embarrassing questions before the body got safely buried.

Meanwhile I had to fold the thing, skin side in, and put it in my pocket, for Amanda was returning now, her face paler than ever. Throwing up had relieved her of some of her earliest feelings, and what she says sternly now, including the other two boys, was "What were you doing off school grounds without permission? And what are you doing *out of uniform?*"

"Let it go, Amanda," I told her. "The boy just saved your virtue and my life."

She turned her rage on me. "You don't know that. I could have dealt with him. Women go through that sort of thing with men all their lives. He didn't frighten me."

"No, I sure saw he did not," I agreed. "That was great, stabbing his leg like that. I'm mighty grateful to you for spoiling his aim. It was you who saved my life first." I did think her a marvel, a young girl from a good family, handling herself so well in a violent situation.

But she wasn't pacified. "He did not have to be killed!"

Meanwhile Wolf had found the pistols dropped by the dead man, as well as the bowie discarded by Amanda.

"Just a minute," I told her, and to Wolf I said in Cheyenne, "You earned those weapons by combat, but you are not among the Human Beings right now. You are a boy and a student at a white man's school, and you may not possess those weapons. The same rule applies to the rifle on the horse. But I will arrange for them to be kept until you are ready to leave the school and go home and then be given to you."

He frowned, but next his brown brow cleared, and he said with evident pleasure in his black eyes, "Then I will go home soon?"

"I don't know how soon, but you'll be going home sometime. Where else would you go when you finished school?"

"We thought we would be killed," he says blandly. Which goes to demonstrate a red man's process of mind: white people would take all the trouble to run a school and deal for months trying to get students like himself to learn something, only to put them to death at the end. But you must understand they seen whites kill thousands of buffalo for the hides alone, leaving all the fine meat to rot on the ground, and then send the skins away, not even using them so far as could be noticed. And build a noisy, dirty railroad, the cars of which could only run in a straight line, so if the smallest object lay on the track the train couldn't go around it. And wear continuous pants, crotch joined to the legs, so if a white man wanted to make water, he had to tear open the front seam, and to drop his dung he had to let down the entire garment. For an Indian there was endless examples of how whites didn't make sense, not the least of which was they let their women run them.

The dead man's horse had not been scared away by the commotion and the loss of its master but had just moved a few feet away, where it was standing calmly. I took the Winchester from the boot, and while I was there I opened and looked through the saddlebag on the right side, and the first thing I found was a folded poster showing torn nail holes. I opened it up and seen someone named Elmo Cullen was wanted for murder and armed robbery. A bank in Grand Island, Nebraska, offered $500 for his capture dead or alive. Cullen was described as about 5 foot, 10 inches, weight 165, age 31, "dark complected, heavy long dirty brown mustache, hair dark brown, probably clean shaven, bowlegged."

I took the poster over to the body on the ground, which could have been that of a bounty hunter looking for Cullen. Kind of hard to tell about the bowlegs in his present state, but the rest of the description seemed to fit.

I handed the poster to Amanda, who was still complaining, and said, "Looks like the school's got some money coming."

I suppose it was to her credit that though commonly mercenary for that cause she did not immediately change her tune now. She even added to it something about blood money. But I'll say this for Amanda, by time me and the boys had slung the body over the horse and hauled it into town to the sheriff, she agreed with my simplified story of the episode as being pure defense of her virtue on my part, against an armed criminal from whose boot I was able to pull his bowie, but not without almost being shot through the heart by him, of which I could show the rip in my coat.

I left the Cheyenne boys out of it, for nothing but trouble would of come from them attacking even a criminal white man to save two other whites. At least I never wanted to chance it. So far as the sheriff knowed, them students, dressed the way they was for a school pageant, had just helped us bring in the body, which *was* Cullen, for in one of his pockets the sheriff found a tattered letter from his old Ma, back in Missouri, asking for money, along with an indecent photo of some woman taken in a red-light house, I expect, with "oll my luve to Elmo" scrawled between her naked spread thighs and signed *Saginaw Sal*.

Cullen's horse turned out to be stole from the man he had killed outside the bank he had robbed in Nebraska and had to be returned to the widow. None of the cash he had took from the bank turned up on his person. I believe that sheriff thought it possible I might of helped myself to it. He allowed as how he might have fifty dollars coming from the reward for the costs of identification, telegraphing Grand Island, et cetera, so we let him keep that, and the rest when it come was presented to the Major for the school, by me but in the name of Wolf Coming Out, who never made a claim for any part of the money, on account of he still didn't understand or care what an important place money occupied in civilization, for him and the other boys had not acquired much of the latter from their classes.

You take history, which was taught by a woman with little squinty eyes and a mumbly voice, who was named Miss Gilhooley, which I gave up trying to get the boys to pronounce when they couldn't get closer than *Grr-who*. I ain't going to go through the details of how what she taught in class was transmitted by me to them, but though not literal in the word-for-word, I was careful with the facts, and learned some history myself while so doing. But what would come back when them young Indians was quizzed might be hard to recognize.

All of this was by mouth, for of course they couldn't write. Stands Like a Bear's version of the Revolutionary War: "George Washington stole a horse and rode around telling the Americans that they would all get new red coats if they agreed not to drink any more tea. So they all got drunk on whiskey and started fighting." Walks Last said the Civil War was caused by a big argument between Abraham Lincoln, who was a Black White Man, and President Grant, over a woman.

You might say they didn't care much about white history for it seemed to have no reference to their own lives, but what they was taught about geography, by a big hefty female named Bertha Wadleigh, bothered them boys, especially when she hung a long roll on a couple of nails above the blackboard and pulled down from it a flexible map printed on oilcloth, which was a wonder to them insofar as it was taken as a bright-colored decoration. But when she said it was a picture of the part of the earth on which we lived, in this case North America, them Cheyenne believed she was lying, though for a reason they couldn't comprehend, because walking the same earth as them, she hadn't nothing to gain from pretending it was actually a piece of cloth hanging on a wall. They was getting so riled up about the matter that I thought they might get into trouble, so I just told them Miss Wadleigh was a crazy person who was given this silly job to keep her busy in a harmless way, which is what Indians kindly do to their own nutcases. So once again I weren't no help in what this school was trying to accomplish, and I tell you my conscience was not at peace, especially when it come to the religious classes, which was given by the Major himself. Them boys could readily accept Mary's giving birth though a virgin and Jesus' rising from the dead, and anything else in the realm of the miraculous, like walking on water, turning water into wine, and so on, but they never could make any sense of the central of all Christian beliefs, that God, who ran everything in the world, would let bad people crucify His son, and trying to tell them it was to save everybody from their sins only made it more incredible. Why didn't God just do away with sin?

Well, I have got sidetracked from completing the account of that incident concerning the wanted man Elmo Cullen and its consequence. How'd them boys happen to be out there by the creek to give us a helping hand? For in doing so, they was breaking the school rules for Saturdays, like Amanda had noted, which afternoons they had off from classes but was expected to stay on the school grounds and play sports, which meant mostly baseball, for that was the only kind of equipment the school possessed at the moment, and not enough even so. The one bat was soon broke, after which they used axe handles and the like, but the one ball was finally beat to a state that it could not be stuck together any more, and the substitutes made of wood or tight-wrapped rawhide never were satisfactory. Anyhow, only eighteen players could be in the game at any one time, which meant the rest of the male students had nothing to do but watch, which didn't long maintain the interest of the Cheyenne, who took the opportunity to slip away into the country and play make-believe war, until Cullen showed up and they had somebody to rub out in reality.

Try as I did to explain their ways to Amanda, I can't say she ever found the episode acceptable, even though the Major did, who had been a soldier both in the Civil and the Indian wars, seeing lots of violent deaths and, even as a Christian, having no objection to the death of an enemy in a good cause.

Now I haven't said much about the other students at the school, some of which done a lot better than my boys at picking up what was taught, and most learned passable English, especially the girls. I don't want you to think the place was an absolute flop by any means. There was at least one boy from my time, an Osage if memory serves, who went on to become a doctor amongst his people, and a couple others become preachers in their tribes, and some of the girls went on to teach at reservation schools and be nurses at hospitals for Indians. I never heard of any who got positions in the white world. I guess that practical experience at cookery and, for the boys, plowing, shoeing horses, bailing hay, and so on might have paid off when they tried to make a go of it back home as farmers.

As I said before, it was normal for an Indian from a warlike tribe to boast of such violence as he wreaked on enemies, and such was not looked upon as a blowhard like he might of been with whites, maybe because I never knowed a redskin who told untruths in so doing, whereas with American braggarts the first thing that occurs to you on hearing them is they're probably lying, else they wouldn't have to praise themselves. So young Wolf Coming Out, he sure let the other students hear about his feat, notwithstanding that he didn't speak a word of anything but Cheyenne, and I don't know if I ever mentioned one of the singular facts about Indians was every little tribe had its own peculiar tongue, which frequently was incomprehensible to the tribe right next door, and so the sign language was invented. But words never meant much to young people of any race I was ever acquainted with. I gathered that the others learned as much about the killing of the white desperado as they could have been told, making the other boys real jealous and impressing the girls, which was the desired result.

I saw to it that the medicine knife was returned to its perch on the doorjamb outside my room, never to be taken away again short of another life-or-death situation.

Now, Cheyenne maidens was renowned for their chastity and their courting could be as long and involved with rules as that of Miss Millicent Chutney by Mr. John Longworth Whitfellow, in Boston. But the boys was not obliged to take a similar care with the honor of females from other tribes (like the lads of the three major religions when going interfaith), so the schoolgirls, none of which was Cheyenne, was fair game, as they was to the boys of all the other tribes, which accounted for the solid walls between the two halves of the dormitory building and the separate entrances. The sexes was also kept apart at meals and in recreation, for it was the Major's theory that nothing was more likely to impede the progress of civilization amongst young barbarians than access of male and female to one another before proper marriage by a Christian preacher and not the heathen connection made without benefit of clergy in which these young folk had been conceived by their parents.

I have said that another of the small male staff was a German what taught arithmetic, name of Klaus Kappelhaus. He was also in charge of the ground-floor dormitory and, even though near as I could understand he had emigrated to avoid military service in the Old Country, he maintained an even stricter discipline over his boys than the Major asked, among other things making them polish their shoes in unison each night before going to bed and on arising in the morning recite by heart long sections of the Declaration of Independence, the preamble to the Constitution, General George Washington's farewell address to his troops, etc., all of which Klaus had himself memorized before becoming a citizen. The accuracy of his memory had to be taken on faith by most folks, for his accent was so thick he could be saying almost anything. His version of the Declaration began something like, "Van in duh coze of hoom-ahn ayffents. . . ."

I generally kept out of Klaus's way, for like everybody I have ever knowed who was hard to comprehend by reason of accent, speech impediment, or mouth wound, he loved to talk a lot. But this one evening after the boys was supposed to have gone to bed — though in my case, not being a German, I wasn't strict about the exact schedule, so long as all lamps and candles was out, for safety from fire — I come down to have a smoke out front of the building, again for safety's sake, for when sitting alone at the end of day with a pipe in my mouth I had acquired a tendency to nod, and a few times the lighted pipe had fell into my lap with a spray of sparks. After all, I was approaching the then substantial age of forty, which looking back was only a little more than a third of my life, but how was I to know that at the time?

So there I was, puffing away and watching the lightning bugs flash over the little patch of lawn that had finally took hold but had to be hand-watered frequently by the students, which seemed foolish to them because it wasn't an edible crop and a near drought was always in progress thereabouts.

"Check," says somebody in a harsh whisper behind me, and before turning I recognized it as my name as pronounced by Klaus Kappelhaus, which was useful because aside from the glowing bugs there wasn't much light from the overcast sky and none from the dormitory behind him. (His version of my whole name was *Check Grobb.*)

"Just going in, Klaus," says I, tapping out against an uplifted boot heel what remained of the tobacco embers.

"Check," says Klaus, "iss any of your boyss shneeking into duh girlss' side?" I am purposely making this easier to understand here than it was in reality. Believe me when I say each speech of his was a struggle for me.

"I don't expect so, Klaus," I tells him. "For not only do I keep my door open but I'm a real light sleeper." And I adds, "Plus any such would have to go all the way downstairs past Charlevoix's floor and then through yours, then get into the girls' side without being detected by Bertha Wadleigh." Who was the ground-floor guardian next door, and a hefty person who made even Klaus uncomfortable to be near, for she was husky enough to whip him in a fair fight.

"Check," says Klaus, "duh girl got shits."

I wondered why I had to hear that. "It ain't like Mrs. Stevenson to cook bad food. It's probably something they ate on their own, green apples maybe."

"Check," says Klaus, "she lets duh shits down from duh vindow."

For a minute I still didn't get it. Then: "You mean the girl drops tied-up sheets from a window?"

"Eggzackly! He climbs opp."

"You seen him in the act?"

It was too dark to clearly see his expression, but I reckon he was shocked by the question. "No, I have not zeen dem fickling, and I don't vant to!"

Klaus didn't always get an American turn of speech and had therefore believed "act" meant more than my reference to climbing. I straightened him out on the matter and then asked if the sheets was lowered tonight.

"In duh beck." He meant the back of the building, where he had just come from as I came out the front.

So we went through the ground-floor hallway and out the rear door.

The night wasn't any lighter back there, but with that trick of looking not directly at the object of your interest but rather just to the side of it, I could just make out a long twisted kind of rope made of knotted — they wasn't sheets, which in fact the students were not given and, at least with my boys, wouldn't of used even when the use was explained — blankets is what was tied end to end and hung from a window from the top floor boys' quarters, dangling a couple feet from the ground. And over on the girls' part, another such come down from a window on the second floor.

I had to get the young fellow, whoever he was, out of there before an alarm was raised that reached the Major, who was dead set against any kind of sexual activity for anybody and in the case of his students for all I knew would prescribe the firing squad. At the least he'd expel the offenders, who must then go home in shame, having disgraced their tribes in front of the whites. That's sure how the Cheyenne would see it.

"I'll shinny up," I told Klaus. "God knows how long he'll stay up there otherwise." Before the climb, I squeezed a promise out of Klaus, which wasn't easy on account of how he was about discipline, to let me handle the punishment of the miscreant my own way and not inform the Major or anybody else on the staff. I admit I made use of my boys' rep for savagery, Klaus after all having fled the Old Country to avoid the warlike.

So I goes up the blanket-rope, which was the easiest part of this mission, and I clumb over the windowsill. By now my eyes was adjusted to the night and I could see some, dark as it was, but him I was looking for would of been easy to spot in any event, for he was grunting like a rutting animal. I won't keep you in suspense any longer than I was, for I right away suspected it would be Wolf Coming Out, him having got his man and thus the admiration of them Indian girls, to which he was like a matinee idol would be for white maidens, and no male person can resist taking advantage of such an opportunity.

Now I go over to where he is covering the girl, who I can hardly discern, and in as low a voice as could be I announce myself and call him off.

But Wolf don't stop what he's about nor even change his rhythm, but just says, breathing quick, I should take as his gift any of the other girls in the room, for they all belong to the bravest warrior in the school, namely himself.

So I see strong measures are required, and I haul off and give him such a kick in his naked arse on that low cot that he goes sprawling across the girl, and then with a choke hold I drag him off and onto his feet, where he tries to wrestle, at which Cheyenne boys is pretty good, but they never understood the principle of fist-fighting, so it was easy enough to give him a right uppercut onto the glass jaw all Indians have (as opposed to their granite skulls), and he hits the floor dead to the world.

I pulled the makeshift rope up and inside, run it around his chest under the armpits, and tied it tight. Then I took off my belt and put it around his body to hold the wrists at hip-level, so his arms wouldn't raise when he was lowered on the rope.

Then, using the leverage of the windowsill, I let him slowly down until he hung close to the ground, where Klaus could let him loose.

While I was occupied with this effort, my pants, too loose at the waist to stay up without a belt or galluses, began to move south, and when I straightened up and was preparing to slide down the rope now Wolf was clear, my trousers plunged to my ankles, right at the moment a delegation of female staff members entered the room, each carrying a lighted oil lamp and headed by the burly figure of Bertha Wadleigh. What happened was Dorothea Hupple, the staff monitor for this floor, had been woke up, behind a closed door, by the noise of Wolf's rutting and, scared, had already went down to fetch the others before I arrived.

Now Wolf had been saved, but I was the one in trouble, all the more so because I never had no drawers on, owing to the fact that with the weather too hot for longjohns I hadn't found the time yet to go into the drygoods shop in town and buy summer garments. I should of worn a Cheyenne-style breechcloth! So you can imagine what it looked like I had been up to, in that dormitory full of Indian girls, who had probably been awake all the time but only now begun to giggle and chatter.

Seeing me, Dorothea Hupple let out a scream and almost dropped her lamp, but big Bertha advanced on me like a mad bull, being about that size.

"Now, wait a minute," I says, having pulled up my pants, "I can —"
But didn't get no further before Bertha shifted her lamp to the left hand and slugged me in the jaw with her ham-sized right. I went down.

Standing over me, she glowers down in the lamplight. "Beastly little man! The Major will put you in prison for this."

I roll-dodged the kick she sent my way with a big slippered foot, and quick got up before she could launch another, clutching the waist of my pants, which was threatening to fall again. She and them others was wearing what respectable women put on for bed in them days, which was no less modest or voluminous than the daytime garb, and they had dressing gowns on top of that, but aside from Bertha they all acted like I had caught *them* naked.

"Hold on," I says to Bertha and included the rest. "This looks like what it isn't." But then I reflected that having gone to so much trouble to save Wolf, I could hardly implicate him now. "You just ask these girls if I touched any of them" was the best I could come up with, and it didn't do much for my case, for Bertha allowed as how she had got there just in time to stop me from forcible rape.

That girl Wolf had been topping, who I got a look at finally, had pulled the skirt of her nightgown down and was pretending, alone in the room, to be fast asleep. I believe she was a Kiowa. Wolf wouldn't have knowed a word of her language, but never had to.

Bertha says, "Dorothea, go run for the Major and tell him to bring his gun."

"You want me shot?" I asks.

"You vile little runt," Bertha says, thrusting her big square jaw my way, but I never thought about returning the punch, not wanting to break my hand. "You think this doesn't matter, because they're just Indian girls?"

I could of told her I once had a Cheyenne wife, and a baby what was half Indian blood, but when they're that riled people don't want to hear reasons why they shouldn't be, so I never bothered. But I sure wasn't going to wait around for more abuse, even if I was pretty certain the Major wouldn't shoot me.

I straddled the windowsill and then went down that blanket-rope while holding my pants up with one hand and braking my descent with the other and my knees. I probably arrived at the ground before them ladies started downstairs.

Klaus was still there, along with a groggy Wolf Comes Out. I quickly explained to the former what had happened, and reclaimed my belt. I was in too much of a hurry to wait while Klaus reacted in his Dutch version of English, but got from Wolf a promise not to say anything about the evening's events if asked, which he probably wouldn't be.

"I'm sorry I had to hit you," I told him. "I have to go now."

Being an Indian, what he said in return was only "I hear you." He knew if I wanted to say more, I would of done so. Since I didn't, it wasn't his place to bring it up.

I then departed that school in the dead of night, ending my term there under a cloud of disgrace. I tell you this: I wouldn't have went away in that fashion, as if admitting my shame, but for one consideration. I would of stayed and defended myself, and without betraying Wolf Comes Out too, for I can be right inventive when the need arises, but I knew that one person would never believe a word of mine, and I don't mean Bertha Wadleigh. I just couldn't bear to face the disdain of Amanda Teasdale.

8

Buffalo Bill to the Rescue

NOW I HAVE MADE A LITTLE FUN OF KLAUS KAPPEL-
haus's accent, but he was nice enough on my hasty escape from
school to lend me such money as was in his pockets that night,
which added to the small change in my own, was sufficient next
morning to buy me a train ticket (I spent most of the night hiking to
town) back to Dodge City, of which I had previously thought I seen my
last, but at this time it was the only place where I had any connections,
and I was out of a job and owned only the clothes I was wearing, though
having reclaimed my belt at least my pants stayed up.

On reaching Dodge I went right to the Lone Star, where the evening's
entertainment was in full flower, if that's the word, but I was real touched
when Longhorn Lulu, one of the girls who was particular friends of mine,
screams a greeting at me, climbing off some cowboy's lap, where she was
groping his all but unconscious person though for pocket-picking and
not sexual reasons, and comes and gives me a great big hug.

"Jack, I be damn if it ain't you. We heard the Indians got you, honey."

I had a real warm feeling when I smelled the familiar cheap perfume
from the harlots, mixed with the odors of even cheaper whiskey, worse
cigars, and cowboy sweat, and tried to hear what she was saying amidst
laughs and yells and hog-calling hollers and music from an orchestra
which in time-honored style played the louder the less talented the mu-
sicians, for any good ones would of been over at the Comique or the Varieties. That the Lone Star, already going downhill when I had left some
months before, was the nearest place I had to home might of been embarrassing, but not nearly so much as my last moments at the Indian

school, so I was glad to be back and, throwing down a few on the house, getting the latest news, of which the first Lulu give me was that Belle, my other friend, sometimes called Squinty Belle from her habitual expression, and the one of the two which looked a lot older though wasn't by much, had got married to some drummer, not the kind from a band but a commercial traveler who sold gewgaws, I don't know what kind for neither did Lulu. When last heard from, the happy couple was in Denver, from where Belle had sent a hand-tinted postcard of a bouquet of flowers, much admired by Lulu, who claimed to be able to count at least a dozen colors, but with not much of a message: "We're heer. Its reel hi. Yr pal, Bel."

I returned the card to Lulu, who put it back under her clothes somewhere and from the same place out come a roll of money. "Say, Jack, I don't want to hurt your feelings none, but you might find use for a dollar or so."

"Do I look that down-and-out already?" I says, rubbing my day's growth of whiskers. I was undoubtedly dirty from that latest train ride, from which I was still chewing the grit from them cinders blowing in. I was also hungry again. This train had stopped at eating times, but I never had enough cash left to buy aught but a cup of coffee and a hunk of stale dry bread at noon. I hastened to add, "But it's real nice of you, Lulu, till I get my job back." I accepted without looking what she give me, for she did it real private, our hands down at the side against the bar, so it wouldn't look like I was a man being kept by a whore, which is as low as you can get.

"As long as you want," Lulu says. After some years of harlotry she still could of passed for eighteen if she washed off the paint and put on the clothes of decent girls. She was hugging my arm to the shoulder. "Me 'n' Belle couldn't stop cryin' when we heard you was kilt by them goddam Indians."

"I wasn't killed, as you can plainly see, Lulu. I wasn't even hurt."

"I hope you got some of them," said she, real bitter.

"I guess I ain't made it clear," I says. But to do so, I would of had to explain about the school, and at the moment that was still too touchy a subject for me. "Just you forget about Indians, dearie," I says. "I didn't have anything to do with them. I was just away on personal business. Uh, St. Louis."

Lulu pouted. "You might of sent a postcard. You know how I like to get cards."

"I'm sorry, Lu."

"It don't matter what's writ on them," says she. "I can't read anyhow."

"I'll remember next time. Now I think I'll eat a bite and then get drunk."

Lulu squeezed my arm again and says, real affectionate, "You might go over the barber's and take a bath sooner or later."

It shook me to hear that, considering the hygiene of some of them who shared her bed however speedily. "Yes, ma'am, and thanks again for the loan." I didn't want to keep her too long from her job, whoring being paid for as piecework.

"Oh, Jack, you know who's back in Dodge? Bat."

"I'm real glad to hear that," I says. "Now I'm heading for that bath." Which I done, after throwing down a couple fingers of whiskey, first I had had in months, for the Major never tolerated any strong drink on the school premises even for the male staff, lest the students get hold of it, and for once he was sure right. And after that first one I had a few more on an empty stomach and by time I headed across the tracks I was feeling pretty good, else I would never of so readily accepted Bat Masterson's invite to come along with him to Ogallala, up in Nebraska, to rescue one Billy Thompson from jail.

But let me catch up. Before even getting to the barber's, who should I meet up with on Front Street but Bat himself, looking the same spiffy gent as always, though he hadn't carried that gold-headed cane in ages, having recovered from his leg wound.

"Well sir, Bat," says I, "I'm proud to see you again. I been away myself, and —"

Bat cut this short. I don't think he knowed where I had been nor cared, nor did he want to talk about Leadville, where last I heard he went to gamble, nor about why he was back, having left after he run for re-election as Ford County sheriff and got beat. Bat was not all that popular in Dodge. The respectable people, like them at the church Dora Hand went to, didn't like his friendship with lowlifes, chief amongst them the Thompson brothers, Ben and Billy. And what he now proposes to me, there on the street in front of Dog Kelley's Alhambra saloon, is I come along with him to Ogallala and help Billy Thompson escape from the jail where he had been put as a result of one of his many scrapes and was wounded and under arrest and in danger of being lynched by the local friends of a man he had shot.

Had I been cold sober I would not of entertained the proposal, as much as I owed Bat Masterson, for Billy Thompson was one of them Texans nobody except their blood relatives could stomach. Bat himself disliked Billy, putting up with him only because of Ben, who he liked, the way he tolerated Doc Holliday as a friend of Wyatt Earp's. Friendship meant a lot to Bat, and I can't knock that principle in view of how I myself had profited from it, but it can be inconvenient, that's for sure.

Ben Thompson had lived a life as eventful as any but mine, having been an officer in the Confederate cavalry, then served as a major in the forces of Maximilian, the French emperor of Mexico who was actually an Austrian—don't ask me to explain that. When Max was overthrown and put to death, Ben come back to the U.S.A., where he gambled in various places and co-owned a saloon in Abilene named the Bull's Head, but the sign outside depicted not a horned head but rather an enormous bull's pizzle, and finding it indecent, none other than Wild Bill Hickok, then the marshal, made them change it. Ben never took on Wild Bill, not even when the latter killed his partner, but he was a real dangerous man who fought a lot, and him and his brother Billy had a shoot-out with some enemies in Ellsworth that resulted in the death of the sheriff, but they got off.

Ben was another example of that type that was sometimes on one side of the law but occasionally on the other. Bat believed him the best with a gun who ever held one. You can judge the quality of Ben Thompson's nerves by his principle of gunfighting: he always got the other fellow to fire first. He said the man was likely, through hurry, to miss, and firing second, Ben could claim self-defense.

But why would Bat Masterson be such a good friend to Ben Thompson at a personal cost? The best reason in the world then and now: he saved his life. Ben come to his aid in that fight where Bat lay wounded, down in Sweetwater, Texas, and would likely of been murdered by his adversary's friends.

Now though I was fairly drunk and on account of my own friendship with Bat would of honored any request by him even when sober, I did ask why Ben Thompson himself wasn't going to Ogallala to rescue his brother? The answer was that Ben himself was banned for life from that part of

Nebraska. I never found out what he done there, but the Thompsons generally meant trouble wherever they turned up. What Billy done was him and a man named Tucker shot it out in a saloon called the Cowboy's Rest, over the affections of a harlot named Big Alice. Billy blew off Tucker's left thumb and three other fingers, Tucker falling behind the bar, but when Billy turned to stagger out, Tucker come up with a sawed-off shotgun and give him both barrels in the back, but because his aim wasn't the best, owing to his one hand being essentially a bloody stump, only part of the buckshot found its mark, which meant the bad news, for much of the world, was that Billy would keep his worthless hide on for a while longer, though he was, in sickbed at his hotel, under arrest by the local sheriff, who as a friend of Tucker's was expected to look the other way so Billy could be lynched.

En route to Nebraska I begun to worry about the reception we'd get there as a delegation in support of a man as unpopular in Ogallala as a Thompson, but when I finally bucked up my courage to run the danger of Bat's thinking me yellow and allowed as how the odds might be against us, Bat again demonstrated the kind of mental command that kept him ahead of the game.

"Jack," says he, "the only problem is if Ben has the money they'll ask."

"Come again?"

"If they were in a hurry to kill Billy," says he, "they would have done it long since. They'll only stretch his neck as a last resort, if Ben can't come up with enough to buy them off."

There was Bat for you. I should of known he wouldn't ask me along if he expected gunplay. What he wanted was somebody friendly to drink with while on this job. Since I lacked his capacity to tolerate alcohol I was under the influence most of the time and don't have no clear memory of when we went to Tucker's home, except that the "thumbless one," as Bat called him when talking to me, had a big bandage around what remained of his left hand but wasn't mad at Bat or me and seemed in the mood to deal.

When he was ready to name a figure, he beckoned Bat close with the hand that worked, and mumbled a figure I couldn't hear.

After which Bat nodded and thanked him and said he'd telegraph Ben and get back, but we was hardly out Tucker's door when Bat says, "Ben doesn't have that kind of money. We're going to have to get Billy out for free."

My peace of mind departed when I thought the lead might fly after all, but once again I underestimated Bat's powers of invention. He waited till the night everybody in town including the sheriff, who served as fiddler, attended a dance at the schoolhouse, with the exception of the deputy guarding Billy Thompson's hotel room, and while I waited on the floor below, Bat stood several rounds of drinks for the deputy, a young fellow come not long before from the East who hadn't yet had time to grow a hollow leg like Bat's. Also, what passed for a whiskey sour in Ogallala was used as paint remover elsewhere. Not to mention the possible contribution of that useful Irishman, Michael Finn.

Anyway, the deputy eventually hit the floor and stayed, at which Bat whistled down, and I come up and helped him lift Billy out of bed and carry him, Billy cursing in pain at each jolt, across to the railroad depot, where a train stopped not long after to take on water, Bat having timed it perfect, and we got our load into a coach without attracting any attention in town on account of the dance and not much on an almost empty train.

Having got Billy settled, slumped in a seat of his own and sucking on the bottle Bat provided him with, we set ourselves down, and I mentions the job we was going to have to get Thompson back to Dodge, considering there wasn't no direct rail line yet between here and there. We had had to come by a combination of trains and stages.

Bat passes me the second bottle he had the foresight to bring and says with a smile, "I have made an arrangement with Bill Cody, who's home right now in North Platte. We'll be there in an hour."

"Buffalo Bill Cody?"

"One and the same," Bat says.

"Why would he help us?"

"I asked him to," Bat says between swallows. "By telegraph."

"To help in the escape of a man under a criminal charge?"

Bat pointed the business end of the whiskey bottle like it was a gun. "Bill Cody loves excitement," he says. "And at the moment, living there with the little woman, I'm taking for granted he will be bored."

No matter how often I seen Bat being right, I was sceptical as usual. For one thing, by time the train reached North Platte, the hour was near two A.M. on a real dark night, and we got off, toting Billy, who seemed twice as heavy as before and even more disagreeable, at a place none of us knowed our way around even if we could of seen anything but the lighted saloon across from the depot. Which is where Bat heads us.

So we carry Billy in through the swinging doors and deposit him in the nearest chair, and by golly there's Buffalo Bill at the bar, not only awake this late but with a full head of steam, surrounded by a crowd of cowboys listening to his spiel. He raises his glass to us and we go and shake his hand. Cody was a handsome fellow, best-looking man I ever seen, over six foot tall, muscular and fit, with that shoulder-length hair and mustache and goatee which started light brown and over the years would turn snow-white. The brim of his big hat was swept up over one ear, and his jacket of white buckskin was decorated with extensive bead-work along with three times the normal amount of fringe. His shiny soft calfskin boots run all the way to mid-thigh. There wasn't a single weapon hanging from his big-buckled belt. Never being a gunfighter, Cody seldom wore a pistol except in his shows. Most everywhere he went he acquired admirers much like them here, for he could tell a story so well you would listen to his version of some event as more interesting than the experience you had had yourself at the same place and time. Imagine what Buffalo Bill could of made of being the sole white survivor of the Little Bighorn fight or one of the handful to witness the murder of Wild Bill Hickok.

"Colonel Masterson," is how Cody greeted Bat. "Your reputation precedes you, sir." To me he says, "Sir, you have me at a disadvantage." When I told him my name he lifted his glass and said to us both, "Won't you join me and my friends in a sip of tanglefoot? Name your poison: whiskey, brandy, or Old Tom Cat gin. Meanwhile, let's start on level ground." At that he drains what he is holding and calls to the bartender to take orders from all around.

Billy Thompson, though half passed out from his ordeal and the bottle he drank on the train, yells in his usual foul language he wants another one too.

Cody frowns and says to Bat, "Colonel, would you please inform that gent that cursing is out of order on Dave Perry's premises, at least while I am present."

So Bat does as asked and then returns, by which time the new drinks was waiting on the bar top, where Cody shooed away some of the others so me and Bat could belly up next to him.

Cody begun, "I was just telling these gentlemen of the unexpected availability of ice during the summer in the eastern part of our glorious country, making it possible on the hottest days to enjoy cold beverages. It is cut from lakes in winter and the blocks are stored under sod or sawdust, a method of preservation so efficient, I was told by my dear friend Mr. Augustus Hamlin, the eminent financier at whose luxurious home in New York City I have frequently dined, 'Cody,' said he, 'would you believe that only about ten percent thawing has occurred by the following summer?'" Having emptied his glass again, he skittered it across the shining bar top to Dave and says to us he had to see a man about a horse, and goes, in a mostly sturdy stride, to the back. It took me a minute to realize he went to pee.

"See what I mean?" Bat says. "He couldn't be friendlier."

"All he's done so far is talk," says I. "He ain't said anything about helping us get back to Dodge. And what's this about you being a colonel?"

"A title of respect," says Bat. "Just be patient."

But when Cody returned he resumed the subject of ice. "I'm sure you gents will back me up on this, though the inexperienced may cast doubt, but you will recall if you cross North Platte at Richard's Bridge and proceed past the Red Buttes to the Sweet Water, past the Devil's Gate, to the Cold Springs, if you dig three feet down in the earth you will find ice at any time of the year."

"Is that right, Bill?" asks the nearest cowboy.

Cody solemnly closed his eyes and opened them quick. "On the hottest day of the summer."

He finally got off ice and onto his adventures fighting Indians, the first example of which he claimed he killed when he was eleven. He was right good at storytelling, so good he never made the mistake so many B.S. artists do in having themselves win at every turn. Of course he always won in the long run, else he wouldn't of been here buying round after round. It was enjoyable, to tell the truth, and I decided why should I worry whether Billy Thompson ever got back to Dodge: it weren't my responsibility.

But sometime during the night Cody finally decided to wrap up the party, and he showed he hadn't forgot what we was there for. He got Dave Perry to furnish us a place to hide out till morning, in case a posse from Ogallala showed up, and directed another fellow to bring us out to his farm at the edge of North Platte, next day.

"I'd like to carry you out there with me now," he says, "but for the need to get Mrs. Cody's approval, and I don't like to disturb her at this hour. She is a fine lady of whom I am inordinately fond."

I was surprised to hear he was happily married, out drinking all night like that and running all over the country as he was famous for doing, killing buffalo and Indians, performing as an actor, rubbing elbows with the powerful and wealthy of big cities, but that was Buffalo Bill Cody for you, a real package if there ever was one.

When we got to his farm or ranch next morning, which by the way he called the Welcome Wigwam, which I calculate was only a couple hours after we last seen him, he didn't show no signs of wear whatsoever, but was already dressed in one of his buckskin getups, with black velvet pants, and the hair of his head and face was real glossy in the sunshine.

"Gentlemen," says he, when we climbed out of the buggy, leaving Billy inside, sleeping off his drink. "Won't you join me in a breakfast cup?" By which he shortly proved he meant about an inch of coffee plus two or three of brandy, topped by a douse of heavy cream, which he allowed made up most of his cows' production, which you had to considerably dilute with well water if you wanted only milk. He had the makings on a table on the veranda, for he says he didn't want to disturb Mrs. Cody at her morning prayers.

As it happened we ended up staying a few days around North Platte, for apparently the Ogallala folks decided not to pursue Billy Thompson, who could recuperate in one place as well as another, so long as he wasn't bumped around and even when that happened he survived, having the usual endurance of the worthless, and Cody begged us to stay till a party of foreigners, German dukes and the like, arrived to experience his version of the West, hunting whatever game could be located, wearing sombreros and chaps, meeting some harmless Indians, and of course listening to Buffalo Bill's stories. Now Bat was not the sort to turn down such an invite, besides which Cody promised him the loan of a brand-new phaeton carriage he had lately purchased for his gracious wife, and a horse to pull it, so we could eventually return to Dodge in comfort.

When the European bunch arrived, we all headed out into the open country after a good deal of liquid refreshment, so much indeed that Cody found it difficult to mount his horse and therefore went to sleep in the accompanying mess wagon, being driven by Bat, who was also the worse for wear, to the degree that, missing a turn in the trail at one point, the wagon got turned over, throwing Bat clear, but Cody was buried underneath it and the heavy load it toted, mostly bottled and jugged goods.

The scare sobered everybody up on the spot, and we dug frantically in the pile of spilled cargo, fearing the worst, but when he was finally uncovered, Buffalo Bill sat up, shook his long curls, found and donned his hat, which hadn't seemingly been creased or smudged, and grinning, says, "Let's drink to that!" I'll tell you another remarkable fact: I never seen one bottle that got broke.

When we reached where we was camping for the night and had a big meal of local specialties, buffalo and antelope and prairie chicken, washed down by the usual drinkables plus countless bottles of champagne brung by them foreigners, Cody give a memorable performance of riding, on a horse as tricky as any you seen in a circus, and of marksmanship with both a Colt's and the fifty-caliber Remington buffalo rifle he called Lucretia Borgia, using champagne bottles as targets. He invited Bat to shoot as well, but the latter had suffered a sore lip in that wagon crash and weren't at his best, so begged off. Cody offered me my choice of guns, but as I hadn't discharged a firearm in some years I didn't want to serve as a bad example now in front of them Europeans, so I too declined. Nor did I open my mouth when Cody's stories included his old friends Wild Bill Hickok and General Custer. By the way, he got to calling me "Captain," and like Bat I took the title as one of courtesy.

Now after this brief glimpse of Buffalo Bill we're going to leave him for a spell, after I say I never laid eyes on the often-mentioned Mrs. Cody, whose new buggy we borrowed to carry Bill Thompson back to Dodge, and without her knowledge according to Bat. And one more item: when we shook goodbye with Buffalo Bill he says to Bat that he was about to put one of his traveling shows together and would admire to have Colonel Masterson join him as partner and featured attraction, and he says kindly to me, "And you can be sure we'll find a prominent role for yourself, Captain." Which I thought was real generous of him, since he hadn't seen me do anything but drink, but maybe that was enough.

The trip back turned out not to be as comfortable as we expected, heavy rain falling for the entire two hundred mile, and Mrs. Cody's phaeton didn't have no top, so we was all soaked with water and splashed with mud, with Billy whining and cursing the whole way, plus under them extreme conditions we run out of liquor sooner than usual, on a stretch of open prairie where it couldn't be replenished.

But miserable as his state was, Billy's first act on reaching Dodge was not a meal or a drink or a visit to the doctor to change his filthy bandages or, it not being Christmas in a leap year, a bath. What he had to do before anything else was go to the telegraph office and wire a jeering message to the sheriff of Ogallala about how he put one over on him.

For me things went back to normal. I resumed a job at the Lone Star, though no longer as head barkeep. I moved back into the same hotel but a different and shabbier room with worse cracks in everything breakable like the window, the washbowl, and the thunder mug. There wasn't no pitcher despite many threats to the series of shifty-looking persons at the so-called front desk, a packing crate with some key hooks on the wall behind, each of which denied being the owner. Now wouldn't you think I could at least have afforded to buy a pitcher of my own? The truth was I had fell into a depressed state of mind after that episode at the Indian school, the main effects of which was postponed by the rescue of Billy Thompson, but the heavy drinking I got into on that trip, first I had done in years, maintained after returning to Dodge, made me even more melancholy than I would of been otherwise.

Four decades of age, and what did I have to show for it? It was not exactly a new problem, but it recently got worse. Even Cody was younger than me, and I had been hearing about him for years. Everybody older, like Custer and Wild Bill and most of the Indians I had been close to, was dead. By steady work I had accumulated that sum of money I thought of as a nest egg but in truth was maybe only a couple hundred dollars, which hadn't even earned the 2 percent interest offered by Amanda Teasdale's Pa's bank, on account of I had kept it under a floorboard in my room, fearing a bank holdup despite the presence of them famous gunfighters on the Dodge police force. But then I had spent it all on the legal defense of Wild Hog and his pals. Earning it back would take a long time and wouldn't amount to that much when done. How in the devil could I make some real money? For I become convinced that money was the answer. If I had money I would of gotten more respect from Amanda, even though she thought she disapproved of that which was material. Money might attract hate to them which has it, but never results in disregard.

One idea I never much entertained was getting rich through gambling. I had stopped playing poker after one time in Kansas City when I now regret to say, owing to a pressing need for cash, I cheated in a game with Wild Bill Hickok and come close to being shot by him, and I never tried anything else like "bucking the tiger" at faro, Bat's favorite game, but while frequently winning at it you didn't notice Bat becoming wealthy, and the same was true of Wyatt Earp. Business was the way to do that, I was convinced: providing goods and/or services at a price beyond what it cost to provide such. It was simple in principle, but fairly difficult to bring about successfully, else, though it seemed easier to do in the U.S.A. than anyplace other, everybody would of been rich. Or so anyhow it's easy to say. But giving the matter considerable thought over many decades, I now believe that if everybody had a million, it stands to reason millionaires would be called poor.

I didn't gamble because I wanted to save my luck for continuing to survive the catastrophes from which I had had so many close escapes.

Trouble was, whenever I'd get to planning my next move, my mind needed a little warming up, so I'd take one drink, which wasn't enough, and then one more, which might of been adequate once it kicked in, but I was too impatient to wait that long, so I'd have a third, which was the first step on the road to definitely too much, but by then I would of begun to feel pretty good about myself and able to handle anything, including keeping at that edge without falling over, which I found was the most delusionary state known to man, for when you're there you're already drunk but don't realize it and won't till you've gone too far to recover.

Anyway, I was in a corner so to speak when once again it was Bat Masterson who pointed the way out. He had went away again, this time to Kansas City, where, what a surprise, he played faro, but he came back to Dodge around the first of that year, which was, let me see, '81.

Now Wyatt Earp had been awhile, as aforementioned, with his innumerable brothers, down in Arizona Territory at a boomtown which had sprung up from sheer desert owing to the discovery of silver there a couple of years earlier by a prospector name of Ed Schieffelin, who was told all he'd find in the area was his tombstone, hence the name he give the place, and by 1880 a couple thousand people lived there, most of them having to do with silver mining and the needs of them who did it, which included entertainment of the same type as that provided for cowboys in Dodge.

Silver differed from gold in that individuals didn't go with a pan to a stream and look for nuggets. Silver can't be taken just by picking it up or even digging, but by chemically testing the rocks in which it is always combined with other elements, and if they contain sufficient ore, then a big operation is necessary to get it loose, involving big-scale crushing and processing mills. The Earp brothers went down there to turn a profit on such sideline opportunities as the presence of mines and mills offered, starting out with a familiar idea whenever a new strike in precious metals generated the birth of a new town, as for example Deadwood and the projected enterprise of Colorado Charley Utter and Wild Bill: a stage line from the new place to the largest nearby town already in existence, which in the case of Tombstone was Benson.

But somebody else had beat them to it, so Wyatt, who never liked to dirty his hands at any real work, once again become a law-enforcement officer, as did his older brother Virgil, the former as deputy sheriff of the county and Virge as a deputy U.S. marshal.

But I am getting ahead of myself, for I was still at Dodge with no thought of Tombstone and, as you are aware, no love for Wyatt Earp, when two events occurred. One was that not long after he come back to town again, Bat invited me to accompany him on another of his jaunts.

"Tombstone?" I asks. "Heat and sand and Apaches? It ain't an attractive thought, Bat."

"Drink enough and you won't notice the first two," says he with a snort of laughter. "And I thought you were a great friend of the Indian. Anyway, the Apaches have pulled in their horns. Tombstone's the up-and-coming place for opportunity." He went on about striking while the iron was hot: think the Earps would have gone there if it wasn't the place to be?

"I'm the wrong fellow to ask," I told him. "I only know Wyatt, and I've generally been unfortunate in that."

"Come on," Bat says, blue eyes twinkling above that big black mustache, "Wyatt thinks the world of you." Bat was one of them friends who can't believe you ain't as fond of *their* friends as they are, even though he himself never liked Doc Holliday, Wyatt's pal. "Look," he goes on, "didn't we have a good time with Bill Cody?"

"Yeah, but that was only a few days, and it ain't so far away. How long's it take to get to Arizona Territory? That's to hell and gone. I been in New Mexico, years back." I poured him a refill. This happened so often I don't bother to mention it. I wasn't drinking, myself. I never did while on duty, being a professional.

"You haven't kept up with the times, Jack." He pointed with his free hand in the direction of the railroad. "You take the train to Trinidad, where you transfer to the new Santa Fe line going south. Nothing could be more convenient. We'll travel in comfort."

"That was supposed to be the idea with Mrs. Cody's phaeton," says I. "I'm still picking the mud out of my teeth."

He shrugs and grins. "Look at it this way, Jack: Have you really got anything better to do?"

That got to me. It hurt my feelings some, but only because it was true. So I agreed, never knowing what I was letting myself in for. But now it's so far in the past, I'm glad I did, for otherwise I would not of been able to add still another historical episode to a life uncommonly rich in them. That I was almost killed in so doing only adds to the interest, though at the time I didn't see it in them terms.

Before we headed for Tombstone, a couple days later, this other thing happened which was real unusual. Around dawn one morning I was woke by the sound of pistol fire outside the hotel. A gunshot will always bring me to life immediately though I have been asleep only a couple hours, as was the case then, but after I was awake I remembered previously, while sleeping, the persistent barking of a dog. I can hear certain sounds when asleep that don't wake me up, but I register them all the same. I learned that when living with the Cheyenne: you hear a pony whinny, but it's a different type of noise than the animal will make when being stolen by a Crow who has sneaked into the herd in the dead of night, so you don't bother to get awake. But if you hear the one that says, "Grandfather, don't let me be taken by this bad person, for I belong to a Human Being," you jump up, grab your knife, run out, and sink it in the Crow's heart, unless of course he's too fast and does the same to you.

But I had lost some of this sense, else I would of reacted right away to the barking dog, there on the dirt road out front, though I might be excused in part by the fact that my room was at the rear of the building.

Ordinarily when you heard shots in Dodge, you did better to stay where you was so long as it weren't in the line of fire, for onlookers often took strays or ricochets — and as bad as it might be to get shot by an intentional enemy, for my money it's worse to get hurt by chance in somebody else's fight — but that sixth sense that failed me in not being roused by the barking now come into play, and quick pulling on a pair of pants so I wouldn't be caught again as at the Indian school (though now, in January, I was wearing longjohns) and putting on my boots, I run out in the street, where believe it or not who did I see but old Pard, that dog I left behind in Cheyenne several years before!

It was lucky I got there when I did, for the drunk who had been shooting at him but missed was about to try again. This fellow could hardly stand up let alone point a gun accurately, but he wanted to keep trying and when I objected he allowed as how he'd be as happy to kill me first before doing so to this damned mutt.

"Hold on," I says. "I'm on your side. I can't sleep for that barking. But you're a little under the weather. Let me do it for you."

I held out my hand for his gun, but a man in that condition never believes he has a weakness, so he didn't give it to me. But he hesitated slightly before turning it back on Pard, and I grabbed the weapon off him, kicked him in the shins to bring his face down, and smashed the heavy barrel of the pistol, Earp-style, on his head, crushing the hat and knocking him down and out, there at the edge of the street.

Having unloaded what was left in the cylinder, I dropped the gun into the standing water of the nearest fire barrel and went back to where Pard was waiting with wagging tail and dangling tongue.

"Pard!" I says. "You old son of a gun! How'd you get here?" You know how people talk to dogs, as if they're going to get an answer, but I wanted to distract myself from the guilty feelings I had about leaving him at our camp outside Cheyenne, which, the way these things go, was worse now that I seen him again than when I did it.

Now if you know only the kind of pets ladies keep indoors, or even sporting hounds, and so on, you might expect old Pard to make a greater display than he done when he seen me for the first time in more than three years, having tracked me over hundreds of miles, but just as he weren't the type to bear a grudge, thank goodness, he had lived the sort of life in which the interests of survival tended to hold down emotional demonstrations, in which he reminded me of myself, so we never hugged or anything, but I was real glad to see him, a feeling which alternated with amazement at his feat, which exceeded anything I had heard of at the time, though in the many years since, now and again dogs have somehow followed their families at greater distances on foot while the humans used the motorcar, so when I tell about Pard it might be easier to believe than the experiences I relate concerning historical personages, though all are equally true.

Anyway, I says, "I'm sure glad to see you, partner. You're looking real well." Which was a polite lie, for the tip of one of his ears was missing, with a ragged edge indicating something had chawed it off; his left eye he kept squinted almost shut; his hide was a shade lighter and redder owing to a coat of dried mud; and he limped bad on his left forefoot. Add a few burrs, and a streak of black-green at his neck from some cowflop he had rolled in, as dogs do, and you had the picture. Owing to the last-named, he had an even higher odor than usual, bringing him to almost the stink of that drunk, who now indicated with a groan that he was, unfortunately, alive, so when a deputy marshal showed up in response to them shots, I told him about the illegally carried weapon, now in the fire barrel, and took Pard to a pump back of the nearby stable, where I drenched him with several gallons of water and washed off the filth though it was right cold and him and me was both shivering, but when he had shook hisself, wetting me further with the spray, and I dried him with an old horse blanket, he looked 100 percent improved. I judge that was the first real bath Pard ever had, and he didn't like any part of it. I reckon at that moment he might of regretted tracking me down over all that time and distance, but I made it up to him by buying him a big breakfast heavy on meat.

Now that he had a smell not so high as most of the people thereabout, I had no hesitation in giving him a home in my room, and though the management wasn't too keen on this, it was the off season, the cattle drives generally taking place only during the warmer months, and the extra, and exorbitant, fifty cents a week I paid for Pard's rent was welcome. But I never took him to work with me, even though the Lone Star too was in its quieter season: it was not the place for a decent dog. Anyhow he was an outdoor animal, so he roamed free while I was working, out in the countryside if I knew him, but by the same means by which he had tracked me throughout the years, he always knowed what time I got off even when I put in part of an extra shift if some other barkeep never showed up, and was waiting outside.

First time I run into Bat in the street while Pard was at my heels, I say, "Look who's here."

Bat stares around and then asks, "Where?"

"Right there," I says, pointing down. "Remember that dog I had in Cheyenne? You bought him a big steak."

He nods and says vaguely, "Uh-huh." But I doubt he did.

"This very animal! He followed my trail over all that distance. It took him three years, but he got here."

"Sure he did, Jack," says Bat, with his familiar smirk.

"Dammit, Bat, I'm serious. This is the one."

"Listen, Jack, I'm heading for Tombstone day after tomorrow. Are you on for it?"

"I am if Pard can come along."

"Who's Pard?"

"It's this here dog I'm telling you about."

Bat grinned some more, only now with a certain impatience, nodding his derbied head. "They won't let him on the train."

"Him and me will ride in the baggage car."

"Then who am I going to drink with?"

Having a friend like Pard give me the nerve to stand up to the great Bat Masterson. "Well," I says, "that's the only way I'll go."

Bat thought about it for a minute and then, pushing up the brim of his derby with his gloved thumb, he says, "I admire loyalty. If they let him on, I won't object."

Bat by the way was ever the dandy. For winter he had him a real handsome long black wool overcoat with a thick collar of beaver fur. So you won't think him a *heemaneh* I might just mention that whenever he took up residence in Dodge he generally lived with a sporting woman.

9

Tombstone

GOING TO TOMBSTONE FROM DODGE IN EARLY '81
involved three separate train rides as well as two spells on different
stagecoaches, none of which phases was rapid transit, and all of
which was fairly uncomfortable, inconvenient, and dangerous owing to much of the passage being across hostile Apache territory. I of
course had an additional problem with Pard, whose presence did not inspire good will in many, if any, but him and me made a lot of compromises, me riding with him in freight cars, then him tolerating being tied
on top of the stages, amidst the luggage, and we eventually arrived at
Tombstone only slightly the worse for wear, which was an old story with
us.

The Oriental saloon and gambling house was Bat's destination on
reaching town, for he heard from the shotgun rider on the stage from
Benson, the final leg of our trip, that Wyatt had bought a quarter interest in the gaming room there, but I said I'd be along later, as I wanted to
find a hotel or rooming house where they would let Pard share my quarters, for pitching a tent out in the surrounding desert never appealed to
me, and the dog, coming from the Black Hills, wasn't familiar with the
godforsaken terrain of southern Arizona, looking at which as we bumped
over it on the stage, I wondered what in hell I was doing there. By the
way, on that last ride Bat agreed with me (and it won't come as a surprise
that the driver and the other passengers agreed with what Bat decided)
that the dog required protection against the fierce sun, and Pard rode inside the coach.

Tombstone had been in existence for a couple years by now and thus was almost fancy compared to the Deadwood I had knowed in its rawest days, with two fine hotels facing each other across Allen Street, on a block otherwise occupied almost entirely by saloons, and Schieffelin Hall, around the corner and down Fourth, the local opera house and the biggest adobe structure in the U.S.A. The better buildings was of adobe, a new material to me and right attractive, the trouble was you had to live in a place with a burning sun and a water shortage to use it. The rest, and in fact most, of the center of town was hastily built of lumber, which was true of most everything beyond the center, and it soon occurred to me that the place was a fire waiting to happen, given the dry heat of the air even in what elsewhere would be the middle of winter and the open flames used for cooking and all types of artificial lighting in them days. So one of my concerns in looking for a place to stay was how much of a firetrap it might be, which immediately ruled out anything above the ground floor, for though I could let myself down by rope from the window of a burning room, that might be hard to do with Pard.

You might notice the special attention I was paying to the welfare of a dog and think it foolish or immoral to take an animal that serious, but I tell you I never knowed no other creature who craved my company so much it would trail me for three years and across several states, through territory that, judging from his scars, was not markedly friendly.

We wandered around for a while, taking in the sights, like a restaurant called the Maison Doree, which had a dinner menu pasted up outside listing a number of dishes that looked misspelled to me, like "boeuf" and "porc," though what did I know with no education, and I sure couldn't afford to eat there, for I expect you couldn't of got out the door without spending at least a dollar.

But reading the menu reminded me we hadn't ate in a spell, so I bought a hunk of bread at one store and then got some boiled ham at the nearby butcher shop of a man named Bauer, for to make a big sandwich, and while I was there I asked the butcher, a heavy-set fellow in a blood-stained apron, if he could recommend a place to get a room.

He smiles and says, "Fly."

"Thank you kindly," I says and, there being no ladies present, I reached down to do up the buttons, but it turned out I had misheard the meaning, which the butcher cleared up.

"Camillus Fly," says he. "He takes pitchers. They're good but they cost too much, and then his wife comes in here and complains about the price of meat."

"I don't require a photographer at this time," I says. "What I need is a room."

"That's what I'm telling you," says he, wiping his big gory knife on a wet rag. "His missus lets rooms."

The place was just two doors along Fremont Street, past the assay office where silver claims was filed, and Pard and I strolled there, sharing that sandwich I slapped together while walking, for we was not given to niceties. I did however linger in front of Fly's house till I swallowed what I had chewed. If I wished to bring a dog onto the premises I didn't want to show coarse manners to boot.

But before I had gotten the crumbs brushed off the lapels of my coat, the front door opened and who should step out but my former Dodge City dentist, Dr. John H. Holliday. And after him a lady of the type the French had a name for, I learned when visiting their country with Cody's show, something on the order of *jolly-lard* (though having nothing to do with the English words), which means attractive and ugly at the same time. This lady had strong features but lively eyes and a figure you couldn't miss dressed as she was in clothes that made the most of her bosom and hips.

Holliday give me a cold once-over, no doubt checking for visible weapons, then looked away, showing no sign of recognition, but his female companion smiles sugar and spice, dropping her eyes quick then raising them slow.

"How-de-do, sir," says she. "You got a real nice dog for yourself."

Doc looked like he was gritting his teeth under that mustache of his, but it might of been he was just fixing to cough. Old Pard liked this flirty gal, and he cocked his head with the torn ear and wagged his ragged tail at her.

I just said, "Ma'am," and touched the brim of my hat. I continued awhile to steel myself against a possible late recognition by Doc, but he had undoubtedly been in so many real fights since what turned out to be an empty threat on my part, and killed so many enemies by gun or knife, as to empty his memory of the incident with me, if it ever registered on him in the first place.

So they went on, and I goes to the door and knocks, but when Mrs. Fly opens it she tells me the place is full up at that time, so we never did get into the matter of keeping a dog. But it was Pard who finally found us a home.

We had got out Fremont beyond First Street, where the houses was real close together and so little it looked unlikely there'd be spare rooms to rent, and I was ready to head back when a small woman comes along the road carrying a number of parcels, one of which slips from her grasp as she is turning into a house just ahead, but she don't notice it at all.

"Excuse me, ma'am!" I hollers, startling Pard, who never heard me raise my voice before, and he kind of shies away.

The little woman looks questioningly at me, still not seeing the fallen item, so while saying she's dropped something and doffing my hat, I walk close enough to pick it up myself. It was wrapped in paper and real light.

"Why, thank you kindly," says she. "You are a real gent of the sort I wouldn't look for in this town — excepting my husband of course."

You might say I was disappointed in coming across a woman built on my own proportions, with a nice personality and a sweet face to match, to find her already married, but you'd be wrong. What I felt for her right away was affection of a brotherly kind. Maybe we was related in a past life, like they say. No, she weren't one of my long-lost sisters from that wagon train years ago. However, she did have a connection to somebody I knowed.

But right now, I says, my hat still in my hand, "Ma'am, I wonder, do you know of anybody might rent a room to me and my dog?"

She looks down at Pard and frowns, but what she said was favorable. "Well, you're all right, ain't you?" I reckon this was directed at Pard. To me she says, "If I was you, I'd get me one of them little houses." Still holding that armload of bundles, she nods in the direction of further along Fremont, where there was some shacks of raw lumber. "But if you don't like Mexicans you won't be happy, for it's mostly them from there on."

"I get along with anybody who ain't nasty," I told her. "I seen enough trouble in my life to want as little as I can get away with from here on in."

She laughed quite a bit, and says what I considered remarkable, "Do me and you happen to be related? We sure look at things the same way."

"Let me introduce myself, ma'am. My name is Jack Crabb, and this here's my dog Pard."

"Now, no more ma'am, please, Jack. Just call me Allie. And don't think me forward. As I say, I got me a husband, a great big fellow in fact. When he first asked me to walk out, I says, 'Whyn't you pick on somebody your own size?'" And telling how he laughed, she herself was so amused, tears come to her eyes. Then she settled down and said, "They're asking twenty a month." I realized she meant the shacks near the Mexicans. "But they'll take fifteen, and that's a fact."

"I'm real obliged to you, Allie. And give my respects to your mister, for he is a fortunate man."

She was real pleased at this, but her kind of plain-talking woman in them days wasn't used to praise, seeing it as flattery whose purpose was suspect. "Get along with you," says she, "before the neighbors, who happen to be my relatives, get the wrong idea and tell Mr. Earp."

"Earp?"

"Yes, sir," she says proudly. "My husband."

"Am I hearing you right? You are Mrs. Wyatt Earp?"

She laughs again, but this time it ain't with entirely good feeling. "My man is Virgil Earp! Wyatt's his younger brother."

"Oh, I'm real sorry, Allie."

I had a feeling she was not insulted by the apology, but she just smiled and wished me the best on renting a place, and she went on in her house.

As it happened, me and Pard did get that shack and paid what Allie said we ought to of, to the landlord, an educated higher type of fellow who come to Tombstone to make his fortune the smart way, namely in real-estate speculation and not by working in the silver mines. So living on the same street I frequently run into Virgil Earp's little woman and become the same kind of friend to her as I had been with them working girls at the Lone Star in Dodge, in saying which I don't intend no disrespect to Allie (for if she heard me say that, she'd spit in my face), who was of spotless virtue. What I mean is only I was just her friend and nothing more.

Another person I met was Mattie Earp, who was Wyatt's wife, a modest-looking woman, quiet and reserved, as befitted the companion of an egotistical type like Wyatt, you might say, except that the next female he took up with, and stayed, was completely different. Anyhow, the Earp brothers, and there was even two more, James and Morgan, all lived along the same street, in fact Morg and his woman for a while moved in Allie and Virge's house, little as it was. The Earps was the closest brothers to one another I ever knowed, one for all et cetera, and I don't see that as a bad thing in itself, whatever the era, but especially in that one, and in fact I was real envious.

Speaking of the latter, the furnishings of the shack, left behind by the former tenant, was not much of an improvement on Bill's barrel, which might of made Pard feel at home, but I required at least something to get me off the dirt floor in a region noted for rattlesnakes, gila monsters, and scorpions, so I scouted around town and found a used canvas cot I expect somebody stole off the Army and bought a serape from one of the Mexican women who was my neighbors in the other direction from the Earps, and also a couple tortillas wrapped around a wad of frijoles cooked with chilis, which made me real nostalgic for the time I spent in Santa Fe with a big fat passionate gal named Estrellita, I being only sixteen at the time, with quite a bit more vigor than I had at forty, and often full of pulque, which I hadn't tasted since. It was just my good luck that I hadn't went on to become another Bill Crabb.

After our home had been set up this far, I left Pard to guard the premises and went in to the Oriental saloon, where I had last seen Bat. Well, wouldn't you know he was already employed there, dealing faro for the house, and there was Wyatt Earp, striding around looking important in his role as one of the owners, and when I come up to the table and Bat had a free minute, he says, "They can put you on as barkeep. Go over and introduce yourself to Frank Leslie."

First I should say I had seen a few saloons in my day but never anything as lavish as the Oriental, where the enormous mahogany bar alone, including the so-called altar, the back-bar with its lineup of bottles and fancy etched-glass mirror and a cash register big as an organ, was supposed to of cost a hundred thousand dollars. They kept on hand a framed article clipped from the *Tombstone Epitaph* on the opening a year before, which said nothing like it could be found this side of San Francisco: "Twenty-eight burners, suspended in neat chandeliers, afforded an illumination of ample brilliancy, and the bright lights reflected from the many colored crystals on the bar sprinkled like a December iceling in the sunshine."

Bat told me to go see the head bartender, one Buckskin Frank Leslie, who I had not heard of till then but who had already, like so many of them on the staff of the Oriental, had a colorful life and been an Indian scout for the Army in an earlier day as well as a performer in one of Cody's shows, though he rarely talked about these matters, and had also killed a man in Tombstone the previous summer, which I certainly heard about from Allie Earp next time I run into her and says where I was working.

At the moment though I didn't know none of this but just saw a brushily mustachioed gent in a barkeep's red vest over quite a fancy white shirt with studs of what seemed precious gems and cuff links likewise, who was not just pouring drinks but making quite a show of it, holding the bottle high in the air and at an angle that produced an arc of crystalline liquid glittering in the light of them chandeliers and catching it in a glass held as low as his arm could reach and without a lost drop. It was an amazing performance, and I complimented him on it.

"Mr. Leslie, I've been of the profession myself for a few years, but never did I see such an exhibition of mixology."

He thanked me and when I told him what Bat had said, directed me to put on a apron and start right away if I wanted to.

"Mind showing me how to do that trick?" I asked.

"All it takes is practice," says he. "Better do it outside, with bottles filled with water."

I went around the bar and took the folded apron he found on a shelf. It was freshly laundered and slightly starch. Everything at the Oriental was of the best quality and well maintained. There was more drinkers at the bar than you would of thought for early afternoon and not in a Kansas cattle camp at the end of a drive. I would of thought more of them might be out at the silver mines, but by then there was a lot of other trades in Tombstone that was practiced near the saloons.

Most of the customers on hand stayed at his end of the bar to watch Frank's fancy tricks, of which I had seen only the simplest. Sometimes he'd flip a glass end over end as he was just starting the pouring with the bottle in his other fist, but by the time the point of the high-arching stream got there, the glass would be right-side up to receive it, and always without the least splash. That last effect or lack thereof was the one I never did master, however much I practiced.

Though the drinkers had to wait awhile before Frank could serve them, nobody was attracted to the immediate service at my end of the bar, I was acquainting myself with the bottles lined up along the bottom of the altar and the higher ones alongside the big mirror. Quite a few of the potions available was new to me, for most of what I poured in my time at the Lone Star was the plain red whiskey common to that place and day, and we was not above watering it on occasion when the ready supply ran low or, with some of the characters who worked there, as part of their profit-skimming effort. Gin and brandy was also offered for them with those tastes, and on occasion one of the house girls might take a sip of sherry wine instead of the usual weak tea, but much of the elaborate variety of fiery liquids available at the Oriental I was looking at for the first time. For example, Apache Tears, brewed, said the label, right in Tombstone, and Tanglefoot, Bill Cody's pet word for a drink, appeared to be a real trade name, as was White Mule and Red Dog, Bumblebee, and Prickly Ash Bitters, not to mention a fluid named Cincinnati Whiskey, which of course led me to guilty thoughts of Mrs. Aggie Hickok and the lost money I was supposed to deliver to her.

"Hold on," says someone standing at the bar behind me. "I believe there's an outstanding warrant against you in Dodge."

I turns around and sees the fellow whose idea of a joke this was. "Good day, Wyatt."

"Hello, Jack," says he, dressed in the gambler's black tailcoat. He was not unfriendly, though I seldom seen him smile except at one of his brothers. "Did Bat tell you Luke Short's here with us too?"

Short was another former citizen of Dodge City and a man who enjoyed some reputation as the "undertaker's friend," on account of the habit he supposedly had of shooting his victims between the eyes so laying them out wasn't a messy job.

"Is that right?"

"And Doc's here as well," Wyatt goes on, "and of course Big Nose Kate. Half of Dodge's turning up in Tombstone."

"I see Doc and Kate are staying at Fly's boardinghouse," I told him, if only to seem knowledgeable, for Wyatt always had the air of lording it over you.

He disregards that, in his way of having said the last word on a subject, and asks, "Are you heeled?"

I was thinking about saying, Why, so you could take it away and buffalo me again? But as he was now one of them that paid my wages, I didn't. "I don't own a gun," I says.

"Better get yourself one," says he. "Us Dodge fellows have got to stick together against the cowboys."

"I didn't know there was that many in these parts," says I. "You mean it's just like Dodge all over again? I thought most here was silver miners."

Wyatt frowned, which made his eyes, rarely genial, even colder looking than normal. "The word's got a different meaning hereabout. In this part of the world 'cowboy' is the same as 'rustler.' " Then he smirks and with a head movement indicates the other end of the bar, where Leslie was still showing his tricks. "You want to keep on Frank's good side. He's not only the best mixologist in Tombstone, but he can get unruly when he drinks, and drunk or sober he's a mean man with a gun."

I ought to say right here that me and Buckskin Frank always got on fine together, and I never knowed a nicer fellow, for while on duty at the Oriental I never saw him take a drink. When he wanted to tie one on he went to the other local establishments, where he was known for not only shooting at flies on the ceiling but actually hitting a good many. He and Wild Bill would of had some entertaining exhibitions. The "Buckskin" of his nickname come from the fringed attire he wore off duty, in which I believe he was influenced by Bill Cody when he performed in one of the latter's theatrical shows. He liked Buffalo Bill, so I told him of me and Bat's visit to the Welcome Wigwam.

"Didja ever offer old Bill a drink?" Frank once asked me.

"Never had a chance," I says. "He always did the providing."

"Well, if you done it when I knew him, he would always say the same thing: 'Sir, you speak the language of my tribe.' "

So you see what an amiable fellow Frank Leslie could be, but the year before while romancing the wife of a man called Mike Killeen, so Allie Earp told me, when Killeen come after him Frank shot him in the face. However, as Mike subsequently died of the wounds, Frank by marrying the widow showed he really cared for her, and Allie always approved of romance, and she claimed, surprising me, her husband Virge was of the same sentimental cast of mind, while his brother Wyatt was never nice to any woman not a harlot, which comment was no surprise to me, though I did remember that in Dodge once he was fined one dollar for slapping around a dance-hall girl who had sassed him (while her own fine was put at twenty bucks).

It hadn't taken Allie long to make clear the dim view she took of her brother-in-law. She had been aching to get this off her chest with somebody, and the only other people she had to talk to locally was either Wyatt's brothers, all devoted to him, or their wives, the nearest being Wyatt's own, that crushed woman called Mattie, who he punched on occasion, so criticizing him to her was only rubbing it in. Virgil though was beyond reproach. Allie always carried with her in her reticule or whatever you call it a little card Virge once give her decorated with a border of rosebuds and bearing a poem I tried to commit to memory, for I thought I might make use of it sometime in my own affair of the heart should I ever have one, coarse a man as I feared I was, but there was too many of them words found only in versifying, like "e'er" and " 'twas" and I felt self-conscious even when reading them to myself.

So anyway I had a job and a place to stay for myself and my dog and an old friend in Bat and a new one in Allie, in a new town. Once again I was starting up from scratch, and I was trying to keep from being discouraged by the recognition I had done this more than once. Here I was forty already, pouring drinks for a moderate wage and a good deal less in tips than at the Lone Star, there being fewer spree drinkers in Tombstone, the customers not thirsty after three months of driving longhorns. It would take longer hereabout to collect a nest egg, and meanwhile the opportunities available in a boomtown was being seized by everybody else. The Earps for example had a knack for business, or anyway as led by Wyatt, with real estate in the form of lots on Fremont Street as well as various mining claims of the sort which you don't go out with a pick and shovel to establish but rather, without getting your hands soiled, trade on paper.

By the way, I soon met Virgil, who looked a lot like Wyatt only heavier, and I had a brief scare when Allie, who could be a joker, introduced me as her new boyfriend, and big Virge glowered down at me for an instant before winking and saying, "My sympathies, sir."

And now it was little Allie who didn't right away get the joke, complaining, "Aw, Virge . . ." She really was stuck on him, and I never saw Virgil with any other woman. He was my favorite of the brothers, because he was the most genial, though I should say that didn't mean he couldn't turn ornery when riled. Allie told me they was en route to Tombstone by wagon when the driver of a stage going the other way too close and too fast raked one of the Earp horses, leaving a long gash in its side, and Virgil turned the wagon around and catching the man at the next station beat him half to death. I should also say that Virge was the Earp most often wounded, though one of the others was to be murdered in time to come. Wouldn't you know that Wyatt never suffered a scratch his life long?

On the subject of getting into business on my own, which if you recall had been my idea back in Dodge, which I hadn't had much success at and then had gotten distracted, I figured Tombstone was an even better place to do it, but I needed at least one partner in any sort of venture. Once again I went into the matter with Bat Masterson. He said Tombstone was probably big enough to accommodate still another saloon–gambling hall, but he didn't know how long he'd stay in town, preferring a more northern climate as he did, so told me to talk to Luke Short.

Short had operated the gambling concession at the Long Branch in Dodge, and I was acquainted with him, though not closely. Here at the Oriental, like Bat, he dealt faro.

I didn't intend to bother him while he was playing, but late one night, or early morning, when my own shift come to an end and I was ready to head home, I instead hung around waiting for Luke to take a break, for a fellow in his profession slept all day and wasn't easy to find for a talk.

But when I went into the gambling room, Luke was having an argument with another gambler called Charlie Storms, and it had gotten to a point hot enough to boil over had not Bat Masterson stepped between the men and in his familiar role as the voice of reason escorted Charlie, who was pretty drunk, back to the latter's room in one of the nearby hotels.

Luke had followed along to the sidewalk, it being always a prudent idea to see where an enemy of yours went after leaving you if he was still mad, so I took advantage of this opportunity.

"Luke," I begun, "seems to me a fellow with your experience might want to open a place of your own in town here." Luke Short had the right last name: he wasn't much bigger than me.

But now he wasn't paying no attention. "Bat's coming back," he says, looking down the street. "I guess he got the son of a bitch tucked in." He waits for him and when Bat reaches us, repeats the same thing.

"Let's hope he stays there," said Bat in his usual confident way, then proposes we go have a nightcap, but I beg off, not having been part of this anyway and after a night's work being eager for a sleep and not further association with that which I had been pouring, and smelling, for hours.

So I says goodbye to both men, who had turned to go inside the Oriental, but hadn't taken two steps when someone roughly pushes me aside, grabs Luke's arm, and pulls him into the street.

It was Charlie Storms, who appearing from nowhere and though staggering drunk managed to steal up quiet and unnoticed. I guess town living had again dulled my senses, but the street was unpaved and there wasn't much light except what come out of the Oriental.

Charlie was carrying a short-barrel Colt's, but he did not have full command of himself and was unsuccessfully trying to free the muzzle from its entanglement with the front sight in a buttonhole of his coat. Meanwhile though, he was detaining Luke Short, the smaller man, with his left hand.

I grabbed at him, but Bat pulled me away. "Let 'em finish it out here," says he. He had separated them inside the Oriental so they wouldn't cause any damage to the furnishings. He didn't care what they did in the street.

I'm making the event ten times as long as it took: in fact, by the time Bat told me the above, it was all over, Luke having drawed his own gun, put it against Charlie's side, and blowed a hole in him, and while he was falling give him another .45 slug for good measure, though it were needless, Charlie being dead when he bit the dust.

I guess it was from trouble of this nature that the Oriental had acquired a bad name locally. Allie for example said she was sorry to hear I worked there. She considered it so unrespectable she didn't use the sidewalk in front of it, and this was a place her brother-in-law had a business interest in! Of course Wyatt had devoted friends like Bat and Doc Holliday, but he also made a lot of enemies wherever he went, and it was such he invariably blamed for any difficulties.

One fellow he especially didn't care for was Johnny Behan, who had gotten the appointment as county sheriff which Wyatt had craved but claimed not to have sought due to Behan's promise that if Wyatt didn't contest him for the top job, he would name him chief deputy and then step down in time. How a cynical man like Wyatt Earp could believe a promise of this kind just goes to show you every person has a weakness of mind on certain subjects, me included as you know.

Anyway, Behan once appointed lost no time in handing the job to a crony of his own, and from then on there was one incident after another in which Behan was on one side and Wyatt, which always meant the other Earp brothers as well, on the other.

To run through each episode would wear you out to hear about this long after they happened, for I was often confused at the time of their occurrences, and you'd need a program of the theatrical type to list all the characters, and you still might not keep straight who was what and why, or even identify consistent names, like was Curly Bill Brocius the same fellow as Curly Bill Graham, and was Pete Spence's name really Spencer, and for that matter even the McLaury brothers, principal figures, was sometimes the McLowerys, and then you had a Billy the Kid, who was not the notorious one of the Lincoln County War in New Mexico Territory but a local lout name of Billy Claiborne. Even Wyatt's new girlfriend was called either Sadie or Josie. But I am getting ahead of my story.

Meanwhile me and Pard was living a quiet life out Fremont Street on the edge of the Mexican district, giving me a chance to brush up on the Spanish I had learned more than thirty years before from Estrellita but hadn't used much since, and I would buy fresh-made tortillas from the ladies there, who on learning I was single, could parley in their lingo, and had a better job than any of their men, who worked in the silver mines for low wages and frequently met with accidents, why, they would point out the desirability of the married state and the availability of their daughters, age twelve on, for a man who wasn't getting any younger. But with all respect to them nice women, I still wasn't ready to undertake what would be my third marriage, with still another type of female, in this case with her relatives at close hand, as had been true of my Cheyenne bride Sunshine, which always meant you had family responsibilities you might not of bargained for, and the gal I found most appealing, with her big dark eyes and long shiny black hair, with a hint of Indian blood in the slight slant of her eyes and soft tan color of skin, had a Ma only a decade and a half older than her but weighed twice as much, as well as three little brothers who was snotty unless you give them money.

Now one night I was coming home from the Oriental, having turned the bar over to Ned Boyle, the all-night man (Tombstone saloons never closed), going out Fremont when passing Fly's boardinghouse I hears the sound of someone crying, and it was past midnight but there was one of them bright moons you get in the desert, so I could see the figure of a woman, hand at her face, standing slumped against the side of the house, where between Fly's and the house of a city councilman name of Harwood there was a narrow vacant lot shortly to become famous under the wrong name.

A woman's tears will get to me every time, even when I can't be held accountable for her grief, so I goes up to her and says, "Ma'am, I'm at your service."

She lowers her hands and even in the restricted light I can see her left eye is surrounded by a big black ring that had to of come from somebody's fist.

"The goddam dirty son of a bitch," she begins and then continues with a flood of language as filthy as I ever heard from the foulest-mouthed man, and I was afraid she'd wake up the people in both houses, who would believe it was me she was talking about.

So I done my best to calm her down, but that process was complicated by not only her rage but also her state of drunkenness, by reason of which she was slumped against the building. When she tried to straighten up so as to give further vent to her spleen, she instead crumpled and fell to the ground.

She was somewhat bigger than me, and in one of the mysterious facts of life in which the end wagon in a train has to travel faster than the lead, just to keep up, drunks weigh about ten times what they do when sober, but I got her to her feet and against the wall again.

I says, "Hush now, you don't want to wake up these fine people."

That was the wrong note to strike for sure and only caused her to cuss all of Tombstone for five minutes, finally ending with an indecent reference to somebody named Doc.

I don't know why I was so thick, maybe being tired after a long day's work, but I asks in disbelief, "Doc Goodfellow?" Who was the local sawbones, one of the rare examples of somebody who had a name describing his own character, with an office over the Crystal Palace saloon, from which bullets now and again come up through the floorboards, endangering the patients already there by reason of gunfire wounds.

"Doc Holliday, that ———— ———— ————!" she yells, and only now do I recognize her as the woman called Big Nose Kate. She weren't in so bedraggled a state when I last seen her, also maybe her honker hadn't looked so large at a time of day when it wouldn't cast a big shadow. Fact is, it wasn't that huge at any time. Abusive names for women of her kind was in fashion then, as I said when listing some of the harlots of Dodge. It was either the pedestal or the gutter. You wouldn't of found anybody who referred to Miss Teasdale as Crazy Amanda.

"Oh," says I. "Well, I expect you'll work it out. Now I got to get me home."

But she grabs ahold of me, and she says, "I'm coming along. I'll let you have a free one, and then I want you to kill that low-down bastard for me."

"You're asking me to kill Doc Holliday?"

"Lisshen," says she, trying to get me to walking while her own feet was slipping under her. "Wait till he's cold sober. Nobody can get the jump on that son of a bitch once he's had a few."

I had a few hours to carry out Kate's wishes, for Doc started drinking before sundown and continued to do so while playing faro or poker all night. He was most dangerous, Frank Leslie told me, in the morning whether winning or losing, for that was when he was drunkest and meanest, and not only did he pack at least one hair-triggered Colt's where he could get to it in a hurry but he hung a dagger down his back on a loop of string around his neck under the collar, so you had to watch he never reached back as if to scratch an itch or tilt his hat brim forward, else suddenly a knife handle would be sticking from your chest with blood spouting out around it. Or anyway so they said, which was probably somewhat exaggerated in the fashion of the day, as was the story according to Allie Earp, who didn't like Doc (mostly because he told her to go to hell once when she asked him to look at a bad tooth), that he was run out of his native Georgia after he shot down one too many colored fellows for walking down the same street as him.

As if I was going to carry out Kate's wishes or for that matter collect my reward for so doing! Frankly, I had rather face Doc Holliday's weapons than enjoy Kate's favors, at least at that point. Though as I said she had certain feminine attractions when sober, soaked with liquor as she was now, she smelled too much like what I had been pouring for the previous twelve hours, and I happened not to be aroused by a woman who used foul language.

But the fact was I couldn't get rid of her, for as if she weren't making enough noise to begin with, she really begun to sound off whenever I tried to pry her fingers off my arm, screeching and screaming, and now lamps was being lighted in the adjoining houses and someone yelled from an upper room at Fly's that the next sound we would hear was the discharge of a double load of buckshot, so I never had no choice but to jolly her into if not silence then at least a drunken mutter, by saying I would be pleased to murder Doc.

As we was making our way out Fremont Street, passing Allie's house,

I was praying Kate didn't start up again, for she knowed Allie and fought with her sometimes, blaming the Earp brothers for Doc's problems, which was okay with Allie so far as Wyatt went, but she wouldn't let nobody say a word against her Virge.

But we finally reached my shack without further incident. Old Pard was waiting outside. I don't know what he did all day, maybe went out to the desert and chased lizards or hung around the neighborhood looking for some tail from a Mexican bitch, but he was always there when I come home. Right now, though, he appeared right dubious of my companion and steered clear of her, even to the degree that he was slow to come get the meat scraps I brung him as usual. He never cared for the smell of alcohol, which I think is why he come with me in the first place, to get away from my brother Bill.

Now if I had wanted to have my way with Kate I would of been out of luck, for soon as she spotted that cot of mine in such moonlight as come through the open door, she went and fell onto it with a force I was afraid might split the old canvas, and begun to snore with the sound of a tuba soon thereafter. Pard couldn't take much of that and left the shack.

I didn't have noplace for myself but the earthen floor, which I wasn't happy to sleep on, owing to the easy access of vermin, especially now the dog was outside, but tired as I was I rolled up in the serape and soon drifted off despite the concert.

I was woke by somebody staring at me. I possess that natural trait, I can't explain it, and it's true even when my back is turned to the starer, as now. So I rolled over and there is Kate Elder glaring down, standing erect, showing no sign of either drunkenness or hangover, and in fact making a better appearance by morning sunshine than she had by moonlight, except for that big black eye which was actually various shades of blue and purple.

"You got two minutes," says she, "to explain where you have abducted me to and beg my forgiveness, else I pity you when my husband finds out. He happens to be one of the leading professional men of Tombstone, Dr. John H. Holliday by name, and he don't take lightly to anyone trifling with his missus."

I'll tell you, far from being worried by any threat concerning Doc, I was so relieved she was no longer noisy and disorderly that I scrambled to my feet and hastened to say, "I'm real pleased to see you got over your attack of the vapors, Mrs. Holliday. I'm sorry I didn't have no better place to give you shelter than this dump, but it was real late at night. You must of hurt your eye in the spill you took. May I suggest you stop by Bauer's and get a hunk of raw meat to put on it?"

This pile of buffalo chips struck the right note with her and she smiles and says, "Well sir, you're a real gentleman. I wish you'd call in soon at Fly's and take a cup of tea with me and the doctor, so he can express his gratitude in person. I expect I was a victim of the cowboys."

"Yes, ma'am."

"They're an unruly element, and one of these days my husband, assisted by his dear friends, them fine Earp boys, will have to do something about that crowd."

"May I escort you home, ma'am?"

"That won't be necessary, sir. Just point me the right way."

Pard was waiting outside the door, but he shied away when Kate appeared.

Despite my pointing she looks first in the wrong direction as she steps out, sure on her feet and even dainty, and she sniffs with disdain. "Where did all them greasers come from?"

"They're harmless," I says, "but you go the other way."

10

The Gunfight That Never Happened at the O.K. Corral

THE NEXT THING OF NOTE THAT OCCURRED IN TOMB-
stone in '81, of which the month was only March, though the sun
was hotter than in August of any other place I lived, was an attempt
to rob the stagecoach to Benson, not an uncommon event especially
when treasure was on board, in this case silver valued anywhere between
twenty-five and eighty thousand, depending on who was doing the esti-
mating, and it was probably worth at least half the lowest figure. There
was always a lot of lying in such matters, even when, as here, the holdup
men didn't get the strongbox, on account of a fellow named Bob Paul
was driving, and he wouldn't stop though the villains begun to fire and
they killed Bud Philpot, the regular driver who didn't feel well and in
switching jobs with Paul, riding shotgun, traded a stomachache for a .45
slug in the heart. A passenger also got hit and died later on.

Bat Masterson welcomed the opportunity to join the big posse that
headed out to track down the outlaws. Him and me had been in town
hardly a month, and he was doing pretty much the same thing he would
of done anywhere else, namely, gambling and drinking, but he was already getting tired of Tombstone, which as you might have noticed was
his way. For my part, having lived longer than him, I wanted to locate for
a spell and Tombstone didn't seem any worse than anyplace else if you
liked the climate, and I did once I got used to it, for though the days was
blazing, the air was so dry your sweat dried as soon as it appeared, and the

nights was generally cool. I never had a head cold during my time there nor knowed anyone else who did. Doc Holliday didn't cough nearly as much as he had in Dodge. If he could of kept his nose clean he might of stayed in Tombstone and lived longer.

Another thing I changed my mind about: whereas on first sight I had not taken to the endless stretches of alkali dust and rock where only mesquite, greasewood, and spiky cactus would grow, with rain usually a dim memory, and populated by land creatures whose hides was scaly and not furred, after a while on my day off I got to going out to the edge of town, Pard trotting along, and watching the vast desert sunset, which seemed to have a greater range of colors than elsewhere, and there was mountains in every direction, some rounded and soft in the purple haze and others, such as the nearby Dragoons, which had a jagged look as befitted the Apaches who hid out there from time to time and maybe right now, but as you could see in every direction I didn't think I was in danger and never carried a weapon.

This was probably foolish, particularly with what I knowed of Indians' gift for stealth, but I'll tell you why I did not own a gun at this time: I couldn't be sure what Big Nose Kate might of ended up telling Doc Holliday about the night she spent with me. Enemies generally found out whether one another was armed before trying to kill each other. This hadn't nothing to do with fairness. If you shot down a fellow who didn't have no weapon on him, your chances of successfully pleading self-defense when arrested and tried could not be called good. As it turned out, however, I was in error as to the consumptive dentist's regard for legality. When it came to Doc Holliday, you did well to reflect that he was dying anyway.

Getting back to the attempted holdup of the stage and the killings, the posse rode out of Tombstone including three Earps and Doc Holliday, along with Bat, as well as Sheriff Johnny Behan and his deputies. Behan resented the Earps sticking their nose in local law enforcement, though Virgil always had some kind of official position, being at this time a deputy U.S. marshal for that part of Arizona Territory. Buckskin Frank Leslie, another who liked excitement, left the Oriental bar to me while he also went with the posse.

The wonder is that though the sheriff and his bunch was at odds with the Earp crowd, they found a fellow hiding on a ranch who admitted to holding the horses during the attack on the stage while it was being committed by three men of which the leader was one Billy Leonard. This trio was thought to be connected with the cowboys, which was to say rustlers, who stole cattle down in Mexico which they drove back to Arizona and distributed amongst the herds of the Clantons, the McLaurys, and other ranchers in the country near Tombstone, not all of which was the desert I mentioned before, especially on the higher ground.

The Earps believed Sheriff Behan was too friendly with the cowboys, while Johnny considered Wyatt and his brothers tinhorn gamblers, and there was talk from supporters of each side that the other was in cahoots with the killers and intentionally steering the posse away from the trail. Whatever was the case, the outlaws Leonard, Head, and Crane was never caught by any peace officers, but the first two was shot from ambush by a couple brothers seeking the reward money who before they could spend it was themselves killed by the surviving Jim Crane and his new gang, and then a few weeks later Crane was with a bunch of rustlers driving a herd of stolen cattle through Guadalupe Canyon, near the border, when some Mexican hard cases dry-gulched them and stripped their corpses bare. So you can decide for yourself whether justice was done.

But a mystery remained and does so till this day, and it begins with the fact that Doc Holliday had been a real good friend of Billy Leonard's! So was it likely he could of been seriously helping the posse in the pursuit of same? By the way, Leonard was still another called Billy the Kid.

Bat Masterson not only had had enough of Tombstone by the time the posse came back emptyhanded, but he got a telegram to the effect his brother Jim had run into trouble in Dodge, having lost his marshal's job, and a couple of bastards was gunning for him. Now this was a mission up Bat's alley.

"Sure you don't want to come along?" he asked me as he waited for the stage for the first leg of the lengthy trip back.

"How long since we got *here*, Bat?" I asked. "I have barely got settled." Bat as usual had stayed in a hotel. I don't think he had a real home during the time I knowed him. "Besides, I ain't no gunfighter. I wouldn't give you much help — not that you'll need it."

Grinning, he says, "I can recall the time when you wanted to go for Doc Holliday."

"I didn't know who he was."

"Well, you keep away from him down here," Bat told me, his smile fading. "He's nothing but trouble, but you can't tell that to Wyatt."

I might of said the same for Wyatt, but I didn't want to differ with Bat, good friend as he had always been to me, even though once I accompanied him someplace at his suggestion I never saw much of the man.

I shook his hand and wished him luck, and I says, with some truth, "You know, I have went some interesting places because of you, and I want to thank you."

He gives me the famous Bat grin once more and says, "I'll let you know when I get another good idea."

And just then the stage comes hurtling along the street, horses being driven as fast as they could go, and skids to a dramatic stop in a spew of dust. This was one of the public spectacles in Tombstone for which people waited every day.

Next thing happened a few weeks later when a member of my profession at Arcade saloon on Allen Street lit a cigar while inspecting a barrel of bad whiskey that smelled like coal oil and probably was, for it exploded, not hurting the bartender or nobody else physically, but soon burning all of downtown Tombstone to the ground, for one reason because there wasn't no water to stop it. Given that fact and an early summer afternoon considered right warm even for this place, over 100 in the shade, and real windy, all that remained of the business district in a couple hours was a few empty walls of the buildings made of adobe. All of us at the Oriental at the time did what we could, but the only thing we could save from the flames was one barrel of whiskey. However, by the time the fire had burned itself out, this was the only supply available in the center of town, so Milt Joyce, the saloon owner at the time, had me and Frank Leslie open it up in the street outside, while the flames was still flickering here and there in the ruins, ashes swirling in the wind, and sell drinks to parched firefighters, at inflated prices that kept going up further as the barrel emptied, and by the time it was all gone Milt had made almost enough to pay the cost of rebuilding, which in our case, and in fact that of most of the sixty other burnt-out businesses, begun early the next morning and, believe it or not, was completed in only a few weeks, for buildings of that kind consisted of bare boards nailed together, with the exception of the adobe structures that distinguished southwestern from northern towns. It took a while longer to restore the fancier furnishings at the Oriental. At the time, some of such things as cut-glass chandeliers might first have to travel from the East by ship around the bottom of South America and up the Pacific to San Francisco before heading our way.

Owing to the fire, however, all fireworks and the random discharge of guns was forbidden in Tombstone for the Fourth of July, and what with the rebuilding there wasn't room in the streets for the usual parade, which temporary ordinances, along with the existing laws, would be enforced by the new chief of police, none other than Virgil Earp.

Allie was real pleased by her husband's elevation, but she told me Wyatt had got himself a girlfriend and come home only now and then so Mattie could wash and iron his shirts, which of course weren't none of my business, but when she told me Big Nose Kate Elder was back in town and threatening to cause trouble for Doc Holliday, who beat her up so much, the news give me a turn, I admit. I had heard Kate left Tombstone and was hoping it was for good.

"Why does she keep coming back to him?" I asked.

"She's just crazy about that good-for-nothing," says Allie. And when I shakes my head, she adds, "Jack, you don't know much about women."

"You're sure right about that."

"You oughta get yourself one."

"How do you figure I should do that? By punching some girl in the eye?"

Allie laughed like the devil at that remark, which I hadn't intended to be comical, but then she got serious and says, "Virge wouldn't ever try that, let me tell you. I might be little, but I'm an Irish Mick and would wipe the floor with him, big as he is." But she laughed again. "He wouldn't do it, 'cause he's a real sweetheart. There ain't nothing better than real love, Jack. You oughta try it."

It didn't take long for Kate to make her return known to me, though soon's I heard she was back I determined to avoid passing Fly's boardinghouse, near the corner of Third and Fremont, going across to Second and down Tough Nut Street, and then coming over to the Oriental at Fifth and Allen, a lengthy route the purpose of which was to also avoid the other Allen Street saloons, where she done her drinking. She never come into the Oriental, where she might run into Wyatt, who never liked her any better than she liked him, each believing the other had a bad influence on Doc Holliday. Which was a laugh. As if Doc needed any help in being what he was.

As if avoiding Kate on the sidewalks meant I wouldn't ever encounter her! Fact is, I come home one night not long thereafter, and it happened to be real dark, and I stumbled over something soft on the ground at the doorstep of my shack, first fearing it was Pard, who if he stayed there so quiet must be dead. But some loud cursing in a whiskey-hoarse voice proved otherwise, and when I got a lamp lit and brought out, I seen it was Kate Elder, by now on all fours and shortly standing up though not remaining in one spot.

She looked quite a mess, hair in her face, clothes in the condition you would expect when they had been rolled in the dust after having been dampened down the front by spilled whiskey.

"You son of a bitch!" she says, shaking a fist, which was enough to threaten her balance, so she lowers it. "You run out on me!"

"I believe you was the one who left town."

She shakes her head, dark hair flying. "Who bought you off? Wyatt? Doc don't have no money, I know that. He and them others messed up that stage holdup." She said this with lisps and slurrings of a drunk, so it took me a minute to figure it out.

When I did, I asks, "*What?* You're saying *Doc* was one of the gang?"

"Damn right he was, and I turned the bastard in. Trouble is, they didn't keep him in jail. Wyatt bailed him out, and now he's gunnin' for me."

I didn't believe much if any of this. I have mentioned the suspicions regarding Doc Holliday's friendship with Billy Leonard, but it seemed unlikely that he worked as a holdup man himself, and while the Earps was said to often straddle the line between right and wrong in their business practices, especially Wyatt, it was hard to believe they consorted with common criminals, not to mention that Virge was now chief town marshal.

And how reliable could Kate be? She now went on: "So I wantcha to kill him for me, Ringo. Then I'll be *your* woman." Having said which, she fell onto my bed like the other time and immediately passed out, her head hanging over the side so far I was afraid her neck would be broke, so I lifted it back onto the bed and while I was doing so I brushed the hair back from her face so she wouldn't breathe it in or swallow any, and I seen now she had two black eyes and a split lip to boot. I guess Doc had beat her awful, and I was relieved I didn't own no gun, for I never could stomach the using of fists on a woman no matter how bad she acted, and

I might of felt obliged to go looking for him — ending up like his other enemies.

Kate woke up briefly while I was smoothing back her hair, though she never opened her sore eyes, and she moaned as if I was doing something else, and says, "Oh, what a man you are," in that fake passion harlots sometimes show to please a customer.

But to go back to her earlier calling me Ringo. She could of got me killed while not even knowing my name! There was a real Ringo, first-named Johnny, and he was in and around Tombstone, associating with the cowboy element, and some said he was the deadliest man with a gun west of St. Louie, a claim made at one time or another about everybody, Wild Bill, Wyatt, Bat, Doc, Ben Thompson, John Wesley Hardin, and so on, but so far as I know Ringo never shot anybody in town except Lou Hancock who took a beer when Johnny wanted to buy him a whiskey, so Ringo shot him, which never killed Lou but did make him more wary of his future drinking companions.

Now having been through this before, I expected Kate to wake up next morning in the same mood as the other time, and so as to beat her to it I kept alert for her first stirrings, on hearing which I scrambled to my feet.

"I know you'll be sober now," I says, "and I don't want none of your high-horse stuff about being abducted. You was laying on my doorstep stinking drunk. I took you in and give you a night's lodging, like I did that other time, and on neither occasion did I try to have my way with you." I run on for a time, for I was real indignant.

But she wasn't like before. Once again the night's sleep had refreshed her considerable, though of course them two black eyes and split lip remained, but as it happened she was real humble now. "Sir," says she, setting on the edge of my cot, her woebegone face in her hands, "I'm in terrible trouble and am afeard for my life. Let me tell you what I done. I got mad at Doc Holliday and went and told them he was one of the stage robbers, so Johnny Behan arrested him."

"So that was the truth?"

"It was the truth I turned him in," says Kate, "but it weren't the fact that I really know if he helped hold up the Benson stage or not. I just said what I did to pay him back for being so mean to me."

"I ain't going to kill him for you," I told her. "Get that idea out of your head."

She looked shocked. "Why, I wouldn't ask you for that. I am real fond of Doc and couldn't ever want him hurt. What I was thinking was maybe you could say a word to him on my behalf. He thinks the world of you."

I swear, Doc never even knowed he ever seen me before, and he hadn't much, except for working on my teeth in Dodge, for dealing faro at the Alhambra he seldom came to the Oriental. I told her she was badly mistaken about me, so she should take her appeal to Wyatt or someone else friendly to him.

"Doc ain't got no friends but Wyatt!" she wails. "Everybody else hates him, including the other Earps. And Wyatt hates *me!*" Tears begun to trickle out of them blackened eyes and run streaking down her face. "Doc'll cut my guts out, I know he will. He told me I ain't worth the cost of a bullet."

I felt sorry for her, but I was disgusted too. "Why do you love that fellow?"

"It's just his nature. He can't help it. His nerves is real bad. He told me once the only time he's not nervous is when he's shooting somebody or pulling teeth." She starts crying real hard, digging her fists into her eyes like a little kid, and I think I have already noted that a weeping female could generally get what she wanted out of me.

So I says, "All right, settle down. I'll speak a word to Doc, but don't blame me if it don't work."

Kate advised me to wait till he woke up naturally, not before noon, for having gambled all night he needed his sleep and might come to life shooting at anyone who disturbed him before time, which meant I'd be working, so I said I'd do it as soon as I could, and I guess I would of, for when I give my word I mean it.

But as it happened, lucky for me, before nightfall Kate was drunk again, creating a public disturbance, and Virgil Earp threw her in the hoosegow. Meantime the charges against Doc was dropped for lack of evidence. What I was grateful for was that Kate lost no time in getting out of town again. Reason I never told her I wasn't Ringo should be obvious, and my good sense was confirmed a few days later when I run into Allie at Bauer's butcher shop, where she was buying steak for Virge and I was after a bone for Pard.

On the way home she tells me Doc Holliday found out it was Johnny Ringo who plied Kate with liquor and got her to charge Doc with the stage holdup.

"How'd he know that?"

"Kate told him," says Allie. "She said Ringo took her in before when Doc give her a beating. You know what Doc told her? 'You stupid bitch,' he says, 'didn't it never occur to you Ringo wouldn't have no use for an ugly whore like yourself except to damage *me?*' That's what really hurt her feelings, even more than beating her up again, which he proceeded to do."

I figured Allie included that last observation for my benefit, to teach me something more about females. Ever since I admitted not understanding them, she would give me such tips.

"Thing is, though," I says, "ain't she been connected with Doc for a long time? So how does it make sense for him to knock her so much?"

"Why, the consumption's gonna kill him soon, so what's he care?"

I thought this a peculiar sort of answer but dropped the subject, as did Allie, who had more than one woman confiding in her. She started in next on Wyatt and his girlfriend, who was an actress with a theatrical troupe come to Tombstone, where before long she had moved in with that sheriff the Earps considered their enemy, Johnny Behan.

"So he took her away from Johnny," I says. "That must make Wyatt feel good."

"I'll tell you what makes him feel even better," says Allie. "Sadie's Pa is a rich merchant up in San Francisco." She squints at me. "But if that's so, then why's she such a loose female?" We had reached her house by then, with Wyatt and Mattie's place next door, so she spoke in a lower tone. "Too many of the wrong kind has got too many women, whereas a nice fellow like yourself is all alone. I'd sure like to find a girl for you, Jack, 'cause I know you'd treat her right."

I joshed her a bit. "How'd you know that? I might be civil to you only because your man is chief of police."

"Why," Allie says seriously, "I can tell from the way you look after your dog. You can always tell about people how they treat their animals. I used to have a spotted dog I named for my little brother Frank. An Indian give him to me."

"Is that right? I think Pard might of been an Indian dog."

"This boy brought him around to our cabin, and Frank he just run in and jumped on the bed and wouldn't come down, so the boy left him there. Best dog I ever owned. He always wanted to sleep on the bed with Virge and myself, but he wouldn't touch a piece of fallen meat till you told him he could have it."

Pard was just the opposite. He didn't have no interest in my cot, but anything eatable that fell near him he would catch before it hit the ground.

Now, I have mentioned that fire in Tombstone. Hardly had it burned out for lack of water and was rebuilt than the rain begun to fall, as it rarely done in that region, and in such quantities that the resulting floods made the roads into town impassable, stopping goods deliveries and the mails, and undermined some buildings. Tombstone was a place of extremes, including its two newspapers, one, the *Nugget*, favoring the so-called cowboys and the second, the *Epitaph*, on the side of the tinhorn gamblers also sometimes called the Earp Gang by the other side. Law enforcement showed the same split. Whereas at Dodge City there had been cooperation between the county sheriff and the marshal of the town, both being members of the Masterson family or their pals during the time I was there, in Tombstone them two officials was totally opposed, and each was supported by a faction with a reputation for violence. Let me say I never belonged to either, not being much attracted to the Earps even when Bat was in town, and I had never in my life had a lot of regard for cowboys even when they wasn't outlaws. I'll admit to a prejudice, having no doubt seen only their worst side in saloons and whorehouses, when it is a rare man who would make a good impression and then only if he come to sell Bibles. I realize now when they was working, on the three months of the cattle drive, they was doing more for the betterment of the country than almost anything I personally had accomplished, in effect feeding lots of people including me. So looking back I expect I ought to apologize for my narrow-mindedness.

However them they called cowboys in Tombstone was up to no good so far as I could see then or now, and if I speak more about the Earps, much of it critical, it's due to my associations and not because I was ever inclined towards their adversaries, which now included fellows named Frank Stilwell and Pete Spence, who robbed the stage to Bisbee and was caught by a posse of Earps but was immediately bailed out by the Clantons. And the McLaurys was mad that Stilwell and Spence had even been arrested, and talked of getting revenge.

The enmity between the two crowds got worse than ever when Ike Clanton accused Wyatt of violating a confidence, which Wyatt probably done, but the fact was the secret that Ike wanted kept quiet probably wouldn't have become known to many people had he not made such a fuss about it.

Back some months earlier, Wyatt Earp had gotten the bright idea that though the Clantons and McLaurys was friends with the outlaws that had attacked the Benson stage, they would gladly lure the three back to be captured if he saw that Ike and Company got the reward money, while Wyatt himself took the glory, which might get him voted in to replace Sheriff Johnny Behan next election. You might say Wyatt understood the criminal mind so well because it was as cynical as his own.

But of course the deal was off once them outlaws was dead by others' hands, so the Clantons and McLaurys not only didn't profit, but if it come to be known to their other lowlife pals, they wouldn't be trusted by nobody — if allowed to continue to live.

There I was one evening in the fall of the year, eating supper at the Occidental lunchroom, when through the front door comes Doc Holliday, which was never good news, and behind him there's Kate Elder, which might be worse. She was all spiffied up, I'll say that for her, hair piled high and fancy clothes, and she's got that superior look a person of her kind alternates with the woebegone expression appropriate to laying in a gutter.

Whenever Kate was in the rare condition of being both sober and not showing evidence of recent beatings, she considered herself an aristocrat who had strayed by accident amongst the peasants. Allie told me Kate claimed to have been born in the land of Hungary, where everybody belongs to the nobility, but maybe she just said she was hungry.

Which I sure was, chewing my steak, but I lost my appetite when I seen that pair, though being down the counter a good ways from her, Kate didn't sight me as yet. But the situation proceeded to worsen, for I have neglected to mention that another person eating at the Occidental that night was Ike Clanton, who I barely knew by sight and hadn't even yet recognized now till Doc Holliday, spotting him, calls out his name accompanied by "son of a bitch," Doc meanwhile reaching into his coat for the shoulder-holstered pistol, the nearest of several weapons he usually carried.

There being no place for me to hide, and I didn't dare make a sudden move that might spook Doc into action, I just froze, along with the others not involved on both sides of the counter.

Doc hadn't drawn yet. He first wanted to explain to Ike why he was going to kill him, which you might see as a sort of courtesy though expressed with a deal of foul language, for it was my belief that Doc generally shot first and left the palaver for later. He was also being unselfish, his complaint against Ike not concerning himself personally but rather what Ike had supposedly said about Wyatt.

Ike managed to save his life by yelling, "I ain't heeled!"

Then, as if the place ain't already crowded enough with troublemakers, while honest folk was just trying to fill their bellies, in come Wyatt and Morgan Earp.

I ain't said much about Morg, the youngest of the Earp brothers then in town (as there was the oldest, named Jim, a gambler and businessman who didn't involve himself in the others' fights), but he was a younger version of Wyatt who looked a lot like him and was a bit more agreeable though more hotheaded.

Now seeing Doc taking on Ike, Morg also goes inside his own coat, and Ike gets called a son of a bitch once again, and again he had to repeat, even more anxious, his little beady eyes blinking and goatee twitching, "*Goddammit, I ain't heeled!*"

At this point Kate, cold sober, had enough sense of self-preservation to leave by the front door, which I tell you relieved me of an even greater worry than of being hit by a stray bullet, and in fact Wyatt now stopped his people from going further and shooting down an unarmed man in front of so many witnesses, and he told Ike to get out of the place.

Which Ike proceeded hastily to do, though at the door he turned and said, "I'll thank you not to shoot me in the back." And then he run out, followed by Doc's and Morgan's renewed curses and strong suggestions he arm himself for their next meeting.

I had lost my appetite for food but badly needed a drink, and headed for the next-door Alhambra saloon, which you could enter off the Occidental. But first thing I saw up front inside the Alhambra when I got there was Kate's high-piled hair and hat on top of that, so I quick reverse-marched and went out through the lunchroom, on the sidewalk in front of which Wyatt and Morgan and Doc had been joined by Virgil, who was friendly enough to me on account of Allie.

So now when Virge bids hello to me in a genial fashion and steps away from the group, I says, thinking I might hear from him more about this feud between his family and the Clanton bunch, "We're heading the same way, Marshal."

"Oh, I'm not going home yet," Virgil says. "I'm going to play some poker." The only complaint I ever heard Allie make about him had to do with these all-night card games. "Say, Jack," he goes on, "you want to play? So far there's only Tom McLaury, Johnny Behan, and me."

The full significance of that table never hit me till afterwards, but even at the time I thought I'm damned if I ever understand what makes the Earps tick: they considered the McLaurys their bitter enemies and despised Sheriff Behan, yet Virge would stay up all night playing cards with the same people.

Thinking back, I have sometimes regretted not playing a fourth hand that night, just for historical purposes, but I never did, not wanting to lose any of the nest egg I was building up again, and besides I had been superstitious about poker games ever since seeing Wild Bill get shot in the back while in one.

So I begged off, telling Virge I was all-in after a long day at the bar, and went along Allen Street in the direction of home and was just across the street from the Grand Hotel when out of it come Ike Clanton, a pistol in his hand.

He glares over at me, and remember it's night and easy to misidentify a person, so though I don't know him personally, I quick crossed the street, hands away from my body, and come closer so he can see I'm unarmed.

He don't shoot me, but he ain't too friendly either. "You seen Doc Holliday? I aim to kill him."

"I expect he went to bed," says I. "You might want to sleep on it yourself."

"I can't sleep till I kill at least one of them sons of bitches," Ike tells me. "They all ganged up on me while I was trying to eat my supper, and I wasn't heeled." He pushes past me and goes down the street with a stride that is both determined and none too steady, not the best condition in which to head towards trouble.

But in fact what Ike Clanton ended up doing that night was, if you can believe it, making a fourth in the poker game with Tom McLaury, Johnny Behan, and Virgil Earp!

Well, there wasn't nothing I could do about it except to steer clear of all who was armed with blood in their eye: one of my bedrock principles and maybe the best reason why I have lived as long as I have. So when Ike started off down the street in one direction, I continued hastily in the other, with only that worry that Kate Elder might find my shack again. But she didn't.

That trouble at the lunchroom was worked to Pard's advantage: due to the interruption, a large hunk of the steak remained, and I brung it home for him.

I had now lived in the world of saloons and gambling halls so long it seemed normal to stay up most of the night and sleep through the morning, so next day I got up not far before noon, by which time Pard, who kept his usual normal hours, had gone about his business, such as it was, hours earlier, and I went downtown to get me a bath and a shave, and would you believe it the first person I run into, on Fourth Street, was Ike Clanton, and he had a wilder look in his eye than ever, and now had added a rifle to the revolver he carried previously.

I never knowed then he had played poker all night in that game with Virgil Earp, but he looked like he hadn't gotten no sleep, with his squinty red eyes and drawn pale face.

He glares at me. "You seen Doc Holliday?"

"No, I have not," I says.

"Well, I aim to kill that son of a bitch," says he, brandishing his Winchester.

Now who should come around the corner right then and start towards us but Virgil and Morgan Earp, but Ike's back is turned that way and he don't detect them. I didn't see no personal advantage in telling him. I just looked for a route of exit. Anyway, he goes on about how he has took his last insult from the Earps and their friends and how he ain't scared of them bastards, bring 'em on one at a time or all together, and he is so deaf to anything but his own bluster that the brothers are able to walk right up unnoticed behind him, where Virge slams a Colt's against his head, knocking Ike to the ground, and the Earps take his weapons away, arrest him for carrying them without a permit, and pulling him up, drag him into the recorder's court, situated conveniently nearby.

Now there was at least two versions of what went on inside the court, according to what side you favored, and I wasn't there so have had to figure out what was likely, and I believe Ike and Wyatt exchanged more threats of mayhem. But Virgil was town marshal and Ike broke the law, so the judge fined him and the marshal carried Ike's rifle and pistol over to the Grand Hotel and put them into the custody of the barkeep. It was illegal for Ike to have firearms on his person in public without a permit, but they remained his possessions and he had a right to reclaim them when leaving town, which he was urged to do now.

I went on to the barber's, and when I left there after my bath and shave, I should mention I wasn't alone on the street that famous day. Plenty of other people seen what happened too.

Anyway, I turn the corner onto Fourth Street and just after exchanging good-days with Bauer, that butcher, who had stopped to talk with another fellow, I spot Wyatt Earp crossing the street on a diagonal from one side to meet Tom McLaury coming from the other, and no sooner do they meet than right away Wyatt punches young Tom in the face with his left hand and with his right draws the Colt's and does what he done so often to so many, including me, that it ought to be called not buffaloing but rather Wyattizing: hits him over the head with the barrel.

Tom falls in the dust in the middle of the street, and Wyatt continues on to the sidewalk, right near me. He still has got his pistol out, holding it down against his leg, and he gives me a cold, grim stare like maybe if I wanted to object it wouldn't be wise.

One thing about buffaloing, it didn't kill nobody. After a little while, probably waiting for Wyatt to get out of sight, Tom McLaury got up from the street, found his hat where it had rolled, dusted himself off, and begun to walk in a pretty groggy fashion, in the other direction to Wyatt's. He had not been carrying any visible armament. I assure you from experience, him and Ike had bad headaches, which in Ike's case lasted all day. Tom never had that long left to live.

Now, not having ate at all well the evening before, I decided to splurge and get me a good feed at one of the finer restaurants in Tombstone, the Can Can, regardless of expense, so I did so and got the whole business from soup to nuts, which was literal and included amongst its many courses fricassee of chicken, luxurious eating in them days, and custard pie, costing me fifty cents all told.

When I left the Can Can after the meal, there's Sheriff Behan talking with Marshal Earp, standing on the opposite corner, out front of Hafford's saloon, Virgil holding a short-barreled shotgun, and alongside him is his brothers Wyatt and Morgan, as well as Doc Holliday, on whose skinny frame hung a long heavy gray overcoat, which nobody but him would of worn in Tombstone at midday. Doc was also carrying a cane, which I never seen him do before, but somebody later said he was feeling weak from the consumption. If so, shooting people would buck him up, as would shortly be seen.

I never paid no attention to this bunch, nor them to me, and being inside the Can Can I had no way of knowing that Wyatt had not long before had another run-in with the Clantons and McLaurys outside George Spangenberg's gun shop, a couple doors down the street, and Johnny Behan, who generally took the cowboy's side in any difference of opinion, was likely doing so now.

As usual I had some leftovers from my meal wrapped in a bandanna as a treat for Pard, who by the way was eating so good he had filled out real nice since showing up all tattered skin and bones in Dodge. The only thing I worried about was if he wandered into Hop Town, the Chinese section of Tombstone between Second and Third streets, where, operating hand laundries, they was the hardest-working folks I ever seen. The white saloons might never close, but the people employed there got time off, whereas every Chinaman I ever saw in a laundry seemed to work all twenty-four hours, at least there he was, with his pigtail, amidst clouds of steam every time you passed, night and day, and they done all of this on an occasional bowl of rice — and maybe cooked dog, according to what them drinkers at the Oriental bar said, which ordinarily I took with a grain of salt, but having ate that dish myself while amongst the Cheyenne, I admit to having some concern.

Well, I was going along Allen Street in the homewards direction, and when I was passing the O.K. Corral I seen, directly across the street at the Dexter stables, a group of fellows including the Clanton brothers, Frank and Tom McLaury, and that Billy Claiborne I mentioned a while back for being one of the many who liked to be called Billy the Kid. This bunch was conferring together in a way that reminded me of the Earps and Behan, back on Hafford's Corner, but I didn't have no reason to connect the two groups, especially insofar as these boys seemed to be collecting their horses, ready to leave town for their ranches.

Seeing the open yard of the O.K. Corral, I decided to cut through there over to Fremont, in the alley between the Papago Cash Store and Bauer's butcher shop, on account of I preferred the shops there as opposed to the stables of Allen. The only hazard was in passing Fly's boardinghouse should Kate Elder be in residence, but the time being only early afternoon, she was probably still sleeping it off from last night, and in peace if Doc was where I last seen him.

Well, I was wrong and here's what happened. I got past Fly's all right, but between that house and Harwood's was the vacant lot, and who's in it now is not only Kate Elder, but she's bending down to talk to — Pard!

If you recall the times she was at my place, Pard left and stayed away till she was gone, but she was paying a lot of attention to him now and using that kind of lingo dogs seem to like when it comes from women, maybe it's the maternal touch, them animals having a childish streak all their lives.

Anyway, there's old Pard, head cocked to the side, listening with every evidence of pleasure to her say stuff like "Oo, ain't um a real nice doggy." In fact he was so taken with this that he never paid no attention to me at all for a few seconds, and I was torn between what I admit was jealousy and a temptation to keep going before Kate noticed me. But Pard couldn't afford to long neglect his main mission in life, to eat as much as possible, for what was only a novelty, so that black nose of his twitched on picking up the aroma of the pieces of chicken I was carrying in the bandanna, and he leaves his new friend and runs to the old one.

"Say there," Kate says when she sees me emptying the contents of that bandanna on the ground, "that ain't chicken, is it? Don't you know them bones will get stuck in a dog's throat?"

I couldn't as yet tell if she had been drinking or not. I said without looking up, "That rule don't apply with this here animal, who's a cross between an Indian dog and a coyote. He'll kill and eat a prairie chicken every part but the feathers."

"I been thinkin' of getting a nice pooch for my own self," says she, smiling real sweet, and she adds, "For when I'm lonely, which is an awful lot." She comes closer when I straightened up, and her smile has got warmer. She wasn't drunk, so she didn't remember she ever seen me before.

Pard of course had swallowed the food immediately and, seeing I never had no more, turned and loped off in that stride which could of been mistaken for a coyote by someone not too careful about what he shot, yet that dog had survived in a world full of menaces.

"Yes, ma'am," says I, "and now I got to get me to work."

"I expect you own one of the richer mines," Kate tells me, moving near enough so I can smell her scent, though I should say as I had been smelling it since I was twenty foot away, it was now like my nose was in a perfume bottle. "A man important as you makes his own time."

At this point along Fremont comes the Clanton boys, Ike and Billy, Billy leading his horse, and they stop in front of the lot where me and Kate was standing. Ike is talking to his brother, all worked up, and don't pay us no attention, but Billy Claiborne, who had followed along behind, grins at Kate real familiar. I don't know if he knowed her or not, but Allie Earp had told me he was always after every female he seen.

Kate sniffed and tossed her head. "Come on," she says, "let's move away from these cowboy trash."

So her and me step out to the sidewalk, passing Ike and his brother, who walk into the lot, along with the horse. They still don't pay us no heed. Ike's doing the talking, and at this minute he mentions Doc Holliday, with obvious hatred.

Kate hears him too, and self-centered as she was, she interprets his use of the name as referring to herself, and with credit, and she grabs my arm and says confidentially, "It is true that Dr. Holliday is crazy about me, but I claim the right to make my own friends."

She's bigger than me and has a grip on my upper arm that is all but lifting my foot off the ground on that side, and right about the time I'm wondering that if to get free I'm going to have to stamp on her foot or something drastic, she gasps and says, "Oh, my God! Here he comes."

And as I'm being pulled into the door of Fly's house, I look down Fremont and see, a block away, coming in our direction, that bunch of tall Earps last seen at Hafford's Corner, and alongside them is the slightly shorter figure of Doc Holliday.

Inside Fly's I don't get out of Kate's clutch till she has slammed the door behind us.

"Goddammit, woman, will you get off me?" I says, prying off her fingers one by one.

"Go out there then and get kilt!" she yells. "He's crazy jealous, I warn you."

"I ain't touched you!" says I with heat, and open the door and look out just as the McLaury brothers arrive at the lot, Frank leading a horse, so now there's five men and two large animals in what's a pretty narrow space, and if that's not enough, added to the collection already present comes Sheriff Behan, a refined-looking person compared to the other principals, balding with his hat off though it was on now, but he always looked more like a merchant to me than an officer of the law, at which at least in appearance the Earps had the edge on everybody, especially when they was walking together, three abreast, wearing black.

Johnny Behan says something to the cowboys, which I couldn't hear but believed was likely to be friendly, and next he walks down to stop the Earp bunch in front of Bauer's meat shop and either warns them off for their own protection as he later claimed, or in Wyatt's version, to assure them he had disarmed the cowboys, a damn lie that could of got the Earps killed.

Anyway, whatever Behan said, the Earp boys and Doc Holliday resumed their stride and would of walked right over him had he not gotten out of their way. As marshal, Virgil had jurisdiction in town, and he claimed later he had deputized his brothers and Doc.

At that point Kate hooks her hand into my belt in back and yanks me into the house. "I ain't gonna let you die for the crime of loving me!" says she. "C'mon, I'll hide you out in the photo gallery." Meaning the building behind the rooming house which Camillus Fly used for his camera work. And she tugs mightily, lifting me off my feet for a second. I'll tell you that woman was a caution, and I might of popped her one had I not remembered that was Doc's way, so instead I says, "Dearie, I'll be obliged if you let me walk on my own," and as soon as she let me go I was through the door and into the street, which you might see as out of the frying pan, but I didn't want Kate hampering me if there was going to be a gunfight in the near neighborhood. The thin walls of a Tombstone building wouldn't protect much from flying lead, not to mention I liked to see what was going on when guns were likely to be discharged in my vicinity.

So I trot across the street and get behind a wagon parked there, just past the shop of a dressmaker named Addie Borland, and I watch the Earp delegation approach the lot full of cowboys and horses.

Virgil's in the lead now, and he's carrying what looks like the same cane Doc Holliday was using earlier, whereas Doc, walking at the outside, has got that shotgun formerly held by Virge, holding it inside the overcoat with his left hand, which can be seen when the breeze blows back the coat flap. In Doc's right hand is a nickel-plated six-shooter. Morgan Earp has also drawn a pistol. Wyatt's hand is within a pocket of his black tailcoat.

There was other uninvolved people on that block of Fremont Street that day, like a fellow name of Bob Hatch, which owned a billiard parlor, and Billy Allen and R. F. Coleman, with some watching from neighboring buildings like Addie Borland and a judge named Lucas who was looking out his office window down the street in a structure known as the Gird Block, and all of them saw a part of the action, and everybody give a different version of it at the coroner's inquest and the subsequent murder trial, but the only true account of what really happened follows right here, and ain't never been heard before because I never testified anyplace, which failure will be explained I hope to the satisfaction of all.

When the Earp bunch reached the edge of the lot between Fly's and Harwood's — at the outset of the fight miscalled the Battle of the O.K. Corral, whereas them cowboys as I have said only took a shortcut through the O.K. and never even kept their horses there — they stopped, and Wyatt says in a loud voice, "You sons of bitches have been looking for a fight, and now you've got it."

But Virgil, who's in official charge of the party and is showing only that cane and furthermore holds it in his right or gun hand, says, "You boys throw up your hands. I want your guns."

Now at this point Doc Holliday lifted his nickel-plated pistol and shot Frank McLaury in the belly at a range of no more than six feet.

Virgil yells, "Hold on," at somebody though it's hard to tell who.

A split second after Doc's first shot, Morgan Earp shoots Billy Clanton in the left side of the chest, from no more than a foot away, Billy being blown back against the side of the Harwood house, and he slid down to the ground, ending up in the position of a Mexican sleeping against a wall. His horse moved calmly away.

Frank McLaury had been holding the reins of his own horse, which was standing behind him, and though wounded bad by Doc, he never let go of the mount but pulled it with him as he staggered out into Fremont Street, coming close to where I was crouched behind that wagon, which had a solid wood bed but its spoked wheels wouldn't of stopped much lead, and looking down at them who do I see but my dog!

"Jesus, Pard," I says, "why'd you come back here now?"

He wagged his tail at me, displaying an animal's lack of foresight for this type of danger: people shooting at one another across the street didn't mean nothing to him. But I couldn't pay no further mind to him at the moment.

Meanwhile there had been more gunfire. Doc had emptied his pistol and fetching out the shotgun from his coat, he blasted a double load of buckshot into Tom McLaury's chest at the usual close range, and that was the meanest weapon of all, its shells packing nine pellets each as big as a .38 slug, so it was a wonder Tom could hold himself together with crossed arms while lurching out of the lot and getting as far as the corner of Third before he fell.

Now all the shooting had happened real quick, and none of the cowboys had yet to pull a trigger, nor had either Wyatt nor Virgil Earp. Billy Claiborne by the way had run out of the lot when the action started and jumped into Fly's rooming house, which would of put him at close quarters with Kate, if she was still behind the door.

Now Ike Clanton grabs at Wyatt, yelling, "I ain't heeled, goddammit!"

Wyatt's got a pistol out, and he might of shot Ike down, for he was outraged that the fellow who more than any other caused this fight would be the one who was unarmed when it came, but Ike kept yelling so that everybody watching could hear, and Wyatt pushed him away, and Ike too runs into Fly's to join Billy Claiborne and, I guess, Kate Elder.

Though fallen against the Harwood wall, Billy Clanton had drawed a pistol and begun to fire back at the Earp party. In addition to the wound in his chest he had another in his right wrist and was therefore using his left to shoot, but was doing real damage to his enemies, hitting both Virgil and Morgan, each of which fell then got up, Virge joining Wyatt in returning Billy's fire, while Morg and Doc come after, running out into the street after Frank McLaury, who was desperately trying to get the Winchester out of the scabbard on his horse, but that animal, quiet till now, was veering away and finally panicked as they will under too much urgency without no rider in the saddle, and it reared and broke and galloped away down the street, raising a cloud of that lime dust for which Fremont was noted except when it rained, so Frank drawed his pistol.

With Doc and Morgan advancing on him, he took time to boast to the latter, "I got you now!"

Doc replied with some profane abuse, and Frank sent a shot that would on a better day for the McLaurys have struck the dentist square, but when your number's up nothing goes right — I seen that with Custer — so the slug hit the several layers of thick leather of the belted holster and hurt Doc only slightly, and having emptied the shotgun he had traded it for another of his pistols, and him and Morgan kept up a fire that drove Frank across the street, right past me, the lead snapping by uncomfortable close, some thudding into the side of the wagon. I could feel Pard finally taking this serious and huddling against my boots.

Frank reached the corner of the adobe building next to Addie Borland's and was shooting back at his attackers, but he was weak now from that slug he had took at the start, which was not a whole minute earlier but seemed like an hour before, and having to rest his wavering pistol on his good forearm, none of his shots hit their mark, and when he turned and looked down to reload, one of the multitude of bullets sent his way by Doc and Morg went into his head just behind the right ear, and Frank McLaury fell down dead, though Doc wouldn't believe it and come running gun in hand, cursing the fallen cowboy and would of shot him further when, though unarmed and taking my own life in my hands, I had seen enough, and I walked away from the wagon and says, "Skin it back, Doc. The man has died."

Doc lowered his gun and still glaring down at Frank's body and not my way, asks real disgusted, "What took the son of a bitch so long?" And then he made a statement probably only Doc Holliday in all the world would of said, in its mix of indignation and wonderment. "That son of a bitch shot me!"

Well sir, that was the so-called O.K. fight from start to finish so far as the shooting went, though across the street Billy Clanton, who had taken one hit after another and now laid flat on the ground but was trying to lift his head, was also still trying with dying fingers to cock his single-action Colt's and keep fighting. He might of been a good-for-nothing, but it had been him who after taking a slug in the chest at close range and having his gun hand disabled by another, had used his left to wound both Virgil and Morgan Earp. Not to mention that his big brother had run away.

I went over there once the shooting had stopped, along with a number of the other onlookers, and we was joined by Camillus Fly, the photographer, who come out of his house now, toting a rifle and yelling at everybody else to take Billy Clanton's gun away, but not wanting to get plugged nobody paid him any mind, so Fly finally done it himself, at which time Billy says, in a voice that was weak but clear, "Get me some more cartridges."

Somebody decided to carry him inside the house on the other side of Harwood's, and I volunteered to help but three or four bigger fellows did it, Billy between howls of pain asking them to pull off his boots, for he had promised his old Ma not to die with them on. I had heard that expression before, but never did figure out what it meant.

Tom McLaury was still laying where he fell, and they carried him into the house too. Of them on the field of battle, he alone had displayed no weapon whatever, to my observation, and none was found on the street, so if he had a gun it was presumably on his dead person, but in fact when the coroner got there not long after, he didn't find no weapon on Tom either. There were them who, excusing the Earps, claimed though Tom had left his regular pistol at the Capitol saloon earlier in the day, he was carrying a hideout gun, but if so, he never showed it in the fight and it disappeared thereafter.

The truth is that Doc Holliday and Morgan Earp shot Frank McLaury and Billy Clanton before either of them had reached for a weapon, and then Doc emptied his shotgun into Tom McLaury, an unarmed man.

In the gathering crowd, there come Allie Earp, in her sunbonnet, asking anxiously what had happened to Virge. She had heard the shooting, their house being but two blocks away on the same street. I took her to the hack what had been quickly brought, where a doctor was probing Virgil's leg for the bullet that struck him.

The people gathered around didn't want to let her through, but some big fellow pushed a passage through, saying, "Stand back, boys. Let his old mother get in." I tell you for me that provided a light moment, but Allie, four or five years younger than her husband, was right irritated and but for worry about Virge would have got after that man, I'm sure.

Back of that carriage was another hack holding Morgan Earp with his wounded shoulder. Of all that participated in the fight, only Wyatt had went untouched. I imagine that with his high idea of himself he believed that was only as it should be.

Now Sheriff Johnny Behan comes up to him on the sidewalk and says, "Wyatt, I am going to have to arrest you."

But Behan couldn't never again get the edge on Wyatt since tricking him that time into withdrawing from the sheriff's election.

"Johnny," says Wyatt, with his cold stare, "you said you had disarmed those boys: you lied to us. I'm not leaving town, but you or your kind won't arrest me."

Somebody was asking what become of the cowboys' horses, and that reminded me to look for Pard. I knowed he could take care of himself and never liked crowds so probably had went off, but I was somewhat bothered by recalling how he had unaccountably showed up right while the shooting was heaviest.

Responding now to the question about the horses, somebody else says Frank's had run up Fremont but he didn't know about Billy Clanton's, which maybe had wandered back of Fly's photo gallery, and then he added the words that chilled my blood.

"Lead was flying all over the neighborhood. A couple shots hit that wagon parked up in front of Bauer's, and a stray dog got killed under the one across the street."

11

Wild West

T HERE PARD WAS LAYING, EYES CLOSED AND SNOOT FLAT
in the dust. He had been hit in the head, which was one big smear
of blood. I gathered him up in my arms, where as a limp weight he
was quite a burden to carry the couple blocks home. I hadn't ever
lifted him before. At least he hadn't turned cold yet. I thought about
how he had traveled so far to find me after I left him behind at
Cheyenne. I never had no human friend would of done that, and I didn't
blame humanity: I might be just the kind of person whose best friend
naturally was an animal, on account of my shiftless ways, but the fact was
I did have a dog who had been a fine pal, and now he was dead.

To relieve my sadness I developed quite a hatred for the Earps, the
cowboys, the gambling, drinking, robbery, and killing that Tombstone
consisted of for me, not remarkably different from Dodge in that respect,
and now this goddam foolish fight, which was more like a slaughter, in
which three young men had been gunned down mainly because Ike
Clanton had shot his mouth off and couldn't back it up.

I was even resentful of Bat Masterson for having led me to this town
and then soon left himself. Why didn't I go with him? Because anyplace
was much the same as all, insofar as my life went. To be fair to Dodge and
Tombstone and wherever else I had wandered, including even Deadwood after a while, I'll bet, they all had or was developing a respectable
element with decent ladies, children, schools, churches, and business activity in something other than whiskey, faro, and sporting women. In
Tombstone right at the same time as all the mayhem I been telling you
about, there was Sunday school picnics, ice-cream socials, private musi-

cales, a wedding dance at the Cosmopolitan Hotel with a quadrille band (of which occasion the *Epitaph* waxed poetic: "Love looked love to eyes that spoke again, and all went merry as a wedding bell"), and even an organization called the Tombstone Literary and Debating Club. But why didn't I participate in any of that uplifting activity? Because I was coarse and ignorant and half illiterate, as I have said many times before, and would of been ashamed to show up. Then why didn't I try to improve myself? I tell you, I didn't know how. You seen how I tried to do so, in my own way, in the case of Amanda Teasdale, and that was quite pathetic when you looked at it. I was sure it would take a woman to make me better than what I was and would likely stay if I associated with men only, and not just a female but a lady, and what specimen of the last-named would put up with me except to carry her luggage?

Well, I finally got Pard back to the shack that had been home to me and him, and put his body down and begun to dig a grave in the rear of the lot, or tried to in the material that passed for earth in that part of the world, but not having no pickaxe I had to use a broken-handled shovel I found someplace and managed to make only a fairly shallow hole in the ground which was sunbaked hard again despite the recent rains, and wrapped old Pard in my best shirt of blue-and-white check, and laid him to rest. Now I have always considered myself a religious person at the core, despite my lifelong avoidance of church (except when forced to go as a kid, and when besotted with Miss Hand), and I said a word or two commending my faithful friend to the Everywhere Spirit who made him and me, and then I apologized to Pard for not being able to bury him in his home ground of the Black Hills, after which I covered him with the dry dust I had scratched up.

But this arrangement didn't look too secure against such living dogs, rodents, et cetera, as might catch the scent of his remains and make a meal of them, animals having no sentimentality whatever towards the dead, so I went looking for a boulder, hunk of iron, or other weight to batten down that grave, for I didn't have anything of the sort at hand.

In my search I had gotten as far as Virgil Earp's house without finding what I needed when who do I encounter but Allie just coming out the door.

"Virge will live," says she though I hadn't asked. "The bullet just went through the calf of his leg and didn't hit no bone."

"Glad to hear it," I says. "Say, Allie, you wouldn't know where I could find some big rocks without going out to the desert?"

"I expect you're heading the wrong way," says she. "You ain't likely to find any from here on. They would of cleared them away when puttin' up the buildin's."

"Yeah. I should of thought of that."

"Say Jack," she asked, "what's wrong with your eyes? Get a faceful of dust? They're right watery."

"My dog got killed, Allie," I says. "He was an awful good fellow."

She wasn't wearing her sunbonnet now, though the sun was as bright as ever: I figured being taken for Virgil's mother was to blame. So when she squinted, I thought it was due to the glare, but in fact it was not. She was staring past me.

"Jack," she says, "this ain't the day for jokes."

I hadn't no idea of what she meant, and considering the situation I might of made an equally testy reply had I not heard at that moment a familiar whine and spun around in disbelief and saw Pard, his bloody head now caked with dust, trotting along lively as ever and producing that sound which in his case was one of triumph and not complaint.

Well sir, you can imagine what a joyful occasion it was, probably more for me than for Pard, who took everything in his stride including death when it come, but it hadn't yet, and he seemed to consider being buried, coming to, and digging himself out as an entertaining puzzle I had arranged for him, and he was proud of having solved it.

I explained to Allie what happened, so she wouldn't think I was trying to make a fool of her, and she says, "Well, I'm glad for you, Jack, for I know what a nice dog can mean to a person, but I still say you ought to get yourself a good woman too. Now I'm going down and fetch some soup meat from Bauer's to put some strength back in Virge. I'll save the bones for your pooch."

I squatted down and examined Pard's wound. His skull had been creased, and he had been coldcocked by the impact, but the bullet just tore across the skin of his crown without penetrating the solid bone underneath. "You was saved by your thick head." I told him, and he twisted his face around and licked the hand I was examining him with and then runs off a little and back, like a puppy at play. Being near-killed seemed to of made him younger!

The events of that day hadn't done so for me. I felt a deal better than when I buried him, but Pard's coming back from the dead hadn't changed my feeling about my way of and place in life, and from that minute on I was studying what I could do to improve it. I didn't take long to come to the conclusion that to get a clean start I needed to get out of Tombstone, but not just to go to another town of the same sort. And so I probably hung around too long, which is what Allie said about her and Virgil too, and in their case it was worse than mine, as I will relate directly after I quick run through the other notable events of the fall of '81.

After the big fight the town was more divided than ever between the two factions, that which supported the Earps, and them what favored the cowboys or anyway thought they got a raw deal, and there seemed to be more of the latter than before.

Billy Clanton and the McLaury brothers had the biggest funeral Tombstone ever seen. They was laid out in dress suits, in coffins trimmed with silver and fronted with glass, and was so displayed in the window of Ritter's undertaking establishment. The Tombstone Brass Band led the two hearses along Allen Street to the cemetery while watched by an audience of just about everybody in town.

But a coroner's inquest failed to find the Earps to blame for the battle, and when Ike Clanton nevertheless brought murder charges against them and Doc Holliday, a justice of the peace named Spicer, a friend of the Earps (as was the mayor, the publisher of the *Epitaph*, and the postmaster, all of which was the same man, John Clum), found them justified in what they did, Virgil being chief of police, and they never went on trial except for these two hearings, in which each side produced eyewitnesses at variance with one another. Probably because I hadn't been noticed back of that wagon, nobody from either faction called me to testify, and I sure didn't volunteer. I never cared a whole lot for either side, but if I had told the unvarnished truth like I done here it would of served mostly the cowboys' argument, so I would be helping thieves who was friends of holdup men and murderers and also offending Allie and Bat Masterson when he heard about it and maybe getting myself gunned down by Doc.

Not everything went the Earps' way, though. The town council suspended Virgil as chief marshal, and believing their enemies might be plotting to kill them, the brothers and their families moved out of the Fremont Street houses and into the Cosmopolitan Hotel. Virge and

Morgan was still recovering from their wounds. I rarely run into Allie after that move.

Speaking of wounds, Pard's healed up before a week was out, but a new scar was added to his collection, this one like a part in the hair on the head of a person. His ways however had gotten tamer, and he hung around the shack more than before and wanted to be petted by me. Unfortunately that brand-new check shirt I had used as his burial shroud was a dead loss.

One brighter happening during this time in Tombstone was the opening of the Bird Cage Variety Theater, on Allen near Sixth, where only a year before Curly Bill Brocius, himself now not long for the world, killed the then marshal Fred White. Given my earlier ambitions to own a place like this, I would of been right envious, for it was real nice, with a saloon on one side and a theater on the other, the latter lined on both walls with hanging private boxes, to which bar girls delivered drinks, singing while they did so, but the main entertainment was on the stage, with all manner of performers, including in the future even the great Eddie Foy, who like so many of us come there from Dodge City, but I was gone by time he arrived, another violent event having hastened my overdue departure.

One night just after Christmas, Virgil Earp, leg healed now, was crossing Fifth Street right outside the Oriental, when several shotguns was fired at him from out of a building under construction across at the diagonal on Allen Street, the buckshot slugs shattering his elbow, and them that missed went into the walls and windows of the Crystal Palace saloon and some up through the ceiling into Doc Goodfellow's office above.

Virge wasn't killed, but his left arm had been made permanently unusable, and he was laid up worse than when he had the leg wound.

Three men, not identified, was seen fleeing the unfinished building on Allen, but had long disappeared by time pursuit was mounted. Wyatt might of been right to blame it on the cowboy element out for revenge, led by Ike Clanton.

I myself saw the incident as a strong suggestion that from now on this sort of thing would be a regular occurrence, with resultant sprays of lead throughout the neighborhoods where I lived and worked. Damn if I wanted to be maimed or killed in somebody else's quarrel.

So I decided to leave soon as I could, and in a while I'll tell you where I was heading, but first I'll wind up my story of Tombstone.

I didn't have no more possessions than I had brought with me a year earlier, but I had accumulated another nest egg of several hundred dollars, most of which I sewed into the tails of the new coat I bought me at the Summerfield Bros. Dry Goods rather than stuff it in my boots like some did, only to have to take them off and shake them upside down for a holdup man who stopped the stage, and I considered getting some armament for the journey, particularly for getting out of Arizona Territory, which had gotten so wild as to even upset President Chester Arthur, who wanted to police it with the Army, but hadn't fired a gun for so long now I doubted my proficiency up against practiced outlaws, and the Apaches had quieted down, so maybe if held up I would pretend to be a preacher.

I went to the Cosmopolitan to say goodbye to Allie, who was looking after her husband in their room there. Virgil was sleeping at the time, so she stepped out in the hall for our conversation. He was going to recover, she thought, but had lost a lot of blood and would not ever again be able to do much with his left arm.

She then looks up and down the hallway, for the other brothers had rooms there too, and she lowers her voice and says, "This is the second time Virge got hurt lately. He got shot in the War too. But ain't it funny Wyatt allus goes untouched?"

"I sure hope the marshal gets well soon," I says. "I come to say that and also to tell you so long and thanks for being my friend while I been in Tombstone."

"Well, Jack," says she, "I don't know what I done for you, but I'm proud you're happy about it. And I'll say this, I just wish Virge was strong enough so we could leave too. We should of got out when the gettin' was good. Now I don't know if we'll ever get away."

She looked more worried than I ever seen her, so I says, "Oh, sure you will."

"I just have this feelin' it's going to get worse."

"You're a superstitious Irishman," I says to cheer her up.

"God bless you, Jack," says she with a grin, "and don't forget what ole Allie told you: git yourself a good woman. Then if you are ever shot, you'll have yourself a nurse." Her grin was fading into a weepy look, so wishing her and hers all the best, I left.

Now before dropping the subject of Tombstone, to which I won't be returning, let me tie up the loose ends, though everything from here on is hearsay.

Allie was right in her foreboding, though nothing further happened to Virgil in the way of physical damage. In March of that year, Morgan Earp was playing pool at Hatch's billiard parlor when two shots come through the glass-paned door behind him, the first cutting through his spine and killing him, the second hitting near, but naturally just missing, his brother Wyatt.

Wyatt subsequently collected a gang including of course Doc Holliday and still another brother, Warren, and in the ensuing months pursued and shot down, sometimes in cold blood, a number of men he rightly or wrongly believed responsible for the back-shootings of his brothers, and Sheriff Behan again tried to arrest him for murder but as usual got nowhere, for now the Earp gang left the Territory. Meanwhile Allie and Virgil moved to California, where I believe Virge despite his impairment once more become a town marshal someplace.

A few years later Doc Holliday coughed himself to death from consumption up in Colorado. As to Kate Elder, I had the good fortune never to encounter her again, and I never heard what become of her except for a somewhat indecent account of her death which I never believed and won't repeat, for you know my principles regarding the fair sex, except to say she was supposed to of been shot to death by a chance bullet that left no unnatural opening on her body.

Now given my occupation in both towns, I haven't talked no more about silver mining at Tombstone than I did about longhorn cattle at Dodge, though these was respectively the main reasons them places existed, but I'm ashamed to say I never knowed much about such professions and won't pretend I did, just so long as you don't forget that my account of shooting and drinking, poker, faro, and calico queens doesn't represent the whole of or even most of life in the Old West: it's just the part that people seem to enjoy hearing about. In fact, before long it become all that Tombstone was remembered for by the rest of the world, for a few years after my time there, water, scarce on the surface of the earth in that region, got so abundant underground that them silver mines flooded and the veins of ore could no longer be reached, and pumping the water out cost more than the mined metal would fetch, silver being so expensive to extract and prepare. So the mines and assorted operations closed down, and the town was about to make the familiar change from boom to ghost when somebody come up with the bright idea to market what Tombstone had in abundance, and could never be taken away, namely, the history of a lot of bloodshed, and I hear still today the tourists come to watch regular reenactments of the killings around the corner and down the street from the O.K. Corral.

Now before I forget let me say while I was at Tombstone I had sent back by mail that money Klaus Kappelhaus loaned me on my hasty departure from the Indian school, and I did the same in the case of Longhorn Lulu of the Lone Star in Dodge, along with one of them postcards she loved to get, in this case showing a picture of Schieffelin Hall, which I called my house: she'd get a laugh out of that when it was read to her.

I didn't send any money to Mrs. Agnes Hickok, to replace that of Wild Bill's I had lost, on account of I never had an address for her.

So where did me and Pard head on leaving Tombstone? Well, you might recall when me and Bat was up in Nebraska rescuing no-good Billy Thompson, helped by Buffalo Bill Cody, the latter had spoke about a traveling show he was going to put together and had invited both me and Bat to join him—he really wanted Bat and probably included me just to be polite, but I thought of that now and figured though I didn't have any special talents at riding, shooting, and the like, I could make myself useful and was willing to work as a flunky if I could get some association with entertainment, which the more of it I seen as a spectator, the more alluring it was to me. I don't mind admitting I could put myself in the place of that fellow in the story who give enemas to circus elephants and got beshat a lot but stayed at the job because he couldn't give up show business. That halfway offer of Cody's seemed the best chance I'd ever have.

So I'll skip the details of our trip up to Nebraska now and go direct to North Platte, where I figured right in looking in on Dave Perry's saloon first before going out to the Welcome Wigwam, though it was only midmorning, for there was Buffalo Bill, belly up to the bar, and as usual in the midst of a number of fellows listening to what he was saying. His subject at the moment was patriotism, George Washington and the cherry tree, Ben Franklin's kite, Paul Revere's ride, and the like, and lifting his glass, he says, "Let's drink to Tom Jefferson, who was known for taking a beaker of good cheer on occasion."

Then he spots me, who he hadn't seen in a couple of years and besides had paid most of the attention to Bat at that time, and what I had been worried about was that given all the people he had dealt with since, traveling around the country performing in plays, not to mention his heavy drinking, he wouldn't believe my reminiscence of the last time I was in his town. But Cody was a remarkable individual, as I hope I will be able to convey.

"Good to see you again, Captain!" he says heartily, and to the crowd around him, "Step aside, boys, and let Captain Jack wet his whistle." And he gives me one of his big handshakes that made anybody else's seem weak. "And how is my friend Colonel Masterson?" He was wearing one of his buckskin jackets, even fancier than the ones I had seen before, with fringes on top of fringes, beadwork on beadwork, and embroidery likewise, and an enormous white sombrero which must of been part of his stage costume, for it was certainly impractical garb elsewhere, though Cody probably could of wore it untarnished through a mud storm.

After a decent interval I brought up the reason I was there. "You might not recall it, but the time me and Bat was over here you mentioned a show you might be —"

"Let me head you off at the pass, Captain," he says, motioning the others to close in again now I had been given entrance, for Cody loved to be crowded especially when drinking. "Not only do I renew my personal invitation to you to join me in that endeavor, but the first phase of it is already at hand. You could not have arrived at a more opportune moment, sir. Let's drink to that!" After several big swallows, he elucidates. "To my unpleasant surprise, nothing by way of local observance had been planned for our nation's birthday, which will arrive before you know it. No redblooded lover of the country could stand by while the Glorious Fourth was treated as inconsequential. I couldn't look my wife and family in the face again, let alone the multitude of fellow Americans who expect better. I have therefore been drawing up some preliminary ideas. Given that the season will be summer and the fact that while we here in North Platte have no indoor stage large enough for what I envision, which would include a simulated buffalo hunt, riding, roping, shooting competitions, and the like, there is a fenced racetrack at the edge of town which should be ideal. I am about to persuade a number of our generous businessmen" — he tipped the brim of the big white hat at Dave Perry, back of the bar, who thereupon refilled every extended glass — "to invest in some prizes."

I took note that he put everything in a positive way, which no doubt had something to do with his popularity, for it tended to make people feel good. Take that "invest in" instead of just saying they was donating sums of money like it was charity. He made it sound like a profitable business opportunity, as in fact it turned out to be.

Now the interesting thing about Cody's optimism is that it generally started out sounding like exaggeration, but when it was applied to entertainment it usually proved to be on the modest side. He thought his blowout for the Fourth of July would attract maybe a hundred contestants. Instead, more than a thousand showed up when the time come, and most everybody else living at the time in western Nebraska, northeastern Colorado, and upper Kansas showed up as audience, so in fact the local merchants did turn out to have invested in a successful venture, with what the visitors ate and drank and bought in North Platte.

And I had a part in this, as well as a place for me and Pard to stay in one of the outbuildings at the Welcome Wigwam. Now though adequate enough at both, I never claimed to be a dead shot nor a champion rider, and all my life I been sufficiently clever not to pretend to be something I ain't if there is a great likelihood I will be put to the test. So at this point what could I do that Cody would find worthwhile? For though he had that lavish manner he was no fool when it came to getting the best from the people he associated with, and soon enough he established which of my capabilities was most useful to him at this moment. You might snort when you hear what it was. He figured I could serve him best as his personal, well I guess the right term would be bartender, though he give me the respectable title of quartermaster.

You might wonder why Cody needed someone to provide a supply of drink when he spent so much time in saloons, but when planning outdoor shows he had to spend time outdoors. You got to know this about Buffalo Bill, his entertainments would never of been so successful as they was did he not apply himself to them in the ideas and the applications. I never knowed anybody worked harder than Bill Cody, and he seemed to take energy from a quantity of drink that would of paralyzed the average man.

But he couldn't be seen with a bottle, for kids had already begun to look up to him, and besides he didn't want anybody to think of him as a drunk — which you might laugh when I say he wasn't, but I never saw him worse than what could be called feeling real good, certainly never the real low-down and dirty drunkenness which was common enough in them days by many whose intake was less than his.

What he done was get me a cart that could be pulled by one horse, and it had a canvas cover on it like a miniature covered wagon. The inside was fitted with a little desk and some boxes full of papers, ledgers, and the like, so he could call it his "field headquarters," for Cody always had to give a special name to everything associated with him. It was big enough to climb on board and sit down at the desk as though he was going to work on the business records, but underneath the papers was bottles of different kinds of spirits and wines, each type in a box of its own with the outside labeled according to a code known only to me and him, like "Accounts Payable" might signify gin and "New Expenditures," brandy, and so on.

I would park this vehicle near that racetrack where the Blowout was being readied, and then during the events themselves, and Bill would visit the interior from time to time for reinforcement for his energies. He was so pleased by how I handled the job that he offered me regular employment on a similar basis with the traveling show he begun to prepare now on the basis of that commemoration of the Glorious Fourth.

Now I was pleased to have found a new direction for myself, but not thrilled to be doing essentially the same kind of work I wanted to get away from, though truly it wasn't no longer in a smoky room full of gamblers ready to go outside at some point and shoot one another down. Cody's shows was real wholesome from the first, decent entertainment for families, and you never heard no filthy language from the performers even amongst themselves, nor unruly behavior, and that was just the kind of association I wanted at this time of my life. What I had to do was come up with an idea that would appeal to Cody beyond this wagon full of wet goods, but I was unequipped for fancy horsemanship or spectacular shooting, and I tell you, seeing the performances in the various events at the Blowout, and by amateurs, I realized no mere practice would elevate me from mediocrity. There was ordinary cowboys who could make their horses dance on hind feet, and ranch hands who ordinarily pitched hay and shoveled manure but with a pistol could hit a silver dollar thrown in the air.

So I had to employ my brain, which had gone unused too long else I would of left Tombstone earlier. What I come up with now was such a good idea that Cody had already gotten it himself and in fact had already arranged to carry it out by means of a well-known man of that day, Major Frank North, who back in the '6os had organized the Pawnee Scouts what become part of the U.S. Army and back when the railroad was being built across the plains, when I hired out as a wagon driver, I met North, who didn't think much of me, and at least one of his sharp-eyed Pawnee recognized me from being on the other side in a previous fight they had had with their traditional enemies the Cheyenne, and I felt real uncomfortable until everybody's attention was claimed by a battle.

Yessir, the idea I had for Cody's show was to include Indians in it, and by Indians I of course meant them who I knowed best, the Cheyenne, who was wonderful riders, though they never did a trick on a horse unless it had practical value, like hanging on the far side of a galloping pony's neck if being fired at, and was also remarkable shots with a bow and arrow while riding, which called for controlling the animal with the legs alone. I figured there was white audiences, especially in the cities where Cody was planning to take his troupe, that would find such a demonstration real entertaining without no danger to the audience, while on the Indian side it would be a way to get paid for showing prowess at activities they was discouraged or even prohibited from doing on the reservations.

Well, it was such a good idea that as I say Cody had it himself, and as always with that pertaining to public performance, he took it much further than my limited concept.

Seated at that little desk in the wagon, he says, "Madeira wine, Captain, if you please." He pounded himself in the area of his stomach. "I'm off my feed today." I found the bottle under some ledgers in the box marked "Matters Pending" and poured him a tin cup full. After a big swig he says, "As for your suggestion, I welcome it." He smiles broadly and raises his cup in a toast. "Major Frank North will join us with a band of his Pawnees."

"Pawnees!" I said with an instinctive disgust which might of been noticed and inquired about by another person, but Cody disregarded anything of a negative nature.

"Fine fellows," he says. "We go back a long way." He referred to the battle of Summit Springs against Tall Bull's band of Cheyenne, and so far as North himself went, him and Cody was also partners in a ranch up on the Dismal River, so I wouldn't be able to talk him out of this arrangement, and if the Pawnee was there, I sure wasn't going to want to invite some Cheyenne, in view of the old enmity between them two tribes.

Frank North was not just going to bring Pawnee warriors but also women and children and set up a village at the show grounds, wherever they happened to be at the moment, so white folks could see at close hand how redskins cooked and ate their food and how they spent the night, and in the show itself the Indians would not just ride their horses like my idea but would attack a stagecoach, shooting blanks of course, and be driven off by Buffalo Bill and his white scouts and cowboys, and later have a big scalp dance, and then in a grand finale would surround the cabin of a helpless settler and his family and be about to burn it down when Buffalo Bill and his bunch show up once again in the nick of time. It was real ironic that the Pawnee would be acting these parts, for in real life they was the white man's ally. What they'd be doing in the show, you might say, was playing Cheyenne.

The first season opened up the following spring, and I won't go into it day by day but just touch the highlights, many of which was unfavorable, beginning with the rehearsal of the Indian attack on the Deadwood stage-coach, conducted by Major North and them Pawnee, with the mayor of Colville, Nebraska, and several town councilors as passengers. Now the Indian charge, with screaming war cries and much firing of blanks, spooked the mules and they stampeded, which excited the Indians even more, and it was quite a while before anyone but the driver and them in-side the coach knowed anything had gone wrong. When the vehicle was finally brung to a stop, the mayor jumped out and, though on wobbly legs, wanted to whip Cody's arse for what he believed a practical joke.

Then in Omaha in late May of '83, Doc Carver was suffering from a hangover and missed a lot of the glass balls thrown into the air as targets for the shooting exhibition and was booed by the crowd, who called for Buffalo Bill to take over, which embittered Doc, but I forgot to explain who he was in the first place. W. F. Carver was a fellow Cody had met in New York while performing in a stage play, Carver himself being a cham-pion shot who traveled as far as Europe with his marksmanship shows and could put up enough money for Buffalo Bill to take him on as a full partner in what was now called Cody and Carver's Rocky Mountain and Prairie Exhibition.

Carver also claimed to of had extensive Indian-fighting experience, a close friendship with Wild Bill Hickok, and other distinctions, all of which was lies as anyone who could of made genuine claim to them things but did not (guess who?) could tell right away. Cody privately told me once that Doc "went West on a piano stool." And guess why he was called Doc? He was another damn dentist! On top of all this, though he wore decorated buckskins and sported long hair like his partner, he couldn't hold his liquor like the latter, and every time I seen him he was notably under the weather. Yet when he broke with Cody at the end of the first season, he says it was on account of Buffalo Bill was drunk throughout.

More reliable marksmen, and easier to get along with, was a man name of Captain Bogardus and his four sons, and Cody himself was a fine shot from horseback, which even if you never been mounted you can imagine as an achievement, hitting 75 out of 100 glass balls at twenty yards while at the gallop. There have been some who discounted this, as well as the other feats of exhibition shooting in them shows, for loose shot and not solid bullets was used even in the rifle and pistols. Well, they started with lead slugs, until they busted windows half a mile away and nearly plugged a few citizens, so from then on used a half load of powder and a quarter ounce of Number 7½ shot, in case you want to try it, but my advice is don't do it at home, not even with a BB gun, for you're likely to put an eye out with it sooner or later.

Then Cody had some bad personal fortune. We was at Indianapolis at the time. In the buffalo herd, which at every show was chased around a fenced enclosure, individual animals getting roped and not killed, was one big bull who nobody even tried to put a lariat on, him being so strong and mean to begin with and getting meaner, having at every performance to get run around like that. But never letting anything go untried, Cody asks the leading rider, Buck Taylor, billed as "King of the Cowboys" and an enormous fellow six foot five or six, to not only rope and throw this big devil but climb on and ride him!

"Hell, with that," Buck said, meaning the riding, but him and Jim Lawson got ropes on the bull, who was called Monarch, and managed to throw it.

Now I could repeat for almost every episode that Buffalo Bill produced more hot air than anyone I knowed, but he also really done a lot of things that took more nerve than was common or even sensible.

He now comes over to where Monarch is down but struggling so hard to get free that it was all Buck and Jim could do to hold onto the ropes. As a joke Cody once again asked Taylor to climb on, for he liked to kid him, but then he admitted that not even Jim Bullock, the lead steer-rider with the show, would come near old Monarch.

"So," says Buffalo Bill, "I guess that leaves only me." And don't you know, he got on the back of that enraged animal, which when allowed up, the ropes still trailing from it, took maybe three steps, then bucked with all the force of its massive, hairy body, big brute head lowered to the ground, snorting through wide-open nostrils and beady eyed, and Cody flew high into the air and come down so hard he didn't breathe for a spell nor could talk at all.

The audience give him a mighty cheer, believing this a part of the spectacle, and the other performers, including the Indians, had been prepared by Bill himself to go on with the show no matter what happened, so while he was being taken to the hospital the redskin attack on the settler's cabin proceeded, the only difference from the usual being that Cody didn't lead the rescuers, for he had no stand-in. How could there be a substitute for Buffalo Bill?

He stayed in the hospital a couple of weeks and joined us in Chicago, fully recovered from the stunt, but then something a lot worse occurred. He had to hurry back to the Nebraska home where he spent so little time, on account of the sickness of one of his children he saw so seldom, namely little Orra, only eleven. Now while living winters at the ranch I had hardly seen his missus or the little daughters, so far did his wife Louisa, called by him Lulu, keep aloof from anybody or -thing associated with Bill's career, believing it beneath her, and she might of been right about that, but it did not bring them closer. And now little Orra died, though at least he was there for that sad event and not too late as with the little son who had passed away previously.

Cody's absence from the show meant I never had anything to do, for I had still been providing his drinks, either in his tent or his private railroad car. By the way, Pard was still with me, and we traveled, him and me, in a little section I walled off at the end of one of the cars that carried the livestock, in this case horses, which stank less and wasn't so noisy as the steers and buffalo. I stayed apart because I didn't want them white performers to complain about him, and I didn't want to go near the Indians on account of my fear they might eat him.

Speaking of the Indians with what since Carver's departure had been called Buffalo Bill's Wild West, I have so far mentioned only the Pawnee of Major Frank North's bunch, who I avoided for reasons stated, but in fact Cody had managed to get ahold of a small contingent of Sioux as well, and like the Cheyenne they was historically hostile to the Pawnee and had always fought against that tribe. Yet with the Wild West the two groups camped peaceably side by side at each of our stops. This encampment was considered part of the show, and the public came and watched them, the Indians actually living in those tepees, cooking their meals on outside fires, and once in a while babies would be born in the traditional redskin fashion and not in a hospital and carried on their mothers' backs while being called "papooses" by white visitors.

I got to know a young fellow name of Gordon Lillie, then an interpreter for the Wild West, as he had worked at the Pawnee reservation in Indian Territory, and he told me the two tribal groups while feeling a natural rivalry in this situation, like baseball teams, tolerated each other and never come close to quarreling in his observation. Which caused me to reflect that even I tended sometimes to underrate the red man. He was getting plenty of grub here, a decent wage for the time, and admiration from the white public merely by pretending to be who he once had been, in the fake attacks on stagecoaches and settlers, and after the performance, being who he really was, a person with a wife and family and a portable home — two more things than me. He didn't have no more territory to contest over, and no horses to steal or be stolen, so there wasn't no reason for fighting.

Lillie by the way later on took the name of Pawnee Bill and for a while had a traveling show of his own.

When the Wild West closed its tour at Omaha that fall, I told Cody of my old connection with the Cheyenne and proposed to go up to their reservation and hire a bunch for the season to open next spring, and he says sure, the more the merrier, which reaction was typical of the man. We was back at the ranch in North Platte, along with a big bunch of others from the show, even an Indian or two, and Cody, full of drink and wearing a battered plug hat he had borrowed from somebody, was telling the stories for which he was noted but which, oddly enough, in various examples wasn't as remarkable as some of his true adventures, as I learned only in later years when many of the Army officers who he had scouted for wrote or spoke of exploits of his he rarely or never mentioned and in fact called him modest. My own opinions changed as I knowed him better, and at any given point here I am trying to tell you how I felt at the time.

In my earliest impressions, based on hearsay, I believed him just a blowhard. I had been wrong. If he were not the inventor of a new style, then he perfected it, and of course by now it is a pretty standard mix in which the true and the false are so intimately intertwined as probably never to be told apart, and anybody tries to figure them out will get thrown so off balance as to fear for his reason. I expected it's only owing to this state of affairs that anybody ever gets elected to public office in this country.

12
Little Mrs. Butler

S O TOWARDS THE END OF THAT WINTER I TRAVELED UP
to Montana Territory, and I recruited a group of Cheyenne, of
which most was men but some was women, all the latter married
and with children, and brung them down to St. Louis, where the
Wild West opened its second season.

Now, thinking about Buffalo Bill Cody and his habit of presenting the
brightest side of matters, and also with regard to the people who still live
up there today, I ain't going into detail about the Tongue River reservation, for while no doubt it was an improvement over where the Northern Cheyenne had first been sent down to the Nations, Indian Territory,
it was not the place they would of been living permanently if they had
my right to live anywhere I wanted.

I wasn't overwhelmed by the crowds of Indians who wanted to go off
to parts unknown and join some kind of entertainment put on by the
people who had slaughtered so many Cheyenne and taken away their
land.

I tried to explain these weren't the same white people who done that,
but I was hampered in this by my own conscience, for in fact the two
main Indians Cody was credited with personally killing during his days
as an Army scout, Tall Bull and Yellow Hand, *was* both of them
Cheyenne, so the best I could come up with was the bury-the-hatchet
argument, and them Sioux had come with the show after all, not to
mention the Pawnee: why should both their friends and their enemies be
profiting when they wasn't? But they answered easily enough that they

was too polite to comment on the taste of their friends and allies, but as to a miserable tribe like the Pawnee it could be said anything done by such would turn the stomach of a Human Being.

Now I had went to a certain amount of effort in getting there, for with Cody's help I had to obtain the Government agent's okay to talk to these people at all, and it had first to be confirmed by Washington, and if you expected Indians to listen to you, you did well to bring them presents of a decent quality, for they had long since been too advanced to accept a handful of glass beads, so I invested in bolts of nice cloth and foods of the sort I knowed they liked, some of which, sugar and coffee and bacon and such, they was supposed to be issued by the Government but the rations was often short owing to the dishonesties all along the line of distribution.

I don't want to complain, for this was my own idea, but the point is I wasn't getting far with the people who I was trying to lend a hand to, and I might of ended up with the bitterness so often felt by the rejected do-gooder had I not got unexpected assistance.

First I ought to say that amongst the Indians gathered in the area near the agent's office where I had parked the wagon full of presents and give them out, I didn't recognize a single soul from either my old days with the tribe or from that little band of prisoners down in Kansas, Wild Hog's bunch, who had been sent up here after the charges against them was dropped, but then the last-named had not taken to me much even when I helped them out and maybe to see me now would only remind them of a rotten time and they stayed away. And my old friends was probably dead.

But just as I was about ready to quit and go back emptyhanded to Buffalo Bill, having proved my sole talent was in filling a glass from a bottle, who should make his appearance as a latecomer, hailing me with warm feeling, but that young fellow from the Indian school run by the Major and Amanda Teasdale, Wolf Coming Out, who if you recall I had got out of the Kiowa girl's bed in the females' dormitory but was caught myself in what looked like compromising circumstances.

I clumb down from the wagon and shook his hand and said I was sorry all the presents had been handed out.

"I'm glad to see you," said Wolf. He was a few years older and his hair had growed long again. He was wearing the mostly white clothes with some Indian touches of them that lived on the reservations, moccasins and beaded vest over a blue cloth shirt and pants of wool. "Nobody would tell me," he went on, "where you went when you left the school."

"Well, that's past now," I says, not wanting to remind him, and in fact myself either, of an embarrassing incident. "How are things at the school? Are you back home on vacation?"

"I was thrown out and sent back," Wolf says with a grin of apparent approval. "It took me a while to tell Gold Leaf that I was the one who caused the trouble, because he speaks only English. He can't even talk in the signs. It was too bad you left, because everything was all right after that, and you could have stayed."

"How could it be all right if you were expelled?" I asked, though knowing just what he meant: he was real happy to leave a place he never liked. But his response was not as simple as I expected. You always had to allow for that with an Indian. He seldom approached things like a white man, but not because of stupidity or ignorance as such. He was just answering another question than the one you thought you had asked.

"Because I had learned enough by then," says he, serious now. "It's an excellent school, and Gold Leaf is probably the smartest white person in the country, along with your woman, of course."

"My woman?"

"*Heovo-vese.*"

"Yellow Hair wasn't my woman!"

Now he was smiling broadly. "Oho, she was Gold Leaf's woman? Is that why you ran off? He was going to shoot you?"

"She wasn't anybody's woman." And then, since he was joking with me, I kidded him about the white man's clothes he was wearing, the pants and shirt of cloth, and right away I regretted having done so.

"When the leather clothing wears out, we can't replace it nowadays," he said. "There isn't much game around here any more."

By the way, the rest of the Cheyenne, most of them also dressed in white style, gingham dresses on the women and the men in jeans and that high-crowned style of black felt hat I never seen on anybody but an Indian, had drifted away by now, having gotten the presents and politely listened to my pitch, but Wolf had not yet heard it, so I went through it again. "The food is plentiful, and it is of excellent quality, with lots of meat. Cody provides all the clothing, and it's buckskin, with authentic decorations of the tribe. The women will be given the materials they need to make it, or he'll have it done by people who work for him making costumes. Everything is provided, including the horses and guns, and Cody also pays twenty-five dollars a month to each warrior. If he is married and wants to bring his wife and family along, they get an additional fifteen dollars every moon."

"I am glad to hear the men get paid more than the women," Wolf says. "Whites too often are run by their women, as in the case of Yellow Hair at the school and the other female teachers."

"The reason here," I says, "is the warriors perform in the show, attacking stagecoaches and white settlements."

Wolf frowns and asks seriously, "Where does this man find the white people willing to get hurt or even die to entertain others?"

Now, nobody was more familiar with Indian ways than me but I was rusty. I begged his pardon for neglecting to say all these fights was fakes, with blank cartridges, and then I had to explain what a blank was, for he had never heard of ammunition without bullets, which couldn't do nothing but make noise. Indians rarely had enough cartridges, and of course couldn't manufacture none, so they was careful of what they possessed, often using arrows at short range, to save their bullets for the long.

"I'm not married," Wolf says next.

I figured he was thinking about that extra fifteen dollars he would not get as a single man, and I says, "I'll offer you thirty-five dollars a month for yourself, if you can talk a group of Human Beings into coming with the show." And I threw in an appeal to his vanity. "I noticed at the school that you were a natural leader."

He nodded solemnly. "That is true, but only among those of my own age and younger. The older men might not be willing to follow someone who has never been in battle." He showed me a sensitive look. "My parents wouldn't let me fight at the Goat River. It is not true as some whites have said, I understand, that so-called suicide boys went to the battlefield to distract the attention of the soldiers so our men could kill them more easily. The Americans were easy enough to kill as it was: they were all drunk. I went over there only when they were all dead. Having been to that very fine school and learned many things, I now know what money is, of course, but I did not in those days and neither did the rest of us, and the money belonging to the dead soldiers was blowing all over the field. Some of the girls used it to make dolls' dresses."

"Greasy Grass" as I have said was what the Little Bighorn was usually called by the Indians, for that was mostly Sioux territory and the name was in the Lakota language, but the Cheyenne had previously known it as the Goat, and though young, Wolf had become a man of tradition.

"I didn't know you were there." I decided for the moment anyhow to continue to be silent as to my own personal experience.

"Only as a child. But many of the grownups were as ignorant as we children. A warrior named Rising Sun took a thick gold medal from a soldier's dead body. It was at the end of a chain and made a ticking sound, so he hung it around his own neck. But when the ticking stopped, next morning, he believed its medicine was good only for white men and bad for a Human Being, and he threw it into the river." Wolf's teeth glistened in his dusky face, his color having darkened now he was mostly outdoors. "If I had been to school at the time I could have told him it was a watch. Gold Leaf had one just like it."

Well, after some more talk, and a meal prepared by his relatives from the gift eats I had brung — he lived with them in a tepee made of shabby old canvas on account of buffalo hide was scarce, and they was waiting for a government shipment of lumber to build a shack, and they had a mean patch of land on which to grow crops when and if the seed arrived — after eating and then of course smoking a pipe on the matter, Wolf collected a little bunch of nine fellows, six of which was married and brung their wives and some little kids, including babes in arms, and after the necessary permissions had been granted, with telegrams back and forth to Cody and him to his pals in the Government, we made our way down to St. Louis by steamboat and railroad, which none of them except Wolf had ever rode on, so he could confirm his superior position, and let me say though I have made clear my high regard for Indians, they was altogether human in such things as envy and self-interest.

Now don't think Pard was forgotten. He stayed on at Cody's ranch in Nebraska while I went up to Montana. Buffalo Bill liked him, and he got on all right with the hired hands and the other dogs on the property. I didn't take him with me this time, for I was concerned the Cheyenne might be hungry for their old delicacy.

When we reached St. Louis and I met up with Pard, who Cody had brung along with him, I took the precaution of asking Wolf Coming Out to keep himself and the other Human Beings from licking their lips when seeing my four-footed pal if I wasn't always there to protect him.

To which Wolf says I needn't fear for the animal, because his uncle once had a dream he would die if he ate dog and, having done so anyway, was killed next day by a bolt of lightning, after which everybody in their band regarded that sort of meat as bad medicine. "Besides," he says, "that dog of yours is too old to eat." I took some comfort in that fact: it was true that their preference was for puppy-dog soup.

In the encampment at the show grounds, the Cheyenne set up the tepees Cody provided, next to the lodges of their pals the Sioux, and it was only then that I learned Wolf could talk Lakota. It seems his aunt on his Ma's side was the wife of an Ogallala, like more than one Human Being woman, intermarriage being one of the practices that caught on after the first one or two done it, and it kept going. At the Greasy Grass the two camps was adjoining. Despite this longstanding connection, the two languages was totally different from each other, and unless an individual learned the other fellow's tongue they had to converse in the signs. I never knowed till I got over to Europe that pretty much the same thing was true of the French and the Germans, but then they wasn't all that close friends.

So I asks Wolf if he would translate if I ever wanted to talk to the Lakota, and he says sure, but maybe I'd want him to learn me the lingo and then I could practice it with the Sioux contingent.

"Oh," says I, needling him, "go to school as you did? I just hope I can be as good a student."

"You have to be as smart as I to learn that much," says he, and I swear he was altogether serious, "but whatever you learn will be worthwhile."

I thought it would of been nice for the Major to know what a high opinion Wolf held regarding the institution, but I was embarrassed at not being able to use good enough English to write him in, and not so much for his sake as if he showed it to Amanda.

Now having broke up with Doc Carver, who immediately started a rival show, Cody went into partnership with a fellow name of Nate Salsbury, who had been a stage actor for a long time, but with the Wild West he handled the business end and never performed any more though I bet he would of liked to be a star like Cody, but there wasn't ever no one else in existence, then, before, or since, better at what he did than Buffalo Bill.

The first thing Salsbury done was to get a promise from Cody to stop excess drinking. In view of the job I had been hired for, and maybe to his mind still held in addition to being interpreter for the Cheyenne, I guess it made sense to read me the letter he had wrote to Nate when they signed the deal.

I had to keep a straight face when he promised not to drink no more while they was partners other than the "two or three" he would take to "brace on, today." Now that could be taken two ways, but maybe he wasn't being devious but just trying to fool himself as well with a vow that, the way I read it, said he could take three drinks a day without specifying how big they could be, and in fact this promise become part of the Cody legend in later years, with just that supposed limit at the heart of it: you had people saying he swallowed three beer buckets of whiskey every twenty-four hours, and next it become barrels. All I can honestly say is I henceforward never saw him drink no more, and — I guess you can see this coming — no less.

"Lucky I have this other job now," I told him.

"Oh, we'd have found something else for you to do," he says. Cody was loyal to the people around him, his employees usually becoming his personal cronies, who was closer to him than his real family. "Tell me this, Jack. Do those Cheyennes of yours carry a grudge because I killed some of their people in the past?"

"They don't even know you did it." It might of been my imagination but I thought he looked a little disappointed.

"Say, Jack," says he, "that's a fine dog you have. While he stayed with us at the Welcome Wigwam I noticed he was a very bright animal. Have you taught him any tricks?" I allowed as how I never thought of it. "Well," Cody goes on, "you might want to consider the matter. People like trained dogs, especially the children, and such a feature would be quite edifying, demonstrating the benevolent domination of the higher type of mentality, as in the human, over that of the beast, to the betterment of both."

I says I would think about it, but whether I could get Pard to do it was another thing, for though I never knowed how old he actually was, he was getting a bit grizzled under his pointy chin, and I figured it had been a while since he was a candidate for learning new tricks.

With this second season the show seemed to be doing better due to Nate Salsbury's business sense, but a couple misfortunes happened.

Major Frank North, Cody's old friend from Cheyenne-fighting days, was throwed from his horse when a saddle girth busted during a performance at Hartford in Connecticut, and he got badly trampled. He never did fully recover, and died the following year.

The next trouble was only temporary, but highly inconvenient and not without expensive damage. We had give well-attended performances in the major cities of the East, including even New York, where I hadn't ever been before and on this occasion never saw anything of beyond the Polo Grounds where we was camped, because like most places we went that season it was but for one day after all the effort in getting there and setting up. I ought to mention how big the Wild West was getting, with the troupe of cowboys, all the Indians, as well as now a bunch of Mexican *vaqueros*, the buffalo herd, horses, mules, and donkeys by the hundreds, the Deadwood stagecoach and other wheeled vehicles, the collapsible scenery including the settler's cabin that was attacked by the Indians at every performance and canvas backdrops of painted mountains, crates of ammunition, extra weapons, costumes, saddles, horseshoes, ropes, and nonperishable foods, the fresh having to be purchased wherever we stopped. It was a traveling town in every sense of the word.

Well, this whole shebang got dumped into the Mississippi River that winter, when Cody and Salsbury decided to keep the show going during the months it would usually be closed, performing at Southern places where the weather was warm enough, so we all loaded onto a steamboat at Cincinnati, the name of which always reminded me uncomfortably of Mrs. Agnes Lake Thatcher Hickok and the money of Wild Bill's I lost, but I didn't have time to look her up right then.

We went down the Ohio River, joining the Mississippi at Cairo, Illinois, stopping at various places on the route to New Orleans, but the attendances was disappointing, and then our boat slammed into another at Rodney Landing, Mississippi, and sank, taking with it a lot of livestock, much of our wheeled equipment except for the Deadwood stage, and a deal of other stuff, but fortunately no human life, and not Pard, who I never saw swim before but who did a real good job with churning paws. As is obvious, I too made it to shore.

Soon as we all got in and was counted, Cody found the nearest telegraph and sent Nate Salsbury, in Denver at the moment, a wire as follows: OUTFIT AT BOTTOM OF RIVER PLEASE ADVISE. And when Nate telegraphed back, GO N ORLEANS REORGANIZE, why that's just what Buffalo Bill did in eight days, getting hold of another herd of buffalo, more wagons and all, and opening when it had been announced for weeks earlier — and then it rained in the Crescent City for the next forty-four days straight, keeping most people away, and the show was in the red sixty-some thousand dollars by winter's end. Cody advised Salsbury he had a mind to go home and, *for a change*, get drunk.

Though Buffalo Bill wouldn't call off a performance if three tickets was sold, we had some time on our hands and New Orleans weren't a place without interest, with its mix of all kinds of people speaking different lingos including not only what was supposed to be proper French but a version known locally as Coonass, which hadn't no meaning of colored, for the black folk talked what they called Gombo Zerbes, combining West Indian and African palavers with everything else, and they had also concocted a tasty stew of the same name, which might burn your mouth if you had only previously used salt on your steak, though speaking for myself I had ate a meal or two in the better eateries of Tombstone like the Maison Doree and swallowed stuff with foreign names which underneath it all was usually proved to be the familiar meat and potatoes, but the New Orleans fodder was really different, maybe including even bugs and lizards and so on, but I reckon you could get a taste for it in time. The sporting houses was awful fancy too and offered special features unavailable in the cattle and mining camps — or so I was told by acquaintances.

So far as I was personally concerned, I had got another of my crushes on a respectable female, though you might well ask why I was still wasting my time. All I can say is I was only doing what came natural to me, though in this case you might question what was natural about a man now forty-four being attracted to a girl who looked fourteen, with a fringe over her forehead and long wavy brown hair back of her ears and falling down over her shoulders, and not quite as tall as me, and I will hasten to tell you it was mostly a fatherly feeling, protective and not romantic, she being just the kind of pretty little thing any man would be proud to take care of and maybe write about as follows:

> She's a loving little fairy
> You'd fall in love to see her.
> Her presence would remind you
> Of an angel in the skies.
> And you bet I love this little girl
> With the rain drops in her eyes.

Now, I sure could never write such fine poetry myself, and in a minute I'll tell you who did, but at the first time I ever saw this pretty gal we was still in N.O. camped out beyond Audubon Park in the rain and she was entering Cody's tent accompanied by several men, among them our press agent John Burke, a big heavy fellow also known as Major or Arizona John, for most everybody around Cody had to have a title, nickname, or both, Buffalo Bill even naming each of his rifles.

Having fallen for her on just that glimpse, scoff if you want, I waited till she left and then went to ask Cody whose daughter she was, and I tell you I wasn't uneasy in so doing, given the clear conscience of my feeling.

But he was busy at the time, going over the schedule with Burke, so I couldn't ask him till later and by that time, what with his money worries and all, he couldn't recall much about her except she was a performer with the Sells Brothers circus, which was also appearing locally and also suffering from the weather and about to leave town. I was disappointed to hear that, given the general reputation of females involved in entertainment in that time, which my experience with Dora Hand hadn't gone to disprove, so with the idea that her schoolgirl appearance and demeanor was intended to deceive, and likely she was one of them lady acrobats wearing indecent tights that outlined the limbs, I dropped the matter from my mind.

As it happened Buffalo Bill didn't go home but instead took the Wild West upriver to Louisville, Kentucky, towards the end of April, and one day early in the engagement he called most of the company together in front of his tent and by the hand he brings forward the pretty girl I seen in New Orleans, and for a minute I thought what was the Wild West coming to, was we doing such bad business we had to hire a girlie act?

"Little Missie here is joining us," Cody says. "She'll be the only white woman with our company, and I want you boys to welcome and protect her."

Standing next to me was another newcomer to the show — at least I assume he was for I never seen him before — a good-looking fellow of the middle height, with short, neat hair and a well-trimmed mustache, and I says to him out of the corner of my mouth, "She looks like a real velocipede," which was what you might say in them days to mean quite lively.

And he says, "Sure if she's not my wife, little man, and I'll kick your arse."

I had put my foot in it for fair, for he turned out to be an Irishman named Frank Butler, a sharpshooter of reputation, and this little wife of his was even better though nobody knew at the time that she was just about the best as ever held a firearm, man or woman. Of course I'm talking about Annie Oakley.

I sincerely apologized, explaining I had meant nothing immoral by the word, which in fact I wasn't even sure of the meaning anyway, and thereupon begun a friendship with Frank that lasted all the while we three was with the Wild West, which meant I was Annie's friend as well, for them two was close as could be, Frank being a rare fellow for that day or maybe any other in that he give up his own career to manage his wife's after recognizing her greater talent. And I'll say further that I kept my crush on Annie, who was actually about twenty-five at this point, but even when you knew that, she seemed like one of them young girls whose unstained character you wanted to protect from the ugly traffic of the world as long as possible. In fact there was little about harsh reality that Annie didn't know from the age of nine or ten, when to take the strain of supporting a half-dozen other kids off her widowed mother, she was farmed out to a married couple what managed a poorhouse and insane asylum in that part of Ohio, and this pair put her at hard labor all day long. So she finally run back home, got her Pa's old rifle, and subsequently become the provider of meat to her own family, killing so much small game she sold the excess to hotels and restaurants in the region.

Now with the Wild West the Butlers had their own private tent, which in fact was their only residence at this point, so Annie made it homey as possible, with a nice carpet on the ground and proper furniture, including the rocking chair where she sat between shows, doing fancy embroidery or working on her costumes, of which she made all by hand. Frank wrote more of that poetry of which I give a sample earlier, not all of it romantic, some being what I guess could be called moral instruction, like the one entitled "What the Little Bird Said":

> Life is like a game of cards
> In which we pass our stand.
> Sometimes the stake is a true heart,
> Ofttime it's but a hand.
> Sometimes we take in the trick
> Which we should have passed,

But if you play your cards for all they're worth
You're bound to win at last.

But in case you might think him a henpecked sissy, I should say Frank Butler was a fine enough shot to hold his own with the best, and sometimes he'd compete in shooting contests, apart from the show, keeping his aim keen, but his best talent of all was as a shrewd businessman, a much rarer gift in the world of entertainment than marksmanship. Not only did he set up profitable deals for Annie, both with Cody and in other public and private appearances in between seasons when the Wild West was shut down, but Frank was also a representative for several companies making guns and cartridges. I don't think Annie ever had to reach into her own pocket to pay for a weapon or a round of ammunition. What weren't given her gratis by some manufacturer, as an ad for his product, was sent by admirers first in this country, then all over the world, and the presents included valuable jewelry, silver services, rare china and crystal, and she also got medals everyplace she went.

There wasn't many who was not in love with Annie Oakley, so I don't feel funny about including myself with the majority for once and not joining the few who detracted, usually with nothing more forceful than that she was stingy. I'd call it prudent. The fact was everybody looked parsimonious around Bill Cody, who was a big spender even before he had much money, so if she filled her little pitcher with lemonade from the gallon-sized one in his tent, you can be sure he didn't complain, especially since he kept that fluid on hand only to give to child visitors and maybe to make Nate Salsbury believe it was what he himself was drinking. Though I'll say again, Cody never missed a performance owing to drink, nor did it seem to affect his aim. He might not of been on Annie's level, but there wasn't nobody better at shooting from horseback.

What did Annie do that was so special? Well, she would trip into the arena like a girl returning home from Sunday school, and then as if only just becoming aware there was people watching, shyly curtsy and wave and blow a kiss to all, wearing her wide-brimmed hat with a single silver star on the edge of the upturned brim, and a fringed dress and matching leggings that looked like buckskin but wasn't, Annie considering leather too hot to perform in in summer.

So there she was, a little, frail, helpless figure all alone in the middle of the arena big enough for the simulated buffalo hunts and Indian attacks to follow, and then she'd lift her rifle and begin to shoot, the first noises of which, extra-loud due to bouncing off the grandstand, would always startle the female spectators, who might scream at first, adding to the dramatics of the occasion, but gradually get used to the rapid fire from then on.

What would she shoot? Glass balls, some filled with red-white-and-blue feathers or confetti, and clay pigeons hurled into the air by spring-powered traps operated by Frank. She could bust five balls, launched simultaneously, before any reached the ground. She would wait till the traps sent up two clay pigeons, then jump over a table, grabbing her gun off the top, and fire two shots busting both birds in the air. At times she tied her skirt at the knees, took off her hat, stood on her head, and, upside down, hit everything she aimed at. She shot a cigarette out of Frank's mouth, and a dime held between his fingers at a range of thirty feet. She would hit targets behind her, holding a mirror in one hand and with the other firing the gun over her shoulder and, sighting on the thin edge, slice a playing card in two.

Then, when her act was over, she would take a bow, blow a kiss, and make a cute little kick, a finale which become as famous as her shooting.

But the biggest crowd-pleaser, though frankly I had a hard time watching it, was when she shot an apple off the head of her little poodle named George, and he would catch one of the burst slices in his mouth and eat it. I always feared a big horsefly, of which there was always plenty around due to our livestock, would buzz around when this act was in progress and George might snap at it just as Annie squeezed the trigger. The fact is this never happened, George staying ever still as a dog made of china. But then Annie's reflexes was so fast she might of gotten off a safe shot even if he moved.

Remember Cody's suggestion I train old Pard to do tricks? Damn if I wanted to try that one. I sure never took Pard along when I went to the Butlers' tent for a cup of tea. Just as I feared the Indians might eat him, I suspected he might of gotten the same idea about little George!

Annie was the biggest single attraction of Buffalo Bill's Wild West, which by the way she was wont to call "B.B.W.W.," with the possible exception of Cody himself, and the poster for the show, plastered all over every city we played, usually featured her stanch little person, wasp-waisted and bosom covered with medals, "The Peerless Lady Wing and

Rifle Shot," but she was to get an even better title by which she has been remembered ever since. And this come about as follows.

I ain't spoken about the Indians with the show since bringing Wolf Coming Out and the other Cheyenne to it, but my bunch done fine that season, enjoying the buffalo hunt and shooting at the settler's cabin and the Deadwood stage even if the shots was blanks, and they never got tired of producing the bloodthirsty yells Cody encouraged, which in my experience was louder than what you heard in real fights and also a lot more gunpowder was burned in just one show than in any historical battle, for the redskins never had that many cartridges to burn, whereas the Wild West was better supplied than the U.S. Army, and it was fun for the Indians to be able to fire at whites and get paid and applauded for it. And if you think they might of been upset by having to lose every battle when Buffalo Bill showed up, they was not, for though going so much by dreams and visions and "medicine" like they did, Indians was at the same time rock-bottom realists: having lost the whole country in fact, they wasn't bothered by getting whipped in make-believe fights, but more important was the consideration that Buffalo Bill was paying them and supplying their meat, which by the way had to be beef at every meal unless one of the show buffalo died by accident, and Cody understood such details. I never knowed any other white person who never having lived with Indians got on so well with them as him, and I figure it was some of the same qualities that made him so good a showman that appealed to them: the taste for display and color and noise, and his personal style of being the center of attention without lowering the value of them around him, which was the manner of an Indian chief. So with real admiration and pride Bill could promote Annie's career without any worry it would diminish his own.

Nevertheless it was during that last disappointing engagement at the end of the season that Wolf Coming Out told me him and his bunch wanted to return home.

I made the mistake of thinking their decision had to do with the show. "It will stop raining sometime," I says. "Anyway, we'll be moving north before long and the Wild West will get back to normal."

"We have to return for spring planting," Wolf told me.

"I am surprised to hear you talk like a farmer."

"That's one of the things I learned at that very fine school," says he. "It's hard work and I don't like it very much, but it is what I ought to do.

Maybe I will come back some other time if you ask me, but now I have to go and do the plowing. The agents doesn't want the women to perform that sort of work, because whites think women should be idle."

"The idea is that women are smaller and not as strong," I pointed out, "so men should do the heavier tasks."

He raised his chin defiantly. I should mention this was not long before a performance and he was wearing the red-and-yellow facial war paint for the show, which Cody had them apply extra-gaudy so it could be seen clear from the grandstand. "The women of the Human Beings are stronger than most American men."

You can see how he turned the point I was making. It wasn't easy to argue with an Indian. So I just noted that "Cody says red men are Americans now too."

"I will call myself American when more Americans than Cody call me one." Wolf made two words of *Co-dee*. Indians tended to complicate the simplest white names, so you could see why they wouldn't even try to say longer ones like Winchester and Smith and Wesson. Usually even the non-Sioux called Cody by the Lakota term *Pahaska*, meaning Long Hair, for to an Indian a name always had to have a personal reference to the individual holding it, which is why there couldn't ever be, say, a Bad Bear, Jr. If Cody's Sioux name sounds familiar, it might be because Custer was also called Long Hair, though as I've said earlier he was known to the Crow, who liked him but not so much they stayed to die with him at the Greasy Grass, as Son of the Morning Star.

"I will call you an American if you want," I says.

He frowned under them glaring slashes of color, which was especially bright in that it was not homemade Cheyenne stuff but rather theatrical greasepaint. "Do you have to be American to be white?"

He had asked me a question nobody but an Indian would of thought of, I swear. If you want to know what I consider most valuable of all the things I learned from the Cheyenne, beyond the practical matters like riding, hunting, et cetera, I'd have to say how to look at life from other angles than the obvious.

"No," I says. "There are all kinds of white people on the earth, many different tribes from the Americans. In fact, there was no American tribe in the beginning. It was not created by the Everywhere Spirit but by people, as a big family which everybody can join and get a new start, no matter who he is, what he has, or where he came from." I never waited for him to point out the exceptions to this, at least as it was practiced, but added, "It is a fine dream, and as with all such it is not exactly like life, else there would have been no reason for a dream. But you are right if you think it is a dream of white people and applied first to their own kind."

Wolf smiled, which was an interesting expression on somebody wearing warpaint: if you was seeing it for the first time, you would of thought it extra-ferocious. "It is good to take care of your own kind."

"That is true. But there's also this vision by which all people are part of one big family and therefore should help one another, regardless of color or language or land."

"I don't want to insult you," Wolf said, "if that is your own dream, but it seems to make little sense. The Human Beings are the greatest of all peoples. How can they belong to the same family as the Crows and Pawnees, who are so inferior to them?"

Now if you are white you will usually hear this argument coming from them who dominate others not as numerous or rich or powerful as themselves, and if you are fair you'll have to say, even if you agree with it, that it's the reasoning of the bully. But ever since I knowed them the Cheyenne's successes was momentary whereas their catastrophes had all but brung them to extinction. If you still believe yourself best after all that, it's mighty damned impressive for my money, and I ain't going to try to talk you out of it, for you might be right on some higher level.

"These are matters that must be thought and talked about a great deal," I told him. "Meanwhile go home and do the spring planting. I hope you can come back for the summer season."

"I can't speak for the others," he says, "but maybe I'll wait awhile. Getting money is good, but sometimes your friends and even your relatives feel bad if you make too much." By which he was referring to envy, and I assure you Indians feel it, even when as in Wolf's case and that of most of the Cheyenne with our show, they sent the largest part of their wages back home, in care of the local Indian Bureau agent, who I just hoped was honest.

"I'll miss the Human Beings," I said. And in more ways than one. My job had been looking after that bunch. I knew Cody would keep me on in some capacity, but Nate Salsbury was always searching for ways to economize, and he wouldn't tolerate me going back to being Buffalo Bill's private barkeep.

"You can interpret for the Sioux," Wolf pointed out. "You speak pretty good Lakota by now. You are a better student than I was at Gold Leaf's school, I have to admit."

Nice of him to say so, but I had stuck at it with the lessons he give me, plus quite a bit of practice with the Sioux, around their campfires after supper, for in the days before the show got its own electric-generating rig we didn't perform at night.

"But Cody doesn't need any more translators of Lakota," I says. The head one was a white fellow named John Y. Nelson, who also acted as driver of the Deadwood stage and was married in real life to a Sioux woman and had a number of little kids who looked like full-bloods and also took part in the show.

"But there will have to be a special one for *Tatanka Iyotake*," Wolf said.

"Where's he going to be?"

"Here," said Wolf. "Or wherever *Pahaska* takes the show."

That was some news, and I can tell you none of the whites with the Wild West knowed anything about it yet, I wager to say not even Cody or Salsbury at this early date. True, Bill had tried to get this distinguished person to join the show a year before, but the agent at the Standing Rock reservation wouldn't grant permission.

Cody would reapply later this spring, but Wolf Coming Out already knowed, in some Indian fashion that did not use the telegraph or the U.S. mails, that the second request would be successful and that the next big star of B.B.W.W., to use Annie Oakley's term, would rival even her in popularity for one season. I speak of none other than Sitting Bull.

13

Sitting Bull

B
UFFALO BILL GOT PERMISSION FROM THE INDIAN
Bureau and the agent to sign up Sitting Bull for the Wild West, but
the Bull himself had to agree, and according to Cody had to be
talked into it in person, so Arizona John Burke was going to the
Hunkpapa agency at Standing Rock, Dakota Territory, to see the old fellow — who was about fifty at that time, while I myself was only a half-
dozen years younger.

As to "Major" Burke, I expect that rank was give him by "Colonel"
Cody, who had if you recall made me on first acquaintance a captain, but
at least I had had some association with the Army (mostly through having been attacked by it while living with the Cheyenne), whereas Burke
had only been around show business and newspapers all his life, talking
and writing in an inflated style that put Cody's in the shade though it
might of been the source of some of Buffalo Bill's own lingo. I also doubt
he had ever been near Arizona Territory, but Burke was the type of person who would not of used any rank or title to which he had a real claim,
because his purpose, like the typical press agent, was to make you believe
in something you would not have thought of, and he would of been so
disappointed to know you already believed it without his help he might
of started to argue in the reverse, for what he wanted was power over
you.

I can't take credit for coming to that conclusion on my own. It was
Sitting Bull who commented to that effect after hearing Burke talk for
three minutes in that log cabin of his on the Grand River at the Standing Rock reservation.

First I should say I was there only through chance, as usual, John Y. Nelson, and the others including his eldest son who spoke both Lakota and English, being sick or otherwise occupied, and Cody wouldn't trust any interpreter supplied by the agent, for there had been too many false translations in the past, one of the most notorious being that of Frank Grouard, which, like I said, maybe got Crazy Horse killed.

But he knowed I had been studying the language, so he asked me if I was good enough yet to handle the assignment, and I says sure, though I wasn't certain by any means, but Cody always had so much of the positive in his own manner as to remove your doubts about yourself.

Now when I told Mr. and Mrs. Butler who I was going off to see, Annie says, "Jack, you ask the chief if he remembers Little Sure Shot, and if he does, you give him my regards." Turned out she and Sitting Bull had met once after a performance of hers in St. Paul, Minnesota!

"What was he doing there?" I asked.

"Why," says she, "they took a troupe of Sioux around to a number of cities, Sitting Bull among them."

"So he's already been a showman?"

"Ah," Frank says in his Irish fashion, "he sat there, ya know, and people paid to look at him. He came to see Annie perfarm and was quate taken with her."

Annie give her modest girlish smile. "According to the translator, he said he wanted to adopt me for a daughter, but" — she put her head down — "I don't know about that."

"He gave her that name," said Frank.

I went to the Sioux camp and got the Lakota version of "Little Sure Shot," so when the right moment arrived I could say it correctly.

Now when Burke started to talk to Sitting Bull, I got a little flustered and was forced to substitute a Cheyenne term or two when I didn't know the right Sioux word, and Bull's scowl got even worse than his natural expression, which was normally disapproving when he talked with whites.

And he said a time or two, "I don't speak Shyela."

So I finally took the courage to come out with it. "I am sorry," I says. "I have studied Lakota, but am not as young as I once was and cannot learn as fast as when I was a boy and lived with the Shyelas."

After that admission, he gradually altered his manner with me, for contrary to appearances Sitting Bull was a tolerant and generous man, though he never did warm up to Burke. First he said I didn't look that old, and I got a smile out of him on saying I wasn't all that much younger than him, only small as I was I might not look it. And then he begged my pardon for criticizing my knowledge of the Sioux language, which was really not bad, and next he asked me about my Cheyenne boyhood and the band I was with and the fights and horse-stealing and the rest. I think what he was doing was checking up on my claim, though an Indian was too polite to let on when the subject was, so to speak, exclusively Indian. But he wasn't hesitant to voice his distrust of the Americans.

I reckon he came to believe in me, for he finally says, "Have you been telling me exactly what this fat man says in English, or have you made some changes?"

"I have cut it in about half."

"Still too much of it is empty wind," said Sitting Bull. "You might cut that half in half. Up to now he has been talking for himself."

Thinking his spiel was going over, Arizona John proceeds, "Chief, I assure you that the acclaim which will greet you on each and every appearance with what Colonel Cody modestly calls an exhibition but to the great American public is an extravaganza the like of which has never been known since the dawn of man, bar none, the acclaim, I say, Chief, will exceed any you have received throughout your illustrious career even from your dusky brethren."

"He just said more of the same thing he said before," I told Sitting Bull.

"Tell him I'm going to cut his throat and then scalp him."

Knowing this was his Indian idea of a joke, I admit I found it funny myself, so I laughed.

"Well," Burke says, smiling too, "we seem to be hitting it off nicely."

We was sitting on blankets on the floor of Bull's log cabin. Burke had been forced to lower his load of lard with some difficulty. How he would get up was to be proved. Sitting Bull had asked the hospitable question all visitors got on entering an Indian camp, "Do you want to eat?" I had declined, for though we was overdue for a meal, I didn't want to see Burke hog up a week's worth of the meager rations the Bull would of been issued by the agency. The cabin was just one room, reminding me of mine in Tombstone, except there was Indian stuff strewn about here, blankets and medicine bundles, et cetera, and some things hanging from nails, like a warbonnet and a hunk of bacon. There had been some other

Indians too, females and some youngsters, probably his wives and children, but they was not introduced, and left when I politely turned down the meal. If I knowed kids, these was probably disappointed, expecting to eat some of the food prepared for us.

Now, it wasn't that Sitting Bull was against oratory, coming as he did from a people who admired speechifying almost as much as fighting, but the Bull by now knowed enough about American ways to be aware that Burke, unlike an Indian, was not in it for the spirituality.

So I says to Arizona John, who by the way let his hair grow long like Cody's, a mess of stringy curls down to his shoulders, "He wants to know how much you will pay him."

When I told Sitting Bull what I had told Burke he made that kind of cough Indians do to indicate amazement, for he himself was too polite to have asked that question so soon. "I have been interpreted wrongly many times," he said. "But this is the first time that something that did not come from my lips is actually a question that comes from my heart." At a later point in our acquaintanceship he give me examples of the bad translations he had had to put up with, which he didn't even know about until someone who spoke both tongues, an Indian or the rare friendly white, informed him. One of them was the year before, when him and a delegation of other Sioux was hauled around the East to appear onstage, sitting at a fake campfire in front of a canvas tepee, while a white lecturer talked about the Red Man.

In Philadelphia, Sitting Bull was asked to make a little speech in Lakota, so the audience could hear what savage lingo sounded like. He spoke about how the Indian now had no choice but to walk the white man's road in peace and of the need to see their children get educated. Afterwards a young Sioux student from the school at Carlisle come backstage to tell him the remarks had been translated by the show's interpreter as a bloody account of how he had killed Custer at the Little Bighorn. "No wonder then," the Bull told me, "why I have been hissed and screamed at in some places. But I do wonder why that hasn't happened when I spoke on other occasions. Can it be that I was not wrongly translated at all times? Or is it rather that at some places the people admired me for rubbing out Long Hair?" Sitting Bull by the way, though having predicted the defeat of the soldiers, wasn't nowhere near Custer's part of the field at the Greasy Grass. He never even crossed the river that day. Nevertheless most whites in that time believed he personally killed the General.

But back to the present negotiations. The terms Cody offered was good money for the era, a fortune for someone in Sitting Bull's position as an agency Indian still technically a prisoner of war: fifty dollars a week, plus a bonus of $125, plus all he could make selling his autographs; all this for a season of four months.

But the chief still had his doubts. "I am no fool," he says to me. "I know that money is good to have, but to be given it just to sit and have people stare at you is strange."

"It is interesting for them."

"It seems to be, but I don't understand it."

"If *you* were white," I said, "you would not put Sitting Bull on display. You would rub him out and be done with him."

"That is true, but since I am who I am, it is a waste of time to talk about the impossible."

Now, see, that's another Indian thing: you could speak about dreams, visions, and the like all you wanted, but they figured it pointless to mess with reality. I don't know as how any white person, including even me, can understand the distinction altogether, but there is one. I can't tell you often enough that while talking to an Indian was sometimes exasperating, it seldom failed to refresh my mind.

But anyway so as not to hurt my feelings he says, "The Shyelas taught you well." He meant my knowing he would kill a defeated enemy and not keep him around for show, and he would do this not only for his own self-respect but also for that of his adversary. This concept may not be as nice as you'd like, involving as it might the splitting of a skull with a hatchet, which ain't so neat a means of killing as a lead slug, but there's a human belief behind it and not just stupid barbarism.

At that point I recalled my promise to Annie, and I remembered her to him. "*Watanya Cecilla* sends you her regards."

At which Sitting Bull rose to his feet, real graceful, thickset though he was and not in his earliest youth, and rummaging amongst the bundles that comprised his worldly goods, found something and brung it back and handed it to me.

It was one of them souvenir cards Frank had printed up bearing Annie's likeness. This one was signed with pen and ink:

Thomas Berger

To *Chief Sitting Bull,* with every good wish
from his friend, "Little Sure Shot"
Annie Oakley

"Are you also a friend of Little Sure Shot?" he asked me.

"Yes, I am," I says, "and she will be very pleased if you join *Pahaska's* show."

"Then I will do so," said Sitting Bull.

And that's the way it happened, and he brung some other Hunkpapa Sioux along with him, men and women, and that season of 1885 was a big success for B.B.W.W., finally turning a profit of, so they said, a hundred thousand dollars, having played in forty-odd places including amongst them a number in Canada, where on account of the Canadians was never at war with the Bull, and in fact was proud they had give him and his band a refuge after the Greasy Grass fight, his reception was generally better than in American cities, where he was sometimes booed and hissed for killing Custer, but he took this with what the newspapers of the day saw as the "typical stoicism" of the old redskin.

Finally, though, one place or another in the States — I often lost track of where we was at any given time on a schedule like that, sometimes traveling every second day — in some interview between performances he was asked if he ever regretted massacring the General, the old Bull jumps up from his seat and he points a finger at the questioner. I translate what he said as follows.

"You fool! Custer was not murdered. He was rubbed out in a fight in which he killed as many of us as he could. I have answered to my people for the dead on my side. Let Custer's defenders answer for the dead on his. I will say no more about this matter."

For his performance, which never consisted of more than just riding around the arena on the gray horse Cody give him, Sitting Bull sported an outfit of fringed buckskins and one of them big warbonnets whites thought, and think, all Indians wore all day, and then he went to sit in front of his tepee, where people lined up to buy cards like Annie's with his picture on them, which he signed ahead of time, tracing a signature I first wrote out for him, but when Annie looked at it she sighed and wrote a better one, easier to read, herself, but then Frank allowed as how it ought to be more masculine, so he added his improvements.

Every once in a while a person of the type they used to call a smart-aleck or whippersnapper, generally wearing a real thin mustache and slicked-down hair, would, so as to impress a lady friend, question them ready-to-go cards, asking me with a smirk, "How do I know they wasn't signed back in the tent there by you and not the Chief?"

"He'll write his autograph in front of you, but it will cost an extra dollar," I would say, and sometimes to save face before the lady in question he would have to shell out this sum, for which he could of bought a fine dinner for two, in which case Sitting Bull would "draw" his signature, for with some practice he had gotten pretty good at imitating the letters me and Annie and Frank had designed for him.

Another moneymaking idea of mine come about when some big fat fellow seeing the Bull's beaded tobacco pouch asked if he wanted to sell it.

When I translated the question, Sitting Bull put his hand to his mouth, hiding the smile I knowed he was making, doing this because he was supposed to look fierce whenever the public was watching. "Is there nothing that Americans will not buy or sell?" he asked me.

I'll admit I never myself been averse to turning a profit when one was offered, for while the best way of surviving in a place like Deadwood, Dodge, or Tombstone in the old days was to keep out of the way of flying lead, the best anywhere at any time is making money. But I got his point, and was about to tell the fat fellow to forget about it when Sitting Bull says, "If he needs the pouch I will give it to him. One of the women will make another one for me."

So I says to the white man, who, with a heavy gold watch chain stretched across his bulging vest and a sparkling tie pin not far below his second chin, looked like he could afford it, "Well, sir, you're talking about an article of great sentimental value to the Chief. He was carrying that pouch in his pocket at the time he scalped General Custer."

"I'll give him ten dollars."

I takes the man aside while the line of them waiting for their autographs moves up. This fellow by the way hadn't waited his turn but bought the place from the young boy who had: I seen that.

I says to him I wouldn't translate such an insulting offer, fearing for his safety when the Chief heard it.

Well, who knows how high I could of run him had I not had to get back — some sharper might try to pass off Confederate money or other shinplaster on Sitting Bull — so we settled on twenty-five simoleons, cash on the barrelhead, more than most people in them days earned for a week's work.

"You're getting a museum piece," I told him, "and we're throwing in the baccy."

In succeeding days I kept the Sioux women busy turning out more tobacco pouches and sold them all, not usually getting so much as the first time but once taking more from a drunk, and I was quite proud of myself, for I had to keep this trade from Sitting Bull's knowledge, to do which I would tell the potential buyer that the pouch being offered was the original while the one on the blanket alongside the Chief was a copy.

What I done was add the pouch sales to what come in from the autographed pictures and turn it over to Nate Salsbury to credit to Sitting Bull's account, less what the Bull kept as pocket money though he rarely got beyond the show grounds, because we stayed each place so short a time, but also because Cody was held responsible by the Indian Commissioner for the moral welfare of the red men who worked for him, which meant they wasn't supposed to stray into such fleshpots as was offered locally wherever we was.

But after I had been selling the pouches for a time, Sitting Bull says he wanted more money to keep on his person, so I give him some in coins before turning the rest over to Nate, and he put them in a little bag he carried on his belt, for Indian garments didn't have no pockets. I figured he thought of it like a medicine bundle of the kind Indians keep at hand for what you might call good fortune though it's more than that, until I mentioned the matter to Annie Oakley, and she told me he give quite a bit of money away.

"Who to? The other Indians?" I wasn't with him twenty-four hours a day.

"Why," says Frank Butler, "those ragamuffins that hang around his tent."

Cody would let a lot of young kids who looked poor into the show for free, and in them days there was plenty of such whenever we played a large city. Now, there wasn't no kid rich or poor who wasn't fascinated with Indians in general and Sitting Bull in particular, and if I have failed to mention previously how a bunch would hang around him until me or other whites, never him, shooed them off, it's because at that time they was not noticed except as annoyances. I don't say this to shock anyone of a later time; it's just the truth. Or I should say wasn't noticed by anybody but Sitting Bull.

So I brung the matter up with him soon thereafter, for I found it as strange as some of the white ways that puzzled him.

"If you kept that money it could go to help Hunkpapa children."

"Hunkpapa children don't need it that badly," said he. "They never wander among strangers, as if they have no family or friends, and if they are hungry and in tattered clothing, it is only because that is also true of the rest of their family."

Within their tribe and all the more so within a particular band and then their circle of relations, redskins stuck together in a fashion that the civilized didn't always practice, including myself, and he had shamed us, no doubt about it. But there was another issue here that an Indian couldn't be aware of, unless he was that pathetic kind called Hang-Around-the-Forts, and that was when you started to just hand out money, more and more would show up to get it including finally some who wasn't needy, and the giver might get disgusted and stop giving to anybody. I mention this fundamental problem of the human race because I'm not saying Sitting Bull had the universal answer, just that he was mighty generous to the offspring of the people who stole his land and tried to exterminate his own folk. That meant he was a fine man, but what made him great was he never in any way did anything in disrespect of himself.

Having said as much, I don't mean he was at all grim like the pictures usually show him, with them pouchy eyes, big nose, and scowl. The Bull was real interested in his appearance, call it vanity or pride, and when dressed for the show he braided his hair with intermixed otter fur and his leggings was decorated with porcupine quills. Under the big warbonnet his leathery face was brightly painted. When not attired for a performance, he sported a vest of brocade that reminded me of one Wild Bill Hickok once wore, a fancy shirt the tails of which hung over his pants, and a big white sombrero that was a present from Buffalo Bill. His deer-skin moccasins bore elaborate arrangements of sewn-on beads. Like all such footgear as worn by Indians they was soled with only a double thickness of leather, too easily worn through unless you walked only on the prairie, so I got him to let me have a cobbler stitch on rubber soles.

He wore a red tie, which I doubt he knowed was like the ones George

Custer sported from the Civil War to the ridge above the Little Bighorn River. His favorite piece of jewelry was a brass crucifix hung on a thong around his neck, and I don't mean just a plain cross but the real religious article, with a little pale wood figure of Jesus attached to it, and seeing this Annie told me to ask him if he was a believer.

Sitting Bull said a Black Robe, a priest, give it to him a long time before. He pointed to the little Jesus. "This doll is the image of a man killed by the white people for being too good."

This was on one of the occasions when me and him had tea with the Butlers along with cake, bread and jam, and other sweet things, all of which he favored, along with me, especially the ice cream we had on occasion, which I thought maybe he had never ate before but he had done so several times though he still didn't understand how it could be kept so cold unless the weather was freezing — and in fact neither did I nor do I to this day, except in a electric Frigidaire which wasn't yet invented then. I should also say Sitting Bull could use a spoon and fork just like anybody else, and he sure did so in Annie's presence, and afterwards he enjoyed examining her and Frank's remarkable collection of firearms of all sizes, calibers, and gauges.

The Bull was a real sociable person with an easier way than mine when in genteel surroundings amidst white women. I don't know how he acquired it, but he had a natural sense of how to act. For example, one of the first times he had ever been brung to a white town the people in charge took him, I guess as a joke, to a place like the Lone Star and he saw dancing girls. Now, not only did he tell about this in front of Annie, but he suddenly gets up and begins to imitate the movements of them dancers, kicking his legs and swiveling his hips in a hilarious way, but what worried me now was he had not only wore out his own welcome at the Butler tent but ruined mine as well.

But I tell you Annie laughed harder than even Frank and me when I saw it was okay to do so.

And who would think that the one time I got to the White House it was due to Sitting Bull, but it's true. The Wild West was performing in Washington, D.C., and on an off day Cody led a delegation of our Sioux to the Father's Tepee, headed by old Bull in all his finery, and we was let right in the door, which surprised me even though I knowed Buffalo Bill had a lot of pull by now as a celebrity and also was a Democrat, but as it happened President Cleveland was not home, so we just passed the time of day with a smooth-talking fellow who flattered the Indians without saying anything for which he could be held accountable and give us a tour of the ground floor, which I found real nice though not comfortable-looking.

But Sitting Bull had wanted to ask the Father, which is how the Indians called the President, if he couldn't do better by the Lakotas, and furthermore he didn't think much of a chief's home in which a visitor wasn't fed, so he was not in a happy mood when we went next to the headquarters of the U.S. Army and he had to shake hands with General Philip H. Sheridan, who was credited with the expression about the only good redskin was a dead one, though the Bull probably wouldn't of known that. What interested him was that Little Phil wasn't much taller than me but was about twice as heavy. Sheridan had been Custer's protector before the Little Bighorn fight, pleading his cause with President Grant, who despised him, and his defender ever since, maybe because he had a crush on Mrs. Custer, though I couldn't blame any man for that.

Now when that season come to an end in the fall of '85 at Columbus, Ohio, Cody sat down with Sitting Bull for a smoke and told him he had contributed greatly to the success of the Wild West and invited him to join up again when we started up next spring.

But the Bull had me tell Long Hair that while he liked him and believed himself and the other Lakota had been treated well, and he had been interested in seeing all the white towns, he missed his home so much he did not want to leave it again for so long. "I am an old man," he said. "I would not want to die in a place that is foreign to me." Though most of his homeland was now denied to him, he cherished what little was left, that cabin on the Grand River and a few acres around it.

Cody thanked him again and saying he would be welcome back any time he wanted to come, he made Sitting Bull a gift of the gray horse he had rode around the arena at every performance, which animal had previously been trained by our cowboys to do tricks like sitting down and raising one hoof as if to shake hands, and taking a bow at the end of its performance. The Bull wore that big white sombrero Cody had given him also, along with the rest of his street outfit including the rubber-soled moccasins, when he boarded the train home. Wearing any kind of white-man's hat, he usually put an Indian touch to it, like sticking a feather in the band or pinning a butterfly onto the brim, but this day there was something new.

I peered and asked, "Is that a little American flag?"

"Yes," said he.

"Does that mean you are showing you're an American?"

"It means I have fought against the American Army," says he. As I mentioned, he always had his own original slant on everything.

Me and him shook hands. I had become real fond of Sitting Bull, who reminded me a lot of Old Lodge Skins, the Cheyenne chief in whose band I was reared in my formative years. I says, "I hope this is not the last time we see each other."

"You are always welcome at my house," Sitting Bull says. "You know where it is." Then his dusky face, lined as it was to begin with, crinkles up like the terrain of the Badlands. It was the biggest smile I ever seen on him. "Maybe by the time you come to visit, you will have learned to speak good Lakota and not have to fill in with Shyela and the signs."

How do you like that? I actually begun to think I was perfectly fluent in Sioux, and though I was aware of occasionally using Cheyenne words, I didn't even realize I was also resorting to sign language, the use of which I guess was instinctive when trying to speak in a tongue I wasn't sure of, as in this case, or didn't know at all, like in the old days when us Human Beings talked to strangers. But I was touched by him pointing this out, which with a white person or maybe even another Indian would of been impolite, but by doing so on saying goodbye here, he was demonstrating a close feeling for me.

Me and Bill Cody had come with the group seeing Sitting Bull off on the train, and riding in a carriage back to the encampment, where all the animals was being readied for shipment to his ranch and the equipment crated for winter storage, Cody says, "I couldn't keep the Chief against his will, but he's been the main attraction this season and will be sorely missed. I can get all the Indians I want, but it's Sitting Bull's historical value that is hard to replace. He's the only savage most people know by name. It's that connection with Custer. What does it matter if the Bull didn't kill him? People like to think he did, and that brought all of us a nice piece of change this year."

Warming up on the subject of Custer, he told me about how he once guided the General from Fort Ellsworth to Fort Larned in '67. I had never mentioned my own association with Custer, either to Cody or, for that matter, Sitting Bull, but for another reason in each case. More than once I had heard the former's scorn for the now sizable number of fakers claiming to be Last Stand survivors and wanting him to hire them for the Wild West. As for Sitting Bull, I couldn't of explained to him how though intending to assassinate the General in revenge for the attack at the Washita which killed my Indian wife, I got close enough to knife him but never did.

Buffalo Bill went on to tell me a lengthy but not uninteresting story for them days in which mounts was so important, how him and Custer had a friendly rivalry as to which was the better animal, his mouse-colored mule or the General's horse, and of course the mule's endurance in rough country had it all over a thoroughbred's. Custer was supposedly so impressed by this that he wanted Cody to be his chief of scouts.

"But as we know, that never happened," said Buffalo Bill. "Else he might be alive today — though admittedly that was nine years before the Little Bighorn."

Now while Cody was talking in this wise, I got one of the best ideas I ever had, but before I could pursue it further we had reached the camp, pulling up in front of the headquarters tent, which was always distinguished by the mounted buffalo head hung over the entrance, and he says come and join him for a drink to mark the end of the season.

So I goes in and there is his partner Nate Salsbury and Arizona John Burke, and Nate scowls when Bill asked me to pour for old times' sake, on account of Salsbury thought my job was still private bartender. There ain't much you can do to change the impression others get of you without doing something big to distinguish yourself otherwise, and just interpreting for Sitting Bull had not been enough.

But as it happened — and this ties in with that idea I suddenly got while listening to Cody talk about General Custer — what I had been cooking up for a while now was no less than a plan to put together a show of my own, and I had been saving most of my wages towards that end, rarely leaving our encampment to visit any of the other attractions in the cities where we played. Yessir, this dream had replaced the one of running a dance hall I had entertained throughout the time I was in Dodge and Tombstone. I had long since come to understand that going into business for yourself was the way to succeed in this country, and how all of them big fellows what run things like J. P. Morgan and the rest, or their Daddies, got started. Then if you made a lot of money it would make up for any lack of polish, for if you could offer a better class of woman a life in which she could buy anything she wanted to make her happy, she wouldn't care if at the beginning you talked real ignorant, picked your teeth with a clasp knife, and so on, because she could teach you how to be a gentleman.

So here's the particular idea I got now: I would build this show of my own around a reenactment of the fight at the Little Bighorn, and the emphasis would be on the heroic courage of George A. Custer, a positive value rather than the negative fact that him and his men got whipped so bad. But don't get me wrong, I wasn't going to present anything that would downgrade the Indians. I have talked often enough about my regard for them, and it was my old childhood friend/foe Younger Bear what saved my hide that day at the Greasy Grass. But the truth remained that what whites would pay money to see was their own kind being massacred by savages, only in the end to have civilized principles come out on top. For the fact that it was the subject of a dramatic exhibition at all, performed in the major cities of the country, meant that though sustaining a momentary defeat, the right side soon won again as usual.

If I say this event was made for show business, I'm talking about a different matter than the actual killing of a lot of young men who had that morning of June 25th, 1876, got up, their lives in front of them, and by the middle of the day was corpses, naked and cut so bad nobody's Ma would of known him.

Anyway, at this moment I was feeling real good, having them drinks with Buffalo Bill, who I now started to think of as a competitor. True, it was him who give me my start in show business, and like they say I would always be grateful, but a fellow with the real goods had to strike out for himself sooner or later, the way Cody separated from Doc Carver, who had continued with a show of his own. It was also true that no love was lost between Doc and Bill, who had went to court against each other only recently. I didn't like to think the same might happen in my case, but I had to face the possibility. Successful folks have to put up with a lot of envy from them they surpass.

Well sir, the way I was getting grander and grander in my daydreams seems pretty pathetic at this late date, but there wasn't much wrong with that idea of mine — except that the preeminent showman of his time had already had it.

Cody hoists his glass and he says, "Gentlemen, I have arrived at the perfect solution to our problem."

Nate Salsbury, who the drinking hadn't mellowed on account of he wasn't doing any, asks sourly, "What problem?"

"Why," says Buffalo Bill, "the absence of Sitting Bull next season."

"A stellar attraction," says Arizona John, who was throwing down a deal of drink himself, "winning favor all over this blessed land of ours, 'Foe in '76, Friend in '85.' " He was quoting the slogan he had used to publicize Sitting Bull's appearance with the Wild West.

"It came to me while talking with Captain Jack just now," Colonel Cody goes on. "George Armstrong Custer, you will agree, is a name that rings a bell."

"A hallowed name," says Major Burke. "That of a true martyr of the modern age."

Salsbury, the only one present without a phony military rank, did not experience a rise in mood. "Just tell me what it's going to cost," he says, sourer than ever.

"Nothing," said Cody. "We'll have all the Indians needed, and the cowboys to play the Seventh Cavalry."

My heart falling, I says, "You're gonna depict Custer's Last Stand, ain't you?"

"I only wish I had thought of it while Sitting Bull was with us," says Buffalo Bill. "What a scene that might have provided! The old fellow leading the attack on the soldiers!"

"In all his feathered finery," Burke chimed in, "brandishing a fearsome tomahawk against the golden-haired General and his flashing saber: truly a battle of the Titans."

"At first I assumed I would myself play Custer, for the true-life physical resemblance was remarkable. But the young people would not want to see Buffalo Bill the loser in a fight with Indians. Someone else must portray the General, heroically of course. Buck Taylor is the perfect choice."

This was another example of Cody's genius as a showman. Disappointed as I was, I had to shake my head in admiring wonderment. Buck Taylor was indeed perfect, being six foot five in height and plenty visible to an audience at the distance at which they sat in the grandstand. He was already with the show, where he specialized in the roundup features — later to be called by a name not yet used, namely, rodeo — bronco busting, roping, steer-throwing, and all, and Burke billed him as "King of the Cowboys," who though "amiable as a child, has the titanic strength singlehandedly to hurl a steer to the ground by the horns or tail." Notice how "cowboy" here had lost both its Dodge City sense of a fellow who drove cattle up from Texas and then spent his wages on whiskey and harlots and the Tombstone meaning of outlaw or rustler, and was on its way to becoming what every young American lad wanted to be prior to the age of getting interested in the opposite sex: more than anybody else, Bill Cody was responsible for that.

I tried to salvage something for myself. "That's a real good idea," I told him, "but don't you think somebody ought to go to New York City and ask Mrs. Custer about it, and get her approval? I hear she's real sensitive on the General's behalf." I ought to mention that the Wild West had visited New York a couple of times, but I myself had never yet set foot outside the show grounds. I could of tried to look up Libbie Custer on those occasions, but I didn't. I was too timid, for I didn't have no excuse that sounded believable when I tested it on myself. Now I might have one.

As to why I never set foot in the place irrespective of Mrs. Custer, I'll admit this: I was still bluffed by a town of that size, coming from where I did. I had always thought of myself as smart when it come to the frontier, but considered myself no match for a city slicker when in a big town, especially one so full of foreigners including drunken Irish, though I wouldn't of wanted to say that to Frank Butler.

Speaking of who, him and Annie arrived at that moment, and Bill tells them about his plans for the big finale at next year's performances, and then he says, "Captain Jack here has asked me about getting Mrs. Custer's blessing. Well, my old friend Jack, let me assure you that having sent the gracious lady a written assurance that our exhibition will spare no expense to do credit to her gallant husband and deepen the luster of his glorious reputation as an American soldier and a man, I received her wholehearted sanction."

"So you don't need to send no one to see her, I guess."

Annie in her female way caught the dejection in my voice and, smiling prettily, asks me, "Why, Jack, are you sweet on the lady?"

And Frank says, "Sure, she's a comely one." Annie wasn't ever jealous of him praising other women, stuck on her as he was.

"Why," said Cody, "we all of us are devoted to this noble widow, Missie, and I'm sure I speak for you as well." He offered Annie a glass of lemonade, but she refused it, I think because she had heard about Salsbury calling her too stingy to buy her own.

"Colonel," she said, "there's nothing I would like more than to meet that great lady."

"That you will most assuredly do, Missie," says Buffalo Bill. "She has accepted my invitation to attend our opening performance."

So I'd finally get a chance at least to look at the lady on whom I'd had a crush for all of them years, much longer than the one I had on Annie, which was soon, by the fact of Frank Butler, converted to brotherly affection. But I had to be realistic and remember that it had been ten years since the only time I laid eyes on her, when she tried to board the *Far West* and ride up the Yellowstone to join her husband just before the Little Bighorn battle, having suffered a dream which foresaw his death, a decade of mourning: she might not still be as she was then, the loveliest woman I had ever seen. You will notice what I was doing here: protecting myself from another disappointment.

Well, that was the end of the season of '85, and Annie and Frank headed for Ohio, where her kinfolk lived. Cody returned to his ranch at North Platte, and having noplace other to call home and being welcome there, with anyone else who would drink with Buffalo Bill and listen to his stories, me and Pard went along.

14

Widow Woman

Now I ain't mentioned Pard for a while, but he was still with me and not getting any younger. Fact is, he had turned downright old, as it took me a while to realize, for seeing him all the time, mostly nowadays sleeping in my tent except when I brought in the grub or when he relieved himself, on which trips I went along so he wouldn't do it noplace in the encampment where it would make someone mad. Being with him so much I was slow to notice the gray when it first started on his muzzle, and if he didn't respond as quick as once to what I said, I thought he just wasn't interested in what I was saying or had got miffed because he could smell Annie's dog George on me after I would come back from visiting with the Butlers, not realizing he was getting deaf.

George by the way had died while the Wild West was in Toledo in Annie's native state of Ohio, and her and Frank give him a big funeral at the private property of a fan, burying him wrapped in the satin and velvet banner hung at the show while he was performing, with his name embroidered on it in gold, and the whole troupe come from B.B.W.W., including the Indians, some of whose women made wreaths and chanted their death songs, which you got to admit was more than a slight gesture on the part of people who might of ate him had they been back home.

Back on the ranch, it seemed Cody was so on the outs with his wife that he let her stay alone in the Welcome Wigwam, which meant the people he took home with him from the show had to jam into a smaller house on the property, which didn't rightly affect me and Pard, for we always bunked in a harness room of one of the barns. Bill was trying without success to get divorced from Mrs. Lulu, who hated everything he did including most of all the Wild West and had gotten him to put all his money and property in her name and didn't want to share it with him. Also she was real jealous of some of the female performers that had appeared with him in his stage plays and now, in addition to Annie, in the Wild West.

I might just say here that Buffalo Bill tried throughout the rest of his life to divorce Lulu and never did succeed. It wasn't easy to do in them days, not to mention that despite their eternal quarreling him and his lady had a deep attachment to each other though not hitting it off in the fashion of Frank and Annie Butler.

I thought Pard might perk up some when he got back to open country as opposed to the back lot of the show when camped in some eastern town or traveling in the baggage car every couple of days, but in fact as the weeks went by in Nebraska he seemed to get wearier, spending more and more time wrapped up in an old horse blanket and having to be nudged awake when the time came I thought he should visit the outdoors, like before I blew the lamp out at night, so he wouldn't be woke by the need to make water and blunder around in the dark, maybe getting kicked by a horse, for even his daylight vision wasn't what it once had been, nor his balance.

Pard was at the end of his life, but I wouldn't admit that to myself until it got to the point where he lost most of his interest in eating, for food is a dog's religion, of which you might say Pard was a priest or maybe even the pope: there had been a time when I had to sleep on my leather articles, including boots and belt, lest he chew and swallow such in the middle of the night. I would catch him eyeing many an animal big as a burro, considering whether he might be able to bring him down and have enough meat for the next week — make that two days, for though the size of the coyotes from which I always figured he come in part, he had a bear's capacity for grub, one emerging from hibernation.

Well, not wanting to turn this story of mine into a tearjerker, when so many of the people I was close to had died, most at real early ages, I won't dwell on the death of a dog who nobody had knowed well but me, for I don't count my brother Bill or whoever Pard come from before that, an Indian camp likely. He hadn't lived a bad life, for what dogs require is food and company, and I provided both, with him returning the favor when he could. It was ten years since him and me joined up together, plus he wasn't a pup when we met, so he had put in what was a lengthy lifetime for a four-footed creature of his day, and if you count it according to the difference between dog and man of seven years to one, Pard had lived twice as long as most of the people I ever knowed, Sitting Bull, not far beyond fifty, being ancient.

So one winter morning Pard did not wake up, staying under his blanket even after I had gotten the little iron stove so hot nobody but a dog could of come near it, as he would have if he could, drying his nose till it was like sandpaper, and if you touched it at such a point you would think him sick, but that was when he had been well. I knowed only death could keep him away from a source of heat in the icy season, but I pretended otherwise, patting the blanket and kidding him as a slowpoke who wouldn't get to breakfast before it was all gone into the bellies of others, but all I felt was a stone replica of a dog, hard and cold like it had been outside all night in the snow, but when I wound the blanket tighter and picked him up, he wasn't as heavy as I expected though having turned to rock, or even as he had been when alive, especially in recent years when he got less exercise but ate more. His spirit had obviously been real hefty.

I had quite a job with pick and shovel to penetrate the soil, having first to clear away a three-foot drift of snow and keep it off. The usual wind that blows across the plains, having no natural hindrances, was persistent as ever, but the work went quicker when I got below the frostline, and I kept going to some depth, for I didn't want no animal to dig Pard up and chaw on him.

When the hole was deep enough I let him down by the lariat lashed around the bundle at nose and tail, and I says goodbye to my old comrade in English, Cheyenne, and Lakota, and begged his pardon if he had come from another tribe instead and might of been insulted by the language of his enemies. The important matter was nothing concerned with his death but rather how him and me took care of one another over all them years of life, which death had ended but could not otherwise affect now it become memory. You can think less of me, if you want, for being so close to a dog, but that will matter to me about as much as it would of to Pard.

But I'll be the first to admit my life was wanting for human companionship, especially of the respectable female sort, and while I was sure looking forward to meeting Mrs. Custer when we reached New York

City during the next season, I knowed it would be more practical for me to get a girlfriend who wasn't confined totally to my imagination, and I thought maybe the latest young woman to join the Wild West might be a candidate, for though being a bit on the plump side she was comely, with a head of dark curls and neat little features, and she had a saucy way when talking to you I found quite taking, until I become aware that every other man had that same effect on her. Her name was Lillian Smith, and she was a sharpshooter, real good at that art, rivaling Annie Oakley, but what I didn't care for was her boast that with her arrival Annie was done for.

Of course Annie couldn't understand why Colonel Cody had hired the "California Girl," as Arizona John Burke billed her, for in addition to herself there was young Johnny Baker, who Annie had trained to shoot and was real good at it while having the sense not to compete with his teacher; but master showman that he was, Cody knowed not only that you couldn't have too many sharpshooting young ladies for the public, but the natural competition between them would keep each with a keener edge that she was likely to maintain on her own, for even such a levelheaded person as Annie was not above envy, her being all of twenty-six by this time, whereas Lillian was — well, let me first tell you an ironic particular. If you remember, when I first laid eyes on Annie Oakley only the year before, I took her for a schoolgirl. In the case of Lillian Smith, I figured she was about Annie's age. Fact is, Lillian was fifteen at the time. I reckon it was that "ample" figure of hers that misled me: the term was Annie's, who seldom spoke of Lillian without using it.

In truth Annie never had a good word for her professional rival, suspecting her of loose morals just because Lillian wasn't as prudish as her, and when I says after all the girl wasn't married, that observation put Annie on the outs with me for a while, and I tell you as happened so often with women it was me who lost on that deal, for I had too much competition from the cowboys to get far with Lillian (who within a year married one of them named Jim Kidd) and anyway she was a bit young for me though I never looked my age. Annie was cool to me for a time even after the thing with Lillian was over.

Now we spent the entire summer of '86 in one place, Staten Island, at a resort called Erastina, to which regular ferries come across the bay from the city, passing the newly erected Statue of Liberty. The opening had been preceded by a big parade through Manhattan, with all the Indians, the Deadwood stagecoach, the cowboys on prancing broncos, wagons full of buffalo, and so on, the star markswoman on her horse, wearing a fancy outfit of her own design and needlework, labeled OAKLEY on both sides, prominent enough so it could be read by the crowd as she went by. I doubt she would of gone to this trouble had Lillian Smith not been elsewhere in the parade, for when we was back in camp Frank had to bring the doctor, who found Annie had so bad an ear infection that blood poisoning had set in and she went to the hospital for a few days, rushing back while she was still weak so the public wouldn't have time to replace her in their hearts.

They never did, not taking that much to Lillian, who didn't have Annie's style and charm, nor figure, and while Johnny Baker was a first-rate shot and Bill Cody himself regularly performed, always from horseback, there was something special about a pretty girl with a gun. Men thought it was sexy, and I guess women wanted to be like her.

Now that Sitting Bull wasn't there nor my Cheyenne bunch, I didn't have no particular job, so I made myself useful, throwing up glass balls and clay pigeons for Lillian Smith, Johnny Baker, and Buffalo Bill to break, and giving Frank a hand with Annie's act. I also done some translating with the current troupe of Sioux, headed by an Ogallala name of American Horse. And if they needed an extra actor for the Deadwood stage during the attack by Indians, I might fill in, riding shotgun. Cody usually stuffed the interior of the coach with celebrities, politicians, or visiting foreign dignitaries, who got a kick out of being shot at with blanks and being in mock danger of being scalped.

But when the re-creation of Custer's Last Stand was being readied, I really had to be included. I still never managed to tell Cody of my personal connection with the real thing, how I was certainly the only genuine white survivor in the world. As for the Sioux now with the show, it was hard to tell if any had participated in that fight, for the white feeling against them that had killed Custer was still strong, so any which *had* took part might be leery of admitting as much. On the other hand, there was also plenty of whites, especially in the eastern cities, generally people who though having a horror of violence, admired Indians for being ruthless killers and would reward any as such, buying photos and souvenirs, like with Sitting Bull, so undoubtedly there was Indians ready to confess more than they had ever done. The event was ten years earlier by now: the young men had only been kids then, if they was anywhere near the Greasy Grass that day in June.

It took a while to get everything prepared for this act, like having some artists paint a great big canvas backdrop representing the valley of the Little Bighorn, which probably looked believable if you hadn't never seen the real one, and having cavalry uniforms made, and so on, and meanwhile we had to give the usual shows at the Staten Island site, where the attendance was so good, day and night (with gas, flares, and fires lighted for the latter), that Cody and Salsbury decided to stay in New York for the whole winter, moving the Wild West into Madison Square Garden as of that November, hiring a writer name of Mackaye to design a program that was more like a theatrical presentation than the previous series of exhibitions of riding and shooting.

The result was billed as "The Drama of Civilization," consisting of five separate parts, beginning with "The Primeval Forest," showing Indians and wild animals rented from a circus (some, like the African lion instead of a cougar, not authentic), and going through "The Prairie," with a buffalo hunt, a fire on the plains, and a stampede; the "Attack on the Settler's Cabin," the old standby from the very first show of B.B.W.W.; the "Mining Camp," supposed to be Deadwood, destroyed at the end by a cyclone so forceful it sometimes knocked over the stagecoach in reality, being made by enormous fans driven by steam power. The final act was Custer's Last Stand.

Between each of the above came an interval of the riding, roping, Indian dances, and marksmanship exhibitions from the show as done in the outdoor arenas. Cody, Johnny Baker, and Lillian Smith all did their specialties, but Annie Oakley's nose was still out of joint on account of the California Girl, so not only did she exceed herself with all manner of firearms, pistols, shotguns, and a variety of rifles — the people what ran the Garden had the roof raised twenty-five feet for the sake of the shooting acts — but she added tricks done on horseback, untying a bandanna from around her mount's ankle while hanging from a sidesaddle, picking one of her hats off the ground, and so on, while maintaining her personal modesty with costumes that despite this vigorous activity never revealed more of her leggings than when standing still.

We performed the Last Stand as long prepared for, and of course it was quite a spectacle with the Indians milling around the hillock where

Buck Taylor in his fringed jacket stood heroically, firing his pistol, and around him the cluster of blue-jacketed soldiers, including me as an unidentified sergeant, but of course it never looked much like the actual event or any other fight I ever saw between the cavalry and the Indians, for in real battles awful sights and sounds are interspersed with long stretches like time stopped and nothing is happening, and then you are looking at the fellow next to you, and a bullet hits him in the head and his brains splash all over you.

What I'm saying is not critical of the Wild West version, for in an association of several years now I had become a professional, and this was show business, with no blood spilled and the dying usually represented by the victim clapping a hand to his chest, so the audience could tell where he was supposed to be shot. The firing of blanks was a lot louder within walls and a roof than outdoors, and would of deafened me had Cody, a veteran of the stage, not warned us to stuff our ears with cotton. And of course it was him who come up with that finale which never happened but didn't actually change the historical truth of Custer's death while adding the positive character that Bill Cody always was at pains to represent.

After Buck Taylor clasped the bosom of his jacket and flopped down in fake death, the rest of us having previously gone under (myself taking care to lay out of his range, so as not to have his big carcass falling on me), and the Indians stopped yelling and shooting, in rode Buffalo Bill in a fancy buckskin suit and big white sombrero, leading a bunch of cowboys who scattered the redskins and joined Bill in a sad salute to the fallen while a lighted legend appeared on the canvas backdrop: TOO LATE.

Now if you recall, my own idea concerning the re-creating of the Last Stand had been to use it to get a personal connection with Mrs. Libbie Custer, so I was real excited when I heard she had accepted an invitation to attend opening night, but I had so many chores to do back of the scene during the early part of the show that I couldn't get out and see where she was sitting, which Annie told me on coming off her own performance was a box-seat section for guests of honor all festooned with bunting. And during the act itself, I couldn't look around the audience while shooting blanks at the Indians with my Springfield carbine, and soon there was too much smoke to see through anyway.

Right after the show was as busy for me as just before, for we didn't have as large a company as when outdoors and at moments of commotion everybody not one of the stars had to pitch in, getting the horses into their stalls, putting away equipment, moving scenery into position for next day's performance, so by the time this was done all the audience had long gone, Mrs. Libbie C. with them.

I found Bill Cody in the office him and Salsbury had back of the arena, and I says, "I wonder how it went over with Mrs. Custer."

"Take a pew, Jack," Buffalo Bill says, "and help yourself from the bottle yonder." Over to the side, Nate Salsbury and several male assistants was counting stacks of bills on a table. They was all wearing pistols, and standing to the side was a big officer of the New York police, with tall blue helmet and a handlebar mustache. I couldn't see no armament on him but a billy club. "And while you're there, pour one for Sergeant O'Leary."

"Now, Colonel," said the policeman with a big wink, "you wouldn't want me to defy regulations." But he throwed down the drink I handed him so quick his mustache stayed dry.

"As to the lovely and gracious widow lady," Cody said, "she congratulated us on our exhibition."

"You saw her?"

"She left the premises not three minutes ago, Jack, with her little all-female entourage. The saintly woman remains devoted to her departed husband, ten years gone. Would that she be a model to all American wives." No doubt he was thinking of his troublesome Lulu, but at the time all that mattered to me was I had missed the only person in the world I wanted to meet.

Right at this moment I was so disappointed I didn't care what she thought of the show, but I asked him anyway.

"How could she but admire it?" Cody says, "when its sole purpose was to spare no expense to deepen the luster of her glorious husband's reputation as a soldier and a man." He swished the whiskey around the glass, then swooshed it down his hatch. "I told her, 'Your presence on this occasion will attract the attention of all the good women of America, who will share your pride and my triumph.'"

"That's nice," I said.

"Let me tell you," says he, "how she responded. 'My dear Colonel,' she said, 'your exhibition is the most realistic and faithful representation of a western life that has ceased to be with the advance of civilization.'"

"Is she still real pretty?"

Cody piously lowered his eyelids, then raised them. "The lady is an angel," says he, with a hint of reproach in his voice, like the question was coarse. He was always holier-than-thou when talking about the ladies, and I ain't going to comment on that, except to note that it might of give Lulu a nasty laugh.

As if it wasn't enough to hear how close I missed meeting Libbie Custer with Buffalo Bill, when I dropped in on Annie Oakley, she tells me Mrs. C. had come backstage to personally congratulate her on her shooting and trick riding.

"Where were you, Jack?" asked Frank. "We said afterward, 'Too bad Jack didn't come round.'"

"I was working," I says with some bitterness. "I ain't a featured performer, you know."

I regretted that as soon as it was uttered, but to show you the kind of person Annie was, she says sweetly, "He's teasing you, Jack. Mrs. Custer invited Frank and me to tea on Sunday."

"But I've got an appointment with one of Annie's commercial sponsors that afternoon," says Frank. "I want you to escort Annie."

I tell you, they didn't come nicer than the Butlers. What I suspected from the first was that Frank never had no other business and that he just did it as an act of friendship, knowing of my interest in the lady. But here's the way men can sometimes be even when doing a favor: when later on I told him of my suspicion, he says, "You were doin' *me* the favor, Jack. My idea of a good time isn't lifting a teacup with my wife and some widow."

I worried the next few days I'd break a leg in some strenuous part of the show, like when the Deadwood stage ran into the cyclone or I'd fail to get out of Buck Taylor's way when he bit the dust as Custer, but I survived to dress in my best suit of clothes and a clean shirt with a new collar bought for the occasion and so tight at first I thought any tea I swallowed wouldn't get past my adam's apple, and me and Annie went over to East 18th Street, where Mrs. C. had her flat, Annie for once not in her shooting outfit but looking like a grand lady in a silk dress and a coat trimmed with fur and a great big hat like was the height of fashion.

Well sir, there she was, opening her door herself, Elizabeth Bacon Custer, who I had last seen when she was the lovely young wife of the still living General though his days was already dwindling fast by then, the sweetheart he wrote to most every day when separated from her, on account of whom he had once got court-martialed for joining her without permission in the middle of an Indian war.

He was ten years dead by now, and she had endured a decade of grief, but to my eyes was still beautiful as a forty-four-year-old woman, which was middle-aged for that time, and real old to the likes of Lillian Smith. Her eyes was still of that luminous gray, her hair yet of a rich and lustrous brown, that soft round face still with the blush of rose in the cheeks. She was wearing black, as I heard she done all the time ever since Custer died, but her present dress looked fashionable in its cut. She was of about my own height.

I didn't have no interest in any other human, including even Annie, when in the presence of Libbie Custer, who apart from her beauty and grace I was connected to in the most special way there was, next to having saved her own life: I had been with the closest person to her in all the world when he was rubbed out.

There was pictures of her husband all over the sitting room, atop every table and along the mantelpiece, as well as a marble bust, showing him in one or another of his many versions of uniform, almost always wearing stars, more often the two of the major general than the one for the brigadier, the brevet ranks he had gained in the Civil War and for which he had been called the Boy General, being in his twenties, whereas during the last decade of his career, the one he is best remembered for on account of how it ended, he had been but a lieutenant colonel in the Regular Army, though nobody ever addressed him that way. Officers was generally addressed by the highest rank they ever reached, as a matter of military courtesy, so you can't blame Custer in that regard.

I was, and am, trying to be fair to the man, who I think I made it clear earlier on, had always rubbed me the wrong way from the first I seen him, though I was already prejudiced by reason of his attack on Black Kettle's camp at the Washita, where my Cheyenne family was killed. I didn't like him no better after I seen him die — that, which will happen to us all, being no distinction in itself — but I thought he done it real well. He had lost the fight, his men, his lovely wife, his future, his military reputation, more than enough to ruin a man's sense of himself, but Custer never wavered in his absolute belief that he always done the right thing. If reality said otherwise, it didn't speak to him. I think I would of been fascinated by his case even without a personal connection, for I was exactly the opposite type, as maybe you have discovered, hearing about this life of mine. There has been little of my own motives I was ever sure of, and still less of my deeds. Looking from one angle, my existence has consisted of a series of regrets. I doubt if Custer ever had a single one. I think if God said to him in the Afterworld, "George, I'm going to give you a test. I'm going to turn back the clock to your arrival at the Little Bighorn, and you can do it all over again in the light of what you know now. Would you do anything different?" And Custer would say, "No, sir, nothing whatever."

It ain't that he wouldn't, but rather that he couldn't: that's always the thing to keep in mind about him.

Here I am, meeting Mrs. Libbie after all them years and instead of talking about her I am going on about her husband ten years dead and gone. Well, so it happened on the occasion of which I speak, led by her. She started off by saying how much the General would of admired Annie's prowess with firearms, and how he would share her own approval of the care Buffalo Bill had taken in reproducing the battle so accurately, though she admitted she turned her eyes away for the last moments.

When Annie complimented her about the book she had recently wrote, Mrs. Custer continued on the same subject, for the book was all about the General, and she said she wanted that, and the other writing she was doing now for the papers, to bring in enough income so she could apply most of her efforts into getting rid of the "monstrous" statue of her husband which had been erected at West Point.

When Annie asked her how she liked New York, where she had now lived for some years, Libbie said how kind the people had been to her, but her only truly happy memories was those from when she and the General visited the city, with its fine restaurants and shops and the theater that he so loved.

"Mr. Lawrence Barrett," said she, "was his closest friend, and his picture hung in Armstrong's study in our residence at Fort Lincoln."

Barrett was a famous actor of that day. There was some who said Custer picked up certain dramatic flourishes from him, but I assure you if there was any tutelage it went the other way. Nobody had to teach the flair to George Armstrong Custer, though none of the pictures here on display did him justice in that respect, as in fact most photographs did not, which was real peculiar and not true, for example, of them of Bill

Cody, who was always as handsome in pictures as in life, which I found was generally true of people experienced in performing: I reckon they knowed how to hold their face so it would catch the light.

Now, Lawrence Barrett could probably of taught that to his friend, for the camera of that time didn't do no favors for Custer. His color looks sallow and hair seems drab if not dirty and his mustache in need of a trim. His everyday uniforms look dingy, whereas the fancy attire he had specially designed for himself, with stars and brass buttons all over it, appears foolish. But I guess if you never seen the General on one of the spirited horses he rode, you can never get a sense of the figure he cut, the mount prancing and snorting, Custer giving the impression that he was restraining the animal only by the force of his will, showing what looked like an easy left hand on the reins while his right went to doff his hat and sweep it through the air. Too bad he died before Mr. Tom Edison perfected the cinematograph. (Edison by the way come to see the Wild West on Staten Island, and he too congratulated Buffalo Bill on it.)

Now Annie had introduced me, the way Cody always did when I was meeting someone for the first time, as Captain Jack Crabb. I had gotten so used to the title that I never thought about it, but all of a sudden now I had to do so, and it was an awkward moment.

Having talked incessantly about her husband for the first half hour or so, Libbie Custer suddenly looks directly at me for the first time and says, "Please forgive me, Captain. As the wife of a cavalryman, I am remiss in not asking which was your regiment? I am only certain that it was not the Seventh of my day, for I knew each of Armstrong's officers as if he were a member of my family, for in fact he was."

"Yes, ma'am," says I. "The title's honorary, so to speak." Now no man likes to lessen his credit with the ladies, who quite rightly admired our gallant military men, so I hastens to add, "But I was with the Army in other capacities. . . ." And here I hesitated, for throughout the ten years that I had to prepare for meeting Mrs. Custer, I had still never decided just what I was going to tell her about her husband's final moments. How much of what I could say would only cause pain?

For that matter, I had still to bring myself to a conclusion about the man. If I got to thinking about what I admired in him, I quickly reminded myself of the good reasons to think him basically an enemy. On the other hand, whenever I got to hating his guts as the bastard who, while the regimental band blared "Garryowen," rode down on that peaceful Cheyenne village on the Washita one winter morning, I remembered him all by himself, the way every person dies, on that hill above the Little Bighorn. At least he always knowed what he was, like his Indian adversaries, unlike me.

However, I never needed to worry when it come to Mrs. Custer, who after that briefest of acknowledgments of my presence went right back to her singleminded concern, as I expect she would of done even if I had a distinguished military career to brag about. Fact is, if she thought about it at all, she would probably have preferred me never to of heard a shot fired in anger, so the General could monopolize all the valor in the world.

Well, now you are thinking that meeting the lady at long last, I had all my illusions shattered, that she turned out to be the perfect fanatical widow for the most self-centered man of his time. But in fact I wasn't disillusioned at all and if anything the crush I had always had on her in my imagination was now as strong in reality though of a different nature. I begun to think that there must of been a side to Custer I never knew about, if a lady like Libbie could be so stuck on him.

Annie of course, being a woman and a happily married one herself, was interested in that subject without having my own personal connection to the General, who she knowed about only as the martyr portrayed in the press and also in the description Sitting Bull once give her of Custer, I guess thinking it would please her, for as I said before, the Bull wasn't nowhere near the General at the Greasy Grass: "standing like a sheaf of corn with all the ears fallen around him."

"There is a charming story that has been told by others," Libbie said, "of how my husband and I first met, as children, in my hometown of Monroe, Michigan. Armstrong had come from Ohio to visit his sister. I was swinging on our front gate, and as he walked by, I cried, 'Hello, you Custer boy!'" She made the first real smile since we arrived, aside from the polite kind, and it was like the sun come out. She must of had them dimples already as a little girl. She would of been just the right age to of said the same to me, had I been lucky enough to live on a street full of white porches in Michigan. I could just imagine her melodic voice calling me "you Crabb boy."

Annie too was real taken by this. "And you both fell in love right then," says she, leaning her head at a sentimental angle.

Mrs. Custer was sitting close enough to reach over and lay her hand on the back of Annie's. "Would not that have been delightful, my dear," she says. "But alas! this incident did not happen. It is fictional."

Annie's face fell at that news, and damn if I didn't feel disappointed too. Libbie had a way of taking others into her way of seeing things. So when she goes on and tells how she really met "Armstrong," who now and then, in an especially tender memory, she called "Autie," I got so caught up in the narration that even though I knowed how their courtship come out in the end, I was in real suspense during the account of the many months Custer begged for her hand, first from a reluctant Libbie, who was the belle of Monroe, sought after by everybody wearing pants, including some so bold they tried to steal a kiss but was rebuffed, and then after he had conquered her heart, from her Pa, a judge who was one of the pillars of society in the region.

In fact I still think it was remarkable of Custer to give so much attention to being a suitor when he was at this same time fighting in the Civil War, nowhere near Michigan, and not just serving his time, either. He was just out of West Point, where he graduated last in his class, having done little during his years there but pull pranks and gather demerits, but once he started to lead cavalry charges he become the Yankee J.E.B. Stuart and whipped the Rebs in almost every encounter, the result being he found himself the youngest brigadier general in the Union Army at the age of twenty-three. Finally even old Judge Bacon had to give in and accept him as a son-in-law.

Now, from the side on which I had been acquainted with the man, the aspect presented by his widow was new. I had heard of his brilliant record in the War, but what was mentioned most often by the fellows I had knowed in the Seventh Cavalry en route to the Little Bighorn before they was all rubbed out, was how much higher the casualties was in Custer's command than in any other, so that was another record set by the Boy General. My point in bringing it up here is to say I never thought about it while listening to Mrs. Libbie tell me about her hero, who she at first saw as just another young man she had to keep from being too fresh, also a person of no social standing, from a Democrat and Methodist family, while she was from a quality line and a product of the Young Ladies Seminary and Collegiate Institute.

For a little while anyway I got so involved in this account I was rooting for Custer, a young fellow trying to rise in the world. I felt some similarities to him, even at my current age.

"But at the source of my father's objections," Libbie went on, "was a chance event that occurred early in the War. He was returning home one evening when he saw, staggering along the street nearby, a thoroughly inebriated young man in an Army officer's uniform." She pursed her sensitive lips and looked ruefully into her lap, then raised her head with another smile. "Unfortunately my father recognized that young officer as the Custer boy, whom at that time I had not yet met!"

Now to show you how caught up in this I was, I took Custer's side: he was on leave from a war, for heaven's sake. Who was he to be criticized by some old teetotalling civilian? But I never said anything, and just as well, for Libbie goes on to say though it was true that young Autie was at fault on this occasion, only good come of it.

"It was the very evening that Armstrong's sister Lydia, whom he stayed with in Monroe, saw the same distressing sight, and thereupon exacted from him a promise never to be drunk again. Standing up erect as the soldier he was, Autie pledged, 'Such a promise is not enough! I hereupon swear never again to let any form of alcohol pass my lips.' And," said Libbie, staring at each of us in turn, "he kept that vow to the end of his life." She turned and looked at his bust. "There are many things the world does not know about my late husband. Would you think he would weep at a performance of *East Lynne*? Let me assure you he did."

So there was something I shared with the man, after all: tears come to my eyes during that same show, when I seen it in Tombstone, and I would of been embarrassed had not some of them miners, along with a number of gamblers and other good-for-nothings sobbed so loud at times you couldn't hear the actors speak.

"My husband," said Libbie, "had one fault, and on our honeymoon in this very city he visited a phrenologist who, after a thorough examination of Armstrong's head, identified that weakness."

I admit this statement took me by surprise, for I was slipping under her spell by now. "Is that right, ma'am?"

"Overdoing," she says. "The consequence of having an heroic supply of energy, and bravery, generosity, honesty, and goodness, the very traits in which his critics were and are so woefully deficient." Her sweet face become stern during this speech, only to smile again now. "I should add merriment to his list of virtues. At West Point, Armstrong was habitually last in his class because he applied his gifts to mischief-making and not to his studies. In his final year the subject at which he did worst was cavalry tactics! From which he went into the War and became, in his earliest twenties, the outstanding cavalry commander on either side of the conflict. There can be no question as to that truth. At Yellow Tavern, his Michigan Brigade met head-to-head with the renowned Jeb Stuart's Invincibles, and at the end of the day General Stuart was dead and Armstrong had prevailed."

This was the time when Custer couldn't be beaten and the origin of the famous "Custer's Luck." Now, I had fell into the mood in which I was momentarily eager to help Libbie in her cause. "I heard tell," I says, "the General had his horse shot out from under him more than once."

"Four times," said she. "Once his boot was shot off, and he came back to Monroe to recuperate with a leg wound so slight that we were soon at a dance." Her eyes sparkled. "A costumed dance, I might add. I went as a gypsy, with a kerchiefed head and carrying a tambourine." She leaned towards Annie and said, "You'll never guess Armstrong's costume."

Now if that had been directed to me, I might of said, without any ironical purpose of my own, "An Indian chief."

But what Libbie mentioned was a name I didn't recognize, and Annie didn't neither, for I asked her about it later. I'm going to speak it here the way it sounded, *Looey Says*. Not till some years afterwards, when the Wild West performed in Paris, did I find out what she said — which I remembered due to its oddity — was what the French called their King Louis the Sixteenth. Fellow who told me that was some rich Frenchman who was crazy about cowboys and Indians, like so many of them was, and he never got tired of watching *Coostair* get rubbed out in the show. When I told him of the aforementioned, he says I must of heard the wrong number for the king. It had to be *Looey Cat Horse* or *Looey Cans*, that is, the Fourteenth or the Fifteenth, as nobody would want to be the Sixteenth, for during the Revolution they cut his head off. I was so ignorant at the time that I thought this Frenchie had gotten it wrong: George Washington whipped the King of England in the Revolution, but certainly never chopped off his head.

Though neither of us knowed what she meant, Annie and me joined Mrs. Custer in a genteel little chuckle, and Libbie proceeded to give an example of Armstrong's wit at West Point which in fact I do still think was right clever. It was in a course in the Spanish language, and he asked the instructor how to say, in Spanish, "The class is over," and the teacher told him, so Custer got up and left the room, followed by all the rest of the cadets.

"Once we were married, I was often the target of his teases, and Brother Tom would join him, having been his confederate since boyhood in guying their father, and they were still doing it when he was an old gentleman."

At the Greasy Grass the Indians — some whites said Rain-in-the-Face personally — mutilated Tom Custer's corpse so bad I couldn't of told who he was had not his initials been tattooed on his arm: that's how I last seen him. Along with Tom, most of the other younger male members of the Custer clan was rubbed out: the young brother Boston, and the nephew Autie Reed, son of the sister Lydia to who the future general give the no-drinking pledge, and sister Margaret's husband, Lieutenant Calhoun. You couldn't disregard such a loss, even if you wasn't related to any of them. But the same thing happened to most of the Cheyenne families I ever knowed. No kind of grief is yours alone, no matter who you are, but it's only human to think otherwise much of the time.

But Libbie was thinking of the golden days now, and it was with a girlish giggle that she went on. "All of twenty-two, I was known to those two rogues as the Old Lady. It seems Autie could, by the universal rules of war, have commandeered a certain farmhouse in the Shenandoah Valley as his headquarters, but it was ever his practice politely to request and not simply take by force — after all, so many of his favorite West Pointers were now wearing gray — and on this occasion the old Dutchman whose house it was replied, 'Gentlemens, I haff no objections if you come in, but duh old lady, she kicks aginst it.'"

Well, she had many other stories about her all too short life with the General and I'm told went on to put them into a number of books that covered almost every day of the dozen years they was together, never allowing for no flaw in the perfect husband and peerless military leader, and either convinced most other people or anyway shamed most possible critics of him into silence so as not to rile her, who had suffered so much with no fault of her own, and loyalty in wives and widows was considered one of the prime virtues in a woman of that time. I never heard tell of her ever seeing another man socially in all the rest of her life except in a group. She was as much one of a kind as the late G. A. Custer had himself been, and I'm glad I met her, not only because of my crush, which I kept in that place in the heart designed to preserve such feelings forever, but also to give balance to my sense of the General. Though I doubt I ever could of learned enough to make me actually like him, I could at least see how she viewed the man and even feel for an instant anyway a personal regret that he had never survived that last campaign to go on a pre-planned Redpath Lyceum tour in the fall of '76 and lecture on how he had punished the Sioux and Cheyenne during the previous summer.

Unfortunately, this nice occasion as Mrs. Custer's guest ended on a sour note that probably nobody could be blamed for.

Mrs. Libbie was reminded again, when telling of some fancy dinner her and Armstrong was invited to by rich people, that her husband because of that long-ago vow couldn't taste any of the champagne and other luxurious wines, but never having made such a promise herself, she could and did personally enjoy them. Now, thus far the reflection was a happy one, but suddenly she saddened. "I have reason to believe," she said, "that the tragedy would never have occurred had his subordinates in Montana taken, and kept, a pledge against drinking."

It was true that when it come to Seventh Cavalry officers and boozing, some smelled like walking stills, but I doubt it had anything to do with their defeat.

However, at this point I was so sympathetic to Libbie, I foolishly chimed in, "Some of the Indians claimed a lot of the soldiers at the Little Bighorn seemed drunk." I think I have pointed out that redskins was inclined to say what would make white listeners feel better, and ain't it interesting that people whether red or white think being drunk is a good excuse for any kind of calamity? Whiskey or the absence thereof would not of changed the outcome at the Greasy Grass.

But I had stuck my foot in it to mention Indians in Mrs. Custer's presence. High color darkened her delicate cheeks, and into her eyes come a glint of hatred I wouldn't of thought possible in a lady of such tender sensibilities.

"Please never mention savages in my presence," said she, "or I must ask you to leave. I apologize: you are my guest, but I cannot abide such a reference."

Now you might believe there wasn't no depths I wouldn't sink to in fawning over the object of my besottment, but you would be wrong in this case. I didn't beg her pardon. Custer attacked that big camp on the

Little Bighorn expecting to kill as many warriors as he could. That it happened the other way instead was altogether fair. He got what he had coming, not in terms of revenge but according to the fortunes of war. But I too had had loved ones killed by the enemy, and when this happened as an adult I sure hated the killer — George Armstrong Custer. So I never thought less of her for her feeling.

Well, I had accomplished one of my aims, to finally meet the lady who I had thought about so long, and I was not disappointed by her. Libbie Custer was the sort of woman who a lot of men would of thought was well worth losing their life early for, if God demanded such a swap, and I might of been one of them. It turned out she went on to last almost as long as me, give or take a few decades, living till the 1930s. I never saw her again except at a distance, in a box seat at performances of the Wild West, to which, wearing a jaunty, feathered hat, she was a frequent visitor, but her and Annie become pals, passing many an hour together in embroidering and female palaver, and Annie was the better for it in her efforts to improve herself in genteel ways.

Speaking of Annie, when we left Mrs. Custer's place that day what she says was not about this occasion but rather how I ought maybe get myself another dog on account of missing old Pard so much.

Now I swear I had hardly ever mentioned Pard to her since telling her he died, a year earlier. So whether this was her womanly intuition or she was just reminded of the subject by her own purpose to replace little George with another pooch, I couldn't say.

"Well, if I do I reckon it will have to wait till we get back from over the water," I says, knowing Cody had told her as well as me of his latest bright idea, which for my money topped them all to this point. He was going to take the whole company across the Atlantic Ocean to perform for the Queen of England, the same that when I was a Cheyenne we called the Grandmother, who owned Canada.

Finally, in case you are wondering if Mrs. Custer gave us any tea, all I can say is I think she did, but I didn't pay enough attention to it to remember.

15

Grandmother England

OW AS WE ARE READY TO LEAVE IT FOR A WHILE I
realize I ain't said much about New York, the biggest city I ever
seen up to that point, and the reason I didn't is it wasn't the type
of place where such talents as I had, enabling me to survive out
west of the Mississippi, was very useful. I wasn't so green (which by the
way Libbie Custer called "verdant" when speaking of herself as a young
bride fresh out of Monroe, Michigan) as to buy the Brooklyn Bridge, like
the stories told about, for I knowed it was just newly built and unlikely
to be for sale so soon, and likewise as to the Statue of Liberty, and I was
aware that in a fine eating place like Delmonico's it wouldn't be right to
chew hunks of meat off the end of your knife or pick your teeth when
ladies was present or of course belch, for all them niceties was observed
in the better eateries of Tombstone. But I didn't know much else.

Cody however was as if in his natural element though his origins was
in the same part of the world as mine and he really had guided for the
Army, fought Indians, and shot buffalo. The difference was he had figured out how to get the upper hand over people who was socially superior to himself by being a romantic figure from the frontier, the most
unique American you could find, whereas every country had financiers
and politicians. So he had a high old time, dressed in his fringed buckskins and a hat with a brim so wide it wouldn't of stayed on for a second
in the wind of the Plains, entertained by the grandest people of the day
and their ladies, in what they called salons, which for a time I just
thought was fancier versions than where I spent so much of my life,
namely saloons.

Annie and Frank was popular around New York too, but they went across the river to New Jersey a lot, her being a small-town girl, and was even thinking of buying a house over there.

Fact is, when in the capital of American civilization I tended to revert in my soul to my primitive past, and felt more Indian than I had in years. All them people on the sidewalks and vehicles in the streets, with the elevated railroad roaring overhead, the engines spouting black smoke and hot sparks, and the noise! I could speak a couple Indian languages and what I hope I will be pardoned for calling English, also more than a bit of Spanish, but none of these was much help when trying to make myself understood on the streets of New York, and for my part I comprehended even less of what anyone tried to say to me. It seemed a place where everybody was a stranger to everybody else.

So I don't have much to report on outside the show except what had been true since about the day the Dutch bought the place for a handful of trinkets, namely people so rich their houses seemed like private little countries, with their own armies, and you never saw the occupants except briefly getting in or out of carriages (unless like Cody you was invited to their blowouts), and the roads where they lived was broad and kept amazingly clean of dung given all the horses what went through them, and then there was the other streets, the dirty, crowded ones, sometimes right around the corner from the nice ones, where at all times day or night you saw everybody who lived there, for they was all outside, jabbering in tongues I couldn't make head nor tail of, and the kids was the freshest I ever seen, cursing, spitting, swiping stuff from pushcarts, even relieving themselves in public.

Also there was a lot of politics in New York, or so I heard, for that's what you get soon as a lot of people gather together, and if it was bad enough in Dodge and Tombstone, think what it would be here.

But you can see me and New York having little in common as only to be expected in an ignorant hick like myself, and I won't disagree. After all, Mrs. Libbie Custer found it the place where she could live the rest of her life, which ought to be recommendation enough. I reckon my own position on the matter was put by our leading Sioux, American Horse, when he was interviewed by some New York newspaper reporter, me translating.

When asked what he thought of the place, that Ogallala said, "It is wonderful and strange, so much so that it often makes my head spin, and

I wish I could go out in the woods and cover myself with a blanket and try to make sense of what I have seen."

Every once in a while somebody would get the bright idea to expose our Indians to the higher-minded areas of the local culture, and vice versa, and a delegation of them would be hauled around to places like churches, for example that one across the East River in Brooklyn where the Reverend Henry Ward Beecher sermonized at length on Sundays. Now you might think this was cruel and unusual punishment for them, but it was not. As I've said more than once, redskins had their own tradition for longwinded oratory, so they tended to respect others with enough energy to keep a monologue going, irrespective of what was being said, which in Beecher's case they couldn't understand a word of, and I couldn't translate while he was talking and in fact didn't see no purpose in even summing up when he was finally done, but they enjoyed it though being uncomfortable on them pews of hard wood, till I told them it was okay to take their blankets off and sit on them. But when they did so, they was naked to the waist and shocked some of the old biddies in the congregation, who complained to me.

Another time we visited a school for children, and the Sioux sang their songs for the pupils, but when the principal wanted them to do a war dance, I turned him down after only pretending to ask them, for though they would of done it to be polite, I didn't like them to be thought of as entertainers aside from their professional work with Buffalo Bill's Wild West. I mean, when Indians danced to work themselves up for war, it was serious: afterwards they went out and killed enemies and scalped them, which ain't something that should be suggested to entertain American school kids, even though the children would of liked it.

The Indians enjoyed such excursions, which included visits to the notable sights around the city like the Statue of Liberty, which took a bit of explaining on my part: no, there was never a real white woman nowhere near that big and it wasn't a representation of George Washington's wife or Ma or Grandmother England who ruled Canada, though some who had seen the picture on the Canadian medals give to them what went north with Sitting Bull swore she looked like the same person, who if she was so powerful a woman must be of a giant size (what a surprise they got when they met the real little Queen Victoria a few months later!). And while they was naturally homesick when in such foreign territory, they liked all the beef they got to eat and the money they made just for being Indians. Unlike the whites with the show, they wasn't acting, except insofar as shooting blanks in the stage battles went. When the performances was over, Annie put away her guns and was Frank's wife, and Cody went out to dinner with his swells, but the Indians stayed Ogallala and Pawnee. This might be why when they started making movies in Hollywood about the West, the leading redskins was seldom played by the real McCoy but rather by white actors who was gangsters in other pictures, because Indians playing Indians wasn't make-believe.

Maybe I should explain that better, but I want to get on with the story here and say that all of a sudden Buffalo Bill's Wild West was attacked in the House of Representatives by some Congressman from Brooklyn for taking the Indians off their reservations to appear in a degrading spectacle for private profit. In that they was wards of the U.S. Government, this "Drama of Savagery" was being given under its auspices.

Now Cody lost no time in getting his influential friends to counter this with testimonials as to the educational value of his "exhibition" for both whites and Indians, amongst them another Congressman who said bringing savages to the East to see its wonders would convince them of the foolishness of ever again becoming hostiles. And of course nobody was better at shoveling it than Buffalo Bill when defending his favorite cause. "The so-called savage sports," he told some reporter, "are simply their everyday form of amusement in their own country." He pointed out that what the Indians did while in New York, visiting churches and seeing uplifting sights, was morally elevating. And then he added what he seen as the clinching argument, since he couldn't of said it for most of the whites with the show except Annie, least of all for himself: "Not one of them out of seventy-five or eighty has ever been known to be drunk since they came to this city."

Cody was especially concerned at this time, for the Indians was with the show only by permission of the Secretary of the Interior, and he wanted an okay to take them to England, along with the rest of the company, to perform daily for six months at a big American trade fair to be held during the celebration of Queen Victoria's half-century on the throne, the so-called Golden Jubilee. This was the most ambitious stunt he ever dreamed up, and the North Platte *Tribune* come right out and said he expected to make barrels of money from it.

Well, being such a successful public figure by now, he soon got the Government's blessing, and we all sailed for the Old Country on the last day of March in 1887, more than two hundred strong, of which almost a hundred was Indians, on the S.S. *State of Nebraska*. There was also a dozen and a half of buffalo on board, a herd of deer and elk, a number of longhorn cattle, and a couple hundred horses, mules, and jackasses, along with the Deadwood coach and tons of painted backdrops representing the terrain of the American West.

Now most of the Indians felt real queasy about this trip from the first, though as it turned out they wasn't worried near enough about crossing the ocean, for we was in for a ride even the sailors admitted later was rougher than usual — and let me say right off, there wasn't nobody on board no sicker than me. Like the Indians I begun the voyage with a sense of bad medicine. Most of this was because me and them hadn't never been afloat on a body of water too big to see across, but I personally also felt superstitious when our Cowboy Band, up on the top deck as the boat pulled out into New York harbor, started playing "The Girl I Left Behind Me," which happened to be what I heard the regimental band, not themselves going on the campaign, played as Custer led the Seventh Cavalry out of Fort Abe Lincoln towards the Little Bighorn. Not even thinking of the well-known indecent words to it, invented by forgotten soldiers, eased my mind now.

It took only one look at the crowded aisles and tiny compartments in the innards of that ship to convince the Indians to camp on the open deck, and I joined them, but it was uncomfortable even before the big storm hit us about halfway through the two-week crossing, lasting a couple of days, and I tell you even worse than being seasick is being so while hearing Lakota death songs for forty-eight hours and seeing Red Shirt, the leader of the current Sioux contingent, examine himself every day to determine whether the dream he had was true: that going over the water would cause his flesh to decay and fall off his body.

Even Cody was under the weather, no doubt soon learning, as I did, that though alcohol was the cure for snakebite, gunshot wounds, and consumption, it only made your heaving worse when you was tossed around on the briny. But wouldn't you know the person who would come through it best was Annie Oakley, who wrapped in an oilskin, spent her time on the captain's deck, watching him deal with the problem of keeping the ship afloat with a smashed rudder in an Atlantic storm. She was only disappointed at having to postpone the target practice she done from the deck on better days.

Well, we finally reached England without loss of life, human or animal, but it took me a few days on land before I stopped feeling I was still walking on a rolling ship and my appetite returned, but the Indians and Cody was quicker to recover, the former when it came to eating enough beef to replace what they had been too sick to swallow on board the boat, and Buffalo Bill regained not only his land legs but they was once again hollow when his English hosts was pouring at the big welcome celebration we was given.

The Wild West encampment and show grounds was at a place name of Earl's Court in the district called Kensington, west of what I thought of as downtown London, but the local English had their own terms for everything, such as the "City" as referring not to London in general but to their Wall Street. Anyway there was a lot of open land at Earl's Court, and we occupied twenty-three acres of it, setting up a sizable American town there of tents and tepees, Old Glory flying from the flagpole, with thousands of English, children and grownups, gawking at us from the sidelines even during the times between performances.

Cody was in his element with the British, even more so than he was back home, where he did have a certain competition from others also of frontier experience, but over here he was as special as you could get, and even before the official opening, a lot of swells cultivated his acquaintance and most of these had titles, beginning with the Prince of Wales, who got a dress rehearsal for himself and party, four days before anybody else got to see the show, which I believe come under the principle of "nobleness obliged," that is, if you're in some country where they got people with inherited ranks, you are obliged to please them, though I personally drawed the line at kissing anyone's hindquarters and so wasn't real happy when Cody asked me, of all people, to serve as guide or escort to the Prince while he was on the premises of the Wild West.

"Aw, Bill," I says, "I'm a redblooded American and don't bow down to no foreign thrones, or however it goes. Ain't you got nobody with better manners? Annie, for example."

"Missy has enough to do with her performance," says he, "and so do Little California, Emma Lake, and the other riders. As to the cowboys, they are all pretty crude." He said that to butter me up. "Besides," and here he raised his goatee as if in pious thought, "I don't know how close we should let our ladies come to His Royal Highness."

We had already heard of the Prince's rep concerning the fair sex. "Annie's got Frank to look after her," I says. "And Lillian's married now too."

Cody pours me another drink of Scotch whiskey, having exhausted the American stock as shipboard medicine for seasickness. At first it tasted bad enough to be used for a tonic, but it would warm you against the English weather, which had been rainy every day since we set foot in the country, shades of our time in New Orleans, though here the rainfall if not as forceful was even more persistent. "I don't believe that makes much difference, Jack. He'll be the next king of England, and we're in his country and in fact need his patronage. I believe all purposes are best served by having somebody like yourself act as his escort and my personal representative. After all, you've been with the company since the outset and can explain every aspect of the exhibition, and you can interpret if he wants to meet the Indians, which I am told he very much looks forward to doing."

Before royalty went anywhere, I soon found out, a lot of flunkies got everything arranged in advance: where they will get out of their carriages, where they will walk and sit (and relieve themselves, which can't be anyplace near where normal people do), and what to say when they talk to you, for you was supposed to wait till that happened and not start palavering on your own. Cody told me all of this, but I proceeded to forget most of it, being indignant that while it was true England was the Prince's country, we was his guests and ought to be protected against making mistakes by the natural laws of hospitality, which I tell you Indians sure observed if you went to their camps.

But before I get to my time with the Prince I want to speak of another concern. Cody had mentioned an Emma Lake as being amongst the female trick riders in our company, of which there was ten or twelve. There was too many people now in the Wild West for me to know them all or have occasion to recognize their names, and I hadn't ever heard this one before. It rung a distant bell, though it might not of done so in any other association, for "Lake" was not that unusual a name, but put it with professional performance of horsemanship . . .

I told Cody I would do my best to show the Prince around but not to expect me to remember every nicety asked for by these foreigners, and he says he had every confidence in me.

Then I asks, "Who is this Emma Lake, Bill?"

"The Champion Equestrienne of the World, Jack. She has appeared in Barnum's Circus. Of course we're billing her not with the name of Lake or her married name of Robinson but rather as Emma Hickok, daughter of my late friend, Wild Bill."

"You're just making that up?"

He winked. "Not exactly. Not long before he was assassinated, Bill Hickok married a former circus owner, herself a renowned equestrienne name of Agnes Thatcher, who before she married Mr. Thatcher had a husband named Lake and a daughter by him named Emma."

"She's Wild Bill's stepdaughter?"

Cody winks again. "Not to the letter of the law, but you can appreciate that she *could* have been."

This news hit me totally by surprise. I hadn't knowed Mrs. Agnes Lake Thatcher Hickok had ever had any offspring, let alone what had followed her Ma into trick riding, but then I never went out of my way to find out a whole lot about Wild Bill's widow on account of losing that money he had entrusted me to give her in case of his death. That had happened so long ago now it was easy to avoid the subject in the forefront of my mind, but it was sure in the back of it somewhere. After bartending in Tombstone and then working with B.B.W.W. I had accumulated another of the little nest eggs I saved up at various points in my life, with that persistent idea of going into business for myself with a Western show of my own, like a number of fellows had done with a certain success though nowhere near Cody's, for example, G. W. Lillie, who had been our Pawnee interpreter for a season or two, as usual acquiring a nickname, in his case "Pawnee Bill," but most didn't get far because, as I thought at the time, they didn't have no famous performers. I on the other hand being so close to the Butlers was sure I could induce Annie to join my show, for she had begun to sour on Cody after he hired Lillian Smith and them female riders like Emma Lake Hickok. Annie was a sweet person except when she had competition, particularly of her own same sex.

However, the arrival of this Emma reminded me of that long-standing debt. I never counted the wad of money Wild Bill give me, and didn't have no idea how much it amounted to. I might put together another roll that was around the size and weight of the first, insofar as I could remember them, but of what denominations? Then too, I got to thinking:

it had been a dozen years since Bill Hickok's death. Hanging around Cody and Nate Salsbury, as I done in my spare time to pick up as much as I could of what I understood least, namely the commercial side of show business, I was aware that money don't sit still over the years, or it shouldn't. It ought to grow, at least getting interest in a savings bank. So I undoubtedly owed more to his widow than Wild Bill give me in '76, however much that was.

More of this subject later on, though, for the job of guiding the Prince of Wales around the Wild West took all my attention at the moment, so I'll tell you about it.

I expected him to show up with more than just himself, for a person in his position travels with servants to open doors and take away his hat and coat, pass him a clean snot rag every time he blows his honker, etc., but I wasn't prepared for a quarter mile of carriages bringing along his Mrs. and three little kids, all four of which was princesses; his brother-in-law, also a prince but of Denmark and not England (which I wouldn't of thought was allowed); and a number of other people wearing silk hats and having titles from all over the place, including I believe France, along with a set of flunkies for each titled person, so the party filled so much of our grandstand it could of been a regular performance.

Cody of course was first to meet them, sweeping off that extra-large sombrero he wore for the occasion and bowing till his goatee almost touched the ground, which was a kind of compromise between the greeting that a member of the Royal Family had coming, but which us Americans, who normally don't bow down to foreign sovereigns, didn't like to give, so Buffalo Bill done what he otherwise delivered from horseback to the entire audience at the beginning of each show.

I'll tell you them people couldn't of been nicer, beginning with the Prince himself, who was a great big heavy fellow with a neatly trimmed beard and wearing regular gentleman's clothes, high hat and tailcoat and all, and not the robe trimmed with snow weasel and the jeweled crown I expected, as the Indians sure did, or anyway some fancy outfit signifying his position.

He was however the largest in his party, and he was quite a bit older than I thought somebody still a prince would be. Fact is, he should long since of been king had not his Ma lived so long, so that by the time he finally got the throne from her, not till '01, he had only seven years of life left for himself. Now the old woman could of retired any time before this, but the talk was she wouldn't do so on account of she never believed he had the right stuff for a monarch, having spent most of his life eating and drinking and frequenting females in the carnal fashion.

But I ask what else was there to do when you were waiting to become king? For that matter, I never saw exactly what there was for an English monarch to do even when on the throne once George III had lost America, after which I understand he went nuts, but that might not of been true, for the same Limey what told me that said George happened to be a German. You heard as many tall stories in Europe as you did in the saloons out West.

Cody as usual introduced me by my phony rank, so when me and the Prince sat down side by side in the royal box all decorated with bunting and crossed flags signifying the brotherhood of nations — the big fellow wanted me right at his elbow so everybody else was shooed away — he asks me what regiment I was captain in and if I fought against the Red Indians.

Now here was my chance finally to tell somebody of what I had kept quiet about for a dozen years now, namely my presence at the real Last Stand as opposed to the representation thereof in the show before him, but I was cautious even though he was an Englishman who would probably believe anything.

So I begun by just saying, "Well, Royal Highness, I have spent quite a bit of time with Indians both for and against, you might say, and been associated with the U.S. Cavalry in more than one capacity."

Before I got any further the show started with the music of the Cowboy Band and the march of the whole company around the area, led by Cody on his white horse, followed by the various contingents, quite a colorful occasion, and the Prince was real interested in everything but especially the Indians in their full regalia, every Sioux wearing a full warbonnet, and the lady sharpshooters and trick riders.

Of the former he says, "Splendid chaps, what? One wonders how they would match up against our Zulu. We had our own Little Bighorn, do you know? only three years after yours."

Ignorant as I was, I knowed the Zulus was colored, but that was all. According to the Prince, they wiped out a British force somewhere in Africa with a name I can't pronounce — it's got "sandle" in it — and then descended on a smaller group of English soldiers at a place called Rorke's Drift, who fought so hard that the thousands of Zulus finally stopped and admitted the English was brave and left without rubbing all of them out. Most of the survivors got the medal named for the person he referred to as "Her Majesty."

Without thinking, I asks, "Would that be your own Ma?" Then I seen the surprised look on his face and corrected myself. "I mean, your mother, begging your pardon."

I tell you when a fellow of his girth makes a hearty laugh, it is impressive, and before he was done one of his arse-kissers come along, I guess concerned the Prince might of been choking, but he waved him off and told me, still chuckling, "Right you are. She's my Ma. And once upon a time I was her papoose." He starts laughing again.

"Yes, sir," I says. "You'll undoubtedly hear a lot of other dumb stuff from me, so I'll beg your pardon in advance. I never tried to talk to a prince before. I hope you don't still chop off people's heads."

He winked and leaned close to me. "I'll send the headsman away on condition that you introduce me to some of your crumpet."

It took me a while to figure out what he meant, for at that time I wasn't yet aware of how the English call women by the names of pastry, like "tart" for a harlot, but I was helped by the fact that Lillian Smith had just passed by in the march of performers and in fact looked our way with a flirty flutter of her eyelashes, and now come the lady riders, headed by none other than the newest one, Emma Lake Hickok, who on passing the royal box made her horse rear up and dance a few steps on his hind legs. She was a nice-looking girl, fortunately not resembling that picture of her Ma in Wild Bill's possession.

"The only thing is, Your Royal Highness, all the ones I know is married."

"Isn't everybody?" says he. His wife was a real attractive lady, and he had them nice little daughters too, but they was all seated some distance away and I never seen him talk to any of them or look in their direction all day.

"Well, sir, you're the Prince of Wales and this is your country, but these girls got their American husbands along, who are cowboys."

"Indeed," the Prince says, "and they all carry six-shooters, so I had better mind my manners? And no doubt the redskin squaws are defended by their braves with tomahawks and scalping knives."

I realized he was having a lot of fun, saying these words. So when there was a minute between the various acts I would teach him some more from the Western lingo like "vamoose" and "hightailing" and "hawgleg" for a gun, and how the Indian name for Buffalo Bill, as well as Custer before him was Long Hair, and in fact I went further, him being a Prince and such a nice fellow: I told him that name was *Hi-es-tzie* in the Cheyenne language and *Pahaska* in Sioux. "Now when you meet the Indians later on, you say that to them and they will be flattered."

"Why," says he, in as close as an Englishman can come to talking normal, though I knew he was joking, "I'll be right proud to, ole hoss!"

"Not bad, R.H.," I says, having gotten tired of giving the whole title every time I addressed him. "And here's one which will give them Lakotas a laugh coming from you: their word for whites is *wasichu*. Now what that means is, 'they won't go away.'" He sure enjoyed that.

The Prince had a lot of questions beside what I volunteered. He already knowed far more of historical information about the U.S.A. than I did. All I could tell him was what a foreigner titled or not wouldn't easily learn, as neither would some American who never had my experiences. But I still never got around to mentioning how I survived the Little Bighorn fight, though he was real interested in that subject, especially when the imitation version started, beginning with the Cowboy Band blaring out with "Garryowen."

"Tell me, Jack," he asks, dropping the "Captain" after I abbreviated his own title to initials, "why are they playing that Irish air?"

"It was General Custer's lucky song," I told him.

"His luck changed, then?"

"I guess you could say that. But 'Garryowen' wasn't played at the Little Bighorn. He left the band back at the fort, along with the sabers and Gatling guns."

The Prince frowned in interest and pointed his beard at me. "You know a great deal about the subject."

Now there was an opening if I ever had one, but at just that moment, our Indians rode howling and shooting into the arena and attacked the little force of bluecoats clustered on the artificial hillock built of earth and rocks that had been carted in from the English countryside, in back of which was the painted canvas backdrop of the Bighorn Mountains, and he naturally wanted to watch that. And when it was over and Cody rode in "too late" and then assembled the entire company for a finale and the American and British flags was flown and the anthems of both countries was played, everybody bowing to the applause of our guests,

Emma Hickok having her horse dip down, one foreleg bent back, well, the moment was gone, for Buffalo Bill brung the principal performers over to the royal box, where he introduced them one by one to the Prince and Princess of Wales and the others.

Annie did something she boasted about later, real proud of her prudishness. When the Prince put out his hand for her to shake she ignored it and shook his wife's instead. I guess she figured he might tickle her palm or slip her a note asking her to meet him somewhere private. She got burned up at me when I says she went too far, but she was in a bad mood a lot these days on account of being jealous of Lillian, who by the way was real eager to give the Prince a long, warm handshake along with googoo eyes, though I ain't suggesting anything come of it.

After that the whole party went back to the encampment of tepees and met the people the Prince and all the English called Red Indians, and I didn't know why till somebody pointed out they owned that country of India, over in Asia, where the folks was brown, and in fact while we performed in London some Indians from India come to the Wild West, some in turbans and the rest of their native getup, but a number in the finest British suits, speaking real good English, in a musical accent often easier to understand than some of the whites over there. One of them told me a "cheeky" boy stopped him in the street once and asks, "If you're an Indian, where's your bow and arrow?" Even though I got the point, he figured I might be too stupid to do so, and explained, "Hell's bells, he took me for one of yours, you see?"

Great Britain also owned a lot of Africa full of black people, and I heard there was more in Australia who had been there all along, even before a bunch of white criminals went out from England to join them, and then of course the British had more than a toe in several places with yellow-colored folks, but the U.S.A. and the Spanish and Portuguee in South America had a monopoly on Red Indians, which was probably why the Prince was so keen on meeting them.

Red Shirt was the leader of the Sioux, and with Indians it's just the same as with whites, and wolf packs for that matter: when the top dogs meet, it's different from if just you and me palaver. For one, it's politer, and both sides are real careful in what they say, which is mostly flattery.

So the Prince allows as how he enjoyed seeing the Red Indians perform, splendid horsemen that they was, and dressed in their handsome costumes, very fit and manly chaps, and he was happy to see they brought their families along, and he found a place to work in the word *wasichu*.

In reply Red Shirt give a lengthy speech, to which the Prince listened as if he was fluent in Lakota and thereby showed he could do a king's job when the time came, which is to say look like he's fascinated by what he don't understand or care about, which probably pleases more people than if he knowed or cared.

Red Shirt never stopped for me to translate until he had finished all his remarks, which was a break, for I could trim away all but the essentials, which would of disappointed Red Shirt to know but relieved the Prince from hearing the whole works twice.

Now amongst the Prince's own remarks was how the Princess of Wales joined him in welcoming the Indians, so Red Shirt politely returned the favor. "He says," says I, "he wants to thank the Big Chief's wife for her nice words." When the Prince didn't get this, I explained. "He means Mrs. Princess." I called her that so as to differentiate between her and them daughters, who held the same rank, but I could see the Prince thought it was real funny, though again he demonstrated his command of the situation by not laughing lest Red Shirt think it was at him.

I then asked the Prince if he had something on him that he could give Red Shirt. "I'm probably out of order," I says, "and I beg your pardon, but you see, that's their custom when a great chief visits."

"Of course it is," he says quickly, and he was real mad at his assistants who should of made provision for gifts (referring to these people as "queeries" though that didn't apparently have anything to do with *heemanehs*). "What would be suitable, Jack? Perhaps my pocket watch?"

But I told him that or any gewgaws he was wearing, cravat pins, cuff links, or the like would be so luxurious they might embarrass the recipient and with his usual delicacy the Prince could understand that point. "You wouldn't happen to have some tobacco on you?" I asked him. "He likes a good smoke."

The Prince pulls a sizable cigar case out of his coat pocket and empties it into his hand and in the exact fashion of them tobacco-store Indians, extends it to Red Shirt, who takes them, making the sound of approval, "How, how."

The Prince drawed me aside while the rest of his party was getting back into the line of carriages drawn up at the show grounds. He had already thanked Cody lavishly and told Arizona John Burke to make free use of his name in promotions, for it was the finest thing he had ever seen. To me he says, "Jack, I think you are aware of how much we, the entire party, have enjoyed ourselves today, and I am personally in your debt for an educational and entertaining commentary. I can't wait to tell" — he starts laughing — "my Ma that she should make time in the fiftieth year of her reign to see this marvelous spectacle."

"Well sir," I says, "thanks for tolerating my ignorance, your R.H. You're a real nice person and I bet will make a fine king."

Now I'll tell you, I been arguing with myself about whether I should say any more about the Prince, for it's of an intimate nature. He never asked me to keep it quiet, but then the kind of fellow he was, he was probably assuming I'd act like a gentleman, even though I wasn't one. But he's been dead a long time now, and anyway I'm an American, so I'll just make a compromise and say he sent one of them "queeries" around in a day or so to invite me to a party which turned out to be in a grand private house, with the Prince and the other gents in shirtsleeves, along with a number of girls in less, and the food and wine was so rich I was sick next day, and that's all I'm going to report about it, except that the Prince was supposed to be incognito, so he wasn't called Your Royal Highness but rather "Bertie." He sure knowed how to enjoy himself.

Speaking of Red Shirt, he was as fine a looking man as I ever seen of any color and quite a dandy in Indian or white clothes. He also never minded talking to anybody who wanted him to, so them English newspaper reporters was always interviewing him and printing what he said at third hand, for he first spoke it in Lakota and then I translated it and finally they wrote their version in correct English — and by the way the English think because the lingo's named for them, they're the *only* ones who really speak it — so by the time it was printed it didn't sound much like what Red Shirt had said.

Once I translated it back for him from the newspaper, figuring like me he would be amused, but instead he was right proud of having spoke so beautifully, so you see Indians was just like anybody else when it came to vanity, and I wouldn't be saying this about Red Shirt had I not been vain myself about a mention in the press that said, "In the Sioux language Red Shirt is called 'Ogilasa,' as was pointed out by Captain John Crabb, an authority on Red Indian languages and the official interpreter for Colonel Cody's exhibition."

I made so much of that clipping in fact — or as they said over there, "cutting" — that Annie got tired of hearing about it, for fond of her as I was, I have to say she liked to shine alone like that star on her hat brim, and she wasn't in the best mood these days, even though she got a lot of attention from the English, who wrote about her as a "frontier cow-girl," with a "real Western drawl," though Little Sure Shot, born Phoebe Ann Moses, never went west of Ohio before she become Annie Oakley and never past Kansas afterwards.

The Sioux visited a number of places around town in their off-time, generally with me, and we seen a lot of famous sights like the Tower of London, where they used to lock prisoners up, which Indians didn't do, and kill them later on, which Indians of course did to their enemies as soon as they could. Also a museum full of dummies made of wax but you wouldn't of knowed it without being tipped off, so real did they appear, and while all the Sioux was amazed by this exhibit some didn't feel good about it, seeing it as a place of bad medicine, where they learned something new, namely that while the usual danger was that your spirit might be stolen from your body, in the white world the reverse was also possible and your body could be stuffed and mounted in a place where strangers come and stared at it. I don't think they believed them figures was actually made of wax, even after the people who ran the museum let them touch it.

Another time the Indians was invited to see a famous actor named Mr. Irving perform in a play about a German who sold his soul to the devil, and they was asked to put on their full warpaint as well as the feather bonnets and the rest of their savage getup, so they did, and we was seated in the royal box seats, where Bertie's Ma sat when she came, Grandmother England, which impressed Red Shirt and the others, and they enjoyed the tea and sweets served during the intermissions, but the drama never made no sense to them, Indian afterlife lacking in the idea of a nasty place where folks went when they died, for being bad.

However, Red Shirt, who had a knack for being gracious in whatever circumstance, told Mr. Irving afterwards he thought the play was a very interesting dream.

As might be expected in them days, when religious people was as active in England as they was in America, we was also hauled around to see a lot of churches, and over there these was considerably older than them at home, one for example being St. Mary's Rotherhite where the Pilgrims worshiped before sailing on the *Mayflower*, which I didn't identify for the Indians because I would of had to explain too many details some of which might of been uncomfortable.

And another time we was taken to Westminster Abbey, which ain't only a church but also a great big tomb for a lot of Englishmen who was real important in their day, so there's a lot more clutter than in even a church like H. W. Beecher's in Brooklyn, let alone the plain board building in Dodge where Miss Dora Hand went of a Sunday.

Now the Sioux took an interest in the fact that all them bodies was under the floor or in marble boxes with statues of their occupants sleeping on the tops, some wearing armor also fashioned of stone, for they wrap their own dead in a blanket and put the body on a scaffold someplace away from camp, so it can by natural means, including buzzards, gradually rejoin the elements from which it come, but they figured the English kept these important bodies here so they could display them from time to time at Madame Tussaud's waxworks.

Speaking of armor, they took a dim view of it, either in marble or in the original iron suits we seen at museums, once I explained it wasn't just a show costume you took off for an actual fight, for the Sioux thought a man cowardly for covering himself up so he couldn't get hurt, the purpose of going to war — except against the white man — being to gain honor, which was the opposite of keeping danger away. Also they wondered at the horse that could carry a man of that compounded weight, until we come upon some painted pictures of them huge chargers half again as big as an Indian pony, but they must of been mighty slow, too, and how in the world could a fellow in armor climb on a horse in the first place? Another thing that occurred to *me* was how did they take a leak?

But Red Shirt always thought well of Westminster Abbey, for he had a vision in which he seen girls with wings, and there they was, in stone figures at the abbey, and he give a serious speech on the subject to the newspaper reporters. I don't know if they believed him, but they liked to print what he said, for of course he had a different slant on everything they knowed, which was worth listening to if you wanted to get the most out of life, though I am aware that some people just enjoyed laughing at how simpleminded they thought the savages was compared to themselves. But here's something to consider: the Sioux didn't have no angels in their religion, so how did these get into his dream?

Four days after that dress rehearsal for the Prince, B.B.W.W. had its official opening, and if there had been lots of excitement in London prior to this, it was nothing like what happened after, for like I said it was the fiftieth year Queen Victoria had sat on the throne and everybody was celebrating anyway, and now the Wild West seemed a part of the Golden Jubilee, for both sides forgot our old quarrel with the English to remember America had started as a colony of the British Empire, so the Indians could be seen as originally theirs too, to be added to the blacks, yellows, browns, and them South Sea islanders that I heard a friend of the Prince's say was the color of a "well-roasted sweet potato."

But the highest point of all come five days after that opening show, for good as his word, Prince Bertie had told his Ma it was the greatest thing he ever seen and though her opinion of him was supposedly low, I guess she believed if he knew about anything it was being entertained — which might of been discouraging at another time, but in fact the Queen had been widowed a quarter of a century earlier and not having had to earn a living, could be even more devoted to her dead husband than Mrs. Libbie Custer, so she had mostly stayed inside her palaces all them years, in mourning. Now she had sent a delegation of her own queeries to Cody asking him kindly if he would bring his company to a "command" performance at Windsor Castle, which is how English royalty had to put the matter, not having any actual power (like Indian chiefs, incidentally), but Buffalo Bill replied, with all respect, that the exhibition was far too big to be moved from the grounds at Earl's Court.

Them queeries got all flustered at having to return with such an answer, for English entertainers never said no to the Queen, but Cody considered himself an ambassador and educator, not a showman, so stuck to his guns, and wonder of wonders, Queen Victoria decided for the first time in more than twenty-five years to be seen in public and to do so at Buffalo Bill's Wild West!

She done even more than that. At the beginning of every performance, one of the cowboys rode out into the arena carrying the American flag. Salsbury and some of the others was worried that doing so might insult the current head of the country what lost us as a colony a century before, but once again Cody held to his principles and as usual he was right to do so, for when Old Glory appeared in front of Victoria she not only weren't offended, but rose to her feet and bowed, and the rest of the big party what accompanied her in the flower-bedecked royal box did the same if they was ladies and took off their hats if men or saluted if in uniform.

To which the entire company of the Wild West, including the Indians and the Mexican *vaqueros* and everybody else sent up a cheer so loud I bet it was heard all over London. I don't think there was anything greater for Cody in his whole career, and afterwards he couldn't stop saying how it was the Wild West what finally buried the hatchet of the Revolutionary War.

Now the Queen's flunkies had said she could stay only one hour flat, so we should make sure the performance never went a minute over, but no attention was paid to that limit, either by our company or by Victoria, and we give the full program and she not only stayed for what ended up half again that long, but after the big finale she asked to meet the principal performers, amongst them Annie of course, and Lillian, who showed the Queen how her Winchester worked, and a number of Indians foremost of which was Red Shirt, with me interpreting.

When it was our turn, I forgot the instructions the queeries had give to Arizona John Burke to pass along to everybody about how to act when in front of the Queen, bowing or whatnot and waiting for her to talk first and when leaving to do so while not turning your back, for I always been polite to ladies, especially when they was old, and she was that all right as well as being real fat, but she had a real sweet face of just the kind you'd want in your own Grandma. What I ain't said up to now was the important thing about her for me: when she stood up for the American flag, I seen she was as short as a real young girl. It was heartening to know a person not even as tall as myself could rule the British Empire, and a personal surprise given my acquaintanceship with her great big son.

Anyway, I just stepped up to the royal box and says, "How do you do, ma'am, my name is Jack Crabb, and this here is Red Shirt, chief of the Ogallala Sioux, and I'm interpreting for him."

When I moves aside so he can step up, I seen a quick look of fear flit through her eyes, for though I was so used to the red-and-yellow streaks of warpaint on his face and the rest of his getup, which was much gaudier than he probably would of worn for a real battle, regular people attending the Wild West for the first time was not, especially if English, and the lady boss of the whole British Empire was worried for an instant when confronting this savage.

But Victoria hadn't been queen for fifty years for nothing and she recovered her natural manner right away, just the right mix of motherliness with authority, and she says, "Please tell Mr. Red Shirt that I am very happy to meet him and that I greatly enjoyed his performance."

I passed this on to Red Shirt, and he says, "Grandmother England, I have come a long way to see you, and I am glad I have done so." And then he walks away in the formal stride he put on for ceremonies.

I spoke quick, before Victoria or the others around her could get the wrong idea of this incident. "Ma'am," I says, "he's doing what Indians do to show great respect. He don't want to take up your valuable time. I know he has talked a lot to reporters, but it's their job to listen to a lot of windy palaver. You on the other hand have got to run England. Red Shirt appreciates that."

The Queen was smiling, as was the others in her party with titles, while them who was only in attendance on her scowled. "You are Captain Crabb," she says. "The Prince of Wales speaks highly of you."

"Yes, ma'am. I like him too."

Some of the flunkies grunted or gasped at what afterwards I guessed they thought was too free talk when it concerned royalty, but the Queen come close to chuckling. Having often had that effect on American people of note, from George Custer to Bat Masterson, I was accustomed to being taken for a character. I might of gone over better with Libbie Custer had I acted like the eccentric her husband in fact thought I was, but in general not being taken altogether serious give me freedom to say things others might not.

"He tells me that you are an authority on the Red Indians and have lived in their wigwams."

"Well, ma'am, I lived with the Cheyenne as a boy and I've known a number of Lakota, and I've fought against the Pawnee and the Comanche, and now you take the Arapaho — excuse me, missus, I'm running off at the mouth, but I ain't never talked to a queen before. Say, would you like me to take you around to the Sioux camp?"

The question caused more consternation amongst her attendants, but not on the part of old Victoria. She stands up, all not quite five foot of her, and says, "I should very much like to do that, Captain. Lead on!"

So there I was, a fellow with no education and no great place in life, steering the head of the British Empire around an Indian village in London, England. Tell me if that ain't as remarkable an event as ever happened.

Well sir, it was a real success for all. When we run into Red Shirt again, he had relaxed some from his official formality and he asked the Queen how come she hadn't brung her warriors with her, and she says because she knowed she was coming amongst friends. He liked that answer and everything else Victoria said to him, for she might of been old and English but she was real smooth in handling people. I could see where Bertie got his own technique, even if his Ma wasn't aware of it. Red Shirt told me that after speaking with the Queen he could understand why these people were led by a little old grandmother: she had a great heart. But of course all I passed on to her was the last portion of that commentary.

Being a woman, Victoria was interested in the Indian females, and they returned the favor for the same reason. One of them, Rain Bird, had seen her likeness on a medal and now asked why she wasn't wearing her crown, and another Sioux woman asked if she was an actual grandmother in addition to being one for all her people — which I thought was a real sensible question — and Victoria answered everything with the gracious good humor I guess royalty specializes in, at least since they lost the ability to abuse their power, though it would be hard to think of Queen Victoria chopping off anybody's head even if she could of.

When she got through shaking hands with all the Indian kids which somebody white had put in a lineup according to height, she had me tell them what lovely-looking children they was and how proud she would of been to have them amongst her "subjects," which was the British word for anyone in the empire regardless of color, but I found it hard to translate into Lakota, so said simply, "to have you among her peoples." Now to at least one of the older boys, in his teens, this got transformed into the Grandmother saying she wished she owned the Indians, for she would of treated them better than the Americans had. But for all that I was impressed by the Queen, I knowed the real reasons Sitting Bull was treated better for a while in Canada was two: first, there wasn't many other redskins in that part of the country, and second, there was even fewer whites. Even so, he was eventually invited to go back where he come from, for Indians usually proved to be a pain in the arse if you wasn't one of them, on account of their stubbornness. Show them railroads, electric light, New York City, steamboats, St. Paul's cathedral, Buckingham Palace, these folks who never found the wheel on their own and lived in hide tents, and they still insisted on staying Indians.

"Captain Crabb," the Queen says when she was ready to leave, "as heartily as my son recommended you, he was not quite enthusiastic enough. Without your help I should have understood little of the Red

Indians and should probably not have had the courage to visit their squaws and papooses, for I confess I was alarmed by the war dances of the braves, with their shrieks and wild contortions, and thought their faces cruel, and the sham battles were even more frightening. Poor gallant General Custer!"

"Congratulations on being Queen for so long, ma'am. I think people our size tend to last longer." I might even of winked at this point, for I felt at ease with her: shows you how being ignorant is almost as good as being short. I added, "Well, it was real nice of you to come see us, and now I'll say what the Texans do: y'all come back, y'hear?"

Queen Victoria liked the Wild West so much she commanded another performance the following month, this time at her out-of-town castle at Windsor, where she preferred living over Buck House, as one of Bertie's pals called it, and having made his point on the earlier occasion, Cody now complied with her wishes and went to the considerable trouble of transporting a number of his people and animals out there.

At the Windsor train station the Indians got out and it was somebody's idea they walk to the castle in a double file through the little village. This sure had an effect on the townsfolk, who, like their queen had been, was scared and thrilled and having the time of their lives, especially them little English kids, the fairest-headed and palest-skinned any of us had ever seen, owing to the fact that the sun was almost as rarely encountered in that country as a Red Indian in paint and feathers walking along the High Street.

Well, I'm going to wrap up this account of that first foreign tour, with a lot still untold, for I still got quite a bit of my life to relate and I don't know how much time is left in which to do so, so just let me conclude with a few notes of possible interest.

Bill Cody continued the kind of social life he had in New York, only over here his friends was both rich *and* titled, and as to females I mention only an actress named Katherine Clemons he saw perform and thought fine-looking, and I do that only because I don't know he was on a personal basis with her though later on he did lose money financing a flop play she brung to America. I probably wouldn't mention *any* women in connection with him was it not for Lulu, his storm and strife, accusing him of being too intimate with a number, including Queen Victoria! But I doubt he could of been too active with the English ladies on that trip, for much of our time over there his daughter Arta, an attractive young lady, was in London with him and enjoyed the same high-society life and you can be sure was kept away from the cowboys and of course me.

We stayed over there almost a year and after the first months in London went all over the country, which ain't in fact all that big, something the English got tired of hearing especially from the Texas cowboys, but otherwise B.B.W.W. continued to be all the rage in the Jubilee year, when there was also plenty of celebrations for Victoria, with illuminations and fireworks, and souvenirs such as teapots modeled after the Queen's head and canes with similar knobs and a lady's bustle what had a music box concealed in it which when she sat down played "God Save the Queen."

Nor did our Indians lose their appeal, and they was invited everyplace, and wherever the Sioux went I was sure to go as well, so can thank them for social life on a higher level than I could ever of gotten in on by myself. I'll just mention a couple examples.

There was a bunch of men who had what back home would of been a lodge, only over here they was of a better class, and they met to eat dinner once a week at the Savoy Hotel, wearing dress suits, calling themselves the Savage Club. Now it seemed like a good joke to invite some actual savages to a function, so they asked Buffalo Bill to bring along some of the Sioux, which he done, and I wouldn't of participated if the Indians was treated with disrespect, but they wasn't, the club having been named for one Dick Savage, an old poet of years gone by who come to a shameful end, so the joke was actually on the whites and self-inflicted, which type of humor appealed to the English. Anyway, the Sioux liked the meal, on account of there was lots of beef, and Red Shirt give the members a nice speech and said when he got home he would send them a pipe to hang on the wall to remind them of their Lakota brothers.

Another place the Indians visited was the British Parliament, where we set for a time in the gallery, and the Sioux, I expect, understood as much as me, but though they liked oratory of a religious or spiritual character, which they could identify without knowing the language it was in, they hadn't no taste for the sort of thing legislators talk about, and when later some Lord from the House thereof asked Red Shirt what he thought about the place, he says to me, in Lakota, he didn't think highly of it.

Ordinarily I would of translated it in my own style, but at this moment I had gotten tired of that redskin's superior airs, much as I admired him, so I asks, "Don't you think it is rude to say that when you are a guest in this big beautiful council lodge where for hundreds of years chiefs like these have met to discuss the affairs of their people?" Naturally I didn't add, *And not in some tattered hide tent with their faces all painted and dried scalps hanging from their belt.*

"No," Red Shirt said in his literal way. "He has asked me what I think, and I have spoken the truth. This is not his personal home, is it? It belongs to his whole tribe. We are just looking at it. We are not guests, for they aren't feeding us. Answering a question truthfully cannot be bad manners. If someone thinks he might be insulted by the answer to a question, he should not ask it."

In all my association with Indians, I won mighty few arguments with them, I tell you. So I turns to this Lord and shrugs. "Begging your pardon, sir: in regard to what you asked him, 'What does he think of Parliament?' he says, 'Not much.'"

We was in the lobby of the building and surrounded by other Lords as well as the newspaper fellows who followed the Indians whenever they left the encampment, and when this man busts out in a great big haw-haw and repeats Red Shirt's words in a loud voice, the whole bunch roars with laughter and shouts, "Hear, hear!" And being polite folks, all the Sioux joined in as well though that wouldn't normally be the kind of joke they could recognize as such.

Buffalo Bill's Wild West shipped out for America from the port of Hull in May of '88 and thank heaven the ocean was not so stormy this time, which the Indians believed was due to our heading home, a more natural thing than going to perform for strangers, though they never regretted doing the latter.

Not being seasick, I could give some attention to that obligation I owed to Wild Bill Hickok's widow, for here I was, on the same vessel as her daughter Emma, so first time I seen her on deck alone, standing at the rail, looking at that endless expanse of water, something I did myself on occasion, I stepped up and told her I greatly admired her talent on horseback. "I been riding since the age of ten myself," I says, "but I could never come close to what you do." She could dance the Virginia Reel on her mount, and make the animal stand up on its hindlegs and bow, all this while riding sidesaddle, which our female riders done in the modest style used for family shows, straddling a horse being considered indecent by many in that time.

Emma was a real nice-looking dark-haired young lady, and always on the lookout for a respectable woman who could put up with me, I regretted she was married, for we had a connection, unbeknownst to her, through my friendship with her late step-dad.

She thanked me now and says she too had got started early, but in her case she had the advantage of having as teacher her Ma, who was a famous circus rider.

"Why," says I, "she wouldn't of been Agnes Lake Thatcher? The one what played in *Mazeppa?*"

"One and the same," says Emma, real pleased. "She will be happy to hear that you remember. Did you see a performance?"

"Indeed I did," I lied. "In St. Louie some years ago. I believe I heard she is retired now and living in Cincinnati." And when Emma says that was true, I asked, "If I wrote your Ma a letter about how much I admired that play, would you send it along to her with my compliments?"

"That," says Emma, "would be very thoughtful of you. As a performer yourself" — she believed me a member of the cowboy troupe — "you know how much it means to be remembered." Then she says why don't I just write direct, and gives me the address which she knowed by heart and I took down with a pencil stub on my shirt cuff, which was one of them detachable kind, along with collars, so you didn't have to get the whole shirt washed every week.

Now all I had to do was try to figure out what I owed the Widow Hickok and send it to her.

So that is my account of the first visit to the Old Country by Buffalo Bill's Wild West and also me, except for two more items. The first is that one of them fellows that went to the Prince's parties asked me if I was related to "that chap George Crabbe."

I replied in an expression I picked up in England and thought clever at the time, "I haven't the foggiest," and said I never kept up with any relatives except one brother and one sister and had regretted that.

Having taken another gulp of champagne and squeezed the ample figure of the girl on his lap, he spouts the following:

"Fled are those times, when, in harmonious strains,
The rustic poet prais'd his native Plains."

I finally got it out of him that old George, now bygone, had been quite a poet in his day. Sounded like he might of been a cowboy as well. So I might of come from a more distinguished family than I thought.

The other matter is that when we was well out to sea Red Shirt happens to mention to me, sort of by chance, that some of the Sioux had gotten left behind in England.

"Are you sure about that?"

"No," says he. Indians was never strong on counting and in consequence tended to be cheated by white traders, and especially Government officials, who was geniuses at manipulating numbers.

"I'll look into it," I says. Who was responsible for the Indians in our company was always doubtful, so far as I could see. I believe Cody and Salsbury thought it was Red Shirt, but Indians didn't have a concept of authority like whites: they didn't tell one another, whoever they were, what to do. So in boarding the ship, they would leave it up to the individual to do it or not. Also they never did anything according to the clock, so some might show up after the ship had sailed. Now you might think I was the one what should of herded them up, but though I have just said that Red Shirt didn't have the authority a white man would of had in his position, nevertheless I wouldn't want to usurp it. If this seems a contradiction that's because you don't know Indians as well as I did.

Anyway, I took the matter to Nate Salsbury and he did some checking around and come back and said that was right, a half-dozen Sioux couldn't be found after a thorough search of all decks and even the engine room of the *Persian Monarch*.

I went back to Red Shirt and so informed him.

"So I told you," says he.

"We're too far across the water by now to turn back."

"I think they'll stay over there," says he. He didn't show any worry: they was Sioux warriors, with the same high idea of themselves as the Cheyenne. Also, had they not been big hits with the British? Red Shirt said they could go to the big camp, by which he meant London, and be fed at the lodge of the Untamed Society, which is what he called the Savage Club in Lakota.

16

Her Again

UFFALO BILL RETURNED FROM ENGLAND AS THE
"Hero of Two Continents," so called in the papers, and most
everybody in the troupe felt so good about our success in a foreign
country that when he said he wanted to open right away at Erastina
on Staten Island, they all was real keen to do so except for some of the
Sioux who was homesick and went back to the reservation, though more
stayed on.

My friend Annie Oakley had left B.B.W.W. after the London engagement and her and Frank went over to Berlin, Germany, where she performed for the German version of the Prince of Wales, namely Crown
Prince Wilhelm, the same who later become Kaiser Bill and fought
against us in the First World War. But that was in the future. At the time
of which I speak, the Butlers come back on their own to the U.S.A. and
Annie went on Tony Pastor's vaudeville circuit, doing her shooting act
in various theaters around the East.

All I knowed was that they had fell out with Buffalo Bill, I figured on
account of Lillian Smith, though they never said so and I didn't ask. After that tour Annie even joined the competition, in the form of a rival
show run by a fellow name of Comanche Bill and then switched to that
managed by Pawnee Bill Lillie, our old friend from B.B.W.W.

Now Pawnee Bill already had a lady sharpshooter, who happened to
be his own wife, but the Lillies was shrewd enough to give Annie top
billing.

When in New York, Annie and Frank stayed at the apartment they
had rented opposite Madison Square Garden, and I visited them there

on occasion, as did Mrs. Libbie Custer, though not at the same time, and by my request — which was out of respect for the lady.

Now, as to my plans for getting in touch with Mrs. Agnes Lake Thatcher Hickok, I hadn't yet done so, for I wanted before making any monetary payment to determine how much cash I had accumulated in the North Platte bank to which a certain portion of my Wild West earnings had been sent from time to time. More of that later. Right now I'm going to get to the subject of a closer connection.

We had been back on Staten Island only a month or so when after one of the daytime shows I was in Cody's tent, having a drink with him and Arizona John, sitting in a camp chair facing away from the entrance, when behind me comes a voice I recognized immediately but with feelings that couldn't of been more mixed, so I won't even try to name them all even if I could, aside from the one that made me want to hide.

"Colonel Cody, I should like to speak to you about an important issue."

Buffalo Bill lowered the glass and rose to his feet. "By all means, young lady. Please do come in and sit down. Captain?" The last was for me to vacate my chair, for there wasn't any other except that occupied by the ample rear end of "Major" Burke. "And may I offer you a glass of iced lemonade?"

"Thank you, no, Colonel, but I'll accept the chair."

All this while my heart was pounding, and not only in fear. I kept my head lowered as I got up from the canvas chair and moved over to the side of the tent, not holding the seat for her nor even looking in her direction.

I guess she waited till she sat down before saying the next. I wasn't looking. "Colonel Cody," she says in that cool voice I remembered so well, though it had now been ten years since I last heard it. "My name is Amanda Teasdale, and I am director of the New York chapter of Friends of the Red Man."

Cody always put on formal airs when encountering respectable members of the opposite sex, and I expected him now to make the introductions, but he didn't even introduce Burke, which was considerable relief for me. The stern tone in Amanda's voice had took him by surprise. Remember, he had just returned from England, where Queen Victoria had fell all over him — by which I don't mean what Lulu accused him of but rather that Her Majesty had been real flattering.

So all he says was, "Yes, Miss."

"I don't know whether you are familiar with our work," Amanda says. Cody had recovered to the degree that he could say, "And invaluable work it is."

"I'm delighted to hear you say that, Colonel. Frankly, I had assumed perhaps unfairly, that you would be hostile to our organization."

"Young lady," said Buffalo Bill, now back at full strength, "as I am my-self both an admirer of the fair sex, and I expect one of the original best friends of the American or, as our British cousins say, Red Indian, I as-sure you that the combination of the two names is one to which I pay the greatest honor."

And Burke, silent until he got the cue from his boss, chimed in with, "Hear, hear," another expression picked up in England.

"Oh," Amanda says, "I thought your first claim to fame was as an Indian-killer."

If when fighting redskins Buffalo Bill was as cool as he showed himself under this kind of fire, he done a good job at it. "Miss," says he, "with all respect, you may be mistaking me for others. Far from killing our red friends, I give them gainful employment, with higher wages than many white men receive for hard and brutal labor, chopping at a vein of coal a mile under the earth, breathing noxious vapors, or in hazardous employ-ment in some foundry, splashed by molten steel, or in a manufactory —"

At this point Amanda interrupts him. "Please spare me the rhetorical flourishes, Colonel. I of course refer not to your show but to your boast-ful accounts of killing Yellow Hand."

"My dear young lady," Cody says, in just the tone to annoy her, whether he knew it or not, which is to say a kind of pitying patience, "I was defending myself. *He* was shooting at *me.*"

"Indeed? Yellow Hand had come to seize *your* home?"

John Burke spoke up at this point. Ever the press agent, he says, "Miss Teasdale, I am setting aside a block of tickets for yourself and any num-ber of members of your organization. Lately the delightful term 'Annie Oakleys' has been coined for such free passes, taken of course from the name of the little lady who has brought nothing but honor to your sex. Let me explain the derivation of the term —"

"I have just seen the show," said Amanda. "A large part of it consists of shooting at Indians and having them play dead. It's the most degrad-ing spectacle I have ever seen."

Cody spoke in courteous exasperation. "It is not a *show*, miss, but rather an exhibition of great historical and educational value. We have made every effort to be absolutely accurate in our depictions, and we have been rewarded by universal commendation from those who participated in the actual or similar events."

She spoke sneeringly. "How many Indians have been heard from?"

"You must recognize the name of Sitting Bull," said Cody. "Once the most implacable foe, he was happy to join our company two years ago and stay an entire season, profiting handsomely in both money and acclaim. A pity he's not at hand to correct your mistaken impressions. But a number of Sioux remain. You are free to go back to their encampment and speak with them without any supervision from myself. If you are not fluent in Lakota, Captain Jack here will be pleased to interpret."

So the moment had come. I turned and said, "Good day, Amanda."

She had started out real comely ten years before and only got better-looking in the interim, rather than the usual reverse, at least in them days when time took its toll quicker, her hair a richer and older gold, her eyes of an intenser blue, her features more clearly defined without getting harsh, and she had filled out some without putting on an ounce in excess. Also she was now real fashionably dressed in the fashion of Mrs. Libbie Custer though in livelier colors, in her case a lavender dress and a fancy hat. You could see why Cody had started off not as glib as usual. I only wondered why he hadn't stayed that way longer, but as you know, I was always at a disadvantage with that girl.

She now gives me a glance of little regard and asks, "Do I know you?"

"Well, it was some time ago," I says, "and I —"

"Move out of the shadow, please," says she, squinting.

So I did as asked, and I took off my hat. "I got more forehead now and also this mustache. Name's still Jack Crabb."

"Why, Jack," says she. "Of course it is." And she smiles nicely, something I don't recall seeing her do much if any back then as a real serious young woman, which in fact was my crude fashion of telling a respectable girl from one who wasn't, if appearances was otherwise deceiving: the former didn't have much humor, whereas you could always get a laugh out of a harlot.

Now you recall how I left that Indian school, in a fairly disgraceful style, and though Wolf Coming Out had told me he explained to the

Major that I had not been at fault, he didn't know no English, and the Major no Cheyenne, and that would of been a complicated thing to convey in sign language, so despite Amanda's nice manner I remained uneasy. I also considered it quite possible she didn't remember me, for I didn't know why a person on her high level would of done so. I had gotten to having a high idea of myself, the way I went over with not only Prince Bertie but also with his old Ma the Queen, but all it took was one sight of Amanda to lower myself in my own eyes.

Not wanting to remind her of the school, I asked, "How's your folks? They still live in Dodge?"

"My parents are no longer alive."

I expressed my regrets, and Cody and Burke done so as well, but Amanda was finished with that topic. She stood up from the camp chair in one graceful motion without apparent effort, and in that fitted satin dress she was as stately as any of them titled females I seen in Great Britain and a good deal handsomer than all.

"I'll take you at your word, Colonel," says she. "Lead me to the Indian camp, Jack."

Now Cody returned to the surprise he begun with. "Then you really do know our friend here?"

I have just been saying how small my opinion of myself was when in Amanda's presence, but when Cody agreed with it I was irked, and raising my nose says, "Miss Teasdale and me was colleagues at an Indian school." And then of course could of bit my tongue.

But she never batted an eye at the reference, just inclined her head at Cody, ignoring Burke to whom she had not been introduced, and swept out of the tent with a *swish* of attire as majestic as any I heard at Windsor Castle.

I caught up with her outside. "Amanda, we'll meet the Sioux directly, but I just want to explain how I happened to leave the school the way I did."

She walked as fast as she had when younger, on them longer legs than mine, but with a more conscious sense of herself, and a number of the cowboys from the troupe was hanging about and didn't fail to gawk at her, though they would of been scared to say anything aloud, for she was obviously a lady of high class. But I knowed I'd get kidded next time they caught me alone.

Amanda glanced at me now and said, "I believe it was self-explanatory."

You might think that remark relieved me, but it was so indifferently spoke it made me question whether she had any idea what I was talking about. So I persisted. "I was just worried about what you might of thought, with all that commotion." She made no response to this, so I tried a more general approach. "The Major is a mighty fair man, I'm sure of that."

"The school closed some years ago," Amanda says. "The missionary fund ran out of money and Government policy changed, for the better in my opinion. Religious bodies were really at a disadvantage in dealing with the problem, as demonstrated by the Major's experience, for by no means could he be personally blamed for every difficulty."

She might of got more beautiful over the years and finer dressed, but she had acquired a way of speaking like somebody who sat in an office and talked only to others of their own kind.

We had went past the tents of the white performers and was approaching the Indian camp, and that's what Amanda's attention was fixed on right now.

She stopped for a moment and shook her head. "Must it be so shabby?"

"If you ever seen a real village in the old days, you'd call this luxurious," I says. "There ain't no scalps hanging from a lodgepole, and everybody's got plenty to eat, good beef, not dog, and they're getting paid for just being Indians, not doing anything that could be called work, not to mention that white people buy tickets to watch them."

A lot of this was hypocritical, for having lived with the Cheyenne I didn't have no horror of scalps, and in the days when there was plenty of buffalo and we could get to them, the periods of hunger wouldn't be long, and as for dog, it was good eating and done only on special occasions. Finally, Indians never needed money till the white man took over. But I was giving the arguments Amanda could understand, having been educated.

However, she did not. Like most people with a cause she heard only herself giving her own side.

"They're treated as animals!" says she, tossing her hatted gold head in indignation.

"Come on, then," I told her. "Let's talk to some of them and hear what they got to say."

I led her to the tepee where Two Eagles lived, on account of he had a real nice wife named White Bear Woman who was a good cook if you liked Indian grub, and I did and ofttimes had a meal with them, for I also enjoyed the company. I'm not saying only Indians appreciated their vittles — you should of seen the Prince of Wales tying on the feedbag! — but they applied themselves to food with the wholehearted focus of them who even in the midst of plenty allowed for the possibility of future want.

White Bear Woman had a fire going in front of the lodge and a pot of something already cooked and placed at the side of the hot coals to keep warm while she made fried dough in a skillet.

She was a plump woman with a round brown face, and she smiled at me when I greeted her and said the most frequently repeated phrase in any Indian language I ever heard of: "Do you want to eat?"

I says to Amanda, "She's inviting us to supper."

Amanda was staring real sorrowful. To me she says, "Can you find some polite way to refuse? Please don't hurt her feelings."

I told White Bear Woman that Yellow Hair thanked her but was at that time of the month and didn't have no appetite.

Just as I expected, this Indian female says, "But that's the best time to eat, to replace the strength that is lost! She is too skinny to begin with."

The Indians never had that theory about feeding a cold and starving a fever: there wasn't any disorder they didn't treat with grub if they had any.

"I don't want her to think I am spurning her food," Amanda says, now smiling nervously down at White Bear Woman, who wasn't looking up but rather testing the hotness of the skillet with a fingertip she quick withdrawed and sucked the heat from in her lips.

"You can be sure that would never occur to her," I says, "for she thinks she's eating better than you do."

Now White Bear Woman's several kids had begun to collect for the meal, but though they had been with the Wild West for a time, the littlest having in fact been born during the first season when Sitting Bull was with us, they had been brung up to be polite and not pester white visitors unless of course the latter wanted to buy the pictures of themselves and their offspring which the Indians sold.

Which didn't mean they wasn't staring at Amanda.

Now let me give her credit for not acting like many white women who visited the Sioux encampment: she never exclaimed about how cunning the little girl looked in the fringed dress and beaded headband or spoke to them in "Indian"— *me give heap wampum*, and so on — or worst of all, talked like they wasn't there, for by now all the Sioux could understand some English words, especially when applied to themselves.

On the other hand, Amanda was stuck with the idea she brung with her that these people was being misused, so the presence of them kids made her feel worse.

"I see that we've come at an inopportune time," she says.

"It wouldn't be if we sat down and fed with them."

Amanda frowned. "Let me explain. It's not that I think I'm too good to eat with them, nor is it I have a distaste for their diet. I'll take your word they have food they enjoy eating and in sufficient quantity. But if I joined them, I would be certifying that I believe their being here is right."

"You put more meaning in a pot of stew than it warrants," I says. "Indians deal a lot with the spirit when the situation calls for it, but I never knowed them to be anything but direct when it comes to food. They eat whatever is available, for you got to eat to live, and you got to live to die. That last might sound idiotic on the face of it, until you realize that for them life is a circle."

"That may well be," Amanda says, "but you are speaking of the past. The Indian's situation was changed altogether by the coming of the white man. Whether or not that was deplorable, it took place and we must deal with it as a fact. Putting the red man on display as a performer is not the solution to his plight. Instead, it maintains him as a hopeless anachronism, by celebrating the savagery he must put behind him else he has no future whatsoever."

You couldn't doubt her sincerity. After all, Amanda had been at this work of saving the red man for years, a cause that had little interest for most whites and none at all for many. It's just that if you knowed Indians at all and how personal they was, by which I mean they was actually human, talking of them only as a problem, even when you was watching them get ready to do the most essential thing anybody living can do, namely eat, seemed to miss the beginning point.

Right now we had to move upwind of the skilletful of hot lard, in which the raw dough was sizzling away under a cloud of steam and spitting grease drops at us.

White Bear Woman looks up from her squat and says, "You ought to get a healthier woman to sleep with. You could cut yourself on Yellow Hair's sharp bones."

"You have too keen a tongue. Two Eagles should give you a good beating."

I got to explain that me and her was kidding one another, and I had mentioned her husband, to which she said he'd get hurt bad if he tried it. Sioux women wasn't easily mistreated.

Amanda didn't get any of this, of course, and might not of understood even if she had spoke Lakota: I reckon it was a coincidence that she now asked about the head of the family.

"I reckon he's inside the tepee or playing cards someplace and will show up when the food's all ready to swallow," I says. "The cooking is not his business."

Amanda looked around at the rest of the camp. There was females in front of the other lodges, doing the same as White Bear Woman, and kids as well, and where the meal was ready, the whole family including the menfolk was sitting on blankets, eating.

"It's real homey when you get onto it," I told Amanda. "This is pretty close to a real village. It's more comfortable than it might look. If the weather was wet, they'd all move indoors and make the fire there. The smoke goes up and out the top, where the lodgepoles cross."

"It is all very quaint," Amanda said, "but is this how people should live in the United States of America at the end of the nineteenth century?"

"They're Indians, for heaven sakes. They always lived like this and don't see nothing wrong with it."

"But they can't continue to do so," says she, her chin firm and her eyes fixed, "except in a show like this. It's all make-believe. Their old way of life is dead and gone."

She was right, no doubt about it, when it come to the long run, but I had learned by that time in my own existence to take what advantages was offered by the short run while waiting for the long to come about, else you might end up without nothing, and if anybody was skilled at making the most of what lay at hand, it was an Indian, just as it was whites who specialized in the future. I seen myself as a mix of the two, though better accommodated to the redskin way of making the best of what was available, for there was no getting away from the fact that it was less complicated.

"Amanda," I says, "if we hang around much longer we're gonna have to eat."

"There was no point in my coming here," said she. "Colonel Cody simply wanted to evade a discussion of the issue. That these people might stoically accept their lot or even think it's better than some is beside the point."

I expressed my regrets to White Bear Woman, who had just flipped the fried dough over on the other side, with less spattering this time, for it had soaked up most of the grease, which is what made it so tasty. The smells of that and the stew, as well as the roast meat being cooked over the fire in front of a neighboring tepee, had set my mouth to watering.

"Speaking of eating," I told Amanda, "I want to do it someplace. We don't have a performance tonight. Would you want to eat supper with me?"

Now this might not seem so earthshaking an event, until you understand I had never before in my whole life asked a woman out in the city sense of that term, I mean, I had ate many a meal, under various conditions, with various females, including of course my white and Indian wives, but never asked any on a "date," as such, and I was a man of forty-seven years!

I reckon I was fortunate she never took me up on it, for though I had hung around with the likes of the Prince of Wales, I had never doubted my position was as an entertainer and it didn't matter if my manners was bad, but I sure wouldn't of wanted to give Amanda any more reason than she already had to look down on me by not knowing how to feed in a fine New York eatery.

Now till this moment Amanda had been so distant that I still doubted she remembered me, or anyway I preferred that doubt to thinking it didn't mean much to her whether she did or not, but all of a sudden now she saw me as a person.

She even produced one of her rare smiles. "I'm sorry, Jack. I've been preoccupied. Yes, let's eat together, but not at one of those over-priced restaurants." I had an impulse to tell her price was no object, in case she thought I couldn't afford it, but was checked by the suspicion that her real reason might of had to do with my manners or appearance. She went on, "And they are much too noisy for conversation. Why don't you come home with me to my flat? I'll make a meal, if you don't mind something simple."

"Why, Amanda," I says, trying to be easygoing about it, "that's real neighborly of you." But I was in a state of great feeling. I won't say excitement as such in case you might believe I mean indecent, which wasn't it at all. If I never before asked a lady out to eat, neither had one ever invited me to her house: that the first such turned out to be Amanda was the kind of thing I never could of imagined.

By the standards of a later day it took a long time to go anywhere at that time, but relative to that era, moving around New York was swift. We steamed across to Manhattan on the ferry and then took the elevated railroad uptown. I didn't marvel that a girl from Kansas knowed her way around the city, for Amanda always had a natural authority when it come to civilized matters, but she told me it had took her a while to get on to the best way of handling herself in New York, where it was more than a simple thing of avoiding the areas and persons who seemed unrespectable as in Dodge, for there was too many of both here and ninety-nine percent of the people you encountered was strangers and didn't care what nobody thought of them.

The style that seemed to work best was to act at all times like you knew what you was doing and nobody else did. She says that both parts of that was necessary for it to be successful: neglect one, and you left a gap for somebody to ride through and trample you down — the language is mine, but that was her theory, and I expected she was right but thought it too bad a young woman of such refinement had had to become so cynical here in the East.

It seemed to me her flat wasn't too far from Mrs. Custer's, though I never was sure where I was in any city, even Manhattan, where north of the Wall Street area the streets was regular as a gridiron. I could find my way across untracked prairie or forest where I had never previously been, but I needed a guide when in New York or London or Chicago, where I was distracted by the presence of so many people, vehicles, and buildings higher than two stories, and when you got traffic, you had a lot of noise: cursing and the cracking of whips, and whether you was on that elevated railway or anywhere in its vicinity, you was made deaf to any other sound. How any human person could stand to live permanently in such a place was beyond me.

I thought the outside of her building was ugly, being covered by a scaffolding of iron fire escapes, but Amanda's flat was real nice, with bright gaslight and pictures on the walls of the parlor and thick-holstered furniture in green plush.

"This is real comfortable," I says, instead of complimenting her on the furnishings, which I thought was nicer even than Mrs. Custer's but I was afraid she might think worse of me if I said something dumb about them.

I was wise not to go further, for she says with disdain, "It is certainly ugly." It turned out she had rented it in the furnished condition. I guess she didn't spend much time there, at least not in the sitting room. The surprise to me, though, was she proved to be a good cook, producing as fine a plate of scrambled eggs and ham as I had tasted, and I mean no faint praise in saying as much, for that was a dish I ate a lot at cafes all over the country, and too often it was like a leather glove, but Amanda's was fluffy as a cloud.

We ate in the kitchen, which was my idea as being more homey, but Amanda with a skillet and wearing a plain apron over her finery was still not in the least domestic — unlike Annie Oakley who was, wherever her and Frank hung their hats, but was also a lousy cook, so though she done a lot of needlework at home, they ate most of their meals out.

Amanda's coffee weren't bad either, though I would of preferred it boiled a little longer on account of that was the way I had drank it all my life, cooked down real bitter and then dosed with as much sugar as it would soak up, and I'd spoon out whatever residue was too thick to drip onto my tongue, holding the cup over my mouth. Which I mention, though I never done it in public even in some of the dumps I ate in out West, because it was all I could do to keep from doing it here, so warm did I feel being with Amanda, and while I was aware she was friendlier than I had ever known her, she was a cool customer, I reckon by nature rather than upbringing, for her Ma if you recall was a woman who believed she might even at that late date have a career in singing in a music hall in Dodge City. Her Pa had been a banker who she accused of frequenting the Lone Star harlots. I guess in Dodge he was well-to-do but in New York, where Bill Cody had friends like J. G. Bennett who owned the *Herald* newspaper and sent Stanley to find Livingstone, and Leonard W. Jerome who lived on Madison Square and was grandpa to an energetic, talkative English boy who come to see the Wild West when we was in London, name of Winston Churchill, why Mr. Teasdale wouldn't of been of so high a place as to warrant the putting on of airs by his daughter.

I had to conclude she was just born that way, with a sense of her moral superiority, in which she was by no means alone, for Wyatt Earp was like that, except with him it was for selfish ends, whereas so far as I could see, Amanda had little interest in personal gain or possessions. Later I found out that satin dress didn't come from any of the fashionable places along the Ladies' Mile but rather from a cut-rate drygoods shop downtown: it just looked like a million dollars on her.

Since leaving our encampment she hadn't talked any more about the Indians and had not volunteered any personal details, nor asked after mine, but just offered observations on New York, of which she was a harsh critic for somebody who wasn't compelled to live there.

But when I pointed that out, with all respect, she says, "This is where the money is." Meaning, not in the sense of making a living, which was why Mrs. Custer came there, but rather in getting people to contribute to the Friends of the Red Man, which like Annie with her initials for Buffalo Bill's Wild West, Amanda generally shortened to F.R.M. "But we have ferocious competition from every other organization of social betterment."

"I can't rightly speak for him," I says, "but if I know Cody, he will give you a nice contribution. Despite what you think, he ain't against Indians."

"How could that be accepted in good conscience?" Amanda asked. "Would it not be like accepting in the fight against Negro slavery funds that had been made by selling cotton picked by slaves?"

She had a real fine mind, no question about it, to come up with such a twist. "I guess you could look at it that way, but you could also see it as turning to the good some of the money which in your opinion is at present going only to a bad cause."

"Let me clarify the point, Jack. We don't begrudge the Indians the wages paid by Colonel Cody, or for that matter his earning a personal profit from a business enterprise. The issue here is not about money as such. What is so objectionable about the Wild West show is its presentation of Indians as savage and primitive. Paying them to be so actually makes it worse. Without pay they would not degrade themselves. They would settle down on their acreage and join American society, and educate their children in proper public schools. The Indian will never be civilized until the importance of the tribe is diminished." She opens her eyes wide. "I know that might sound heartless, but what alternative is there?"

Here was a reverse of the usual, with the woman representing reason and the man, namely me, being the person dominated by feeling, but much as I admired Amanda for strength of character and even suspected deep down she was probably right from the historical point of view, I knowed the tribe was the best thing the fighting Indians had going for them, and if you was ever part of one, like I was during my formative years, and then went on to another way of life, with nobody to rely on but yourself, you tended to be lonely, and I had been white all the time.

But the fact was Amanda and her bunch really was trying to do some good for people who needed a hand, whereas for all my regard for Indians they was benefiting me more than I was them, which happened to have been true since I first hooked up with any, aside from maybe paying for the defense of them Cheyenne charged with murder back in Kansas.

Now you might be able to see from this little account of my meeting with Amanda again what never occurred to me at the time, and that is that my thinking on this subject now, which I previously avoided doing because of its hopelessness, had more to do with my personal infatuation than with sympathy for the red man considered as a cause.

"I don't want to pry into your private life," I says while she was pouring me more coffee. "But I was wondering what you done after the Major's school closed."

"I went back to Dodge City," she said in her crispest voice, "where my father's bank failed because he had embezzled money from it, but before he could be tried he shot himself to death, and my mother died the following year, probably from shame. One of my sisters married a cattle broker and moved to Topeka. The younger one followed a man to San Francisco and has not been heard from since, which means reality fell short of her expectations, otherwise I would have heard from her. I think it's more likely she's walking the streets."

I was sorry I asked, unhappily reminding her of these matters. There was deep feeling behind the slightly resentful yet cool manner Amanda had always displayed since I first met her. She just had the self-control not to advertise it to others. Sometimes she could get too harsh, but maybe that was protection against being weakened by sadness.

It was not good manners to ask a spinster if she ever come close to being married, so I did not do so, though I would of liked to know about that more than anything else. "I'm sure sorry to hear of all the troubles you been through," I says. "I admit I used to think of you as a rich girl." Amanda's reactions never could be predicted, at least not by me. "Yes," she said, "I suppose so, relative to the place and time. But all of a sudden I had no source of income but what I could find on my own, and I refused to get married to acquire financial security. I might have taught school, but no local positions were open, and any employment associated with the church was out of the question after my father's scandal."

I just wished I had knowed about her difficulties, as I could of helped her out, but on what basis? It sure could not look like she was a kept woman. In case you ain't reached that conclusion on your own, I might say Amanda was a real difficult person to know how to deal with, especially if you was uneducated and her social inferior.

"Necessity forced me to review the lady's education to which I had been subjected. I assumed it would be a vain effort to find anything of practical potential, but wonder of wonders" — her eyes sparkled — "I actually found something! I had received years of piano lessons. Of course, that meant Scarlatti and Chopin, but I wasn't talented enough to give public performances of such music. However, I was sufficiently gifted to play in a saloon."

"You didn't," I says.

"I did," says she.

"Which one?"

"The Pink Horse."

Which was pretty much of a whorehouse, pure and simple. I don't think they had any other entertainment than that battered old jangly piano. Nobody even went there to gamble. I tell you I almost choked at that point, which was easier than saying something.

Amanda had elevated her chin defiantly. "It was an excellent job. In addition to my wages, I got tips, sometimes lavish if the men were drunk enough. The requests were more often than not for songs of a sentimental sort rather than what I would have expected in a place of that kind, but the women who serviced our customers told me many men were sentimental in the bedrooms. Of course, some were brutal. What surprised me most however was the deference with which I was treated by these cowboys. I kept a revolver on top of the piano, and a knife in my clothing, but in my time there I never had cause to use either one. Not only was I never touched, but only rarely was I ever asked if I might be hired for a private performance, and even then it was put so discreetly I could have interpreted it to refer only to music."

"They was scared of you," I says.

She shrugged. "Oh, I doubt that."

"To them kind of fellows anybody with a musical talent is real special. A man in that job is always called the Professor. A fine lady playing the piano would be a wonder."

I had suspected it but now it was proved: Amanda could walk through a mud puddle not only without getting besmirched but not even being interested in why. So she says, "Be that as it may, it was profitable employment and as honorable as anything else I might have done, perhaps even more than most. I was also given an opportunity thereby to make the acquaintance of prostitutes."

I hastily says, "Well, there are all kinds," and hoped to change the subject, being discomforted by the association, Amanda having represented for me that which was exalting, as far as possible from saloons and harlots.

"To try to find," she went on, "just what attracts men to them."

"It's just that they're there."

She didn't take no account of what I had said, but continued. "What I found was that these women for the most part avoided reflecting on their profession in a general way, though being ready enough to give particular experiences in detail."

Hoping to steer her away from getting into the subject of sex, if that was where she was heading, I says, "Looking at things according to a theory is done only by educated people, on account of only they know how."

"I can't say I learned much," said Amanda, "except that most of these women neither particularly liked or disliked what they did, and that their predominant feeling about men was that they, the men, were foolish, and that they, the women, believed they were in the dominant position because men paid them. There is a great difference between this and the way nonprostitute women look at the issue."

"Yes," I says, trying to sound intelligent, "I have found that to be the case, myself." I was hoping she'd get off the matter. "So when did you get back to the Indian problem?"

"I had not lost my faith in the social gospel," Amanda said. "The church may have its hypocrites, but its aims are noble. I am no longer religious in the doctrinal sense, if I ever was, but I believe more than ever in working for justice. Ironically, the immediate reason for my returning to the cause was the cleaning up of Dodge City, led by the forces of respectability. The saloons became soda fountains!" She had a way, at least with me, of acting as if I wasn't present and she was addressing herself, but now I was real pleased by an acknowledgment of my presence by name. "You wouldn't recognize the town, Jack."

"It could use the improvement," I allowed, and I was sincere. I might not of been part of it, but I thought normal life was the right thing for the country. I just wished it didn't call for the mistreatment of the Indians, but I didn't have no idea of what was the best way to avoid this. Hiring all of them to perform with B.B.W.W. and the other imitations thereof, like Pawnee Bill's, now that Cody had proved so successful, might not be possible, but the Indians who *was* hired seemed to like it, which is more than could be said by most who tried what the Government thought up for them.

It wasn't no use telling this to Amanda, however, who after playing piano in a whorehouse out West, come East to get back to doing good and took up with the people around Philadelphia, mainly church folk, who had an interest in the plight of the red man, and applied pressure to the federal Indian commissioners and Congress till that Dawes Act got passed. Now the same folks, in organizations like this one she had started up in New York, was trying to get the Indians out of show business.

So that was the outline of Amanda's story since I last seen her, but what was missing altogether was anything pertaining to her private life, by which I mean men friends of the personal type, not just the old preachers she had worked with on the order of the Major. Though I had never knowed her exact age when we was at the school, I figured she would now be in her early thirties, an old maid by the standards of that time and living until recently out West, where women was usually at a shortage. But ladies as beautiful and smart as her was not in great supply anyplace on earth, at least not where I had been, and by now I had been a few places.

Well, I'll tell you this: if she didn't have no suitors it did not pertain to her appeal to men or lack thereof. It was due to her low opinion of the opposite sex. I guess what Amanda had seen of men give her little respect for them, but it probably never occurred to her she only looked at the wrong ones or that there was part of everybody human that maybe should be overlooked as long as it wasn't actually criminal. But for that matter it's the way of the world that them who don't run it find fault with them who do: it's a way of getting even. Still, it's too bad if only that.

But all this was just supposition, for I never knowed anything about Amanda's private associations, and you didn't inquire into the subject with a lady. I did allow for other possible surprises, judging from the one I had gotten on hearing about the whorehouse piano-playing, and I decided there wasn't no need to learn more. The important thing was I had re-established a connection with her, and I didn't intend to squander it.

Sitting there across the kitchen table from her, drinking only that real weak coffee, here in the heart of New York City where I always felt so out of place, especially when visiting Mrs. Custer, but even at the Butlers' flat, I got the first feeling of intimacy I had had since old Pard died, and I don't mean no disrespect to Amanda for bringing up the memory of my dog, given the closeness between me and him and the way we took care of one another.

"I'm going to quit Buffalo Bill's Wild West," I told her now, "and work with you folks."

If you think I had at last gotten Amanda's attention, you would be wrong. I don't know what I expected, certainly not that she would gather me to her bosom, but maybe it would occur to her that for her sake I was putting myself out of the best job I ever had.

You see how besotted I was when it come to that girl. It wasn't till a long time later that I could see she would of disapproved had she believed I was doing it for her and not from a sincere belief in the rightness of the cause.

So all she says now was "I'm happy to hear that, Jack. I do hope you understand that the F.R.M.'s budget usually doesn't cover our expenses as is, and most of those who work with us do so as volunteers."

"Oh," I says, digging the hole deeper in my elation, "I meant to make it clear I wouldn't take no wages under any condition." Now that I wouldn't have no current income whatever, my worldly wealth consisted of them savings in the bank at North Platte, which I hadn't totaled up in a while but expected was a couple hundred dollars, not exactly a fortune even in them days but enough to live on for a time even in New York, where you could eat breakfast for a dime and free lunch with a nickel beer. However, at that moment I never had a practical thought in my head: I was just occupied with how I looked in Amanda's eyes. Which is why the next thing I done was seemingly contrary to my interests in being close to her.

I got up and thanked her for the supper and said I had to be going.

If I was hoping for her to urge me to stay longer, it didn't work, but in fact, though I might of liked to hear her say as much, I really did want to get out before overstaying my welcome, and I intended to demonstrate that though we was a male and a female together in a private place, I wasn't the sort of fellow who could take that to mean she was a loose woman.

Anyway, she gets up from the table soon as I did and politely leads me to the front door. Then she says something I figured explained why she hadn't been more pleased by me wanting to join her bunch.

"It has been very nice to see you again, Jack. Perhaps it will be hopeless, but I would be grateful if you continued to remind Buffalo Bill of this issue."

She either hadn't heard or didn't believe me when I said I was going to quit B.B.W.W. in favor of F.R.M. I took the blame for not making myself clear and tried again.

"Amanda, I aim to leave Cody's show and join your bunch if you will have me. He's been real good to me, and I want to give him notice and not just walk out before he can find another interpreter. If you'll tell me where to show up and what to do, I'll be there soon as I can."

She was smiling. "Good for you, Jack. I was giving you an opportunity for second thoughts."

She went away for a minute and come back with a card that had a street address on it and also another number, and she says I could telephone the latter to make sure when she was in.

Now I hadn't never yet used a telephone, though that device had been around for a while in the larger cities. In fact I had thus far been scared to try lest I electrocute myself, so it was just as well I had never had a need to do so. But I realized if I was to gain the respect of Amanda, I would have to get up to date in modern life, for her theories as to Indians could also be applied to myself: it was time I got civilized.

Speaking of which, I now had to ask her how to get back to the Staten Island ferryboat, which would of been hard enough for me to find in the daytime, but it had gotten dark by now, and them streetlamps, being all alike, only confused me. I wasn't fond of braving that city at night and maybe having to tangle with a gang of toughs or drunks lurching out of a saloon or, worst, a bunch of foul-mouthed Bowery juveniles, for how would it look if I was fighting with some kids even if outnumbered. I'll tell you, I would rather of wandered horseless and unarmed in Crow territory while wearing Cheyenne paint than be by myself at nighttime on certain streets in New York.

17

Paris, France

NEXT MORNING I WAS ANXIOUS TO GET GOING ON THE
next phase of my life, but it was useless to look for Cody until late
in the forenoon, given his social pursuits of the night before over
in Manhattan, where he stayed at a hotel. I lived in a tent on the
compound at Erastina, right near the encampment of Sioux tepees, so I
went over there.

The Indians remained early risers even in London and New York, and
by now a bunch of men was already occupied with what they did until
the performance started, namely, playing poker, which some of the cowboys had taught them and for which they was keen, having a natural
taste for gambling as they did.

A group of the women also was collected together, sitting on the
ground in a circle, in their case sewing up some of the souvenir articles
they sold, little coin purses, belts, watch fobs, and the like, decorated
with beadwork, and gossiping as did females of whatever race and profession, from Lakota wives to the calico queens of the Lone Star —
though I couldn't imagine Amanda doing so.

White Bear Woman come out of her tepee, carrying a piece of deerskin, so I went over to her and said I was leaving the show pretty soon,
but I didn't want any of the Sioux to think it was because I no longer
cared about them.

"You are going with Yellow Hair, I think," she says, with a round-faced
smile of approval. "That is good. At your age you should be married and
produce some children and not just get drunk and pay bad women to go
to bed with you."

I'm not going to comment on what she said, aside from noting that married Lakota women, like Cheyenne wives, could be outspoken without being thought coarse.

Her advice was the same as that from several ladies I had been uninvolved friends of, beginning with even some at the Lone Star and then Allie Earp and Annie Oakley, and I told her she was right, that I sure wanted to do so as much, but I doubted Yellow Hair would have me as a husband, so meanwhile I was going to try to show her I was a good man.

"She should believe herself lucky to have caught your eye," White Bear Woman said. "Skinny and pale as she is, how many men would want her?"

Well, you had to excuse her for having the redskin approach to this matter. Next she would want to know if Amanda was strong enough to skin a large animal without taking all day at it. And just let me point out that she wasn't so weakminded that after a couple years amongst the whites of two countries she thought their women had the same job as Indian females: she just didn't think much of what they did. There wouldn't of been no point in mentioning in return that Amanda considered *her* a kind of slave condemned by savage tradition to a life of degrading drudgery. I have found females whatever their race or station in life to be usually more critical of their own sex than men are, either of women or other fellows.

When Cody finally got in, I went to his tent and sincerely thanked him for the job he had give me for the past five years.

"And you calculate," says he, with a slow smile and a pull at one end of his mustache, "it's more than time for a raise in pay. How about an elevation in rank instead?"

He was in a good humor, so I joked back. "But if I was raised to major, then Arizona John Burke would have to be colonel, and you'd be a general."

"As a matter of fact, the governor is preparing to name me general in the Nebraska National Guard," says he. "But I don't know if I should accept the star, having become known as colonel throughout the civilized world." He wasn't conceited in the way this might sound: what he meant was what professional effect the change of title might have. "General" didn't sound as suitable as a title for a showperson, unless applied to somebody like that little bitty midget of Barnum's called General Tom Thumb.

"I didn't intend to ask for money, Bill," I says. "What I want to do is leave the Wild West."

"What in the world will you do then, Jack?"

The question could be seen as insulting, I guess, but from his point of view it was sensible enough. I never had no previous trade so far as he knowed but bartender, and who would want to return to that after traveling with the Sensation of Two Continents, being celebrated by royalty and all?

"Bill, it's time I stayed in one place for a while. I've really enjoyed being a part of B.B.W.W., and —"

"Let me give you a piece of advice, Jack. I know you have a few years on me, but I believe it's reasonable to point out that I have more experience in the ways of the larger world. With all respect, that type of girl can mean trouble for a man like you."

The question riled me. "Did I mention a girl?"

"You didn't have to," he says with a smug movement of his goatee, which by the way I noticed was showing signs of gray. "I won't make the mistake of saying I know women, for no man can, but I have made a close observation of that sex. Your golden-haired friend is the kind who tends to expect more than can reasonably be delivered. Take my word for that, old friend."

I was still irked. "Miss Teasdale is an acquaintance," says I, "and nothing further."

"If you're speaking of her feeling about you, then you're right," says Buffalo Bill, leaning back in his chair. He was yet a fine-looking man though getting a bit of a belly. And he still had that shoulder-length hair, which was also now showing some gray. "But," he adds after a pause, "*you* are besotted with her." He cleared his throat. "I could tell all that from the way you looked at one another."

Later on I realized what I found so offensive in his commentary was I knew deep down it was correct. "Dammit," I says, "you might know how to B.S. an audience, but that don't mean you are an expert on my life, which by the way has included a lot more than pouring whiskey and interpreting for show Indians. I could start up my own exhibition just on the basis of the places I been and the famous people I knowed at the most important times so far as history goes."

Cody raised his eyebrows and showed a big smile. I doubt he believed me, but he says, "I'm proud to hear that, Jack. But you'd better stay here.

Pawnee Bill's business hasn't gone well and is about to go under. And you'll be interested to know that Little Missy's coming back to us."

He meant Annie. I didn't like hearing that from him either, but I had fell out of touch with the Butlers since they went off with the show run by Bill Lillie. "That's just fine," I says, "but I'm giving my notice."

"Then Miss Teasdale has replaced Missy in your affections?"

I refused to let him rattle me further. "Frank's a personal friend of mine."

Cody become serious. "That's why it's a better arrangement, Jack. Miss Teasdale doesn't have a husband to protect you. These willful women are hard to handle. You don't know what Frank Butler has to put up with, unless you've seen Missy's mean side. Not that I don't have my own problems with Lulu. That woman's set on my ruination, and not only financially. She's trying to turn my own daughters against me. Yet you saw how much Arta enjoyed coming to London."

I seen Arta only once or twice during that trip and only at long range. He kept her away from the men in the show and I think had hoped she'd find a husband amongst the English swells.

But I wasn't going to be sidetracked from my own concern. "Couple weeks be enough notice, Bill?"

"Jack," says he, removing the big hat to wipe his forehead with a blue bandanna, "do what you have to do and when. And remember, there'll always be room for you at the bar." He swallowed as if with difficulty. "It gets hotter in New York than on the Plains. My whistle could use a wetting. How about you?"

Since I was standing and him sitting, I could see when the sombrero was off that his hair though long as ever was getting thin at the crown. I had lost only a little of my own, but at forty-seven I was acquiring some gray, and didn't like it, so I admit I'd mix some coloring into the pomade and comb it into both my sideburns and the mustache. I was fond of thinking this plus my shortness of height made me look a lot younger than I was, not that I was all that much older than Amanda, putting the difference at about a dozen years, in a day when it might well be as much as thirty if the man had money and the girl hadn't none, which of course wasn't the case in the present instance.

Speaking of money, by working another couple of weeks I would make enough to get by for a little while without immediately retrieving any of my nest egg from North Platte, and maybe I could find some outside work in addition to the unpaid job with the Friends of the Red Man, like tending bar in one of the plentiful saloons in Manhattan, but I still didn't feel I could at this time afford to send Wild Bill Hickok's widow the money I owed her to replace the roll I had lost, though I was sure going to do so soon as possible.

Well, I don't want to stretch out the telling of this episode, though when I was enduring it, them two weeks seemed to go on forever and not just be the "fortnight" they would of been called by the English. At my present age fourteen days pass in about an hour, but when your heart is still young enough to have some function beyond just beating, the clock is slower than you are. I just wish I hadn't been so yellow about using the telephone, for I could of called up Amanda at her office not to bother her with a lot of palaver but just to remind her of what I had said I would do, if she was in any doubt. As to sending her a note, I tell you I was too worried about how ignorant I was in the use of words, when it came to putting them down in pen and ink.

So I remained out of touch with Amanda throughout this time, and didn't even have no intimates to talk to on the subject, by which I mean a woman pal like Allie Earp, for if you speak to another man about being stuck on a girl he would think you soft, the way Cody done.

But the time eventually arrived, and having already said my goodbyes and collected my final wages the day before, I left the Wild West early one morning in late June and rode the ferry across towards my new life, wearing my city suit and hard-collared shirt, topped by a derby, and carrying a carpet bag containing what was left of my worldly possessions, having give what wouldn't fit in to Two Eagles, White Bear Woman's husband, including my wide-brimmed hat.

The water was a bit choppy in the breeze you always get on a stretch of ocean water even when contained in a bay, which was welcome for on land the day was fixing to get hot, which in the beginning surprised us Westerners with our idea the East always had mild temperatures to match its tenderfoot ways, but we was wrong on both counts: it could get as hot on the sidewalks of New York as in the streets of Tombstone, and as cold in winter as Montana Territory, and the habits of the locals, especially the kind of Irish who owned and also patronized the saloons, was as rough as anywhere beyond the Mississippi. And added to all of this was way too many people everyplace you went. But that was where, on account of a woman, I was going to make my life, and I thought on passing the Statue of Liberty that for me it was a giant image of Amanda.

I had my usual difficulty in finding the address, the streets being downtown in that part of the city that wasn't laid out at right angles and being all named and not numbered, and the men I asked directions of either spoke with an accent I couldn't understand or seemed to find my own speech hard to savvy, and I was afraid a stranger stopping a woman might be taken for a masher, so never done it.

But finally, more or less by chance, I found myself on the right block and located the building, which lucky for me wasn't tall as some, for another thing of which I was leery was an elevator. I never cared how safe Mr. Otis was supposed to of made them: I never could see any reason why one stayed up, so I always walked. Fortunately in this case that was only four or five stories. But first I should say that down on the sidewalk, at the entrance, I run into some old fellow just unlocking the front door, and he was in a disagreeable mood most everybody who didn't know you was in in New York all the time, unless of course they wanted to sell you something, though even then they was barely civil. I guess they just had to deal with too many strangers in a crowded town like that.

Anyway, this fellow, who as I say was old but maybe not more so than me at that time, it's just he was so gray-faced and slow-moving, when he turns to shut the door and sees me behind him, he first flinches and then, seeing I ain't there to rob him, says in a surly voice, "It's too goddam early. There ain't nobody here yet, for Jesus' sake."

Since this was Amanda's building I didn't want to make no trouble, so I just says I'd wait outside the office of the party I was meeting, and he turned his back on me, so I went on in and found the room number for F.R.M. on the directory board in the entryway and undertook the climb, which was a lot more strenuous due to the regularity of the stairs than mounting a comparable height outdoors. That was undoubtedly why there was so many weary-looking city folk: life there was more exhausting for the human body than in the prairie, mountains, or even the desert. An Indian who could survive hunger, cold, and bloodshed on his own terrain wouldn't of lasted long in the wear and tear of Manhattan or what had become of it since the white men bought it.

So by the time I got to Amanda's floor I was all tuckered out and panting like old Pard after he had a good run, and when following the numbers in the unlit hallway I come to her office, the letters painted on the frosted glass panel of the door, FRIENDS OF THE RED MAN, was big enough to see, but my vision was still too wobbly as yet to make out exactly, in the dim light, what was on the piece of paper stuck below, wrote in ink by hand.

So I had to wait a while before understanding that the office was closed not just for today but all week, no reason given. Any packages was to be left with the janitor.

Not only was I disappointed, but I was worried about Amanda. Maybe she was took sick suddenly. But if that happens, a person ain't likely to specify a precise time when they'll be back. I reckoned, or at least I hoped, it was more likely a vacation. If so, what would I do with myself for a whole week?

I clumped down them many steps and found that janitor on the ground floor, where he was pushing a wet mop around.

I was careful to stay on the part that was still dry, so as not to rile him before getting some information. I began, "Friends of the Red Man. I was wondering —"

With the usual New York impatience, he says, head down, "Closed," and continued to swab that dirty mop in big circles without rinsing it in the nearby bucket.

"I know it," I says. "But what I was wondering, due to sickness or vacation?"

His mouth went down in a sneer though he still didn't look at me. "It's her wedding."

"She's getting married?"

"Shit," says he, "if you're going to walk across this clean floor, then go and goddam do it."

I had been brought too low by the news even to consider what I swore I'd do next time one of them city folk was nasty for no good reason: kick him in the arse. Fact is, at that point he could of kicked mine without fear of retaliation: I wouldn't of felt it. I couldn't even ask him any further questions, whether he would of answered or not, for I didn't want to know any of the details. Now, these many years later, I can look back and see that Amanda hadn't made no arrangement with me to do what I done. She hadn't promised me a job or in fact even said she looked forward to seeing me again, professionally or socially. I myself had concocted that entire business out of thin air and overheated feelings. I had a tendency in that direction, but this was worse than with Miss Dora Hand, in that I had put more store in it, though of course not so bad insofar as Amanda was not shot to death, only married, but I was in the same fix, since I wouldn't be seeing her again. I didn't need another married woman friend like Annie.

My reaction to this was not noble. I went to what I believe was a number of saloons but due to my state of drunkenness I couldn't keep track, and it's always possible I stayed in the same one, and what changed was only the other customers and also my state of consciousness. I do recall at around the point I was two and a half sheets to the wind, like the sailors say, I got real bitter about how nobody in New York City knowed I was the sole white survivor of the battle supposedly shown in that picture the Anheuser-Busch brewery hung in every saloon in the U.S.A., "Custer's Last Fight," and it was back of the bar in each of them I visited now, unless it was one and the same place, and I got real mad looking at Custer wearing long hair and wielding a saber, neither of which he had that day, and I begun to tell, probably at the top of my lungs — though at the worst of it I could hardly hear my own voice — what really happened at the Little Big Horn, eventually getting so worked up I throwed my glass at the picture, and I guess I really did go to more than one place, for next day I retained a memory of being bum-rushed into more than one street, and the last time it happened, probably while I was laying facedown in a gutter full of filth, my wallet was lifted, along with my pocket watch and chain, my new derby, my boots, and even my celluloid collar. Whether my carpet bag was took at the same time or I had lost it earlier, I never knowed.

When I come to next morning I didn't recognize the neighborhood at all. It wasn't where I had started out, but seemed to be all slum, with dirty little kids running around and big dark buildings in solid walls from one end of the street to the other, and so crowded and noisy with people and pushcarts, with now and again a skinny overworked old horse pulling a battered wagon while its driver cursed it and everybody in the road, that I thought I was in a drunken dream of Hell or maybe had died and gone there. Anyway, there was enough commotion so that nobody paid any attention to me.

I was such a mess I would of stood out anywhere else, but here I was amongst the better dressed and groomed, and when I asked one of them little kids with holes in his pants and dried snot on his face if there was a public bath in the vicinity, he never had no idea of what I meant, though he could speak English, for he asked me to give him a penny, and when I searched my pockets and found I had lost every cent, he called me the dirtiest name I ever heard.

I walked till I wore through the soles of my shoeless socks, and finally I come to a commercial area with a lot of businessmen on the sidewalk, and picking the friendlier faces, though frankly you didn't see many of such, I would say, "Excuse me, sir, I'm a respectable person irregardless of my present appearance, which is due to an unfortunate accident. I was wondering if you might extend me a loan of ten cents, along with your address, so I might return it promptly."

I repeated this to several people but nobody listened to it much past the "Excuse me, sir," most of them not looking in my direction, but one big fellow with a red nose says he would get a policeman to run me in, and another, the nicest, told me to go to such-and-such mission and get a free pair of shoes.

There's nothing like physical privation to call your attention away from distress of the feelings. When you get uncomfortable enough, you can't remember your other troubles. The summertime pavement of New York ain't the place to walk barefoot. My feet got fried, and when I reached one of the rivers that flow around the island and found a dock low enough to sit on and dunk my hoofs, I hadn't been there long before a big-bellied cop come along with his helmet and truncheon and says, "Be on yer way, or yuh'll rigrit it."

Finally I did end up at a mission on the Bowery, where they give me a used pair of shoes which was too big and with worn-through soles but served the purpose, and all I had to do for them was sing some hymns with the others, to the accompaniment of a piano played by a lady with a sorrowful expression who later said a word to each of us, taking me for just another tramp, and I never let on because at that moment, feeling lower than a snake's belly, I figured I didn't deserve better, at my age to make a fool of myself over a young woman; furthermore, a woman who was herself blameless. I mean, she wouldn't even know of my feeling for her. . . . On the other hand, if she didn't know, then I was not humiliated before her.

I have found throughout my long life that the older I got, the easier it was to deal with matters of pride, at least if they was not bad enough to shoot yourself over right away. I couldn't blame my current predicament on any of the saloons I got thrown out of, but still the experience soured me on any idea I might of had to return to my barkeep career, at least when it come to New York, and I had demonstrated no talent whatever at panhandling, so unless I wanted to hang permanently around a mission, singing for suppers of thin soup and stale bread, I never had no sensible choice but to get back to the Wild West if Cody would let me.

So I found my way by foot to the Staten Island ferry landing and just lingered there till some of the cowboys showed up, returning from an overnight spree in the city, and they staked me to the fare when I told them I had gotten beat up and robbed in an outnumbered fight when I stood up for Texas amidst a crowd of Irish micks, squarehead Germans, and Eyetalian greaseballs, on account of they was always getting into such commotions or anyway claimed to.

I used the same story to explain to Buffalo Bill, only omitting the fight, for he was not himself a pugnacious drinker. I just had one, I says, and then another and so on, until I was blind drunk and busted, a state of affairs which he regarded as normal enough though I never did see him in it. In fact, I never seen him actually drunk, I expect because by time he was under the influence, everybody around him was so much drunker he seemed sober.

Anyway, he says sure my job was still there, and then he adds something I probably should of been offended by had I not been so shaken by the matter of Amanda. "The Wild West is home to you, Jack." I knowed he meant it in a friendly way and probably would of applied it to himself as well, for he seldom stayed with his blood-family in Nebraska, but I didn't have no alternative.

I drew an advance on my wages and bought new boots and replacements for the other clothes I had lost, except for the derby, which would only of been an unhappy reminder of the new life I wasn't going to have, so I would of had to get me a hat had I not run into Two Eagles before doing so.

He was wearing the sombrero I had give him on leaving. Now he would never ask me why I was back, as he hadn't inquired as to why I had been going away. But he did look at my bare head now, which was an unusual sight outdoors in them days with white men.

"Do you want your hat back?"

"I gave it to you," I says.

"Yes," says he, "but I think you need it." And he takes it off and hands it to me.

I mention this because it's a twist on what white people call Indian giving, and maybe demonstrates the redskin angle on the subject of personal possessions.

Well, so much for my imaginary love affair. I can shrug it off here, though it took me a while to get over it at that time.

That winter in North Platte the separate house Cody had built on his property and named Scout's Rest was all finished and ready to move into, with fifteen rooms and big porches ten foot wide, and he had a special room upstairs fitted out for drinking, with a sideboard full of bottles and glassware arranged like in a bar, and a big bed for the use of any guest who was so drunk he passed out. His wife Lulu continued to live in the old Welcome Wigwam house, and as usual I never saw her all winter long.

I was back at my vacation job of personal bartender to Buffalo Bill and the many visitors he invited and also the passing cowboys, drummers, drifters, and all who dropped in without being asked but was whiskeyed and fed just like they was, some of them staying around for weeks, on account of Cody was always in the market for company and missed the show crowds. I myself for once welcomed having a lot of people around, for it was cheerier than if I had only the company of my disappointments. Also I missed old Pard real bad and often would go out to where he was buried and say hi to his bones, which I was relieved to see had not been dug up by any animal, for the grave could not be distinguished by now from the surrounding ground and the grass had grown evenly across all.

There was less money than I believed there'd be in the savings I kept at the local bank, not that they stole any, but I guess I hadn't sent back as much as I thought and also not a lot of interest was earned on an account like that.

Cody seemed to have the golden touch, with his successful show, and I ought to say his ranch was a real one and profitable as run by his brother-in-law Al Goodman and several dozen working cowboys, and I decided if I was going to be lonely at least it wouldn't be so bad if I was prosperous as well, so I asked Buffalo Bill to do me a favor and let me invest the modest amount at my disposal in the next project he come up with.

When he acted none too keen about that proposal, I got sore and, with some whiskey under my belt, accused him of being selfish. If I had been working for any other employer, my arse would have been kicked out the door at that point, but if there was anything Bill Cody was not, it was selfish or stingy or intolerant of the ranting of a drunk, so he says all right, but what I should know about the business ideas of Doc Powell was that they didn't always make as much money as it seemed they might at the outset.

He was referring to an old pal of his who lived now in Wisconsin but showed up from time to time over the course of many years, in fact since Bill had met him when Powell worked for the Army as a physician at Fort McPherson long before. Unlikely as it seemed, Frank Powell was a genuine doctor and sometimes practiced as such, but he was also a character after Cody's heart, a heavy drinker and a big talker, a sharpshooter who sometimes did an Annie Oakley act, an honorary Indian with the name of White Beaver, and a specialist in schemes designed to enrich himself and his fellow investors, among them the merchandising of such patent medicines as White Beaver's Cough Cream, the Great Lung Healer, which was guaranteed to cure any complaint of the chest, from the congestion of a cold up to and including consumption.

Doc Powell's latest project sounded sensible enough, at least when I was drunk, and also remember that Bill Cody was his partner: it was to colonize a couple million acres of undeveloped land down in Mexico that was free for the taking. Now, sneer if you will, but at the time it sure seemed like just the kind of thing that might appeal to a lot of foreigners in Europe who would want to get off to a fresh start in the New World, and this spot would be the newest part, starting from scratch. White Beaver was going overseas with us to sign up colonists.

That's right, Cody was taking the Wild West across the ocean again in the spring, this time to Paris, France, and another celebration, which had a French name pronounced *Eck-spoh-ziss-ee-awn Oon-ee-vair-sell*, spell it as you will, and we'll get to that directly. But first I want to dispose of the matter of money, though I can't do it as thoroughly as my own savings was disposed of in this scheme: in a word, though this is jumping ahead some, Doc Powell couldn't find nobody in Europe or anyplace else who wanted to colonize that acreage of Mexican desert. I had nobody to blame but myself, and Cody lost a lot more than I did. But he had a whole lot else.

Now I know what you're thinking at this point: you're tired of hearing how once again Mrs. Agnes Hickok never got reimbursed for Wild Bill's roll which I lost while in hot pursuit of his murderer Jack McCall. It's beginning to sound like I made all this up! Well, I was ahead of you, way back then. I myself got sick of being a welcher. Before giving a cent to White Beaver, I divvied up my savings into two equal portions. In five years with the Wild West, I had saved almost two hundred fifty dollars. I know that don't sound impressive these days, but in that age you could buy a meal for ten cents, so such a sum was not to be despised. What I done was round out Mrs. Aggie's share to an even one twenty-five and send it off in cash to the Cincinnati address I had gotten from her daughter Emma the Champion Equestrienne of the World. I hope it reached her. I never knew. I included a note in which, after apologizing for poor grammar and worse spelling, I said I had been a pard of Wild Bill's many years before and owed him a poker debt, which I was long last able to return. I never said it was a dying request, for I was ashamed to have taken so long to fulfill it, and for the same reason did not sign my name.

So I had finally accomplished both the obligations I had took upon myself on leaving Deadwood a dozen years before with regard to the two widows, Mrs. Custer and Mrs. Hickok, though as usually happens in life the realization was somewhat different than the intention. I don't know what I had in mind in connection with Libbie Custer before meeting her, beyond being her sincere friend, but I had not exactly hit it off with the lady. As for Agnes Hickok, I had wanted to provide her with a considerably larger bequest, regardless of how much was in the roll Wild Bill had entrusted to me, but it was the best I could do.

Now, getting back to B.B.W.W., off we went to Europe again on the same *Persian Monarch* we come back on the year before, with two hundred persons, almost half of which was Indians, some fifty buffalo amidst an animal cargo of three hundred, the Deadwood stagecoach and the other equipment, and while the crossing weren't as rough as the first time, I never got used to traveling on water. I had first went West as a young boy in a so-called prairie schooner, but I tell you, going over the bumpiest ground, you could stop at any time. Stop on the ocean, you're still there.

You got to bear with me when it comes to French names and places. "Paris" was simple enough to figure out even though they said it with an *ee* at the end, and the harbor where we landed, the "Harve" (though

Americans would of said "Harb") made sense, but where we set up the encampment on reaching Paris was in a park with a funny name on the order of "Annoying," though I gather it didn't mean that in French, and the iron tower what had lately been put up, so high you could see it from everyplace in town, had the right name in the English version, the "Eyefull," but even the Frenchmen who liked it called it something that sounded like "Awful." And by the way, a lot of them hated it even though it was the tallest manmade structure in the world, which was true of them people on almost every subject. Whereas in England everybody seemed to agree on basic matters, at least in public, the French made a specialty of disagreeing with one another on almost anything.

Eventually I found out that some of this was not what it seemed, but due to the language, which is more excited-sounding than ours and makes a lot of next to nothing, like "Good morning, sir" is just a mumble compared to *Bone-JOO, mess-YEAR*, which can be like a song. And a good many of their words though sounding like some in English, have different meanings, for example to us "assassin" would be John Wilkes Booth who killed Mr. Lincoln, but in Paris it meant only the driver of a cab whose trotting horse almost run you down when you tried to cross the road.

They had a lot of funny ways, which shouldn't of been surprising, because after all they was French, and though they was nice and hospitable when we got to Paris, I had the feeling they was suspicious about what it was exactly that a performance of ours consisted of and whether they should like it and why, for I found there was nobody like a Frenchman for taking nothing for what it appeared to be and reserving judgment till he decided if he was being made a fool of or not. So at the opening performance, with their President, Mr. Carnot, and a lot of other big shots on hand, for that Exposition commemorated their Revolution of a hundred years earlier, there was an audience numbering twenty thousand people, and they wasn't unfriendly, but neither did they show anything near the excited expectation that always greeted us at home and maybe even more so amongst the British, who was supposed to be restrained, as opposed to the hotblooded folks across the English Channel, which by the way ain't called that by the French, who was always thinking about food, but rather the "Munch."

As promised, Annie and Frank was back with the show. They had straightened out whatever difficulty they had with Cody, and Lillian was gone now, so there was Little Sure Shot, waiting for her entrance into the arena in Paris, and me and Frank was in attendance, ready with her guns, ammunition, a supply of them glass balls, and other equipment for the act, and I tell you she had stayed as pretty as she was when she first joined B.B.W.W. but had become even more accomplished as a performer, having acquired an ability to take hold of a crowd by simply walking in in her demure way, wearing that fringed outfit and star-marked hat, them neat little shoes and leggings, curtseying like a well-brought-up schoolgirl of the kind Libbie Bacon must of been not too many years before she married Autie Custer. Long before Frank handed her the gun and I throwed the first glass ball into the air, Annie would have an audience eating out of her hand.

But on this occasion, with the French still reserving judgment on the Wild West, Annie took it as a personal challenge to take them on, all twenty thousand. She had noticed that for the opening ceremonies, the audience applauded only when certain persons posted here and there throughout the arena give them the okay to do so by starting up the cheering. Later on we found out that every show in France, from circuses to highbrow plays, hired fellows of this type, who was called "clackers," and once some Frenchman told me, with typical Paris humor tending towards the cynical, that after an act or two you could tell from the level of noise exactly how much the clackers had been paid on each occasion.

Anyway, Annie took this as an affront to her professional pride.

"Go on, Frank," she says, "you and Jack tell them to keep quiet."

Knowing Frank didn't want to rile her before a performance, I took it upon myself to point out there was a number of such people: the show'd be over before we went through a crowd that size.

There was sparks in her eyes. Annie wasn't really a shy schoolgirl. "Well, Jack," she says, "if you ever bothered to look, you could see the main ones are right close. You go over to them and you tell them to hush. Now is that too much to ask of you two?"

If you have had experience in entertainment, you know performers are real highstrung just before going on, so I quick followed Frank, who being married to her had already started off, and being a clear-thinking man, had already figured out a practical answer to the problem, neither of us speaking French: he got one of the English-talking officials assigned to us to deal with the matter, and it was taken care of.

Which meant Annie come into the center of the arena to absolute dead silence. There wasn't even any applause from the President's box, where I heard later they thought Miss Oakley wanted complete quiet for some safety measure when shooting her firearms.

Well, them show guns, even with their light loads, made enough noise to startle city folks when they first went off at every performance, and the Frenchies wasn't any exception. Fact was, they turned out to be just as excitable as supposed, only took a while to show it, but pretty soon their yells and cheers was even drowning out Annie's guns, and before her act was over, the whole bunch was on their feet screaming and throwing hats and parasols and scarves into the arena and at one another, and in general going nuts for her. It sounded like another revolution had started, a century after the first.

If Annie was the toast of the town in New York and London, she was even more in Paris: the French toast, I called her, for them people always went any dish one better, like dipping it in egg, being crazy on the subject of food: you couldn't get a piece of *cheese* in Paris, you had to name the kind, out of several hundred. You couldn't buy *butter* unless you specified the fat content, for again there was a big choice. Incidentally, you couldn't get "French toast" over there, where they call it, in their lingo of course, "lost bread." And who else in all the world would eat liver raw?

You ought to know the answer to that one: Indians, of course, though it would probably be that of a hairy four-footed animal rather than a goose, but sharing that trait weren't the only connection between the red man and the French, who from the first had a spot soft in their hearts for Indians and generally got along better with them in the New World than the British. The French and Indian War was even before my time, but I know that them two was allies in it against the Redcoats, like the Americans was a little later with the French against the same enemy, so though the French was peculiar, we had old ties with them on our side of the water, including even many tribal names, among them Sioux, Assiniboine, Nez Percé, Iroquois, and others, for they was first visited by Frenchmen in the market for furs and also priests, who had enough sense to tell an Indian he didn't have to quit his heathen beliefs to become a Catholic: God would let him be both, at least until he learned better.

Speaking of Indians, who would turn up in Paris but Black Elk, one of them Sioux who, if you recall, missed the returning boat to the U.S.A. the year before and was stranded in England. Cody was relieved to see he was in good shape, for this was the kind of thing the reformers like

Amanda could use to discredit putting Indians in shows, and invited him to take his old place in the troupe, but Black Elk said he was pretty homesick by now though he had had a nice time since the Wild West had sailed away without him, being hired right away by a fellow named Mexican Joe who run an imitation show of Cody's though smaller, and they toured Germany and some other countries including one with a mountain which had smoke coming out of its top and sometimes, according to the people who lived there, it shot out flames and burned up the towns around its base.

"Yet the people continued to live there," said he. "Because it is their home."

"Tell my friend," Cody says to me, "the name of that country would be Italy."

So I did so, and Black Elk says, "But most of the time we were here with the French, who treated us very well, and a young woman became my friend and took me to meet her family, but I missed my own home so much I got sick and fell down and, so far as these people could see, I died, not breathing and having no heartbeat, and they were getting ready to bury my body when I finally woke up, because I had not died but rather had flown across the seas to the Black Hills and then to Pine Ridge and visited with my mother before coming back here. I told her I would return in the body as soon as I had the money for the boat."

Cody now demonstrated again why the Indians liked and trusted him. "You'd better get started, then, for a man must always honor a promise he makes to his sainted mother." And he give him a return ticket and ninety dollars, and got the French to provide one of them cops they call John Darms to go along and make sure he got on the right train and then caught the right ship on time.

Now, just to follow up on that vision Black Elk had, I heard from some other Pine Ridge Lakota with the show in later years that having talked with her son in the same dream, Black Elk's Ma knowed he was coming home and exactly when, and I had no reason not to believe that, having many times known like results from the dreams of Old Lodge Skins, the man who taught me most everything of enduring value I learned in life.

In Paris, as in London, the B.B.W.W. Indians was taken around to see the sights, and reporters followed them everyplace, but not knowing the French language I couldn't say whether the stories they wrote was any truer than anyplace else, but I doubt it, given the difference between the way an Indian looks at things and a fellow who tries to put it down in writing, for example when Red Shirt and some of the others went up to the top of the Eiffel Tower (me too, holding my breath on that elevator ride), Arizona John Burke went along with us and looking down remarked on what I guess there wasn't a white man ever went atop any structure and *didn't* say, which is how the persons below looked like ants, Red Shirt's observation was how if the people down there looked so little from high up where he was, then how much smaller all people must look from the height of *Wakantanka*.

Now that's the way I translated it for Burke, who asks, "Where's Wakanna?"

Distracted from the view and also still shaky from that elevator, I done a careless job. "Sorry," I says, "he means God."

And Burke says, "Here, here," again using the British expression, and then I heard him tell the reporters what devout Christians our Indians all was, which was news to me, and Lord knows how it come out in print, for I never run into a Frenchman who claimed to know English who actually did, and the same thing was true in reverse, according to the French, who claimed there wasn't anybody not born and brung up in France could hope to speak their tongue.

As you can tell listening to this story, I couldn't be called fluent in English, and Sitting Bull wasn't never impressed by the quality of my Lakota, so on Judgment Day, talking to the Almighty, maybe I'd better stick to Cheyenne. Anyway I guess I was pretty pathetic with French, and them people prefer you didn't even try it if you was going to butcher their beautiful language. What really went over in Paris was being as Western American as possible, that is, if you couldn't be Indian, which was best of all, and everywhere you went you saw the locals wearing sombreros and headbands with feathers and riding horses on American horned saddles, and little kids with bows and arrows.

So I had a real good time in that country, the details of which I won't go into, but I was recovering from a great disappointment in the usual way a man does that, by means of what women see as empty frivolities though they usually figure in them, along with drink. Speaking of drink, Frenchmen do that all day long but generally with wine, so they ain't really drunk but they ain't cold sober either: they're just French. And yessir, they really do eat frogs, though not at every meal.

But France nor any other foreign place wasn't much to Annie Oakley's liking, she being of the old-fashioned red-white-and-blue sort of girl with an eye open for un-American immorality, but one thing that concerned her personally she found good for a laugh. The King of Senegal, a colored country in Africa owned by the French at the time, while visiting Paris attended a performance of the Wild West and was so taken with Annie that he come around to Buffalo Bill's tent after the show, a real big heavy person in his fancy robes of spotted furs and gold jewelry, with a bodyguard of husky young black fellows and a white interpreter who translated his French, and what he says was he wanted to buy Annie for a hundred thousand francs.

Now I know Cody thought this real humorous, but he pretended to be insulted, so the King upped the ante, until Bill lifted his hands and called quits.

"Madame Butler," says he, "nor any other American lady can never be for sale, sir!"

The King speaks to the translator, who then tells Cody, "His Majesty says, 'Oh, what a pity!' "

Bill turns his head towards me, with a hand covering his mustache and the top of his goatee, but got himself under control and turned back. "Ask him what he wanted to do with her."

"To keel teegers," the Frenchman says after consulting with the King, who now is smiling eagerly with a display of perfect teeth.

"Pardon?"

"Wild bists. To shoot dem."

"To kill tigers?" Cody asks.

"*May wee,*" says the King, and the interpreter explained, "They eat too many of his pipples."

"Captain Jack," Cody asks me, "will you be so good as to go to Miss Oakley's tent and fetch her here to receive this offer? It's too attractive to dismiss out of hand."

So I done as requested, and the King repeated his proposal, and I'll say this for Annie, she never got mad but just said politely she could not accept due to prior obligations. At which His Majesty parted his leopard-skin robe and, amazingly graceful for a man of his bulk, knelt down on one bare knee, took her little surprised white hand in his big black one, raised it to his lips, and kissed it. Then he stood up, squared his shoulders, and marched out of the tent in a brisk military step, followed by his burly retainers.

As soon as the group could be expected to have gone beyond earshot, Cody let out a big guffaw, and he says to Annie, "I know for a fact there aren't any tigers in Africa. That's according to my personal friend Mr. Theodore Roosevelt."

Annie didn't have no better education than me, but to show you how sensible a person she was, she says now, "Well, maybe 'tiger' is what you call a leopard in French."

I run into Two Eagles on leaving the tent and asked him if he had seen the big chief of Senegal and party go past.

"Yes," says he, "and I liked his spotted robe very much. I wondered where a Black White Man killed such an animal."

Which is what Indians called colored folk at home, and they didn't differentiate by name between types, so I tried to clear him up on the matter. "He's completely black," I says, "and comes from a place called Af-ri-ca."

"But he is here with the whites," Two Eagles pointed out, getting that expression an Indian will show when he becomes stubborn.

"He's just visiting."

"He is not a captive?"

I hadn't wanted to get into this, for I didn't know all that much about the subject. "He seems to come and go as he pleases."

"Why does he not stay home in his own country-of-the-spotted-animals?"

"I don't know," I says. "But he's probably come here to ask the French to do something for his country, which I believe is actually owned by them, so he doesn't run anything, but they let him stay on as big chief."

"Then it seems to me he can be called a Black White Man," Two Eagles said.

I changed the subject to explain something I felt guilty about. "That hat you returned to me in New York? The reason I'm not wearing it is that I got drunk in Paris last night and lost it." This was always a good excuse with anybody in Buffalo Bill's Wild West, beginning with its founder, except for Annie of course.

"I thought maybe you gave it to some French woman," Two Eagles said, with a trace of grin beneath his big hawk nose.

"You're too smart for me," I told him. Fact is, by the time we left Paris, there was few of us who still had the American stuff we brung along on arrival, and some of the cowboys had to send back home for replacement boots, chaps, sombreros, and all, and Cody had to warn against losing guns, for bringing firearms into them foreign countries was under strict controls and the red tape involved in clearing the show's arsenal on first arrival had been trouble enough.

I should mention that the Lakota as usual when speaking of anybody not an Indian called him some version of *wasichu,* their word for "white man." An Englishman was just plain *wasichu;* a black man was *wasichu-sapa;* a Frenchman, *wasichu-ikceka.* None of them was the normal folks they called themselves.

18

Sitting Bull Again

I N THE FALL OF '89 WE FINALLY LEFT PARIS AND WENT
south in France, down to Marseilles where they drank a licorice-
tasting concoction that turned milky when water was added and ruined some well-known people, well, that and the ailment which each
European country tried to blame another for by calling it by the other's
name, like the "Neapolitan disease," and so on, and their chief food
down there, being on the seashore, was fish, especially a stew containing
a mix of all kinds called *billybase,* which was a little too rich for my
blood, but the Sioux, who never ate fish at home, could get sick just by
smelling a bowlful.

But not sick in reality, the kind you could die from: that happened
however when we continued on down to Barcelona, in the land of
Spain, where I found such Spanish as I had learned from the Mexicans
was looked on as being fairly ignorant, for I couldn't bring myself to lisp
on certain words as they do in that city, but I never had much chance to
do so anyway, for we run into an outbreak of both typhoid fever and the
flu, against which the city was quarantined, so few people appeared at
our performances, plus which a number of the company come down with
serious ailments, including some of the Sioux, and the man who announced the acts, Frank Richmond, died. Annie nearly did too, and
Frank Butler was hit hard.

The only other thing of note was Arizona John Burke, always looking
for a chance at publicity, took a bunch of our Indians to the local statue
of Christopher Columbus and got them photographed there, sending the
picture back to the U.S.A. with a comment to the effect that Columbus

was four hundred years early as an advance agent for Buffalo Bill's Wild West. Burke really done that. But I heared later on that someplace it was told that one of the Indians stared at the statue and said, "It was a damn bad day for us when he discovered America." That never happened, and I was there. The Sioux at that time didn't know anything about Columbus, aside from the fact they never seen him anywhere near Montana nor Dakota territories, and they thought of themselves as Lakota and not "Indians" and "America" so far as they was concerned was the part of the country where the white people, including the black white people, lived.

The further difficulty in Spain was once we got quarantined, we couldn't leave even though nobody was buying tickets, but finally we got out of there in January of the year and went on to the islands of Sardinia and Corsica, the latter being the birthplace of Napoleon Bonaparte, and the Indians did know his tomb was at Paris, for they seen it, and when I mentioned he was supposed to be short, they called him Little Big Man, I believe in all seriousness.

Next came Naples, and a mountain named Vesuvius was nearby. The first day we was there, Red Shirt told me, "That is the mountain that Black Elk saw, the one that belches fire."

"I don't see any right now."

"It's the one," he said with certainty, but I never understood how he could know that.

Some days later we was took to visit the ruins of the city of Pompeii which was being dug out of the ground, having been buried by volcanic ash centuries before, so Red Shirt was sure right about that mountain.

Now at Pompeii in its heyday there had been at least as many harlotries as in Dodge City centuries afterwards, but the difference was they had pictures painted on the walls of the Pompeii whorehouses illustrating the pleasures available. The Indians found these of interest, for they was learning some of this stuff for the first time, but a lot of cowboys, who wasn't, was nevertheless shocked to see it depicted in public and thought worse of the Eye-ties for doing so and said we shouldn't let many of them into the U.S.A. lest our morals go to hell and also them foreigners was so ignorant as to misspell Chris Columbus's name as Cristoforo Colombo and claim he was one of them. I admit I myself didn't know the truth of that at the time, for we had just come from Spain, where the Spanish claimed him, only called the man Cristóbal Colón!

Luckily the Butlers was going to visit Pompeii another day, so I was able to warn Frank to steer Annie clear of the filthy pictures.

Cody had big plans for Rome, wanting to hold the performances of B.B.W.W. in the Colosseum where the gladiators fought and the Christians was fed to the lions, but found it was worse for many centuries of wear and had half fallen down. His idea of going to the Vatican with a troupe of Indians and having a private audience with Pope Leo worked out better.

Now people meeting the Pope was supposed to be dressed formal, meaning swallowtail coats and high hats for the men, but as this was not practical for the Indians — though I can tell you they might of liked it — Arizona John Burke got special permission for the Sioux to wear their regular show outfits, but they went him one better. For the sake of the occasion Cody pretended to be Catholic, but Burke actually was one, and he had lectured at length to the Indians about who and what the Pope was and how to act when they met him: not to get excited and yell, etc. So what they did was break out their very best clothing and jewelry for the visit, a lot of which I never seen on them before, shirts of the finest deerskin and beadwork, the decorated bone chokers and breastplates, the most lavish of feather bonnets.

Of course the old Pope could top anybody in the display department, what with his crown and the fanciest robes embroidered in gold and white and being carried into the Ducal Hall by some big gaudily uniformed fellows in a throne held at shoulder level on a tall man, with horn music and the singing of choirs, having been preceded by a slow parade of cardinals, bishops, and the like, all of them dressed to a fare-thee-well in satins and silks — well, the Indians was more impressed than I had ever seen them be by any sight we had yet encountered in Europe, for a spectacle of this sort, with sound, color, and movement, meant more to them than any building or machine could ever do.

In translating what Burke had told them about the Pope, I had gotten them to take it as solemn, though the exact concepts of white religion — which I can't say I understood that well myself though having both a father and stepfather so to speak in the trade — wasn't easy to explain in Lakota.

It turned out that unbeknownst to me, some of them had been baptized by Catholic missionaries at the Pine Ridge reservation, and Burke hadn't been altogether off when he called them Christians at the Eiffel

Tower, but if so they was of their own sort, for getting back to the encampment after the Vatican visit they found that the only one of their troupe not to go to meet the Pope, Little Ring, who had not gotten up in time, had stayed in bed because he had died of what the Italian doctors said was a heart attack.

Now these Sioux thereupon changed their hitherto mostly favorable opinion of the Pope, for if he was God's spokesman, why hadn't he spoke up and asked God not to kill Little Ring just when the rest of them was about to make their visit in their best clothes? The doctors determined the time of death as occurring during the night, so Arizona John couldn't blame it on Little Ring having decided to stay in bed, thereby incurring the wrath of the Almighty — as I assure you Burke would of, had I not myself made this point.

And having been disappointed by the Pope on that score, the Indians also was emboldened to criticize him further: though he was very rich and lived in the grandest house they had ever seen used as a personal dwelling place, he failed to offer them food at any time during their visit, which meant either he was too stingy to speak for God or that he was ignorant of how to treat his guests, in which case his connections with the Almighty must not be too close.

But in interpreting I didn't pass along *all* this negative commentary to Burke, who had been thrilled to meet the most important person in the world if you was a Catholic, for I didn't see it would do either him or the Indians any good. The Pope had his own ways, and the Sioux had theirs, and to show you how wide they was apart, when instead of putting the question to Burke I took it upon myself to give an answer and said the Pope couldn't feed nobody, but had to get fed himself, for he didn't have no wife to do the cooking, they thought he should get married as soon as possible.

Maybe it was this experience that turned the Sioux against Rome, but they didn't care for the place, believing the people on the street laughed at them, which I didn't know was true or not, for Italians seemed naturally a lively, noisy bunch and maybe they was just trying to be pleasant: I never spoke a word of that language.

Also the Indians didn't like to be asked to buy things all the time, and in Rome this happened everywhere you went, people sticking out hands they wanted filled, not shaken, so we wasn't sorry to move on to the other towns in the country, most of them, after all these years, blending

into one in my memory, for they was all filled with real old stone buildings, about half of which was churches, on real narrow stone-paved
streets. The big exception was Venice, which had as many churches as
anywhere else but the main roads was paved with water.

No sooner did we get to that town than Burke in his eternal quest for
publicity loaded too many Indians, Buffalo Bill, and me into a gondola,
which had sunk to the gunwales before anybody paid attention to the
fact except the front and back gondola drivers, screaming in Italian
which nobody understood, not to mention that normal conversation in
Italy was mostly yelling.

The Sioux though in unfamiliar conditions saw what was happening
but out of pride wouldn't show their concern, but finally we unloaded a
few passengers and floated out on the Grand Canal to have some photographs took, with that fancy building in the background that our cowboys, and me as well, called the Dogie's Palace until straightened out.

Later more pictures in front of St. Mark's cathedral at the end of the
big square in Venice full of pigeons where crowds of people come, I think
to get away from the water for a change, for it's at your doorstep everywhere else in town and sometimes, with a real high tide, so I heard, in
your parlor as well, and a lot of us, red and white, begun to miss home
and the eternal dust-dry wind of the Plains, after a whiff of canal air on
days when it was real thick, most of them.

Germany was the next country we went to, that spring of '90, so still
another language was spoke by the locals which none of us understood,
and there was more old buildings to see, castles as well as villages full of
what looked like big dollhouses, but I don't think there was anybody in
all the world so interested in anything pertaining to the American West
as Germans, where a fellow name of Karl May, who had never set foot in
the U.S.A., had already begun to write fictional stories about the frontier, which I heard later on wouldn't of been recognizable to anybody
who had experienced the real thing, but then the same could be said of
most movies on the subject made in California and not Dutchland,
which was the Germans' name for their own country.

Anyway, of all the places we had went to, Germany no matter the
town give us the heartiest reception of all, for they tend to be real thorough about everything, good or bad, depending on when, and I heard in
later years that man Hitler's favorite writer was Karl May, and Adolf, like

Winston Churchill before him, would likely have enjoyed the Wild West if he ever got the chance to see it as a lad.

But by the time we reached Germany, being admired by white people of whichever country had lost its novelty for the Indians, and they had gotten tired of looking at the wonders of civilization that the whites had come up with before they went across the ocean to a land that didn't have none of them and started from scratch, which didn't make sense.

"Why," Two Tails asked me once, "do it all over again when all these things existed here?"

I told him honestly, "I think that the ones who came over the ocean did not live in these big fancy lodges and have a lot of power, so they went to a new place where they would have a better chance to get these things than if they stayed here. America seemed an empty land to them, not being used by anybody but a few Indians who didn't need all that space."

"I think," says he, "that it might have been all right if there had not been so many whites. I was surprised when I first saw the big towns in America. Within the range of an arrow shot, there are more people in New York than there were Lakota and our friends at the Greasy Grass, the largest gathering of normal people ever. Within the range of a rifle shot, there are more New York *wasichu* than all Lakota, Shyela, and Arapaho in the world, and even including the Crow, Pawnee, and all our other enemies. But the towns on this side of the water look more crowded yet."

"A lot of them are full of poor people," I said, "who don't see much future here. So we can expect more to come to America in search of a better life."

He said he was real sorry to hear that. Like most people I've knowed regardless of color, he was not given to looking from any other point of view than his own. The Plains Indians thought the right way for people to live was in little bands which was freely associated with tribes that in themselves wasn't too numerous, everybody wandering around more or less at will, looking for buffalo. This wasn't how you could build a cathedral, or palace, or a factory or foundry, but of course you wouldn't need any of those.

Anyway, by now we had been on this tour for more than a year, and our Indians was not only homesick, but some was physically ailing as well, and in fact a few, like Little Ring, had died from smallpox, consumption, and the like, not bad treatment or starvation or anything Cody done or failed to do, but it was in Germany he learned he was being so blamed back home by certain Government officials, Congressmen, newspaper writers, and others of who I bet I could name one, and no doubt I would myself of been of that company had I been able to join up with Amanda. The accusations was wrongheaded with respect to B.B.W.W., but ours was not the only show that included Indians. Doc Carver, Buffalo Bill's old partner, had an outfit of his own that went as far as Moscow, in Russia, and there was Mexican Joe's and others, and I don't know about any of them, but I swear Indians could have no serious complaint against William F. Cody.

Yet when he sent five ailing Sioux back to the U.S.A. from Germany that summer, his political enemies got one of them, White Horse, to tell the papers that Buffalo Bill didn't feed them enough food and made them sick and when they was too weak to perform sent them back home as being useless. Now, I knowed White Horse, and I'm not calling him a liar, but none of this was true, so what I figured is somebody got him drunk and told him what to say or, more likely, what he said in Lakota was mistranslated by an immigration official named O'Beirne who claimed to be fluent in the language but I suspect was one of them whose interpretations of others invariably agree exactly with their own prejudices.

We was in the city of Berlin, where if you dig into the ground you will find not earth but sand, which interested the Indians more than additional architecture, and by now they had also seen too many soldiers, anyway in Berlin the U.S. Consul General passed on to Cody a letter from the Indian Commissioner containing a list of the complaints against him for mistreating the red men in his employ.

Buffalo Bill was real annoyed by these accusations, but the kind of fellow he was, he never wasted time on either being mad or getting even, but kept his eye on the possible practical effects. If the Commissioner decided he couldn't have Indians any more in B.B.W.W., that would be the end of the whole shebang, for nobody anywhere in the world would pay just to see cowboys without Indians. If you think of it, anyone could learn to wear a wide-brimmed hat and spurs and ride a horse and rope cattle and shoot firearms though not maybe as good as Annie, but a headful of feathers and painting your face couldn't change you into a real Indian: you had to be born one. And though white people had killed as many as they could and taken away their land, whites seemed universally fascinated with red people, not as performers — for such performing as was done with Cody, in the daily sham battle of the Little Bighorn, could of been managed by white actors in costumes — but as a matter of existence: this unusual folk, someplace between human and animal, they was what made the American West one of a kind.

There was horses and buffalo or the equivalent elsewhere, and mountains and deserts and wide-open spaces all over the world, and other races of various colors and plenty of violence and cruelty on every side, both the stronger and the weaker, but an Indian of the warrior tribes, so long as he wasn't trying to kill you at that moment, was the perfect combination of every quality that civilized people enjoy seeing in savages on exhibition. It was all make-believe in the show, but some of these might of been the same Sioux that slaughtered Custer's command and mutilated the bodies, and yet they had wives and babies and sometimes smiled when selling photos of themselves and always was as polite as Europeans and a lot more so than Americans.

Cody now decided on a typical bold stroke. He moved the white part of the Wild West to Alsace-Lorraine, which was either depending on your sympathies the German part of France or the French part of Germany, and set up winter quarters to await his return in the spring, and then with me, Nate Salsbury, "Major" Burke, and a few others, took all the Indians back to the U.S.A. to answer the phony charges against him on their supposed behalf.

And let me say them Sioux went on to Washington, D.C., when we landed, accompanied by Salsbury and Burke, and while Arizona John conducted one of his publicity campaigns to discredit the critics as effectively as he had promoted the Wild West, the Indians went to the Commissioner's office and said Cody fed them so much they got fat and paid them so well they had a lot of money to send home to their families. If the Government made them stop, them and their families would be poor again. Then President Ben Harrison invited them to the White House.

Whether any of this would of been enough to shut up them who, like so many reformers, missionaries, and politicians in general, know what's better for others even when the others don't agree, the controversy was put aside at that time on account of a much bigger Indian problem had started up out West and, for the first time, involving more than just one tribe and its allies. This one in fact united a lot of former enemies.

It was a religious movement based on the visions of a Paiute out in Nevada Territory called Wovoka, who believed the time would soon come, if enough Indians of all tribes would perform the Ghost Dance, when a great flow of earth would cover all the whites and everything they had brung, square houses, iron road, singing wires, the whole kit and caboodle, and the red men would be raised above it and the buffalo and everything else that was good from the old days would come back.

You might ask, why not let the poor devils enjoy their delusions? Way back when I was a young fellow with the Cheyenne, we was going into a battle with the U.S. Cavalry and it was a theory of a medicine man named Ice that if we dipped our hands in the water of a certain lake, we could hold them up when the soldiers shot at us, in which case the bullets would just trickle down the gun barrels and drop harmlessly on the ground, so we did and they didn't, I mean the slugs, which didn't seem to know about the spell, on account of Ice wasn't fluent in the language of lead, or so I heard was his explanation to them that survived. Being white myself, I quick as I could surrendered to the Army.

My point here is that Indians was coming up with ideas of this sort all the time, and now and again they might even work. But when they worked it was in a particular way, not for a whole bunch all at once, and there sure wasn't nothing dreamed up by a red Messiah that was going to get rid of white people by dancing. What the Army was concerned about was that the Indians would figure that out for themselves and give the Everywhere Spirit a hand by going to war again.

General Nelson Miles was in charge of the Army for the part of the country involved, and he sent a telegram that was waiting for Buffalo Bill at the hotel when we got off the ship in New York. Which proved to be why neither Cody nor me went to Washington with Salsbury, Burke, and the Indians.

"Miles wants me to come to Chicago, Jack," Cody said, on reading the wire. "He's worried about old Sitting Bull."

"What's that got to do with Chicago?"

"That's where the General is headquartered now. He's commander of the whole Department of the Missouri."

"What's the trouble with Sitting Bull?"

"We're both going to find out. I want you to come along with me. You are a friend of his and speak the lingo." He smiled and hoisted one of the glasses a bellhop had delivered, along with several bottles, soon as we had got to his rooms. "Besides, you're a fine fellow to travel with. Have another."

So me and him went to Chicago and saw Bear Coat, which is what the Sioux and Cheyenne called General Miles, who told us all he knowed about the Ghost Dance and this Paiute who called himself Wovoka but was known to the Army as Jack Wilson, and Miles said it was too bad Sitting Bull, who ought to know better, had fell for this nonsense or was just making cynical use of it, but anyhow was preaching it to all the Sioux at the Standing Rock reservation and trying to start an uprising.

Now I never believed this for a minute, for the Bull I had gotten to know during the time he was with the Wild West wasn't the type of person to preach anyone else's cause, having a high opinion of his own self as a spiritual leader who had foreseen the great victory at the Greasy Grass in a vision. But I was never the type of individual to get much respect from a general, even a previously reasonable one like Bear Coat. I would leave it to Cody to make the truth known once we got out to the Standing Rock agency, in Dakota Territory, and talked with Sitting Bull himself, for that's what General Miles wanted Cody to do.

Actually, he wanted him to do something much worse. I couldn't believe it when on the train West, Cody showed me the written order, in which Miles said Colonel Cody was "authorized to secure the person of Sitting Bull and deliver him to the nearest commanding officer of U.S. Troops."

"He wants you to *arrest* him, for God's sake?"

"Simmer down, Jack," Cody says. "No need to take the Lord's name in vain. We'll parley a little with Sitting Bull, wet our whistles some, and soon straighten out the whole thing. I'm betting it's some kind of misunderstanding. Sitting Bull's too good a businessman to involve himself in what sounds like a very shaky enterprise. Miles can think it's an arrest, but I'm going to bring old Bull out for another tour with us."

Which went to demonstrate how far gone Buffalo Bill was in his own sort of showman's life by now and why some people thought he had never actually been west of Chicago but was altogether an invention of dime-novel writers like Colonel Ingraham and Ned Buntline.

Well, we finally reached Dakota Territory, at the Sioux reservation called Standing Rock, where the agency was under the direction of a man named McLaughlin, who considered himself a great friend to the Indians, to the degree that he had a Lakota wife, but like many such, his liking for them was based pretty close on whether they did what he wanted them to, which put him and Sitting Bull at odds from the first.

So when me and Cody showed up at Fort Yates, the nearby post maintained by the U.S. Army in case the Sioux disagreed too much with McLaughlin's ideas, the commanding officer got hold of the agent and showed him General Miles's order.

McLaughlin was not much taller than me, and had a big black drooping mustache over a mouth that was likewise turned down. He looked even unhappier after reading the order.

Cody of course was his usual positive self. "As you gentlemen may or may not be aware, Sitting Bull and I have not only enjoyed a close professional association, but I think I am safe in saying we are warm personal friends. I'm certain the fine old fellow and I can settle this little matter in no time."

The commander there was a real colonel named Drum, and being a soldier knew better than to give any hint of disagreement with his superior back in Chicago. "Colonel Cody," he says, "first let me welcome you to our post here at Yates. Your reputation precedes you, and I don't mean just your distinguished career with the Wild West, but also your prior exploits as a scout."

"Why, thank you, sir, and may I present my associate, Captain Jack Crabb."

I shook hands with Drum and then McLaughlin, who I hadn't thought could get any gloomier-looking but in fact had done so.

Having give me a look of the kind a real Army officer will show to an honorary one without Cody's celebrity and shook my hand in the same fashion, Drum says, "Colonel, your wish is my command. But before we get started on the trip to Sitting Bull's farm, which is a few hours from here, down on the Grand, may I suggest you and your aide accept some refreshment at our officers' club? It won't be as luxurious as some you've no doubt known, but I think you'll find the whiskey drinkable."

Cody's reputation had preceded him, to be sure. We adjourned to the club referred to, which might not of compared to them that the New York swells had entertained Buffalo Bill in, but was comfortable enough, for there wasn't much else for the Army to do stationed at a place like this, and anyway Cody wasn't a snob about drinking, needing only a bottle and a tent, and not even the latter if the weather was clear, so he settled there for what I could see right away would be quite a spell, for a sizable audience of young officers soon collected around him, which meant he would stay until either the liquor was exhausted or the rest of them collapsed, there being nobody in America, England, or the whole continent of Europe with as great a capacity, which he had proved across the world.

I stayed for only a while, for I noticed that soon as the fact was established that Cody was fixed in place for the foreseeable future, both Agent McLaughlin and Colonel Drum slipped out the door. I wasn't in no doubt that they disapproved of his mission and though in no position to oppose it openly, would obstruct it sneakily as long as possible, beginning with this idea of getting him drunk.

I myself didn't share Cody's optimistical idea he could get the Bull to return to the Wild West, to sit in a headdress and sell autographed photos again, for I had heard from the Lakotas who newly joined our troupe from time to time that the old chief was doing right well as a farmer, with quite a few head of livestock and fields of corn, there in the bottomland along the Grand River, which furthermore was home ground to him, having been born nearby, something always important to an Indian though he might of wandered afield.

But neither did I trust McLaughlin and Drum. Having a natural suspicion of them in authority, which you might see as typical of someone who was never in that situation himself, it seemed to me to go without saying that neither an Indian agent nor an Army officer would at all times be acting only for the good of those under them. And if you say, Well, ain't it too bad old Jack had that view of human nature? I'd point out how I experienced many a dangerous episode yet am still breathing at my present age.

What I wanted to do now was find out what them two was up to once out of Cody's presence, and since they was unlikely to reveal it to me personally, I consulted the same kind of source from which I learned a lot about the Seventh Cavalry while en route to the Little Bighorn, namely, an enlisted man. There ain't one ever served who didn't welcome a chance to vent his bitterness against his superiors, which come to think about it ain't only a characteristic of soldiers.

So what I done in this present case was outfit myself with one of the bottles of whiskey Cody brung along in the great amount of baggage he commonly traveled with, which otherwise was filled with changes of attire, for he was never less than Buffalo Bill wherever he went, which is to say on performance, and I loitered around outside Colonel Drum's HQ until some soldier emerged wearing yellow corporal's stripes on his blue jacket and started across the "area," which was the Army term for any space whatever inside a fort — and by the way most of the Western forts wasn't the walled and gated affairs shown in the movies, but just a collection of buildings in the open — and much of what soldiers were put to doing when stationed at any fort or camp was just cleaning up the "area."

As it turned out, I struck gold right away. "Say, Corp," I says to this fellow, "will you tell me where the officers' club is? I got me a wagonload of fine whiskey over yonder I got to deliver."

He points with a stubby finger that had a clean nail, not a common sight then. "Across the area." He gives me a disgruntled stare. "I guess you ain't got none for the noncoms' club?"

From his squared-away forage cap and shined boots, I had took him for having a job at HQ and not merely visiting it to be chewed out by the commanding officer. "No, I have not," I told him. "You know how that goes. I'm an old Army man myself."

"Well, it ain't changed," says he.

"Say," says I, "I got me an extra bottle, and you're welcome to take a taste from it unless you're on duty and can't."

He grins with his broad freckled face, showing one tooth broke off clean at just the halfway mark. "I'm supposed to pick up the Colonel's shirt at the laundry and wait for it if it ain't ironed yet. I got the time. But let's get out of the area."

So we went back to the stables, always a good place to find a quiet corner, and I fetched the bottle out of the coat pocket it had been weighting down, and me and Corporal Gruber had a few sips from it, though actually the sipping was mine, whereas he did the gulping. Anyhow, as Colonel Drum's orderly he was able to furnish me with the information I needed.

Drum and McLaughlin wanted to delay Cody from going after Sitting Bull till they could get orders calling him off, and this would take a while, for they had to take the matter to somebody higher than General Miles, whose idea it was for Cody to come in the first place, and all this had to be done on the telegraph, if it was working and not disconnected somewhere along the thousands of miles of wire.

"I don't know, though," says Gruber, "I think if Buffalo Bill can't do something about Sitting Bull, who could? He's got that show of his, which all my family back East see every time he comes to town, and he's real rich and he's got all the women he wants, like that Annie Oakley I seen pitchers of, she's a pretty little piece, and I'd like —"

"Here," I says, "you have another." For which he didn't need no urging, and while he was a-gurgling, I asked, "Why are they so set on stopping him from seeing the Bull?"

" 'Cause they're feared it might start a war," says Gruber. "Say one of them hotheaded young bucks whipped up by that old bastard would kill Buffalo Bill, then we'd have to go down there with troops and make 'em all good Indians, which if you ask me wouldn't be a bad idea. It really burns me up they're still making trouble after all the times we whipped them."

General Sheridan's saying about the only good redskins being dead ones was a familiar sentiment with soldiers on Western duty, but I hadn't heard it said for a while, for in the East and especially in Europe most whites appeared sympathetic to the Indians and often even friendly in their own fashion, so I was took by surprise, but to argue with Gruber at this point would of defeated my purpose. Of course you did well with Indians in a state of excitement not to put yourself in a defenseless situation. But Sitting Bull had a high regard for Cody and I was sure wouldn't let him be harmed, and as for Buffalo Bill himself, he was a lively fellow but never really reckless.

I urged Gruber to make free with the bottle we was sharing. It was his own affair if he reported back to Colonel Drum stinking drunk and without that fresh-laundered shirt. "I don't know," I says, "I thought Sitting Bull become a farmer. Would he want to start a war?"

The corporal took a long pull at the bottle, then worked his prominent adam's apple. "That smelly old sonbitch does whatever he feels like. Did you hear? He's keeping a white whore down there in his cabin. I mean, she ain't a captive, else we'd ride down and pull her out pronto. Imagine a white woman doing a filthy thing like that, even if she is trash."

It was true enough that the houses of ill fame with which I was acquainted would not accept a customer of another race than white, even them with black girls amongst their offerings, like there was colored barbers who would cut only white men's hair and not that of their own kind. With a Mexican it depended on how Mexican he looked. This seemed altogether normal at that time, so much so it wouldn't ordinarily be questioned. But like everything else I had heard about Sitting Bull beginning with Bear Coat's reasons for ordering his arrest, I found this hard to believe. White people in general seldom really knowed what was going on with Indians, and with the Army that confusion was multiplied tenfold: for example Custer, and he had been a veteran of fighting the red man. The mistake was in looking for white reasons in Indian actions, going from point to point in straight lines. No doubt this was the effective way to work with electricity when inventing the light bulb or telephone, but not when making the old Bull into a war- or whoremonger, despite appearances.

I was fixing to ask then what was McLaughlin's and Drum's plans for Sitting Bull, if they didn't want Cody's help nor to send the Army after him, short of war?

Gruber beat me to it, though taking another big swallow of whiskey first, for I now was letting him keep hold of the bottle. "See," he says, "McLaughlin's a pretty smart monkey. He's been training a troop of Sioux police to handle the problems that come up around here. Indins like that: give 'em uniforms and some authority over their own, and they'll strut around thinking they're big men. Of course, they better not get the idea they are real cops when it comes to dealing with the Army, or they'll next be strutting in the Happy Hunting Ground. But they can free us from the dirty work."

"So he don't want Cody to arrest Sitting Bull, but he's going to send the Indian police to do it?"

Gruber winked a now reddening eye, and he says, "I'll say this for McLaughlin: he knows how to deal with Indins. He's married to a squaw! If you ask me, that's a mighty high price to pay, though." He squints and says, "You going to need the rest of this?" Meaning the bottle. "You got a whole wagonful."

"Consider it yours," says I, and leaves him there.

Then I went around the fort until I found an Indian who was wearing a blue tunic with a yellow scarf that turned out to be the police uniform and not clothes pulled off a dead trooper at the Greasy Grass, which I had wondered about before noticing the badge pinned on him.

Now you put a Sioux of that day into such an outfit, you had a person who was uncertain of himself when talking to a white man, even in his own language. He never wanted to be an arse-kisser of the people who if they hadn't been there he wouldn't of needed to become a cop over his own kind, so he didn't really like or trust the whites he worked for, but on the other hand Indians was as human as anybody else, which meant they did not find it without pleasure to lord it over their fellowman, which in their case could happen only if he was red.

Believe me, I appreciated his position, being so often myself between two standards of judgment, so I spoke in a flattering way about his uniform, which included a black hat with the smooth-dome crown Indians always favored without a crease, worn on a head with as short a haircut as our boys at the Major's school was obliged to have. This was a remarkable style for an adult, Indians putting the high store on their hair as they did. Just think, these fellows was of a people who used to take the scalps of their dead enemies: now they was trimming their own in the service of the same folks.

"My wife," said High Dog, for that was his name, "wanted to make this coat prettier with some beads and trimming, but that is not permitted. She can't understand why we are supposed to all look alike. Women find it hard to think in the new way."

"I see you are still wearing moccasins."

"That is permitted," High Dog said in his stilted fashion. "It is too uncomfortable to wear boots. The hat and coat and especially the pants were hard to get used to, and I take them off as soon as I get off duty and go home, but how white men can wear boots I have never been able to understand. You can't feel the ground through them, you walk on boards. Yet Bull Head is able to do so. I think that's why they made him lieutenant."

"I'm sure that's why," says I, and changed the subject. "What I wanted to speak to you about is Sitting Bull. Long Hair Cody and I are friends of his, since a few summers ago when he was with Cody's show. We have heard he is in some trouble now, and want to help him if we can."

A change come over High Dog's dusky countenance. Where he had been slightly sanctimonious, talking to a white man who presumably approved of him being a policeman, he was now guarded. I sensed he believed me a spy of the ruling power, but I didn't know how else to approach him given the shortness of time available. If I had had a week,

I would of tried to slowly gain his confidence, and smoked and ate some meals with him, but if I knowed Cody I had only until the next morning, after he had drunk all them officers under the table.

"Sitting Bull," High Dog said, "lives on the Grand River with his wives and children and horses."

"So I have heard." I waited awhile for him to go on, but he never. "What I wonder," says I, "is what he thinks of this Ghost Dance that seems to interest a lot of tribes and not only the Lakota."

"I have heard of that," High Dog informed me. "But I don't know enough about the subject to say anything worthwhile, and my father told me when I was a child not to open my mouth unless I had something of value to talk about."

So though I had succeeded in getting information out of Corporal Gruber, I failed to get any out of High Dog. From the Sioux with B.B.W.W. I already knowed that Indian politics had gotten complicated due to white policies. A law called the Dawes Act, a couple years back, had offered a hundred sixty acres of land to every Indian who wanted it, and after them parcels had been distributed, all of the rest of that big hunk of land embracing what today would be most of eastern South Dakota, originally belonging to the Sioux by treaty, was to be made available to white ranchers and farmers at a dollar and a quarter an acre. Most of the chiefs at first opposed this offer, which to go into effect had to be accepted by three-quarters of all the adult males in the Sioux nation, but somehow in the end the Government claimed they had collected sufficient signatures (though how that could be told from what must of been a collections of X's was uncertain at least to me) including those of some of the very chiefs who had originally been against it, but one of them was not Sitting Bull. He was too smart to fall for a deal like that, and too stubborn to pretend to do so. He had compromised all he was ever going to do by becoming a farmer, because there wasn't an alternative left, but he wouldn't ever give whites the okay they wanted to destroy the way of life into which he had been born.

And now this Ghost Dance movement come along, it seemed likely he would support it if only out of cussedness, so the authorities decided to arrest him before he could do any harm.

To my knowledge, the last time a prominent Lakota leader had been taken into custody, he had got stabbed to death in a scuffle that nobody could ever rightly explain. I refer to Crazy Horse. If that fact immediately occurred to me, it would certainly be remembered by Sitting Bull. I figured he ought to be warned soon as possible rather than wait for Cody to empty every bottle at Yates, so I left a note in the room assigned to Buffalo Bill in the officers' quarters and started off for the Grand River, of which I knowed the direction, having if you recall been there in '85 with Arizona John Burke when we signed the Bull up for the Wild West.

Having no mount, and I couldn't borrow one without letting Colonel Drum know where I was going to ride it, I was on foot. It was a thirty-mile walk. I wasn't as young as I once had been, and before long it was nighttime, but the terrain was mainly flat, and I hit my stride after a while under the helpful light of the moon in the clear cold air of late fall.

By first light I had reached the Grand and headed west along the river and inside another hour I looked down from the bluffs and seen a little settlement of cabins and corrals and cultivated fields below.

So I went on down there, not seeing anyone at all or even hearing the barking of dogs, until I come around the corner of the biggest of the log cabins, and there, standing in the open doorway, wrapped in a red blanket, was Sitting Bull.

"Do you want to eat?" says he. And then, "How far behind you is Long Hair?"

"He's still back at Yates," I says. "You dreamed that we were coming?"

"No," says he. "I saw someone's breath on the bluff a while ago. I recognized you only when you reached the cornfield." The high ground was almost a mile away, and the cornfield a good two hundred yards, and he hadn't seen me in five years!

"Yes," I said. "I would like to eat. I've been walking all night."

That weathered face of his, so fierce even in repose, crinkled up further in amusement. "And you're not as young as you once were."

"None of us is." I give it right back to him, and his smile broadened. I mention this because of the idea that Indians, and especially the likes of Sitting Bull, was without humor. "But how did you know Long Hair was coming unless you dreamed it? Can you see all the way to Fort Yates?"

"I have friends," said he, and he did not go further.

"I think you know," I says, "that Long Hair means no harm to you. Bear Coat asked him to come because he likes you." I wasn't going to mention the detail about arresting him. "*Pahaska* wants you to come back to the Wild West." Taking some liberties in what I said, I told him he was the biggest attraction the show ever had; that when I told the

Grandmother, the Queen of England, he had worn a medal with her likeness on it, she said it was her great honor and wanted to tell him so to his face; that Little Sure Shot missed him badly; and that Cody would double his wages from five years ago. As to the last-named, if that wasn't possible, I'd kick in my own salary.

"Long Hair has a good heart," Sitting Bull said. "When we go inside my house I will show you the white hat he told me to take along when I left, and back there in the corral is that fine gray horse that was also a parting gift from him. But I'm an old man, too old to travel to all those towns, to be amidst white people all the time, looking at them and what they have built and what they own." He winced. "My head begins to hurt when I even think about it. This is my home." His brown arm, still looking strong, come out from beneath the red blanket, and he pointed in the direction of the Grand. "Right there is where I was born. I would have put my lodge across the river, but the white man from the agency told me the land on this side looked better for raising crops, and I listened to him, as I always listen to people when they speak about something they know and I do not."

"You have a nice-looking farm," I says, looking around. "I'm sure you're a good farmer." I hoped the amenities wouldn't take too long, for though we still had some time, given that Cody would be sleeping late once he finally got to bed and then would have to make the ride down here, I really didn't know what he would do when Sitting Bull turned him down, for Buffalo Bill had a great respect for the Army and was flattered to be given the mission by General Miles. So I wanted to get to the heart of the problem at hand, but with an Indian that's never the matter of a moment, unless of course you are attacked by force and without warning, when talk would be beside the point.

In all other situations you had to eat and smoke and palaver for a long time, starting out as far as possible from the subject and only gradually closing in on it, for the arriving at a decision was as important as the decision itself. I told this to some bearded fellow in France at one of the parties they give for B.B.W.W. and he says it had an amazing similarity to a theory he was developing about poetry and philosophy, et cetera, there being Frenchmen who spent their lives fiddling with such concerns, for it takes all kinds.

I could see, however, with a falling heart that the Bull was not going to be hurried. He pulls his arms back inside the red blanket and says, "Come in and eat."

So we enter his cabin, which looked pretty much as it had in '85, consisting of one room with log walls on which hung various items on nails, feathered headdresses, weapons of various sorts, leather or cloth garments, medals presented at the signing of treaties, and in a real prominent place so it could be seen as soon as you entered, that big white sombrero Buffalo Bill had give him. Aside from having square corners, the place was pretty much like a tepee inside, for there wasn't no furniture to speak of, unless a number of separate beds made of buffalo robes and blankets, on the floor, qualified.

He invited me to take a seat on a folded hide, and he said, "The woman will bring the food soon. She had to collect the eggs." He sat down himself, across from me. "I own eighty chickens," he said. "The woman would have prepared the meal more quickly, but by the time I recognized you, she was in the midst of the other work."

I reckon he meant feeding the livestock, milking cows, fetching buckets of water from the river, and suchlike, the normal chores for which even white farmwomen would pitch in, but with the Indians of them days would be done entirely by the females of the house.

Which reminded me of what I had heard at the fort about some white woman living with him, but there wouldn't be any polite way to look directly into such a matter, so I didn't try.

And in fact didn't need to, for she herself now come in the door, carrying a tin platter of food. She was dressed in long, real modest garments of the type worn by Lakota women, though hers was entirely of dark cloth, unadorned with ornamentation, nor did she wear any on herself, no necklace, earrings, or bracelet. But the most noticeable of her differences from an Indian female was her pale face, framed in lank hair that, though it could of used a wash, was still blond. Last time I seen it it had been piled fashionably high.

In fact she was Amanda Teasdale.

19

Life on the Grand River

N OW I COULD SPEND A LOT OF TIME HERE ON WHAT feelings was caused to arise in me by the sight of Amanda, meanwhile growing even older, but suffice it to say I had a good many and at a rush, and for a while I was on my own with these, for attending to her job like the Sioux woman she was, so to speak, impersonating, she never met my eyes.

Also, since I quickly poked my chin into my chest, lowering the brim of my hat, she couldn't of seen my face for more than a second even if she had looked. I should mention here that I continued to wear the hat indoors not in any disrespect but because Sitting Bull lived in the cabin as if it was a tepee, and in the latter you wore any head covering you wanted to. In other words, taking off your hat indoors was just a white man's way, and the Bull might of even been insulted if I did it in his lodge.

So Amanda put that platter on the floor between us and went out the door.

I didn't know what to think, and there wasn't anything I could of said that wouldn't sound improper, so I kept silent. I also must of ate some of that food, but I wasn't even aware of doing so, such was the turmoil in my mind.

The Bull chewed with great gusto, smacking his old seamed lips. Since this would of been real late for his first breakfast, it must of been the second, and I reckon he was pleased by my arrival if only for the excuse to eat again while feeding a guest.

He chewed for a time and then said, "That is the first white woman I ever knew who could cook a good meal."

As I say I hadn't even noticed let alone tasted what I guess I too was eating.

He went on. "The other one wasn't any good at cooking, but she could paint nice pictures. I'll show you one of them afterwards."

I was grateful for a peg to hang my attention on. "There was another white woman?"

"She went away," he said. "She did not approve of the Ghost Dance, and like a white woman, had to tell me as much though it was not her place to do so, even after Seen by the Nation and Four Robes explained it was not proper."

Them last two named was his Indian wives of many years, and they was sisters. Annie Oakley never liked to hear they was bought by him for one horse each, though Frank always got a big laugh out of that fact. Annie never had trouble understanding that it was quite a high price at the time, but what she couldn't believe was that a man could care for a wife obtained in this manner, let alone two. But she wasn't an Indian.

"I didn't run her out," the Bull says, I guess in case I would think him a mean man. "She got mad and left."

I remembered why I come here. My personal feelings had to be put aside. "Bear Coat thinks you are causing trouble with the Ghost Dance, and so do the agent and the soldiers at the fort. They all agree you should be arrested. Good as this food is, I think we should get out of here as soon as possible."

Sitting Bull nodded and chewed some more. "Don't worry about it. Everything has been decided."

I had been afraid he would come to some such conclusion, based on my early experiences with Old Lodge Skins: you couldn't talk an Indian out of what he seen in a dream or heard from an animal. In the present case it turned out to be a meadowlark, *sdosdona*, for that breed is, as everyone knows, fluent in Lakota (and he took time out here, even on this solemn subject, to kid me about my supposed faulty command of that language). Birds had always been his friends, since one saved his life once as a boy when he was attacked by a grizzly bear, by telling him to play possum.

"If *Sdosdona* saved my life by speaking truly, he can prepare me for my death," said he. "He did not say when I would be killed, but he told me who would do it."

It didn't matter if I believed it or not, and I tell you I did and I didn't, for I had been raised Indian but had since went to many of the major cities of the world and met queens and popes and went up in the Eiffel Tower and rid on railroads and steamboats and stood next to someone talking on the telephone, while here he was, setting on the floor of a crude log cabin eating with his hands, damn superstitious dumb redskin — tears come to my eyes as I'm telling this, as they might of at the time, for I feared he knowed what he was talking about, for at bottom we each live in our own situation.

"You believe the soldiers will finally kill you?" It might be the way he wanted to go, in one last fight.

He shook his heavy head, braids swinging, and he snorted. "The soldiers have never concerned me my entire life. They are only another enemy, one much stronger than the Crow and Pawnee, but still just enemies. Those who will kill me, the meadowlark said, are my own kind."

This I could not believe. "He could not mean the Lakota."

"Yes," said Sitting Bull, "and he spoke the truth."

It didn't matter if I believed him or not, for *he* sure did, which of course could and maybe should of been the end of the matter for me. I liked him but I doubt he had any special attachment to me, and I never owed him nothing the way I would of had he been Cheyenne: he weren't family.

But I have always admired a man of whatever color for standing up for his own point of view while the rest are falling all around him. You will recall that principle applied to my feeling for George Armstrong Custer, who I otherwise never cared for. The attitude he had of regarding as pathetic everyone who could not be Custer stood him in good stead at the end. So with Sitting Bull: if a bird told him how he would die, he regarded that as one more proof he was spiritually superior to his enemies, white or red, in which case being killed could be seen as the greatest success.

But I wasn't going to stand by and let another of my friends get slaughtered after having had a premonition of approaching death. If I let myself think about it, I still could not evade some blame for failing to stop Wild Bill Hickok's murder.

But before I could deal further with this matter, Amanda come in the door. My back was to her, but I could feel as much as see her shadow.

Sitting Bull said, "Yellow Hair has not learned much Lakota. Therefore it's difficult to tell her what to do. Two Robes and Seen by the Nation have taught her some things, of course, but if she wants to be useful she should speak our language."

Notice he did not ask me to interpret between her and him. It was up to me to offer, but I could hardly get out of it, and anyway I'd have to identify myself to her sooner or later, dreading the moment though I did.

So I asked Sitting Bull what he wanted to say to her now, and he asked me if I wanted more food, and when I replied I did not, he said, "*Henana.*"

So without turning my head, I says to Amanda, who was still behind me, "He don't want no more."

So she comes and squats to pick up the platter, and this time she looks at me, being low enough to see under the brim of my hat, but she still didn't say a word.

"Good day, Amanda," I says.

"Good day, Jack," says she, and rises without visible effort and leaves.

Sitting Bull didn't comment, either, but I felt I should explain. "We know each other, she and I." And then since he still said nothing and for all I knowed might of assumed we belonged to some white tribe of which all the members was acquainted with one another, like his Hunkpapas was, I expanded on it in a simplified way, saying we had met in New York, which after all he had himself visited with the Wild West in '85.

"If you'd like to take her with you, you may," he said. Though old and fairly portly due to meals of the kind he just ate, he too rose to his feet in quite an effortless style.

Whereas I, who was still slender as a boy, felt my years and lack of recent practice at sitting on the ground to feed. My knees was not as flexible as they once had been, and I had walked around thirty miles overnight and was stiff. I wasn't sure of how to respond to his offer when I finally got to the standing position.

So I says, "I'll talk to her later, if you don't mind."

"That would please me," said the Bull. "I did not invite her to come here, but I can't very well throw her out. She seems to be an agreeable person, but having her around makes me uncomfortable, and the other

Hunkpapas don't like the idea, particularly at this time of the Ghost Dance."

Now I got to explain why this famous chief and wise man of the fearsome warrior nation of the Sioux found himself not able to expel an unwanted guest: it was them laws of hospitality. An Indian of the old days was at a disadvantage if his bitterest enemy got inside his lodge: he might slaughter him anywhere else, but he was forced inside his own home to treat him as a guest, feeding him and putting him up as long as he wanted to stay. One of the worst sins to a Plains Indian was lack of generosity.

You take that bunch in Italy called the Borgias, who I heard about when the Wild West was over there, for they had a lot of power around the time some of them old palaces and churches we visited was built, supposedly they was famous for inviting folks in for a meal and then dropping poison in the food and drink. No Indians I ever knowed would do such a thing, which should be pointed out along with their failure to contribute much to the history of architecture.

"You must take a look at the picture the other white woman painted of me." No doubt he referred to Amanda's predecessor. "It is in the other cabin, where the women can look at it."

"What was her name?"

"I can't remember," says he, "because it's hard to pronounce. But you will see it written on the picture when you look at it."

"Yellow Hair's white name is Amanda Teasdale." I don't know where the impulse come to mention that: it wouldn't mean much to him.

"I would be happy if she went away," said he. "If you want to, you might suggest that to her."

"All right," I said, and knowing what he meant, I added, "I'll let her think it is my idea. I'll do that right now so I don't forget." I stepped outside.

I welcomed the excuse to go talk to Amanda, now that I seen I wouldn't get anywhere in urging Sitting Bull to get out of there before Cody showed up, which by the way ought to of been pretty soon, judging from the position of the sun. That meal, at which I couldn't remember eating anything, had obviously taken quite a while nevertheless.

There was some Indian women coming and going at the other nearby buildings or lounging about if they was men, and young kids running around at play, all of them closely related to Sitting Bull as it would turn out, wives, daughters, sons, sons-in-law, and grandchildren, though some of the youngsters was of his own offspring. It was just like all the Indian camps I ever knowed, except the lodges was square, made of wood, and not portable, and the Sioux no longer was allowed to do the two activities all Indian life had previously been arranged to further, namely, hunting and war — unless of course they joined Buffalo Bill's Wild West and did them in make-believe.

I found Amanda around the corner, tending a cookfire. Now I could see her in full daylight, her face was smudged with soot on one cheek, I guess when she cleared a lock of wispy hair from her eyes with a dirty hand as she bent over the embers. The hem of her skirt showed dried and hardened mud, being too long for this life, dragging on the ground, and I reckon the whole dress was filthier than it looked, for twice while I approached she wiped her fingers on the skirt, but luckily it was so dark nothing black showed though anything lighter did, such as the yellowish mud and then in back was something looked like one of the babies had spit up where she last set down.

She was poking at the glowing coals with a stick, separating them so they'd burn out quicker. I guess Sitting Bull's women taught her that. A white person would be likely to drench the fire with water, plenty of which flowed in the nearby Grand, but if you done that the charcoal wouldn't be of any use till it dried out and you might need it sooner, and you would also squander the water which had to be fetched by bucket. The stick kept catching fire at its end, at which she would pull it away and extinguish the flame by screwing it vigorously into the ground.

I tell you, I couldn't spare the time for anything but the most important question, at least to me. "Amanda," I says, "where's that husband of yours?"

She straightened up, swiping at her cheek again with her left hand, leaving behind more smudge. "Husband?" says she, them deep blue eyes looking real puzzled. "I don't have one."

"You never got married back in New York?"

She made a face like a little girl's, corners of the mouth turned up, eyes rolling, an expression of hers I never seen before and a specially unusual one to see in her present situation. "Jack," she says, "I did not get married in New York."

"I went to that Friends of the Red Man office," I says, "and there was a sign on the door saying it was closed, and the janitor told me —"

"Oh," says she, "*now* I know what you're referring to. When my asso-

ciate Agatha Wetling was married, the wedding took place in Boston. I
was maid of honor. We had to close the office for a few days. Aside from
a secretary, there were only the two of us on the executive staff." She
sniffed. "All too many people were on our governing board, though,
most of them men. It wasn't long afterward that the organization was dis-
solved." She lowered her head, scratched the still smoldering stick on
the earth, and murmured, but then raised it and managed to look proud
though disheveled. "So I finally decided to do what I probably should
have done in the first place instead of trying to deal with the Indian
problem at a distance: go to the heart of the matter."

I immediately returned to my old sympathy for Amanda, while actually thinking she was misguided. "Well," I says, "you come to the right
fellow. There ain't nobody alive who's more one hundred percent Indian
than Sitting Bull, but he's involved in something now that probably nobody can help him with. Not even his old friends like Buffalo Bill, who
by the way is heading here right at this moment."

"Oh, not that awful charlatan," Amanda said in cold disdain. But
then she give me an appealing look. "Jack, can't *you* do something to get
rid of Cody? You know him."

I was torn in several ways. Amanda could get to me usually, plus I
didn't approve of Cody's mission as specified by General Miles, but I
couldn't believe he would ever try to arrest Sitting Bull and just maybe
he could talk him into returning to the show after all. Beyond all this of
course was the unlikelihood of Cody's listening to me unless I was agreeing with him, and whatever he did would be preferable to having them
Indian soldiers show up, anxious to prove they could do a good job of
controlling their own kind.

"Amanda, I'm saying this for your own good, believe me. I know you
mean well, as always, but — forgive me for asking this, it ain't no criti-
cism — I was wondering what you hoped to accomplish coming here
and working like an Indian wife."

Thank heavens she didn't seem offended by the question. "I suddenly
realized," she said, "that I have previously been morally fraudulent. I had
been looking at these people from an enormous distance. That was true
even at the Major's school." She sneered. "And to work for the cause as
far away as New York was grotesque."

A great need to defend her, in this case from herself, come over me.
"Well," I says, "that's where I think anybody'd have to go to raise the

most money, wouldn't they? It's true there ain't many Indians to be seen there, aside from Cody's show, but out here in the West, with plenty of Indians around, the whites generally hate them and ain't going to look kindly on you."

This found a mark with her. "They're horrible. Poor Catherine Weldon! The newspaper called her Sitting Bull's white squaw, living in sin with an old savage. And she was given worse names at Fort Yates — by the white wives, of course."

"There you are," I says. "I bet you was doing a swell job back East, right near Wall Street too." I had no real idea of what I was talking about, but I did so want to buck her up.

She sneered again, though as before it was not at me but at herself, nor was such an expression an unattractive one with a face like Amanda's. "I did such a good job that the money we laboriously collected managed to disappear without a trace, though neither Agatha nor I took any of it beyond administrative expenses."

"I doubt you're the only person to run into crooks on the money side of an enterprise," I pointed out. "Next time you'll know what to look for."

"There won't be a next time," Amanda said. "I've learned my lesson."

First it was Sitting Bull who exasperated me. Now it was her. Why is it people you like are always the most stubborn? It was time for me to get stern. "Now, Amanda," I says, "how long are you going to hang around here working like a flunky? You ain't an Indian woman and you'll never be one. What you're doing is just make-believe, for the reason you can go back to the white world any time you get tired of this." She had thrown her head back and looked away. "And I expect you will do that soon enough, for Indian wives perform all the hard labor of the camp while the men don't do much of anything, and to the white way of thinking that's wrong."

Now she looked at me and said, "Ha!"

"All right," I says, "so amongst whites except for rich people the women do a lot of chores too, but the husbands go out to work. All I'm saying is it's different with Indians, but so is most everything else, except for the fact that they seem to like what they do, which includes, or used to in the recent past, being merciless towards their enemies, torturing, killing, scalping, and mutilating. If you think you can become a squaw as your latest project, then you really ought to think about what it took to cut the guts out of a wounded cavalryman laying on the field at the Little Bighorn." Even talking turkey as I was, I couldn't bring myself to tell her sometimes it wasn't guts but the private parts of such a poor devil, after which they stuffed them in his mouth. "Yet there ain't no mother more tender to her offspring than an Indian, so they're not always different in everything. But it takes a long time to see Indians as a whole, as well as a real strong stomach."

I could never get one up on Amanda. She smiled at me now and, though her face was dirty, spoke with her old assurance. "That was an eloquent lecture, Jack, but as it happens, I already agreed with its points before you made it. I have no intention of impersonating a Lakota woman. I'm just trying to understand what it means to be one, admittedly in white terms. And I think I'll learn more here, though no doubt never enough, than in some Indian-betterment organization, or at some university under the direction of white men."

That was reasonable enough, I figured. But then what?

"Write about it," says she.

I was always impressed by anybody who could just read and write in the common way, being fairly shaky at both all my life, but to write *about* something meant more than a postcard or list of camp supplies. "For a newspaper?"

"Well, maybe," said she. "Or a book."

"Excuse my ignorance, Amanda," I says, "but that would likely take you a few days, would it not?"

"At least." She seemed amused by my question.

"Yeah, well, I doubt you're going to have that long, here anyway. They're aiming to put Sitting Bull out of business in one way or another, and none will be pretty. Please get out right away. I know what I'm talking about!"

One thing this accomplished, if nothing else: she took more personal notice of me than ever before. "Jack," she says quite warmly, "you've always tried your best to help, and it hasn't gone unnoticed by me. You have a good heart."

Hearing that, my good heart fell. Who wants to be praised for his kindness by a woman he takes to? I wasn't no preacher nor settlement worker. But she wouldn't of been Amanda without adding a twist, which brung back my hopes after all.

"I wonder whether you would do me still another favor?"

"Anything at all, Amanda."

"My greatest difficulty here has been due to my ignorance of the language. I had expected some of the Sioux to know more English than it turns out any of them do. Of course I have learned a little by pointing and asking what it's called, but that's a laborious process and useless for nonmaterial things such as thoughts and feelings." Her smile though with a dirty face was as beautiful as I ever seen. She gestured towards me, putting out a slim hand. "Could you teach me to speak Lakota?"

"You ain't going to leave?"

"Sitting Bull," said she, "is the greatest living Indian leader. My study is not simply of what it is to be a Lakota woman but what it is to be a wife of Sitting Bull. I'm going to stay near him."

Which meant she as usual wasn't really taking me seriously. However, I had no choice but to say, sure, I would start the lessons soon as she wanted, and she said it would have to wait a little, for she had other chores to do. Now you might wonder, like me, how that had come about if she couldn't communicate no better with the Indians, but I found it was her idea to hang around the women and imitate them, and if it turned out she was in their opinion pretty good at something, like cooking food to please the Bull, why, she was welcome to do it. As odd as Indians often was by our lights, they could also be totally practical.

I don't want to be indelicate, but I admit when Amanda mentioned learning about being a wife to Sitting Bull, I hoped she wasn't referring to sharing his bed as part of her research. Of course I couldn't openly pursue that matter. I'd just have to watch where she slept that night, if in fact I was to know that night as a free or even a living person. I figured Sitting Bull would just politely turn Cody down, but violently resist any attempt by Indian police or white troops to take him away as a prisoner, and while, had I been acting on my own behalf, I would of left before this happened, having done what I could to warn him and thus discharged my moral obligation to a friend, Amanda's presence made it necessary for me to remain and help him, and maybe get myself arrested or even killed in the process.

But so as not to keep you in further suspense, let me go through what did and did not occur that evening and for the next couple weeks.

First, I waited all day for Buffalo Bill's arrival, but he never come. What happened, as I learned afterwards, was that Agent McLaughlin and Colonel Drum had been able to stop him after all by that emergency appeal to President Harrison, who sent a return order telling Cody to lay off and go home.

Nor during that same period did anybody appear who was unfriendly to Sitting Bull, but a number of Hunkpapas did get the Ghost Dance proceedings set up in a nearby field, fallow now in winter and suitably flat for dancing, with an associated sweat lodge, an old-fashioned hide tepee where water was poured on hot stones, creating a steam that would make the naked bodies of the sitting participants perspire, purifying the spirit for the ceremonies. Afterwards they would put on special Ghost shirts of what to a white man would be real good quality deerskin, specially decorated, but finally just leather and not the bulletproof material an ordinary Sioux might well work himself up to believe. But I didn't think Sitting Bull would go that far, and I'm not saying he did, though he went into the lodge and sweated with the others.

It wasn't the kind of thing I could ask him about directly, but just being in the same camp I could pick up enough on the subject to get a general sense of the situation, and most of it come from Sitting Bull himself. He wasn't sold on the Ghost Dance, but he wasn't against it either. What he wanted to do was give it an opportunity. Probably it wouldn't work, but maybe it would, and meanwhile it offered people something beyond the limited existence imposed on them by the victorious whites.

He had heard quite a bit about Christianity, from all sorts of missionaries, including even one who was female, and in fact sometimes wore as personal decoration that crucifix give him by a Catholic priest. But most of what it pertained to was quite distant from him and the Lakota way. What good was a Spirit up to who told you to turn the other cheek to an enemy with a raised hatchet?

He did not condemn white people for having beliefs that to him seemed lunatic, for obviously they derived great power from them, though he did observe that the whites who enjoyed the most power was those who acted as if they believed in nothing but force, which is to say, against the religious teachings he had heard, and this made even less sense and could not be explained by the missionaries except by the idea that this present life wasn't the important one, but just preparation for a better one to come for them what was the losers now, and torment for those who at present was the winners. But it seemed to Sitting Bull that to believe in such an arrangement you had to hate the life at hand, the one you could see and hear and touch and taste, in favor of another that seemed real vague, and it was strange that the very people who controlled the world would have a religion that despised it.

But he admitted there was much here he never understood, and maybe many white people didn't either, for it was on its face a lot simpler than it was underneath, and that's why he was interested in studying the Ghost Dance, to see if it had the profitable complication for Indians that Christianity had for the Americans. For example, the magic shirt might not repel a lead bullet in the simple sense, but give the wearer so much spiritual strength that he would be harder to hit. As was proved in every battle, the bravest warriors was least likely to be wounded or killed. And the predicted great flow of earth that would cover white people while Indians rose above the surface might happen not in a literal fashion but rather be a visionary way of seeing the red man elevate himself over the whites by some means yet to be developed.

I tell you, Sitting Bull would of come to the top of any race he belonged to. I'm sorry he never met Queen Victoria, for I bet they would of admired each other as wise leaders, the best of their kind. I'm not saying he didn't have no weaknesses, of which the main one was vanity, and he did not go without the "envyings" my foster father the Reverend Pendrake used to mention. The Bull believed himself principal chief of all the Sioux, and since the tribe didn't have elections or hereditary titles, that position had to be self-bestowed, which never endeared him to the other claimants, who he then accused of selling out to the white man. I never heard him praise any other chiefs but Crazy Horse, who of course was safely dead. He was least fond of Gall, one of the main combat leaders at the Greasy Grass, where Sitting Bull never took the field. That the Bull was represented as the killer of Custer when he appeared with the Wild West was embarrassing to him on the one hand but probably gratifying as well, putting him one up on the lesser-known Gall, who got revenge by doing better in the complex politics amongst Sioux factions on the reservations.

Which brings us up to date on Sitting Bull's predicament. He had finally gotten on bad terms with every bunch, red or white, and except for the family and friends at his camp, everybody was plotting for his ruination, including some Sioux visitors to the place, hospitably received as guests, who was actually spying for the Indian police.

But before I go on with this, I should say I had been giving Amanda them lessons in Lakota she wanted, but with the chores she had took upon herself she didn't have a lot of time and so had not learned much except a number of names of things she thought it most practical to know first, like "beef," *tado;* "stick," *can;* "pot," *cega;* and so on, mostly pertaining to domestic affairs, along with a few simple phrases, like "he comes," which is just *u;* "we eat," *unyutapi;* "you drink," *datkan.*

I had to try to explain to Sitting Bull why I had not gotten her to leave, but this turned out easier than I thought, for when I brought up the subject he smiled and said, "It's no surprise to me. White men can never control their women."

Well sir, I was stung by this, and I says she was not "my" woman but just somebody I knowed, a friend, almost a kind of sister.

"But you would like to make her your woman," says he. "Anybody can see that from the way you look at her. My wives and daughters giggle about this and wonder why you don't make her yours. But unlike me, they don't know the ways of the whites." That was another of his vanities, that he was an authority on the Americans. I expect he might of been so, in comparison with the others, but he was also not shy about representing himself as such to a white man.

"If you're saying what I think, it's against the law," I pointed out.

"American law, perhaps," says he. "But this is Hunkpapa land."

Now to dispute him on that would be nasty, so I swallowed my pride and just mumbled something about how it wasn't really the way he thought, about me and Amanda; it was just difficult to explain in Sioux.

"I hope you are teaching *her* to speak good Lakota," he says, grinning, "even though you don't speak it correctly yourself." And he adds that he heard her ask a question using *hwo* instead of *he,* which was to say the male form instead of the female. She might of done so, for I admit I was not always as careful as I should of been — and look at my English — but he also might of been kidding, for he was given to that, as I like to give reminders of due to his reputation, like that of most Indians, for being humorless.

As for Amanda, I told the Bull she stayed on not to be annoying but to study him and write a book in which he would be celebrated (though I didn't know it was true she would admire him without condition especially when it come to the woman question, but I expect he was safe, for if he survived the current trouble, he couldn't read anyhow).

If I thought he would seem flattered by this news, I was wrong. His opinion of himself was so high that he naturally assumed everybody else shared it unless they was naturally wicked or crazy, especially women, and being he was illiterate, a book didn't mean to him what it would to someone who could make out what the marks on its pages said. He preferred the paintings of that earlier white woman whose name, according to Amanda, was Catherine Weldon, which he could understand, and he was also a pretty good artist himself, in the Sioux way, having sometime before made a long pictorial account of his exploits in battle as a young warrior. He give that to his adopted son Jumping Bull, originally captured as a boy from the Assiniboine and now grown up, who I got to show them to Amanda, which he wouldn't of done otherwise, being like most of the others, real shy of her.

Me and her slept under the same roof, in the main cabin, though not together. Not real far apart, though, either, for you couldn't be in a place of that size, given all the others who also spent the night there: a couple of Sitting Bull's kids, his nephew's wife, and often enough a man or two from the Ghost Dance, as well as the Bull himself and his wife Seen by the Nation. Being square, the house wasn't as suited to purposes of lodging as a tepee would of been, where the sleepers was arranged neatly like the spokes of a wheel without the problem of corners, but everybody found a place for his or her blankets. Amanda usually bedded down not far from me though could not of been touched unless she extended her own arm towards mine, and there wouldn't of been any call for that.

Naturally I never told her what the Indians had been saying about us — and not out of concern for her feelings so much as my own: I was afraid she too would find it amusing from her own angle.

So that was the state of affairs down on the Grand as of a couple weeks after Cody left Fort Yates. No authorities of any kind showed up at Sitting Bull's settlement, and far from waiting around for the axe to fall, he was going about his life as if he had no enemies in the world. Not only had he been studying the local Ghost Dance at close hand, but now a man come from the Sioux reservation at Pine Ridge inviting him to go down there and visit their own dance, for they expected it was close to the time for victorious results of the kind predicted.

Sitting Bull decided to accept the invite, but to do so, since he was still in effect a prisoner of war, he had to ask McLaughlin, the agent, for a permit.

"I'm going to do this properly," he told me, "by writing a letter that will make my reasons clear for wanting to visit Pine Ridge."

I thought this was a good idea for a change, and I says if he told me what he wanted to say, I would be glad to translate it for Amanda, who would then write it down in perfect English.

Sitting Bull thanked us for the offer, but said with all honor to us, he nevertheless had to turn it down. As the matter was a Lakota thing concerning religion, it would not be proper for him to speak through white people however friendly, so he had decided to have his son-in-law Andrew Fox do the translating and writing.

Now it was all I could do not to groan out loud, for Fox had learned what he thought was English in reservation schools, the same place he got first-named Andrew, probably by somebody like the Major, but was actually near-gibberish, but I couldn't tell that to Sitting Bull, who put great store in the young man, whose wife, the Bull's daughter, had took sick and died only a few years earlier.

Here's what Sitting Bull told Andrew Fox in Lakota, near as I can remember, though I have cut back on some of the rhetoric, which the Bull would of been wise to do himself.

> I met with my people today, and I send you this message. *Wakantanka* made all of us, white and red, and the whites have been more powerful, but now the Father of us all has decided to help the red man. Therefore we are praying to find the right road, and do not want anyone to come with a gun or a knife to disturb those prayers. Praying does not make me a fool. You think that if I were not here, my people would be civilized, but because I am here they too are fools. You did not always think that way. When you came to visit me, you said my praying was good, but now you have changed. Be that as it may, this letter is to inform you I must go to Pine Ridge to look into what they are doing with their own Ghost Dance. I hear you want to take away our horses and guns. Is that true? I will thank you for answering promptly.

Now here's what Andrew Fox come up with for an English version, and he was right proud of it when he showed the laboriously penciled text to me and Amanda. I would say his handwriting was awful hard to read in the first place, but then I never myself been noted for penmanship so ain't criticizing that, just pointing out that we might of misread some of the scribble. Once again I give only the gist and not the entire message, which was even more of the same.

> I meeting with my Indians today and writing to you this order. God made you all the white race and also the red race, but white high then the Indians, but today our Father is help us Indians. So we all the Indians knowing. I wish no one to come in to my pray with they gun or knife. You think I am fool. If I did not here, then the Indians will be civilization. But because I am here, all the Indians fool. When you was here in my camp you was give me good word about my pray, and today you take all back from me. I will let you know some thing. I got to go Pine Ridge and to know this pray. A police man told me you going to take all our ponies, guns also, so want you let me know that. I want answer back too.
>
> *Sitting Bull*

After Amanda read this and then me, both in silence, Sitting Bull beamed proudly on Andrew Fox and says, "You can now see why I wanted my son-in-law to write this letter. It is no reflection on you. He not only knows English so well, but also how to speak to the Americans in a voice that gets their respect."

I was worried Amanda might not of been so diplomatic as me, and spoke up quick so as to forestall any expression of dubiousness from her.

I didn't see no choice but to tell Sitting Bull, "I understand what you mean. Let's just hope McLaughlin does the right thing." Though I for one didn't know what the right thing would of been. I was real fond of Sitting Bull, but I wasn't sure he should be allowed to visit Pine Ridge. He would be taking a chance: with him away from the Grand River, his settlement would be at the mercy of his enemies.

Well, only one of the requests made in the letter was answered in the affirmative: McLaughlin was prompt in responding. Next day he sent back a quick refusal to the main point. No, the Bull was definitely not allowed to go to Pine Ridge or anyplace else. Instead he was supposed to cease and desist from engaging in any more Ghost Dance activities of his own, and to send away all Indians presently engaged in them at the Grand River.

What McLaughlin did not say was him and Colonel Drum had finally set in motion the plans to make the arrest. At daybreak next day, without warning, the entire contingent of Indian police, led by Lieutenant Bull Head and Sergeants Red Tomahawk and Shave Head, was to invade the settlement and take Sitting Bull into custody living or dead.

Bull Head had been at the Greasy Grass fight fourteen years earlier — I guess I should specify, on the Indian side.

20

Death on the Grand

GIVEN THE KIND OF EARLY LIFE I HAD HAD, I WAS GEN-
erally a real light sleeper, but on this morning, maybe having a
premonition that what- and whenever anything happened concerning Sitting Bull, I wouldn't be able to stop it, I was not woke up
by what must of been the considerable noise outside of arriving horses
and dismounting men, and was not brought fully awake even by the
pounding at the cabin door and then somebody yelling, "*Tatanka Iyotanka!*" in a voice full of bad feeling, though I heard it as the trailing off
of an unpleasant dream, from which I'd open my eyes to the crowded but
real homey room full of people on good terms with one another and
whose combined body-heats warmed the place against the outside cold,
for it had snowed some lately and ice had begun to form on the Grand,
and anyway whoever was yelling was Indian, using the Bull's Lakota
name, so it wasn't the U.S. Army attacking like they done when I lived
in Black Kettle's village on the Washita and the Seventh Cavalry rode
down on us.

I didn't know what was going on till after the door was throwed open
and a lot of people come in in the dark, walking over us on the floor,
kicking me in the ribs and stepping on my stomach in the process, and
somebody lit a match and then a candle and when I had rolled off that
foot in my gut and looked across, I seen in the candle glare the recumbent figure of Sitting Bull and staring down on him the profile of a big
Sioux nose under the brim of a police hat.

"We came for you," said the latter in a voice without special feeling,
but then he stepped aside and several others grabbed the old Bull and

pulled him roughly out from under the blanket though he never seemed to be resisting, and got him to his feet, stark naked, his barrel chest covered with the scars of old wounds, and they wrestled him across the room, not stepping on no one this time, for most of the other occupants of the cabin was running outside now, but I hadn't done so on account of my concern for Amanda, who wanted it explained before she moved an inch.

Let me say that unlike Sitting Bull, she slept fully clothed, as did I, in my case owing to the cold.

"For God's sake, Amanda, let's go!"

"Can't you talk to them, Jack?"

"What could I say?" I pressed her to the wall, myself between her and them pushing past. This was the closest me and her had ever been, and even at this hectic moment I was concerned she might misinterpret my motives.

Now there was a lot of yelling, most of it so far on the part of the police, near as I could tell, so she had to shout when speaking to me. "Remind them that they're all Indians!" she cried.

"I think they know that!" I hollered back, near as she was. Amanda's belief in doing good had always been part of what attracted me to her, maybe just because I was myself sceptical in such matters, based on my experience of violence, but allowed for the possibility that such experience might not provide all that could be said regarding human affairs, especially by a merciful woman. "People of the same kind can be enemies," I yells. "Remember the Civil War!"

"You can at least try," she says in a reproachful tone, at a lower volume now because the commotion had moved outside, leaving us alone.

Well, you know the soft spot I had for her, so out I went, where the dawn was getting brighter by the moment, and a crowd of Sioux was milling about in the patches of snow and breathing steam into the otherwise crystal-clear cold air, with the nearby animals doing likewise, the horses of the police as well as the big gray stallion Buffalo Bill had give Sitting Bull, which was tied nearby, ready for the Bull's trip to Pine Ridge reservation, his asking permission for which visit was the immediate cause of this raid.

Except for me the people was all Lakota, forty or fifty of the police and maybe half that many on Sitting Bull's side, relatives and people there for the Ghost Dance, coming out of the other residential cabin and the outbuildings, the women and little children behind them.

Sitting Bull's wife Seen by the Nation had brung out a handful of clothes, but the policemen was still manhandling him so he couldn't put them on.

"Why won't you let me get dressed?" he asked, in a mouthful of steam. "It's cold."

"*We* will dress you," one of the blue uniforms says, and grabbed the clothing from Seen by the Nation, shoving her roughly aside, and a couple of them begun to put the garments on the old man's body each by each, telling him by turns to lift his foot or raise an arm, and so on, like he was a little kid.

And to give you an idea of how great he was, he chose not to show bitterness here but rather, displaying one last time that wit of his, told them ironically, "You need not do me this much honor," with reference, as every Sioux would know, to their practice of helping a chief attire himself on occasions of high ceremony.

Now I had promised Amanda, who was watching from the doorway of the cabin, that I would try to do something, so I addressed the sharp-faced Indian wearing a lieutenant's gold bar on his tunic, the highest rank I could see.

"Why are you acting so disrespectfully to this great chief?"

He looked down his nose at me. "*This ain't your affair,*" says he, in English, in the very flat way Indians speak that language, surprising me.

He was putting me in my place, and though he might of been right, I got real burned up at some redskin "officer" trying to high-hat me — as always I'm trying to tell God's honest truth: I was helping an Indian against others of his race, and the first thing that occurred to me when stopped was being myself white — but to my credit I right away felt embarrassed, and in words that was supposed to sound official, I says, "*Yes, sir, Lieutenant, I am aware of that fact, but what I was thinking was maybe you could use more restraint when taking him into custody.*"

But when he just frowned and moved away, I realized he didn't know English *that* good, and that was the last chance I had, for Sitting Bull was now dressed, and the lieutenant, whose name I should tell you was Bull Head, grabbed him by the right arm, with Sergeants Shave Head and Red Tomahawk respectively on the left and behind the old man, the last-named shoving him along with a pistol into his back.

The other bluecoated police encircled them against the growing crowd of the Bull's people, who was shouting defiance, and one of the most evident was Sitting Bull's son Crow Foot, who usually spent the night with the rest of us in the main cabin. He was the survivor of a pair of twin boys born the night before the fight at Greasy Grass and thus represented big medicine. The Bull had always put great expectations in him, even sent him for a while to the missionary school that female preacher ran at the agency. He was a fine-looking young man fourteen years of age, a time when a boy of any race gets impatient with his elders.

So while Crow Foot had joined with the others in abusing the policemen, he also yelled at his Pa, "Father, if you are a brave chief, why do you let them take you away?"

Sitting Bull had been cooperating thus far, though them policemen was pretending otherwise, no doubt to build themselves up both in their own estimation and the eyes of the onlookers, but hearing the voice of his son, he stiffened his old body, in which there was still a lot of contained force, and refused to move further and though his captors was pulling and pushing him with all their might, his strength drawed its source from deep in the ground under him, like a lofty lodgepole pine with roots going down to the center of the earth.

And he says quietly, "No."

Lieutenant Bull Head was fit to be tied, and he took one hand off his captive to straighten his hat, which in the exertions had almost fell off, and he says, with a pleading note, for he was getting real nervous about the unfriendly crowd, "You *have* to come. I have my orders. I am in charge."

One of the other policemen had untied the gray horse and was leading it forward. This animal had been trained to perform in Buffalo Bill's Wild West, and he still, rode or led, had a dainty show step which you noticed right away.

I had remained in place without nobody's attention. I didn't want to get back to Amanda, for I hadn't been able to do what she wanted, and she weren't in no danger I could see. I judged the crowd would continue to threaten and bluster, but there wouldn't be no bloodshed of Sioux against Sioux, and in the end, having made his point, Sitting Bull would relent and mount the gray horse and be taken in to the agency, where the next step would come when McLaughlin confronted him.

That the Bull would go to jail was unthinkable, but the worst was generally what happened to warriors of such great prowess — they survived all battles to be defeated in peace.

Now at this moment Sitting Bull looked slowly around him, as if taking stock of them all, the policemen and his own friends and family, so like an eagle in glittering eyes and beak, not cruel but so intense and alert he might seem so to those ignorant of nature. And then he seen me, who was alone and out of place and therefore invisible to the others, Indians never seeing what they didn't know how to deal with, so long as it wasn't harming them so's they could notice: that was why whites called them primitive. And the Bull wouldn't of seen me either, but that he had a message for me in that glance, sent in silence through the briefest glint of eye: *It's just as* Sdosdona *predicted.*

And I was thinking, Well, he made too much of it, he was just being arrested by his own people, not killed, so the meadowlark had exaggerated quite a bit, like human fortune-tellers tend to do, claiming they was a hundred percent right when being only ten, and I tell you I was greatly relieved to learn the bird had missed by that much.

Now through the crowd pushed a man called Catch the Bear, holding a blue blanket around himself in the morning cold. He had been one of Sitting Bull's closest friends and followers for many years, but in the same degree hated Lieutenant Bull Head's guts long before this episode, due to a dispute them two had over a matter of beef tongues, which meant it could not of been more serious.

He goes right to the point now, him and Bull Head glaring at one another. "You're not going to arrest *Tatanka Iyotanka.*"

"*You* won't stop me," Bull Head says, in a voice of disdain.

"Come on," Catch the Bear calls to the crowd. "We won't let them get away with this!"

People began to shout in support of his sentiments and press against the ring of soldiers.

Bull Head glanced nervously from side to side, and pulled his pistol from its holster. "I'm in charge here," he says to Catch the Bear, who though still staring at him in hatred does back up some. Then Bull Head called to the policeman holding the horse to bring it closer, for he had been detained by the crowd.

Catch the Bear suddenly gives the Lakota war cry, which no matter how often you heard it would raise the hair on your neck even if you was on the same side. Last time for me had been fourteen years before at the Greasy Grass, and I tell you it struck my soul now, and I might of run if I could, unarmed as I was.

And then Catch the Bear throws off the blanket and raises the rifle he was carrying underneath, and he fires at Bull Head, who falls, but, still alive, lifts his pistol and shoots Sitting Bull in the heart at that close a range, at which Sergeant Red Tomahawk puts his own pistol to the back of Sitting Bull's head and blasts the old man's brains out.

At which lead begun to fly all over the place: a policeman named Lone Man killed Catch the Bear, while Sitting Bull's men pumped more rounds into the fallen Bull Head, and then the shooting got so hot and heavy I didn't watch no more but dropped to the ground and crawled in the opposite direction to the most intense firing, though that changed almost instantly, so I guess I went in circles.

What I cared about most was reaching Amanda, who I could only hope was sensible enough to take cover. I couldn't help her much if I was killed myself. At the moment I wasn't reflecting consciously on the death of Sitting Bull, just saving my own hide, but it had had its effect, and all the more so when I had just decided he was going to be, if not happy, then at least alive. I wasn't only embracing the earth, which meant slush and mud, but I was also shaking violently. In the years since Tombstone I had got out of the habit of seeing what gunfire does to the person it hits: when that person is someone you know, maybe even dislike, it ain't never pretty. When it's somebody you care for and admire, you first feel fear before the least touch of anger.

In my crawl I kept encountering fallen bodies, all Indian, some in blue coats and others in camp clothes. If I looked up I couldn't see much except a fog of gunsmoke. Also, since that was the way to get shot in the face, I tried to keep it down, but then at one point I thought I had been hit anyway, for my cheek was smeared with wet and when I rolled my eye at the nearby earth I seen a puddle of red. I waited for the hurt to arrive, which takes a while sometimes when you don't know you been wounded. I even seen men die without knowing they been touched. But the fact was I hadn't been hit. The blood come from a dead Hunkpapa who laid nearby, his nose smashed in and one glittering black eye still open.

Then all of a sudden there was no noise whatever, which happens in every battle before it's really over. If you kept your eyes closed and pinched your nose shut so you couldn't smell gunpowder and blood, you wouldn't know it happened, but it might be even worse than when the shooting's going on, for thinking you was out of danger can be your last mistake, so I just kept crawling, head down, and when I finally raised it enough to take my bearings, I seen, beyond the bodies all over the ground, a bunch of Sitting Bull's people running for the stand of timber along the Grand River. No one was chasing or even firing at them at this moment, for the policemen was tending to their own fallen.

I couldn't see Sitting Bull's corpse from where I laid, but no doubt it was yonder, beyond where the gray horse was, the show animal give him by Buffalo Bill, and I'll tell you the damnedest thing I ever seen happen in any of the many battles I ever engaged in or witnessed: that horse was prancing and bowing and rearing up on its hind legs, and then doing a little curtsy, right front hoof bent back, taught it maybe for when we met royalty, had not Cody made the present to Sitting Bull. Hearing the guns go off all around it now, the trained animal didn't know they wasn't the blanks used in B.B.W.W. and proceeded to perform its part in the show, concluding by sitting down on its hindquarters and raising one hoof.

While the lull continued I had to take advantage of it, and I got to my feet and dashed for the cabin, where thank heaven Amanda was still unhurt though having stood in that doorway throughout, I reckon being paralyzed by the awful sight she seen.

She was still gasping now. I grabbed her by the waist and pulled her inside and into the farthest corner of the room. It would of been nice to have some piece of furniture to use as a barrier, but there wasn't any.

"They'll start shooting again directly."

"Oh, Jack," she says and hugs me tight, but that was only because she was not afraid but horrified. I never saw Amanda show fear at any time, come to think about it, and I don't say that with unqualified admiration, for it can be foolish not to be scared at the right time. "Jack," she gasps, talking against the side of my head, "how could they do that?"

"They're human," I says.

And just then the door which I had closed was shoved open and in come a bunch of Indian police, carrying their four or five wounded, among which was Lieutenant Bull Head, who though shot many times was still living.

I quick moved in front of Amanda, but Sergeant Red Tomahawk and his men disregarded us as they found places to put the casualties down, and in the course of gathering the bedclothes of them who spent the night there, they come to where Sitting Bull slept next to Seen by the Nation and pulled the blankets off, and there was young Crow Foot, cowering on the floor.

Having seen his Pa murdered right before his eyes, he weren't the cocky young warrior no longer, but rather a scared young boy.

"Uncles," he says, "please don't kill me."

"Get up," says Lone Man, kicking the lad in the ribs, and then asks Bull Head, who was laying nearby, "What should we do with him?"

"Whatever you want," says the lieutenant, in not the strongest voice, for he was still leaking blood from multitudinous wounds. "He's as bad as the others."

Lone Man hit the boy in the head with the butt of his rifle, and Crow Foot lurched through the open door.

Amanda hadn't understood the Lakota words, but when she saw the young man get struck, she pushed me aside and dashed after Lone Man and the rest, who had followed Crow Foot outdoors.

"No," I yells. "Keep out of it, Amanda!"

But she never stopped and was yelling herself at the policemen, in English of course and in a woman's voice, and she got maybe one foot out of the cabin, with me just behind, when Lone Man lifted his rifle and shot Crow Foot in the back, spinning him around, and then a number of the other policemen emptied their guns into the boy as he was falling and even after he was on the ground. By now they had worked themselves up to a state of fury I hadn't seen since the Greasy Grass.

Amanda was still screaming, but luckily none of the policemen still paid her any heed, and now the shooting started up again, with Sitting Bull's people firing from the trees along the river, and the Sioux police from cover behind the cabins and barn, and then come another sound of anguish: Sitting Bull's womenfolk, wives and daughters, had gathered in the smaller cabin and their Lakota wails of grief would tear your heart out.

With the gunfire coming our way from the trees it wasn't advisable to stay in the open, so I tried to pull Amanda down to join me in at least a crouch while I looked around for cover, but she wanted to remain standing and denounce them responsible for the carnage, so we had a bit of a struggle, and being fit and young, she put up quite a resistance till I recalled an old Cheyenne wrestling trick of tripping up an opponent, and she went down, fortunately on a patch of ground not yet touched by the blood flowing from Crow Foot's crumpled body. But it soon would be. Therefore, still grappling, I had to roll us away.

"Goddammit, Amanda!" I finally had to yell. "Stop fighting me! We got to save ourselves!"

I guess she had been in shock, which can happen to a person in the middle of a fight, especially if they ain't themselves a part of it except by accident, but she all of a sudden stopped resisting and says in a reasonable tone, "All right."

And immediately I was embarrassed to be wrapped around her, so to speak, in a recumbent position, though it wasn't personal, and I disengaged and stuck my head up enough to see over the dead Crow Foot, but every structure in sight was being used as cover from behind which the policemen was shooting at them in the timber. We couldn't go back to the main cabin, lest Amanda begin to light into them there for the murders of Sitting Bull and his young son, and though sympathizing, I couldn't of stood listening to the Indian women in the other building mourning for what might be hours, if we was stuck there.

So we just continued to lay on the ground, where it was so cold that Crow Foot's blood soon begun to skim over with ice, and we was only wearing indoor clothes, that same wool dress of Amanda's and in my case a shirt and pants and the boots I fortunately had kept on all night, not being able to sleep when my feet was chilly. When I seen Amanda had been in her stocking feet all along, I rolled over and took off Crow Foot's moccasins, which he wouldn't need any more, and give them to her. He wasn't wearing anything else that wasn't soaked with blood.

I thought it was her who started shivering so strenuously that she looked blurry, so begging her pardon, I says we had to hug or freeze to death, and it wasn't until I had been embracing her for a while and warmed up some that I realized I was the one who had been doing most of the shivering. But she hugged me back without protest, so I guess it was okay.

I don't know how long we laid there in one of the strangest situations I had ever been in in a life characterized by many — it was awful in the obvious way while being also personally remarkable — but it might of been an hour or so, the gunfire tapering off to the point where you thought it was all finished only to start up again, until all of a sudden, in the distance, somebody shot a cannon our way, the ball hitting just alongside the barn. Looking between the buildings I seen a puff of smoke rising from the high ground above the river valley, and there come another, followed by a second *boom*. I heard the thud of that ball when it hit, back of the main cabin.

"How do you like that?" I says to Amanda, hugging her even closer. "Now the Army's shooting at us."

A couple of the Indian police come running out of the cabin, with a piece of white cloth tied around the front sight of a rifle, and waved it frantically at the hills.

There weren't no more cannonfire, and after a little while here come a troop of U.S. Cavalry riding down into the bottomland. We stood up at that point, for the firing from the trees had stopped, and in fact I could see Sitting Bull's men slipping away upstream. In the immediate sense, this hadn't been a fight with the Americans.

Now soon as the soldiers rode into the settlement, Amanda marches up to the captain in charge even before he dismounted and starts in on the crimes of the Indian police.

I guess he had heard she was living with Sitting Bull and therefore thought her at best crazy and at worst a harlot so low she would cohabit with an Indian, but to his credit he was civil enough while not taking her too seriously.

"Missus," he said, "I'm just a soldier following my orders. You want to take your charges to my C.O. at Fort Yates, Lieutenant Colonel Drum. Now excuse me please, so I can attend to my duties."

He strides away with Sergeant Red Tomahawk, who is talking in an excited rush of Lakota, which I doubt the captain could understand a word of but kept nodding.

The other soldiers dismounted and was staring at Amanda, for though far from her best at the moment, having been rolling in dirt and blood, she was still something to see.

I was worried they might say something fresh, which I would have to respond to, though being so worn of mind and heart I could hardly stand straight, so once again I found myself trying to divert her from what came natural to that girl: sticking her nose into the affairs of others to serve the cause of right, which, don't get me wrong, I admired, but which often tended to get complicated. Here you had Sioux killing Sioux to serve white policy, but the whites who dreamed up this policy believed they was trying to help the Indians in a place and era in which many other whites would of liked all redskins exterminated.

"Amanda," I says, "that captain's right. What we ought to do is go back to the agency and report on what happened. We can't do no good here."

"I hate to think that's true," said she, but she did stop and think about it. I don't want to ever give the impression that Amanda though opinionated was unreasonable. "Maybe there's something we can do for the poor women." She started off for the other cabin, where the mourning wails had continued so long that it would of been noticeable now only if they stopped.

When Amanda went I had to follow, and we got to the cabin, where the wives and grownup daughters was sitting in a line on top of a long deep pile of blankets, producing that chorus of grief. Amanda walked along touching each on the shoulder, but what I noticed was the total absence of young kids, for there was always otherwise some nearby.

In glancing around to look for them, I seen hanging on one log wall that portrait of himself Sitting Bull had told me about, a full-length view of him in full feather headdress and best beaded and fringed deerskin clothes, a stark contrast to the bloody body which lay outside now on the cold ground. As he had told me, the picture was signed by the white woman who made it, "C. Weldon," the name he claimed was so hard to pronounce he forgot it. The Indianness of that statement was such that I could of shed a few tears if I thought about it, but I didn't have no time for that, for now a white Army officer come in, accompanied by some Sioux policemen, and the lieutenant, holding his ears, hollered at the women to stop that howling, and Amanda screeched at *him*.

Meanwhile one of the police spotted the painting of Sitting Bull, and yelling in fury that his brother had been shot and killed by the Bull's followers, pulled Catherine Weldon's picture off the wall and smashed in the canvas with the butt of his rifle.

I had to shout to be heard by the young cavalry lieutenant. "I talk Sioux," I says. "What are you looking for?"

He rolls his eyes at Amanda and shakes his head. "Weapons," he told me. "We don't want to get shot or knifed in the back." He pointed at the Lakota women. "Tell them to get their dirty asses up. I want to see what's underneath those blankets."

Amanda says, "You keep a civil tongue in your head!" And then blunts her point by adding, "You foulmouthed bastard."

The officers starts back at that, and thinking she was Sitting Bull's white whore, he might of slapped her face, but my presence gave him enough pause for me to speak to the Indian women.

"He wants you to get up," I says, "and you'd better do it before they yank you up by force."

So Seen by the Nation and her sister Four Robes done as asked, rising in their wrapped blankets, as did the daughters, the married Many Horses and her Pa's favorite, little Standing Holy, just entering her teen years.

The lieutenant had the policemen pull away the top coverings from the heap the women had been sitting on, revealing two young Hunkpapa boys cowering together, naked except for their breechcloths.

I doubt, with the officer present, them lads would of met with the fate of Crow Foot, but Amanda wasn't going to take a chance. She lighted into the lieutenant, threatening to ruin him if a hair on those boys' heads was touched. And whether that were the reason or not, nothing worse was done them than a search of their persons, which uncovered no weapon aside from a broken clasp knife, which was confiscated.

The lieutenant happened to see that picture of Sitting Bull on the floor where it fell, with a smashed frame and a torn canvas, and he says to me, "That looks like a genuine oil painting. Tell them I'm willing to buy it though it can't be worth much with the rip in it." He winked. "Anyway, how would they know?"

That seemed pretty cold to me, since the picture was a remembrance of Sitting Bull in better days than would ever come again, but I passed the offer on to Seen by the Nation and Four Robes, not wanting, for the wives' sake, to put the officer in a bad mood.

But their reaction was a surprise, not because they was Indians, who I thought I knew, but female, who I sure didn't know. Turned out they was only too agreeable to selling the portrait. It finally occurred to me that might of been because it had been painted by that white woman. You notice it had not been hanging in the main cabin run by the senior wife. Anyhow, the lieutenant acquired it for two dollars, to which, without telling him, I added all the bills I had in my pocket, which turned out to be a rash gesture on my part, for I hadn't any money left, and Cody had departed from the region. But I never thought of the consequences at the moment.

The officer had the Indian policeman who tore the painting carry it out for him, and he followed with the rest of them and me. I figured serving as interpreter I might be able to head off any treatment of the defeated that was too nasty, for Indians saw no reason for mercy towards them that had been opponents, even when related.

But I didn't get out of there soon enough to prevent what might practically of done no harm, for the old man was dead, but was as ugly a thing as I had lately seen, and had I been closer I would of put my knife in the belly of the perpetrator.

Them loyal to Sitting Bull had long gone, but there had now gathered a number of non-uniformed Sioux to see what happened, relatives of the policemen what had been killed or hurt in the fight, and just as I stepped out of the cabin one of them was carrying a heavy yoke he had took from the barn, probably for some such purpose as this, and raising it high above the body, brung it down on Sitting Bull's dead face.

Just ahead of me, the lieutenant saw this too, and yelled, "Stop that man!"

And running, I translated it literally, "Nazinkya!" for the benefit of the policemen ahead of us, who of course till then thought it was perfectly okay, and for the perpetrator himself, I added, "Or your guts will be cut out and fed to the crows." He dropped the yoke then.

The features of Sitting Bull's once noble face had been rearranged, and I won't say more except I was just glad Amanda had remained behind with the women.

The disrespect to Sitting Bull's corpse wasn't at an end, but I couldn't interfere in what occurred next, for I understood what was involved. The Indian police intended to deliver the body to McLaughlin at the agency, but they also had four corpses of their own men to haul back and only one wagon. Putting Sitting Bull alongside their comrades in the wagon bed would mean he was a man of equal value, and their blood was still running hot due to the bitter fight.

So they pried his old body from the ground, where its blood had froze and glued him down, and throwed it, the back of the head blown off and the chin where the nose should of been, into the wagon, then carefully placed the dead policemen on top of him.

All I wanted now was to get away from there, and not just from the Indians, who was now so degraded as to act like the whites in Dodge and Tombstone, hating and killing one another of their own kind. I had had a stomach full of that long before and should never of come back West. Hell, I had been on good terms with the Queen and Prince Bertie and a lot of Frenchies I couldn't even understand, not to mention Italians and Germans, all of them civilized to the hilt. I was mostly ignorant at the time of the mass slaughters they held periodically and not only of the various kinds of coloreds in their distant empires but also of one another right on their own ground. But at this period they was in between such, at least in Europe while I visited, no doubt getting ready for the next bloodbath, so it wasn't for a few years yet I come to realize that no matter how old I got or where I went there would probably be a lot of killing sooner or later, and I should remember to accept it as I did when a boy amongst the Cheyenne. Growing up had made me soft. But so be it. At this time I had seen enough people die violently, and I was getting too near fifty years of age.

So I went to the door of the cabin of women, and I asked Amanda to please come outside.

And she done so, saying, "Jack, we've got to do something for these people."

"Amanda," I says, "no we don't."

She stared at me with them big eyes, which in certain kinds of light looked so dark as to be navy blue. "We don't?"

"Mind you," I says, "I'm not saying they ain't in trouble. What I mean is only that you and me are not going to be able to do anything about it staying here except just to witness more of the same. We can't stop it or even slow it down by hanging around. I say let's get out. That book of yours will be a greater help than anything you can do here. You seen quite a bit by now that will be news to other whites, and you know English real good and can tell a story I bet people will read."

"And what will you do?" She actually seemed interested.

"Well, you might not approve, but I'm going back to Cody's Wild West, where a number of Indians make a nice income from shooting blanks. They might just be actors now and not the noble savages they was once, but they don't get killed either."

She had the saddest and also the sweetest expression, for in Amanda them two feelings often seemed intermixed, whereas when she was most pleased she was brisk and cool. "I do learn by experience," she says, "unlikely as that might seem."

I never before heard any self-doubt from her, and in a way I was sorry to do so now, for as I have said often enough I was always impressed by them who was assured. But then most such that come to mind had had unfortunate ends, the latest of which was Sitting Bull, whereas if you seldom knowed what you was doing, like myself, you might live as long as me.

Having give all my cash to the Indian women, I hadn't none for railroad fare, so was forced to borrow some from Amanda, who carried some money in gold under her clothing someplace, and while we traveled together for a short ways, she was going on to New York, whereas I was heading back to Cody's ranch at North Platte, Nebraska, the nearest thing to home I had, where I expected to find Buffalo Bill and tell him the true story of the death of his old friend Sitting Bull, because Lord knows what version he would get from others.

My heart was full on parting from Amanda again, though this time it was on real friendly terms, and unless it was my imagination she too seemed reluctant to say goodbye, shaking my hand a little longer and more warmly than ever before.

All I managed to say was, "I hope we meet again, Amanda. I sure do."

"Thank you for saving my life, Jack," said she. "I want to stay in touch with you."

For an exciting instant, I took that statement literally, but then I realized she probably meant we could keep in contact through the mail. By the way, now she was going back to civilization she had spruced herself up, getting rid of that bedraggled dress and buying nice clothes at a ladies' shop in Pierre including even a fashionable hat.

"It sure would be great to get a letter from you, Amanda," I says, "but I got to admit I myself can't write proper English."

She smiles and says, "I don't have any difficulty in understanding your speech."

"Nice of you to say so, but I don't have to spell when I talk."

She then says seriously, "Such things shouldn't matter between friends."

As usual she was thinking of what ought to be rather than what was, but had she thought otherwise I would not of put her on a pedestal as I had always done.

Now just let me conclude this part of my story with what was not a part of it personally and say that some of Sitting Bull's followers, fleeing from the Grand River, joined up with a band of Minneconjou Sioux led by a chief named Big Foot, and a couple of weeks later, at a creek by the name of Wounded Knee, Custer's old regiment, the Seventh Cavalry, met up with Big Foot's bunch to parley about them turning in their guns and settling down quietly without no more Ghost Dances or anything else of a troublemaking nature, and a shot got fired by somebody, maybe by accident, touching off a scuffle which, unlike the Custer fight, had a satisfactory result for the civilized, in that this time all the Indians got massacred, a couple hundred of them including women and children.

The Minneconjou, if you recall, was camped on the other side of the Little Bighorn opposite Medicine Tail Coulee, down which that day in June of '76 General Custer rode with an idea of crossing the river to attack the big village, only to be drove back and up to the ridge where he died. That shallow part of the river was ever after knowed by the whites as the Minneconjou Ford.

21

The World's Fair

A s it happened, I got to Scout's Rest in Cody's absence. His mission to Sitting Bull hadn't been successful, but Bear Coat Miles had quick give him another. Generals from Custer on had a soft spot in their hearts for Buffalo Bill, so it made sense when he was himself promoted to that rank in the Nebraska National Guard, in which capacity Bear Coat sent him to inspect the situation as to the Indians along the borders of his state, after which General Cody had went up to the Pine Ridge Sioux reservation, where some of the Wild West Indians was working as police, and he joined Miles for the surrender of the last band of Sioux regarded as renegades.

So when he finally come home, he had a lot of the latest events to relate, and Sitting Bull's death was old news. He didn't show no curiosity as to where I had went when disappearing from the officers' club at Fort Yates two months earlier, which was typical of his ways. But also typical was his hearty pleasure in seeing me again.

"Well," I says, "you heard all about how Sitting Bull got killed, but there's one thing you might not know. That gray horse —"

He lifted his glass high and interrupted me to say, "Let's drink to the memory of old Bull, who was a fine old fellow. I'm sorry I was prevented from reaching him, but there were political forces at work."

"He still kept the hat you give him," I says, "and as for that horse, there's a story. It seems —"

"I have made arrangements to buy the horse back from the widows," says Cody, raising his chin so the goatee was pointing at me. "I'll ride in on him at the beginning of every performance, carrying the Stars and

Stripes. What an attraction it will be, not to mention the historical lesson for the children of America."

So I never did find out if he knowed how the animal had went through its show tricks right during the little civil war the Sioux fought on the Grand River, and I brung the matter up here only to demonstrate again how Buffalo Bill's mind operated. He would of saved Sitting Bull if he could of, but since he hadn't, he wasn't going to waste time in lamentation. Instead he would find a practical use for the horse the Bull left behind and, it should be pointed out, bring some profit to Seen by the Nation and Four Robes. This was Cody at his best, when seeing an advantage for himself also brought one to others. That was as American as you could get.

Unfortunately, however, he could only pull this off in show business. I never knowed another financial venture of his that did not lose money, including the modest amounts I was able to invest in them, so you might well ask why I continued to contribute, especially when he himself done all he could to discourage me, being often full of hot air but never a crook. I'll tell you why: all of them sounded too good in the planning to fail in reality, the land-development projects, the patent medicines, and all, for other folks was making big money in them days in similar enterprises. Take that pal of his, Doc Powell, what come up with White Beaver's Cough Cream the Great Lung Healer. He had also concocted a beverage by the name of Panamalt, a healthy substitute for any other kind of drink considered harmful: ladies could use it to wean their drunk husbands off alcohol, which might be wishful thinking, but the idea I thought was a real winner was selling it to the Mormons, who had banned the drinking of coffee.

Another business I was sure could not help succeeding was the hotel and livery Cody started in Sheridan, Wyoming. But all went under sooner or later. Maybe if Bill had been able somehow to apply his genius at make-believe to these ventures they might of done well, but I guess he used that up with the Wild West.

Speaking of which, I'm going to condense the next couple seasons here, for though each had its differences from the others, they was sufficiently similar not to go overly into the details.

We started up in '91 in Germany, which if you remember is where we left off the previous year, and though there was the now familiar efforts by people of the type Amanda had been to get the Government not to let Cody hire Indians any more, they failed once again, and not only did we have a hundred Sioux in the troupe, a good many of them had been the very Ghost Dancers involved in the troubles in Dakota Territory, only now earning good money by entertaining white people, so Buffalo Bill had made his point once again.

But during the winter when it had looked like there might be a coming season without Indians, Nate Salsbury hired a lot of other horsemen to fill the gap, and all of them stayed with the company, which included cavalrymen from the U.S.A., England, and Germany, Russian Cossacks, gauchos from Argentina, *vaqueros* from Mexico, American cowboys and -girls, and the big band, not to mention all of them in support of the performers, among which could be counted yours truly.

At that time there was around six hundred fifty people with Buffalo Bill's Wild West, and foremost amongst them, still the sweetheart of the public wherever we played, though now no longer the young girl she had once been, was Annie Oakley, one of whose feats, a great favorite of the fellow who put himself at risk, was shooting the ashes off a cigarette being smoked by Kaiser Wilhelm, who she had knowed as Crown Prince when she done the same stunt. (Many years later, at the time of the First World War, she said she regretted not having missed for once and put a bullet through his head.)

And then there was the time when she saved the life of some Bavarian prince about to be run down by a bucking bronco at a practice session he was visiting: she tackled the prince and rolled him out of the way, so still another decoration was added to her trunkful of trophies. However, her and Frank professed to becoming weary of travel and talked of building a house for themselves in a place back home called Nutley, New Jersey, which, though dumb cowboys and such might joke about the name, they claimed was a real nice community and urged me to consider being their neighbor and fellow member of the Nutley Rod and Gun Club amongst other local activities.

I tell you this idea had its appeal for me, could I of afforded it and had I had me a wife, for you don't undertake that sort of thing by yourself. But my predicament was that knowing Amanda had made it out of the question that I take up with any of the type of women who I could of got, meaning them on my own level. I wasn't no snob on a social basis. It's just her combination of good looks, education, personal spunk, and an urge to help people made her stand out in my experience, kind of like what Libbie Bacon might of been if she hadn't met George Custer. Then again, maybe not.

The point is, I figured I was stuck forever in the type of life I had lived up to now, and it wasn't bad, being amongst friends white and red, eating regular, making a nice wage, and playing a small part in entertaining the peoples of the world as well as what Buffalo Bill regarded as more important, instructing them in the history of the American West, for Cody greatly loved his country, the only place on the globe where a fellow like him could of done as well, and he appreciated that as did I.

Now let me say something about Germany. Wherever we went in that country, amongst the crowds, adult and children, who hung around our encampment was always a number of officers from the German Army, watching every move of ours in unloading the special train we used, setting up all our tents and tepees, cooking and feeding the troupe, and so on, and first I thought they was fixing to arrest us for not doing things the German way, which tended to be more clean and orderly than any cowboy could understand, not to mention an Indian, but Annie, who always knowed what was going on, explained that the German Army was so impressed by the way things was handled by B.B.W.W. that they was going to copy the procedures for themselves. "If you notice, they're writing it all down in their notebooks."

Then we went to Holland and Belgium and across the water to Great Britain again, performing all over the country including Wales and Scotland, where the speech of the local folks was so hard to understand it made the language spoke by the English almost clear.

Speaking of communicating across barriers, one of the most unusual examples of it I ever seen happened in Glasgow that winter, where we give some indoor performances. Cody had went back to North Platte for a couple months to deal with the management of his ranch and to quarrel with his wife, Lulu, and I was relieved he never invited me along for a change, for after the incident with Sitting Bull I was happy to stay amongst foreigners.

Anyhow, Cody's absence would mean a big loss, for though beginning to turn gray and putting on a paunch, he still participated actively in every performance, recapturing the Deadwood Mail Coach from the Indians, arriving too late to save Custer, and so on, along with the marksmanship exhibition, shooting glass balls from horseback.

A fellow name of Lew Parker, who was booking talent for the show at the time, got the bright idea of hiring a bunch of trained elephants and if that wasn't enough, he borrowed some members of the black Zulu tribe which that man Stanley, who found Dr. Livingstone in the middle of Africa, had brung on exhibition to Europe.

Now of course it didn't take no time for the newspaper people to want the two kinds of savages, Zulus and Sioux, to be put together for pictures, and when that happened, and them tall, fit specimens of the African warrior, with headbands, claw necklaces, and lots of blue-black skin met the Indians in their feather bonnets and beads, a Scotch reporter says it was a pity they couldn't converse together and maybe compare the Zulu victory over the British Army, that Prince Bertie had mentioned previously, with the whipping the Sioux give Custer.

I never cared to make a joke of it, having witnessed the latter, but I thought I'd try something.

I says to Rocky Bear, one of our Lakota, "Why don't you see if you can talk to these black people in the signs?"

He nodded, eagle feathers waving, and says, "I'll speak to them." And he starts to talk in sign language, asking the husky fellow who seemed to be their leader them traditional Indian questions on meeting a stranger: "Where are you going?" and "What do you want?" Followed by "Do you want to eat?"

And by golly if the Zulu didn't immediately comprehend and signal back reasonable answers, which under the circumstances didn't need to be literal but just polite acknowledgments, and the two continued to converse for a while not about fighting whites but on such simple topics as the bad weather in Scotland, their children, the kind of meat they preferred, and so on, for the signs wasn't made for complicated sentiments.

Cody come back in the spring, and the Wild West returned to London where we had not been since the Jubilee year of '87, and while that excitement could not be repeated the season was greatly successful and Queen Victoria, who was older than ever but still on the throne, invited us to do another command performance at Windsor Castle.

I didn't look forward to joining the Prince of Wales in his frolics, considering myself too old now for such, but wouldn't of knowed how to get out of it if asked, for it was Bertie's country, of which he might at any minute become king, so was relieved when one of his queeries got me aside to say His Royal Highness sent regrets to Captain Crabb but wouldn't be able to see him this time for reasons of state. And then this fellow, a cheerier sort than most English of the official kind, winks and says to me something about another prince called Hal who become king and couldn't see a fellow named Falstaff no more. I never understood this reference, but maybe Bertie was expecting too soon to get the crown. His Ma lasted another nine years! By the way, him and me was both the same age, but I don't know if he ever really settled down after he got the throne, and it probably didn't matter if he did, the poor fellow having grown so old waiting to become king, he croaked only a few years after he finally got there.

So we had another successful season in England, but by the time the fall come many in the troupe was homesick and welcomed the announcement that B.B.W.W. was heading back to the U.S.A., where we had not performed since '88. I wasn't personally thrilled by the prospect of returning, but neither did I want to remain in Europe on my own, maybe hooking up with one of the imitation Western shows, usually down-at-the-heels, which wandered around the Continent, especially Germany, living on Cody's scraps you might say.

Now here was Buffalo Bill's plans for the following spring: He was taking the Wild West to the Chicago World's Fair. I was glad he had found a new place for a spectacle, for nothing bucked him up more. He needed to reclaim his notable get-up-and-go, being in a current down-in-the-mouth state that was unusual for him, maybe because he unaccountably took up teetotaling on his return to England, even refusing a glass at Windsor Castle, and when Arizona John Burke told the press, Bill was commended publicly by the Salvation Army, who of course was fine people, but to be praised by them wasn't exactly swashbuckling glamour.

I myself, for the reason indicated, wasn't that keen on going home, much as I admired America over any other country I ever seen regardless of the palaces and castles, on account of it was mine, but at least we wouldn't be locating at New York, which was the last address I had for Amanda.

I haven't mentioned yet that she wrote me a couple letters during the first year of the European tour, sending them to "Mr. Jack Crabb, care of Buffalo Bill's Wild West," which meant they was delivered quickly to our encampment, no matter the country, for there wasn't no better-known attraction on earth. It was in the original letter she told me about arriving in New York, and says she missed me, which lifted my heart till I read on and seen that was mainly because there was so much information I could of furnished her, also that without me her lessons in Lakota had not continued.

In the end I felt worse than if I hadn't heard from her at all, and the reasons for not writing back had multiplied. So all I done by way of answer was to put the money I had borrowed in an envelope addressed to her, along with a note thanking her kindly for the loan. A couple months later she wrote again, acknowledging receipt of the money but chiding me amiably for not writing more of a letter in accompaniment, repeating how useful I could be to her if only by mail, and this time asking a number of specific questions, such as what was the dowry a Hunkpapa girl was expected to bring when she got married, and was there any limit to how many wives a Lakota warrior might have at one time and must they always be sisters?

I'll tell you, I tried to put my selfish feelings aside at least long enough to furnish the requested information, for I wished Amanda well with her book, but if I couldn't write good to begin with, I was ten times worse when I tried now. I couldn't even find an opening sentence that made sense. "Dear Amanda, in reply to yours of the 11th instant let me assure you of my estimation in the highest . . ." "Kindly excuse my epistolary degeneracies . . ." "Asseverations to the contrary withstanding . . ." I won't even go into how this stuff was spelled, and not having much experience with pen and ink, I did a lot of spattering on some words and accidental smearings with my shirt cuff or heel of hand. In point of fact, I sent no reply whatever.

That had been a year and a half earlier. She never wrote again. I can still to this day remember how sad I was about the whole situation at that time. One advantage of living so long is being able to take the long view when looking back.

Now this World's Fair was actually called the Columbian Exposition after the Italian explorer working for Spain, Columbus, Colombo, Colón, who got credit for finding America though the Indians hadn't yet lost it and he never reached the mainland whereas Vikings done so earlier, and finally the place was named not for him but for still another Italian who never set foot on the continent that become the home of the U.S.A. Yet it wasn't the Leif Ericson or the Amerigo Vespucci Exposition. Also, as the four hundredth anniversary of the first Atlantic crossing on the *Niña*, the *Pinta*, and the *Santa Maria*, it was a year late, for as could be expected with any American enterprise, there was a lot of differences amongst all parties concerned. But I'll say this, when it finally opened it was a wonder.

Though the most popular feature connected with the Fair was Buffalo Bill's Wild West and Congress of Rough Riders of the World, as it was now called, being more descriptive of a troupe including Cossacks and the rest, we was never officially invited to go there nor was we permitted to set up on either the grounds of the Fair proper or even the strip of property a mile long running at a right angle to the higher-minded main exposition, known as the Midway Plaisance, which by the way give its name to every carnival midway thereafter though without the French word for "pleasure" which turned out not to be required at the original site, for attractions like the gigantic Ferris wheel and Little Egypt's hootchie-cootchie dance was self-evident.

The reason why the Wild West weren't welcomed by the Fair was they considered it to be mere entertainment for profit, with all the riding and shooting, whereas they had set up Indian exhibits of their own, intended to have educational value as demonstrations of primitive life as opposed to the civilized accomplishments on display at the Columbian Exposition, the main part of which had acquired the name White City for not only the obvious reason but also that most of the buildings was covered with a French plaster so white it hurt your eyes in the glare of the full sun.

But having been welcomed at Victoria's Jubilee and the Paris exposition, Cody was determined not to be euchred out of his place in the premier blowout his own country had to offer, so Nate Salsbury, who had a genius for managing and arranging that matched Bill's for showmanship, come up with an idea that probably worked out better than being admitted to the actual Fair ever could of: he leased an entire block of city land so near the entrance to the Fair that whoever arrived at the latter by whatever form of locomotion had to pass Buffalo Bill's Wild West — and I tell you few did without coming in to see us. I heard there was a lot of people who never went further, and after a performance of ours returned home thinking they had experienced the important part of the Columbian Exposition without seeing nothing else.

I don't want to knock the Fair though, for when I say it was a wonder I mean it, and as you are aware, by then I had seen a good deal of what the world had to offer, insofar as the attractions of Western Europe went, and as a native-born American I was real proud of the great display on the shore of Lake Michigan, where within a year they built as many palaces in one place as probably all the Europeans had done together in centuries, a huge shining white building for every different type of human endeavor, Agriculture, Electricity, Transportation, you name it, and inside these was examples of the latest products or processes in that field, like huge machines running at full speed, or in Mining a statue of Justice made of solid silver from Montana, which also had a banner bragging that more copper was mined there than anywhere else in the country, a fact that despite my own association with that territory, nearly having been killed there on the Little Bighorn, I had never heard of before, which shows you the educational value of the Fair.

And there was considerably more. Most of the civilized countries of the world had buildings of their own, Germany and Spain and France and all, and there was even foreign places to take refreshment like the Polish Café, the Swedish Restaurant, and the Japanese Tea House. Then most of the American states and territories had each its own pavilion in which to put their best face forward, showing what they growed or manufactured. In between and around the buildings, throughout the grounds, was water everyplace you looked, with ponds and basins and canals and in the middle of all was a big lagoon surrounding a wooded island containing among other things real unusual Japanese houses called Ho-o-dens with high peaked roofs that swooped down then turned up again at the eaves. Then there was fountains everywhere, some called "electric" since they was illuminated at night, but so was the outsides of them white buildings, along with extra searchlights, and the result was a nighttime glare that rivaled high noon.

And you had all of Lake Michigan right there offshore, looking big as an ocean, and some of the visitors arrived by steamer. There was a good deal of boating on the internal waterways of the Fair itself, with electric or steam launches and real gondolas, poled by actual Italians, like the one me, Cody, and the Indians rode in Venice.

Then there was several historical vessels, or reproductions thereof, at anchor in the South Inlet: them three ships of Columbus', towed over from Spain, along with a Viking boat of the kind in which the Scandinavians claimed their forefathers preceded Chris: the Norwegians actually had sailed this full-size model across from the Old Country. By the way, them ships, Norse or Spanish, was tiny: you had to hand it to those who would go to sea in the old days, not knowing what was on the other side if there even was one. I'd sooner face any human enemy no matter how badly outnumbered or underarmed, for there was always a chance, slim though it might be, to bluff your way out. Having sailed across the Atlantic several times by now in the latest type of steamship, I ain't never felt so helpless as when suspended in sheer water, with the same element on every side for many days in every direction, and that in calm weather.

Well, I could go on about the marvels of the Fair, but all of them have been exceeded many times in the years since, so if somebody from today was magically transported back there it would all seem pretty quaint as to the technology that then was new. Mind you, no one arrived by airplane or even automobile, or listened to news on the radio, let alone TV, et cetera, et cetera, the wondrous devices of that day being the telephone of the American Bell Company, which could call from Chicago to New York, and T. A. Edison's Kinetoscope, an early form of movies, viewed from a peephole only one person could look through at a time.

This I considered something worth waiting for, so joined the long line in the Electricity Building and to pass the time during the considerable wait chewed the fat with the skinny young fellow just behind me, and he turned out to be real knowledgeable about a lot of the electric exhibits in the place, and specifically of those, like the improved phonograph, of Tom Edison, for he worked as an engineer at the Edison Illuminating Company in Detroit, though he had not yet had a chance to view the Kinetoscope.

He was real patriotic, reminding me of Cody in that, though this fellow put his emphasis on mechanics, machinery, electric power, and so on rather than riding and shooting, and when he warmed to the subject he told me something I found hard to swallow even standing there in this temple of technology: that one of these days an American was going to build a carriage that run by itself, that is, without a horse to pull it. And when though trying to be polite I looked dubious, he said he knowed what he was talking about, for the American who was going to do it, says he, was himself. But then he frowned and added something he never got a chance to explain further, for right at that point came my turn at the Kinetoscope, and I tell you it was awe-inspiring at that time to watch pictures of moving persons and things, like the prizefighter J. J. Corbett and the well-known dancer Carmencita, along with walking elephants and other animals, so I never got a chance to talk further with this fellow, who when we had exchanged handshakes introduced himself by the name of Henry Ford.

The remark he made was an expression of worry that his work on the horseless carriage might be stole by an international conspiracy of Jews plotting to take over the world. I had been going to invite Ford to come see Buffalo Bill's Wild West, but in case my old Pa was right, that the Indians comprise the lost tribes of Israel, I refrained from doing so.

There was also all kinds of art at the Fair, both inside and outdoors. All I have to do is look at an oil painting or a marble statue and I am rendered speechless, so don't expect me to expose my ignorance on the subject, though on the European tours I had looked at quite a bit of art, so didn't confuse the best kind with the picture of the half-naked woman a lot of saloons hung over the bar for drunks to slaver over. On the other hand, according to what I seen across the water, the real serious artists never passed up a naked lady either, especially if she had a lot of flesh on her.

Anyhow, at the Fair there was outdoor statues of men, women, gods and goddesses, horses, eagles, polar bears, and other critters real and imagined, and of course Chris Columbus, everywhere you looked, and many of the stone ladies wasn't wearing shirts. How they got away with this when young kids was admitted to the grounds, I can't say, but I didn't approve, and I can tell you this: neither did the Indians, though by now them with B.B.W.W. had seen enough of cities to know how low white morals was.

As many sculptures as was outdoors in the middle of fountains, all over the fronts of buildings and atop the roofs, lining walkways, posted at either end of the bridges and all along the railings, you name it, there was even more inside the buildings, and finally the biggest collection of all, counting paintings, could be found in an enormous place called the Palace of Fine Arts: no less than nine thousand pieces of work from all over the world. It was a revelation to me, more than anything in Europe, where you could expect them to have a lot of culture, having worked at it since Year One. This was my own country, and I for one was real proud of it, given all the time I had put in in the likes of Deadwood, Dodge, and Tombstone.

The Chicago Fair opened on the first of May of '93 and luckily the overnight rainstorm stopped in time for the procession of two dozen open carriages to make a grand entrance carrying President Grover Cleveland and a lot of other big shots including the governor of Illinois, the mayor of Chicago, and numerous other politicians, a couple Spanish ladies, one of royal blood and called an "Infant," though she looked growed-up to me, and of all people, old Bear Coat, General Miles, who was real popular with the crowd due to having answered the Indian question at Wounded Knee. The Sioux of our troupe of course didn't recognize him by appearance, but neither could I find any who even remembered his name. I keep telling you stuff like this to emphasize that the individual identities of even their enemies held little interest for Indians unless they had personal association with such. They never looked at life in the *general* way that when done by white people resulted in history, progress, culture — in other words, the Columbian Exposition — nor understood that the visitors thereto considered them part of the exhibition, as examples of the savagery from which superior humans had climbed up to the White City.

The opening ceremonies was held in the heart of the Fair and the single most impressive sight, the Court of Honor, a continuation of snow-white, columned, porticoed, balustraded, statued, bric-a-bracked edifices around a pool called the Basin, with an enormous sculptured figure standing in the water at the far end, which a lot of folks who hadn't never seen the real one thought was a replica of the Statue of Liberty but wasn't, and at the head of the pool was the high-domed Administration building behind the Columbian fountain in which a bunch of goddesses, angels, and the like rowed a stone boat with long stone oars.

There was balconies at various levels of the Administration building and it was to the highest of these that Buffalo Bill led a bunch of us from the Wild West in opening day, most of which was Sioux warriors, dressed in their feather-bonneted finery also displayed at Windsor Castle, the Eiffel Tower, and the Vatican, and from there we could look over the entire Court of Honor and beyond to where the U.S. Navy had sent battleships down Lake Michigan to salute the Fair with firing cannons, puffs of smoke followed by the booming reports, which I felt I had to explain to the Indians, fearing they might think we was being shot at.

But here was a case that reminded me they had learned some things without my help.

"I think they are shooting the same kind of blanks we use in the make-believe battle with Custer," said Rocky Bear, "only bigger." Then he shrugged. "Americans do strange things, but they don't build all of this and then send war boats to blow it apart."

I felt like a fool when he put it that way, and so as to regain authority I pointed out the ships might of been sent by an enemy.

"But *we* don't have any boats," said he, showing how narrow his Indian focus was and his ignorance of the greater world, unless he was having fun with me, which was entirely possible.

In the foreground way below us was the dais where the President and the other dignitaries had took their places, along with a grandstand accommodating several thousand people, and a big band played patriotic tunes while the multitude of fountains shot plumes of water high into the air. It was quite a grand sight, but though Cody shushed us when various folks took the podium below to give speeches, we was too far up to hear much, which I would call my good luck, for otherwise I would of had to translate a lot of hot air, though the Indians might well have liked it, given as they were to their own windbag oratory.

Also they got a favorable impression of Grover Cleveland, whose stout figure in tailcoat and striped trousers was recognizable even at a distance and in a day when few public men was skinny, and Rocky Bear praised him for it.

"A man that fat and rich-looking is probably a good president."

Next day Cody was real happy to see the Chicago papers include mention of this B.B.W.W. appearance at the ceremonies, for it had achieved just what he wanted, the most effective kind of free publicity.

"Listen to this, Jack," he says, and putting on the spectacles he should of wore at all times, especially when doing his marksman act (but instead used shells with a broader shot pattern), held up one spread newspaper and read excerpts from it. " 'Could it be mere coincidence that as from the vast assemblage below rose the glorious swell of "My Country 'Tis of Thee," a painted and bright-feathered line of American savagery moved along a balcony high above, colored blankets like flames against the alabaster dome. These remnants of a bygone primitive majesty waved their congratulations to cultured achievement and submissive admiration to a new world.' " Cody lowered the paper and took off the steel-rimmed specs. "I don't think it could have been better expressed."

Well, it sure sounded poetic, as did a lot of newspaper writing at the time, which has deteriorated since, more's the pity, but this particular example described an episode that took place only in the writer's imagination, like a lot of what has been wrote about events which I have personally participated in or witnessed. You should always allow for that possibility no matter what you read — unless the God's honest truth I am talking here is ever transcribed into print.

Now I have referred earlier to that Midway Plaisance, which was the kind of amusement-park annex to the high-toned body of the Fair with all the white temples and reflecting pools. Whoever thought that idea up was brilliant, for the Midway wasn't only fun but could also be educational while providing it: for example, that dance by Little Egypt, which our cowboys called the hootchie-cootchie and sung the smutty words somebody made up to go with the tune that was real catchy, "Oh, the girls in France / They don't wear no underpants," wasn't properly no dirty show but rather a demonstration of what the Ay-rabs see as respectable entertainment, including the outfit she wore, though it was thought real raw by some, particularly preachers and women, showing a bare belly button between a band of silk across the bosom and a filmy skirt giving the impression you could see through it.

And there was dioramas and panoramas of the Destruction of Pompeii, the Swiss Alps, a Hawaiian landscape with erupting volcano, not to mention models of sights which us of B.B.W.W. was familiar with the originals, the Eiffel Tower, St. Peter's Basilica, a German village, and so on, as well as a lot we nor most other civilized people ever before had occasion to see, like the Samoan Islanders who supposedly, at least when they was at home in the Pacific Ocean, favored a diet of human flesh, and black Africans from a place called Dahomey, also reputed to be cannibals, but whether this was true or not, some prominent American Negroes complained at how their race was represented, so them that run the Fair promised to add Colored People to the list of nationalities which each got a special Day of their own, German, Polish, Italian, and so on including one even for Catholics, and furthermore offered, as a gesture of good will, to provide two thousand watermelons for the occasion.

But the foremost spectacle of the Midway was the one you couldn't miss even if you never rode it, namely the gigantic revolving wheel made by Mr. George Ferris, and it could be seen as representing technical achievement as well as offering a then unique entertainment, two hundred and fifty feet high, carrying two thousand passengers at a time, I don't think it has ever been surpassed by anything else of its type. For half a dollar you got to travel around twice. For a while I spent most of my off-time on that wheel, along with my ready money, finding it well worth the expenditure just to get the view at the top of each revolution. That might of been childish, but it made me feel good to travel in that big slow loop in the company of a multitude of my fellow men, women, and children: each big car held more than three dozen seated, with others standing, and you could bring food along and eat your meal off the provided counters.

It took me a while to talk the Indians into riding the Ferris wheel. They was fanciful about a lot of life, but mechanical devices tended to make them overly literal. At first they figured it might be exciting to rise into the air that way, but when the wheel come around it would naturally roll over the passengers, and even though I had them look and see this never happened, they remained stubborn, but finally changed their minds and once they did, you could hardly get them off it even at show time. They next thought if it turned long enough it would come off its base and roll down the street and on through Chicago, and they never wanted to miss that ride.

The wheel was right next to a replica of the Eiffel Tower, which at only twenty foot high was another thing that puzzled those of our Sioux who had took the elevator up the real one in Paris a few years earlier. Why had it shrunk if it was the real one? If it was an imitation, then why was it so short? For the sole point of the real one was its extreme height. The special construction, which I wager to say would be what took the eye of the typical white man, held no interest to them, even though in some respects you could say it was more of an iron tepee than an actual building. But it wasn't nobody's home nor burial platform nor the pole used for a sundance, the only types of structure having a practical purpose, and it couldn't move like the Ferris wheel, so in the end it wasn't that much in the big game that I decided they saw civilization as, maybe because though Buffalo Bill's Wild West had traveled throughout half the world, everyplace we went there was either a fair in progress or we brought our own.

Well, sir, I could go on about *this* fair, the sights, the sounds, the smells, and by the way the last-named was pleasant, coming usually from hot popcorn or the pancakes fried by a stout, handkerchief-headed colored woman at the Aunt Jemima pancake demonstration, or if passing a chewing youngster, Juicy Fruit gum, introduced there along with Dr.

Welch's Grape Juice, Shredded Wheat, and Pabst's Blue Ribbon beer. Luckily Chicago's famous wind usually blew in from the lake, so we didn't smell the equally famous stockyards or the stinky Chicago River, which was so thick with filth you had to stare hard to see a current. The reality of that city give you little incentive to leave the make-believe of the Fair. But then that was pretty much my feeling wherever I went with B.B.W.W. After much experience in the actual world, I preferred the imaginary. And if I had had any doubt on that question, seeing Sitting Bull shot down would of removed it.

By the way, I should say the next season after that happened, Annie Oakley was so affected by the Bull's death I spared her the details of it. Annie wasn't no Amanda with a lifelong mission to fight injustice, but she had stayed mad about what she called a murder which, had the victims been white, somebody would of got hanged for the crime.

Reason I mention this is because of an attraction further along the Midway than anything I've yet described. I hadn't even heard of it yet, having never got past the Ferris wheel, the replica Eiffel Tower, and the Street in Cairo, with the minaret and Little Egypt, about halfway along. There was so much to see, and of course we had our own performances to do.

So it wasn't till we had been in Chicago for a few months that one day I was helping Frank set up Annie's act, readying the glass balls, the playing cards and other targets — she handled the ammunition herself — when he says she was real upset and maybe I should try to console her, knowing Sitting Bull as well as I had.

I didn't know why this should be now, for he had been killed three years earlier, but I went to where she was loading the various pistols, rifles, and shotguns she used, a job that required great care, so I waited until she was mostly done before mentioning Frank's concern.

Annie was no longer the young girl she had been on joining us in New Orleans eight years before, but she was still pretty, with her curls and bright eyes, and that wide-brimmed hat with the star on the brim.

She was biting her lip now and blinking. "Jack," she says, "I guess I should thank you for not telling me about Sitting Bull's cabin."

"Well," says I, thinking for some reason she had got to brooding about the sorry event of three years earlier, "I didn't see it would do you any good to hear more. He can't be brung back."

"I mean that cabin of his on the Midway."

I hadn't no idea of what she meant until finally I found out somebody told her Sitting Bull's house had been dismantled log by log at the Grand River site and shipped to the Chicago World's Fair, where it was rebuilt and on exhibit down at the far end of the Midway.

"I never knowed anything about that," I says. "Our Sioux probably do, but the Bull's death is a painful subject they don't talk about. These people do their lamentations at the proper time, but that's the end of it." Also, Lakota tribal politics was involved: some probably did not have friendly memories of Sitting Bull. But I never mentioned that.

"Is it supposed to be educational?" she asked bitterly, and broke open one of the shotguns and angrily popped shells into the barrels. "I call it a dishonor."

What I was thinking was how did Cody miss out on the idea and fail to acquire Sitting Bull's cabin for the Wild West? The act was ready-made, like "Custer's Last Stand": the fight breaks out between Sitting Bull's people and the Indian police, and the Bull is killed, only in the re-creation most of the brutality done to the corpse could be omitted for the sake of the children in the audience, and then Buffalo Bill rides in at the head of his cowboys, Too Late Again. . . . I answered myself: how many would pay to see Buffalo Bill try to rescue the Indian who killed Custer? Which is how Sitting Bull was still seen by the normal white person of the time.

"I agree with you," I says. "I'd go and burn it down if I didn't think people would take it as revenge for the Little Bighorn. Also, they probably paid the widows a few dollars for the cabin, which they might try to get back if it was burned."

But Annie snapped the shotgun closed now and scowled at me. She was too straitlaced for such talk. "No, Jack," says she. "Destruction of property can't ever be right. I'm going to put the matter to some people I know."

I reckon she meant folks like the many public officials who was fans of hers, for she remained one of the best-known celebrities in the country. I expect she did as promised, for Annie always spoke to the point, but Sitting Bull's cabin stayed where it was for the rest of the Fair, which in fact had only a few more months left to go, a far shorter time than any politician can get anything done provided he even wants to.

Right now she swore she wasn't never going over there to look at it, and again I agreed with her. In my case, added to my moral disapproval of them making a commercial spectacle of it was my own personal and painful memories: I had slept in that place and ate there, as a guest of my friend, and then seen him shot down and his dead body dishonored on the frozen ground outside. This sorry event joined all the others I tried not to relive in memory: I seen too many die in my time.

When I brought the subject up with Cody, I guess his reaction was typical, though at first I considered it unfeeling. "Why, sure I was aware of that exhibit, Jack. I always keep one eye cocked for the competition, but we don't have to worry. They won't take a penny away from us."

"It just seems immoral to me to put a man's home on display after he is dead," I says.

"Look at it this way, though, Jack: you can go to Mount Vernon and see all George Washington's personal effects including his false teeth. I don't think old Bull would mind, and I can claim to have known him better than most. He had quite a head for business. I assume you know he sold his one-of-a-kind personal tobacco pouch several times a day to eager souvenir-collectors, and kept the women busy making replicas thereof."

Say what you want, Cody always managed to make me feel better about things. He would of saved Sitting Bull if he could. After all, he had tried in his own way. And in the light of his principles he wasn't being disrespectful now to the old chief's memory.

Right here let me correct an omission that comes to mind: since the beginning of our engagement at the World's Fair, Buffalo Bill led the procession around the arena that begun every performance riding on that big gray stallion he had give Sitting Bull, the one that on hearing the gunfire at the Grand River shootout had went through the tricks learned him during his previous time with the Wild West. Cody had bought the horse off the widows. But I didn't find this objectionable, for the horse started off with us.

"Frankly," he now goes on, "I wouldn't want that cabin, which gives the wrong impression. There's nothing uplifting about it for the youth of this country. I feel the same way about Comanche."

"How do the Comanche come into it?"

"Not the Indian tribe," he says. "The horse of that name that was the only living survivor of Custer's last fight."

"Oh, yeah," I says, "Captain Keogh's buckskin gelding. I recall —"

"Exactly," Cody says, "the one found wandering amongst the bodies on the Little Bighorn battlefield, wounded so badly that the Indians didn't want him. But he was precious to the Seventh Cavalry and they nursed him back to health. When he finally died a couple of years ago the animal was stuffed and put on exhibition at the state university. Now he's on display in the Kansas Building over at the Fair. Back when Comanche was alive, Major Burke suggested we include him in our recreation of the battle, provided of course that I could have borrowed or rented him from the Seventh, but I surely could have, given the reverence with which I celebrate the memory of their late great commander and mourn the greatest tragedy in their or any other regiment's history." He had spoke too long without taking a drink, so he did so now.

I hadn't ever found a better time to try again to get into the matter of having been at the side of the dying Custer, at which I had made innumerable though more and more halfhearted attempts throughout the years, but by now I lacked in sufficient energy. And I got no further than saying, "You know, I was —" when Bill resumed.

"But after due thought I decided against the idea of having this mount in our dramatic presentation, standing there in good health, for I doubt if a horse can be trained to act wounded in a believable way. Also there's the matter of creating the wounds, with theatrical makeup, to be visible from the grandstand. Beyond this, what I didn't care for was the negative associations the animal would bring with him. The essential message of the re-creation is the eventual triumph of the American people as symbolized by the arrival of Buffalo Bill and his men."

Which of course never happened in real history, but the way I come to understand him over the years is that it was even better that it hadn't, for if he had actually come with reinforcements in time to save the day at the Little Bighorn, there wouldn't of been any triumph to proclaim beyond just another routine defeat for the Indians. Custer wouldn't of died a martyr, and civilization, as well as show business, which maybe was one and the same, would not of been furthered.

Let me also clear up Cody's position on Indians, who as I say he greatly liked and genuinely befriended, and as I hope I have shown, they returned the favor. So how could he represent them in the show as being pretty much the same ruthless devils as those who hated them thought they was? This is tricky, or again maybe it's real simple: underneath all the flag-waving, Bill really did love his country and believed he was showing nothing but its true history, and now the smoke of battle had cleared away, the Indians too should come to realize they had played a part in it, and was Americans too and could take pride in the result.

Maybe that was overly simple, but it wasn't exactly simpleminded. And in later years, when the motion pictures showed the U.S. Cavalry ride in to save outnumbered whites about to be massacred, I know for a fact that Indian-reservation audiences might cheer — if you want to take that as confirmation of his point.

Having completed his remarks on the subject, Cody now spoke of the great success of the Wild West in its World's Fair engagement, which exceeded that of any year to date and might amount to as much as a million dollars before it was over.

"And this," said he, "during the Panic."

Once again I had to ask him for a translation.

"Why, the national financial crisis, Jack. I thought you took an interest in money matters. It's in all the papers."

Involved with Indians as I was, I didn't pay much attention to newspapers unless he read me something from them pertaining to our show, but as it turned out there had been a number of bank failures and the gold standard, whatever that was, was threatened, the stock market was falling and businesses going bankrupt, all of which already had got the name of the Panic of '93. But B.B.W.W. was doing better than ever, turning people away at every performance, so this trouble didn't seem to apply to us, except in the sense of some more of them outside projects of Bill's going under, taking along my own modest investments, but of course that usually happened in the best of times.

Now Annie had swore she wouldn't go near Sitting Bull's cabin, and my sentiments was similar at the time I first heard about it, but then I got to wondering about the possibility that it might be only a re-creation or imitation of the real thing, in short, such as what we did in the Wild West. It would sure of been easier to build a fake than to dismantle and ship in the original from that remote spot on the Grand River, and who would know the difference? Unless like me you had experience of the genuine article, and as for me, I'd feel better if it was a respectful counterfeit, along with the midget Eiffel Tower and the model of the Pope's home church.

So I decided I ought to make sure one way or the other before making up my mind what to think. I didn't have no influence on anyone like

Annie did, so it wouldn't matter to nobody but myself — which meant to a person of my sort, it couldn't of been more important, on account of how I'd had to survive on my own so long while not losing the principles I had acquired along the way.

Yet I'll tell you something held me back all the same, like I never really wanted to know. The result in any case wouldn't be heart-lifting, whereas thus far I had been enjoying myself at the Fair. So I kept postponing a visit and who knows how long I might of kept doing so, avoiding the issue forever, had not Annie come up with something else.

"Jack, did you see this?" she asks a few days later, showing me a pamphlet handed out to publicize the attractions of the Midway, with a page opened to a picture of an Indian with a caption saying it was Rain in the Face. She tapped her trigger finger on it. "He's with Sitting Bull's cabin." She waited a second for my reaction, but I was too slow in producing one, so she said, "Didn't he actually kill General Custer? Whereas Sitting Bull was falsely accused of it?"

"It was the General's brother Tom that Rain in the Face was supposed to hate for some reason and said he'd cut his heart out and eat it one day, and then supposedly did so at the Little Bighorn. But I don't know if that really happened." I did see Tom's body after the battle, and it was mutilated worst of any, but I wouldn't tell that to Annie, who had taken on some of the grief, now seventeen years long, of her friend Mrs. Custer.

"I just think this whole business of the cabin is a shame," said she.

"I do too."

Annie kept her eyes on me. "That poem says Rain in the Face did it to Tom."

"What poem is that?" I asked. "One of Frank's?"

"No," says she. "Henry Wadsworth Longfellow, 'The Revenge of Rain-in-the-Face.' "

"I never read it."

"Well, Mrs. C. believes it was him who killed Tom, anyway."

"Rain in the Face?"

"That's right." Annie could be persistent when she took a mind to it.

"So you want me to go over and find out, is that it?"

"I don't want you to do anything you don't want to do, Jack."

"Suppose I find out he did it," I says. "What will we do? Take revenge on the revenger?"

"Well, I sure will complain to the management of the Midway," said she. "But don't you go if you don't think it's right, Jack. I'll have to find me somebody else who speaks Sioux."

She knowed how to appeal to a man's pride. "All right," I says, "I'll go over there. But it won't be as easy as you think. An Indian's idea of politeness is to tell you only what he thinks will please. I can't see Rain in the Face admitting to a white stranger he killed and cut up Tom Custer, especially if he really done it." But she was still looking at me with them sparkling eyes of hers, so I put up my hand and says, "All right, all right, I'll go."

Funny how so often, in fact usually, things have worked out so different from what I expected and, while I can't claim always for the best, given my presence at so many events at which people was slaughtered, my life has taken another turn.

For example, what occurred at this point. Next chance I got, I went down the Midway past the show run by a German circus man named Hagenbeck that I wanted to get around to seeing when I got tired of the Ferris wheel, if that ever happened, for he supposedly had a tiger that rode a tricycle, past the Japanese Bazaar, the Javanese Settlement, the Samoan Islanders, the German Village, the Turkish Village, a big indoor swimming pool called the Natatorium, and the panorama of the Alps, Little Egypt's Street in Cairo, the Destruction of Pompeii (of which if you recall we had seen the real ruins), the French Cider Press, Old Vienna, the Eiffel Tower, the Volcano of Kilaueau, and many other attractions including the gigantic revolving wheel on which I'd rather of been a rider than whatever I was supposed to be on this mission, a spy, an ambassador, an avenger, or just Annie's flunky.

I finally got there. Past the Captive Balloon (which you could ascend in the basket of but was attached by a cable so it couldn't fly away), next to the Ostrich Farm and back of the Brazilian Music Hall, there it was, the log cabin I last seen on the Grand River the day Sitting Bull had been killed and his corpse disfigured.

It looked like the genuine article, though the surroundings was so different, with the background of all them Midway attractions, that the experience of seeing it was unreal. I couldn't certify its authenticity until I got closer, but at the moment there was quite a few white visitors going inside and coming out, along with a few Indians here and there for decoration, for they didn't seem to speak English. A couple of white fellows was selling entrance tickets and acting as guides.

I tell you, everything about it went against my grain, more so now I was here than even when agreeing to come, and I felt indignant towards Annie. I wasn't married to her, after all. She had her nerve, asking me to do something like this.

Now while I was standing there, just outside the area which you had to pay to enter, along comes a heavyset Indian from the direction of the Midway, eating from a bag of popcorn. He was limping. He wore the full warbonnet that was more or less required for all Indians on display at white entertainments in those days. I heard this was true even with Apaches, who normally hadn't never worn feathers, but the audiences demanded this supposed proof of real Indianness. This fellow was an older man and obviously not in prime condition.

I seen from the beading on his buckskin clothes and moccasins he was Sioux, and I asks him in Lakota if he knows where I might find Rain in the Face.

Now from the way he failed to answer this directly, I knowed I was talking to the man himself. Had he not been Rain he would have told straightforwardly where I could find the man. Being the real McCoy, however, he had to go through some devious maneuvers, neither admitting nor denying, and if tradition was to be observed, I would of had to stand there for some time before establishing the truth.

So what I did, startling but also relieving him, was to let him see I knowed and proceed from there.

"Is this really *Tatanka Iyotanka's* lodge or is it an imitation built by the *wasichus?*" I asked him.

"It is real," he said. "The whites took it apart and shipped it here and put it back together. It seemed to me a strange thing to do, but that's the way they are. I am here because they are paying me more than I could make in any other job. Do you want to eat?" He offered me the bag of popcorn.

It smelled mighty good, and I took some. It tasted good too, being warm and buttery and salty, and I made the sounds of approval, "How, how."

"There are a lot of Indians here at Chi-ca-go," Rain says, pronouncing the city's name like the redskin word from which it supposedly come, meaning, so I heard, either "strong" or "polecat." And while I'm on the subject of language, I might point out that Lakota didn't have an actual word for "Indian" as such. Amongst themselves they never needed any in the old days, using tribal designations. But after the white man come, they had to find a general term that made more sense than the name he had erroneously give them and kept even after learning it was the wrong continent for it. So the word the Sioux come up with for "Indian" was the same as for "normal person."

"Yes." I never said more on account of I wanted to keep him talking.

"I hear there are a lot of Lakota in Long Hair's show."

"That is true," I says, chewing.

People was walking past us all this while, gawking at Rain in his head-dress, and one little boy stopped and stared for quite a while, and noticing him, Rain in the Face offered him some popcorn. But before the boy could take any, his Ma come and pulled him away.

"Sitting Bull told me Long Hair is a good man and treats people very well."

"I work for *Pahaska*," I says, "and can tell you that is true."

"I haven't seen the show," said Rain in the Face, "and I'll tell you why. I am told they do an imitation of the Greasy Grass fight. The Americans have always accused me of killing the other Long Hair's brother in that fight, though I did not do so."

"You did not?"

"I didn't see him, and if I had seen him, I would not have known who he was. A white man came to Standing Rock not so long ago and showed me pictures of those two brothers. I did not see either one at the Greasy Grass. I admit I killed soldiers that day, but I didn't cut up any-one on the ground. But the whites think I did, so I won't go over there and get shot if some American gets excited by the imitation of the fight."

"You must do as you think best," I told him, seeing he figured he was safe here at Sitting Bull's reconstructed cabin, where the Indians had lost.

He shared the rest of the popcorn with me, filling my cupped hand.

"A man told me the other Long Hair's widow has never taken another husband."

"She still mourns him."

"I asked if he would send me a picture of her," said Rain, "and he told me he would try, but I have never received it."

So here was another, and an unexpected, admirer of Libbie Custer. "Let me see whether I can get you that picture," I says. "I know a friend of hers."

I had found out what I come for, so I shook his hand and thanked him for the talk and the warm popcorn and fixed to leave. Visiting the cabin wouldn't of done nothing except make me feel bad.

However, if I hadn't glanced briefly towards it on turning away, my subsequent life might not of been what it was: that's all I can say as a sure probability.

Some stout white man, wearing a brown derby, his teeth clenched on an unlit cigar, come out of the cabin door. His stride was that of considerable exasperation, for some blond-haired woman emerged right on his heels, speaking angrily at his fat back.

She was Amanda Teasdale.

22

Doing Good

M Y FIRST IMPULSE WAS TO RUN AWAY AND HIDE. I TELL
you that woman scared me, not in the way you feel when a gun is
pointed at you or a war club is lifted over your head, fearing for
your skin, but in that region of the heart where you feel you just
ain't up to the job, and I sure hadn't never been so with regard to
Amanda.

But for old Rain in the Face I might of made my escape now, and
maybe regretted doing so once I had thought about it, and then returned
and looked for her but never found her again my life long.

As it was, hearing the commotion, Rain looked over at them who was
making it and back at me and says, "Yellow Hair was a friend of Sitting
Bull's. He knew a number of American women. He got on better with
them than with white men, because the women usually wanted to help
him. I think she doesn't like it that they brought his house here, but I'm
not sure, because she doesn't speak Lakota very well."

Up to then I was still intent on getting away, for occupied as she was,
sassing the derbied fellow, she hadn't seen me. But I was touched by the
last thing said by Rain.

"She's a friend of mine, too," I says, "and I should have done a better
job of teaching her the language. I'm going to go over there now, and if
that man is insulting her, I'll kill him."

So that is what I done, went up to Amanda and the heavy individual
in the derby, and when I got there, far from abusing her, he was whining
about her abuse of *him*, which was driving away business, and if she kept

it up he'd have no choice but to call the Columbian Guard, which was the Fair's police force, to come arrest her as an anarchist.

Now that was a serious charge, for some years earlier a bunch of foreigners calling themselves by that name had set off a bomb in Haymarket Square, in Chicago, killing a number of people: even I had heard of that.

So my idea changed about dealing with the present situation. I would only make it worse by lighting into the fat man. As I seen it, what I should do was get Amanda away from there as soon as possible. I didn't think she was likely to traffic in bombs, but this fellow could sure cause trouble with such an accusation.

So I marches up to them, and to Amanda I says, "Oh, *here* you are, sweetheart. Me and the kids been waiting at the Ferris wheel for an hour!" To the big fellow chewing on the stogie, I says, "My wife has a way of wandering off."

Amanda was took altogether by surprise, so much so I was actually able to lead her by the arm off that lot, past old Rain in the Face who looked surprised too but also amused, for Indian men never thought whites knowed how to handle women, and get all the way to opposite the Ostrich Farm, before she reacted.

And then it was not the blowup I expected. I guess she had expended her anger on the derbied fellow. With me it was sullen reproach.

"Do you really think that was necessary?"

"It was the best I could come up with," I says. "I didn't want you to get arrested for being an anarchist."

"I'm not an anarchist," Amanda said wearily. "That was empty bluster."

Neither one of us had said hello, fancy meeting you here, or the like, and it was too late for that now. Nearby, them weird-looking ostrich birds, if birds they was, strutted around on stilt-legs within a fenced enclosure. Beyond it was an eating place.

"I hear the big ones can be saddled and rode like a horse," I says. "But the so-called scrambled ostrich eggs they serve yonder is actually chickens'."

Amanda was suddenly smiling at me, but in a way that was also sort of sad. "Jack," she says, "Jack, what are you doing here?"

"I'm still with the Wild West," says I. "We're on a lot down below the

Midway, at Sixty-second Street, near the Fair but not in it, because the management thinks the way you used to and maybe still do, that showing Indians killing Custer and all does not demonstrate an uplifting sentiment, not to mention a hope for their future as farmers and church-goers and the rest of it, and I expect they're right so far as that goes." At that point I stopped and said, "Excuse me, Amanda, I'm running off at the mouth. There's nothing in the world I'd rather do than see you again, but I was going to run away and hide just now, out of shame for never answering your last letter, but reason I didn't was because I couldn't. I sure tried — but dammit, forgive my language, *I can't write very good.*" Right at that point of embarrassment for me, somebody came to tend to them ostriches, and the birds made a noisy commotion: they can run fast as ponies, you know.

Amanda was not distracted by this. She was still smiling sadly at me. "Yes," she says, "you are at fault, Jack, and you don't even understand why. It's not that you didn't answer my letter. It's your reason for not do-ing so: vanity."

By golly, it hit me hard to get put in my place by a woman more than a dozen years my junior, than who I naturally assumed I knowed more of the basic principles of life. But what hit me harder was that she was right.

I stared down at the toes of my boots. "I guess you got me there, Amanda. I was ashamed of how ignorant I am, so I never sent that in-formation you needed and you couldn't write your book. Now I see it that way, I don't know how I can face you."

"Jack," Amanda said, "look at me." I did so, for there was nothing I had rather do. "Your help would have been important, but it would not have been indispensable. And your failure to answer those questions is not why I gave up."

"Oh." Funny, that took me down another peg. Far from being glad I was off the hook, I guess it was on account of my vanity again that deep down I was disappointed not to have had more effect on her, even if damaging. I was learning more about my character at this moment than I had in all the years before, a pity it wasn't more admirable. "Amanda, them ostriches is bothering me," I says at that point. "Can't we go some-place where we can talk in peace? Up in the Captive Balloon maybe, or on the Ferris wheel? No, they're too crowded, I guess. I tell you, I can't think straight, I'm so surprised to see you." I swallowed hard, and come out with it. "My God, but you are beautiful."

She must of been getting close to what was considered middle age in them days, say forty, but she hadn't failed to improve in every particular through the fifteen years since we first met, her skin and features without a sign of wear, her hair and eyes no less than perfection, her form all willowy grace.

As to the comment I had just blurted out, I think I more or less expected she would be offended, but I couldn't help saying it regardless of the consequences.

In fact what Amanda done was look at me in a way I never seen her do before, call it a mix of earnestness and wonderment and maybe, unless I was just wishing it into being, the slightest hint of affection. "Why, Jack," she said, "that's the first personal word you've ever said to me."

To show you how clumsy I was at this, I couldn't come up with no better response than to gawk and say, "It is? Huh." And then, "Maybe a ride in one of them gondolas over on the lagoon? I've rode the real thing, you know, in the town of Venice in Italy, where the streets is paved with water. Imagine our Sioux seeing something like that. You can't say B.B.W.W. ain't broadened their knowledge of the world." Finally my embarrassment had passed to the degree that I could get back to what I really wanted to say. "Mind telling me," I asked, "how *you* happen to be here?"

After my complaint about them ostriches, we had started to stroll away from them. At the main street running through the Midway, Amanda turned west. "Let's get away from this wretched place," she said, "and walk in the park."

Washington Park was across from the entrance to the Midway, so we went over there and walked amongst the trees on a summer day that was fair but not as hot as some can get in Chicago. Looking at Amanda in the pattern of sunlight that come through the trees I was reminded of some paintings a French person showed me in Paris one time of ladies outdoors. The closer you got to the picture, though, the vaguer it was, coming together only when you backed up. That was not the case with Amanda, who was always in my focus.

"What am I doing here?" she said now. "I couldn't believe it when I read that the cabin had been brought to the Midway Plaisance. I felt like blowing it up."

"Well," I says, "that's likely why that fat fellow thought you was an anarchist. He didn't know it was a figure of speech."

She suddenly put an arm through mine and squeezed it against her. "Dear Jack," she said.

It would of been easy for me to be overwhelmed, but I remembered my place and was proud just to have the other strollers-by see such a fine woman grasping me of her own will.

"I know how you feel," I says, "after what happened on the Grand River. I keep thinking I should of done something to help Sitting Bull, but who could know his own people would do him in — well, *he* knew, he predicted it himself, but —"

Amanda squeezed my arm again. "You couldn't have affected the outcome, Jack. You did what you could when the time came: you saved my life."

I have related the facts of that day, with me and her cowering in the frozen mud under the lead flying above. I didn't think of it as saving her life so much as saving my own while she just happened to be there at the same time. It seemed natural to huddle together. I didn't make this point now, however, enjoying her commendation as I did.

She went on. "I have thought of that morning many times since. In fact, it became an obsession. I couldn't write my book. Sitting Bull's murder kept intervening. But when I decided to confine the subject to that event alone, putting the women's issues aside until I had at least exorcised those awful images, I couldn't manage that, either. I'm afraid I failed at still another of my pathetic attempts to accomplish something worthwhile."

I stopped walking and made so bold as to take her hand in mine, hers being gloved in a slippery material, silk I guess, and real thin so I could feel the warmth of her fingers. "Aw, Amanda, don't you feel that way for one minute! You done a lot of good everywhere you been. Take Sitting Bull, he thought the world of you." You're not much of a person if you can't stretch the truth for someone you care about.

"He thought I was a fool," said she.

"Well, if that was the case, it wasn't *you*," I told her. "He just never saw eye to eye with whites."

"He respected Buffalo Bill, you told me, and he obviously had a high regard for you. Could it be he placed a lesser value on white women?" She took her hand back, but not in an unfriendly way, just slipped it from my grasp.

There was a bench yonder, so I steered towards it and we sat down.

"Well now," I says, "you might not be wrong in one way, but, you know, you was there at his camp for a while, Indian women don't go to college, don't get jobs outside their family and move someplace else, and so on. They stay home and do female chores, which seems normal to them. That's what they like."

"But how does anyone know? Have they been asked?"

"I never thought of that," I says, truthfully. "I guess that's the kind of thing you could of dealt with in your book. All I know is, they ain't shy about complaining and have real sharp tongues, but about particular matters, like if their man don't provide enough food, not concerning the basic arrangement you seem to be against."

"I'm not necessarily against it," Amanda said in her positive style. "I'd just like to understand it, but I came to the conclusion that I never would, and I simply gave up. There's too great a gulf between us."

I knowed she meant her and the Indians, not me and her, though the latter was probably as true as the former, so somewhat down in the mouth, I asked, "Then how did it happen you was over there just now at Sitting Bull's cabin?"

She sniffed. "You're right. I was being foolish, as usual. So far as I could tell from speaking to the Indians there, *they* saw nothing wrong."

"They come to Chicago to make some money and eat popcorn," I said, "have a good time on the merry-go-round and Ferris wheel, if they're like our bunch. Old Rain in the Face, the limping one, he was one of Sitting Bull's best friends."

She looked at me, in the personal manner again. "But, Jack, do you think it's right to have such an exhibit? The bulletholes can still be seen in the walls."

"No, I don't," I says. "But here's the funny thing: that's the white side of me, though the people that brought it here was white. Whereas while an Indian wouldn't ever think of putting the cabin on exhibit, if somebody else does, it's all right with him, if he gets rewarded."

She shook her golden head. "Is that not another example of how we have corrupted that people?"

It was not a question, but I answered it anyway. "I don't know. It just seems natural in anything alive, white or red or whatnot."

"But shouldn't *we* aim higher?"

Now it *was* a question, it seemed to me, and as I was being included in the "we," I was real flattered. But I says, "No doubt about it, if you settle for standing up for your own principles and ain't ruined by the opposition of others."

"Or the indifference," Amanda says, "which is worse."

Maybe that was true from her point of view, but I tell you if you have seen as many people killed as me, you'd have to say it was usually due to real malice and not because nobody cared.

I didn't say this, though, for what I prized most in Amanda was her highmindedness combined with what you really had to call a practicality, for her life hadn't been one of dreaming up ideals inside some library without ever going outside and trying them on for size with reality. It took a lot of guts for a girl like her to go to the Grand River and try to accommodate herself to Indian ways, and when violence come she hadn't panicked. And way before that, you recall that incident back during the time of the Major's Indian school, when the wanted criminal Elmo Cullen jumped us, she put a knife in his leg before young Wolf Coming Out cut his throat. Once she even worked as a piano player in a Dodge saloon and sporting house. She was a durable woman. Yet she never lost that class she had from the first, which I'm proud I recognized right away without having much for comparison beyond my foster mother Mrs. Pendrake way back when, but by now I had met not only Libbie Custer but Queen Victoria, as high up as you could go, and Amanda didn't suffer alongside them.

I wish I could of told her as much, but didn't know how to do so in a way that wouldn't seem humorous, always a problem of mine, so instead I asked her how she come to be in Chicago.

"I was en route back to Kansas," she said. "When in doubt, head for home, I suppose. Though I haven't had an actual home there for a long time, I didn't seem to belong anywhere else. A friend of mine from college lives in Chicago, and I had to change trains here, so I decided to accept her longstanding invitation to visit. Well, it's turned out to be the best decision I ever made. My friend is Jane Addams."

She said this with the kind of expectation of voice and eyebrow that goes with a familiar name, but I didn't recognize it, so she goes on, but not with any disapproval of my ignorance, of which she had had plenty of evidence in the past. "Jane Addams and her associate Ellen Starr founded Hull House four years ago. It's a settlement house in the worst of the West Side slums."

I was still so dumb I wondered what these ladies was doing in a part of town like that if they had went to college and could do better, but I was smart enough not to ask, for it shortly turned out that, as I should of suspected if it had attracted Amanda, Hull House was a place where folks who was down and out through no fault of their own could come and get trained for various vocations and trades, get fed if they was hungry and a bath when needed; board there safe and respectable if they was working girls away from home; put their kids if they was mothers while they went to jobs; belong to social clubs; use the gym to get healthy; and study any number of subjects which if you kept them up would be pretty near as good an education as a university had to offer. Amanda for example taught music, for which she was well qualified from her own college days and also that experience at the piano, though I doubt whether she spelled out the nature of where it had been acquired.

Now most of the people helped was women and children, as most of the staff was female, but Miss Addams was also interested in getting better conditions for workingmen in a time when the work week averaged sixty hours and the unskilled might not earn as much as a dollar per day, so she and her women did a good deal of politicking and had only lately got the state legislature to raise the minimum age for full-time employment all the way up to fourteen.

In short, Jane Addams was a troublemaking do-gooder after Amanda's heart, a fellow ex–college girl reared genteelly, and in Miss Addams's case with quite a lot of money, who figured they had had it easy enough in a life that was real mean for many others, to whom it would be nice to lend a hand. You could see them as a pain in the arse, which I expect they could be, and doing what they did on account of guilt at their own good fortune instead of accepting it as coming from God, and maybe that could be so, and you could doubt what they did made much difference in the long run and instead blow up everything and start over, if you, as the saying went, regarded the right thing as a big omelet and individuals like so many eggs.

Or you might, like me, see them as real kind folks. And if you think there can ever be too much kindness in the world, then you've managed to live in another one than mine. But then I admit I was prejudiced and maybe my own motives had less to do with justice than just being crazy about Amanda.

Anyway, after telling me about Hull House, what Amanda wanted to do now instead of taking my suggestion and going back to the Midway and having pastry and coffee with whipped cream at the Vienna Café, was to take me for a visit over to Miss Addams's place and see all the good that was being done there, and there wasn't any way I could get out of that, happy as it made her to do it and worthwhile as it was. It's just that I would first of appreciated continuing to have Amanda to myself awhile longer rather than going immediately to see how she was helping others who she didn't even know. You see how selfish I was but maybe will forgive me in view of the circumstances.

So we went to the West Side of town, and she had not exaggerated about the slums, which was as bad as them in Manhattan, a comparison that might of pleased Chicagoans who was always in competition with New York, and Amanda took me through Hull House, a big old formerly private mansion on South Halstead Street now used for the activities I mentioned, and I tell you it was a fine thing to see, not tiresome as I admit I expected. It wasn't a bunch of grown men in a sham battle or little ladies shooting at glass balls or doing trick riding, but helping people further themselves in real life had a lot to recommend it.

Of course I was under the influence of Amanda, but before I was there long, seeing them earnest young women, both them on the staff and those being trained in various skills, not to mention the children who instead of fighting with one another or fetching cans of beer for their father from the saloon was learning to play the piano and so on, well, I tell you, I begun to total up my own contribution to the human race, at the age of better than half a century, as nil, and I seen most of the individuals I had frequented as worthless in the greater scheme of things: gamblers and harlots, most of them, leaving aside the entertainers such as Buffalo Bill and Annie Oakley, who I guess did bring pleasure to many folks, and nothing wrong with that, but it didn't feed the hungry or rescue poor women from sweatshops or do anything for the freed slaves come north to live worse than before Emancipation. You name the dirty deal and Jane Addams was trying to correct it while I had been looking in the opposite direction.

So when Amanda took me to meet her, I was ready to ask Miss Addams if she had something I could do that would be of use at Hull House. This might sound remarkable for a person like me, but I was in a state of great feeling from having run into Amanda and had it go so well and keep getting better.

Jane Addams was younger than I expected, younger in fact, I learned later, than Amanda, but looked somewhat older than she was due to being in delicate health owing to a spinal curvature she had since childhood. She couldn't of been nicer. For all her social activism, I got the idea right away that she was more of what you could call diplomatic than Amanda, which you had to be to make a go of a cause like hers in the Chicago of that day, where they could also give New York a run for its money in political corruption.

We had a real pleasant though brief conversation, on account of she was so busy, and as Amanda hadn't said nothing about my connection with Buffalo Bill's Wild West, I didn't mention it either, and Miss Addams got the idea I was just in town to see the Fair, which she said, in her diplomatic way without either praising or condemning it Amanda-style, was quite a spectacle which she was interested in seeing even though her purse had been stole while she attended opening-day ceremonies, at the memory of which she raised her eyebrows while smiling.

"Miss Addams," I said, surprising Amanda, "I sure would admire working here at your settlement house in some way, but unfortunately I ain't got any talents nor no education."

"Why, Jack," Amanda says, lifting her own eyebrows, and she then says, "Jane, he knows more about Indians than any other white man could. He was raised by the Cheyennes."

"There you have it, Mr. Crabb," Miss Addams says, and she forthwith suggests I give the Hull House children a class in American Indian ways and customs and crafts if I knowed any like curing leather and making moccasins and beadwork. If all idealists had her mind for the practical, and vice versa, the world soon wouldn't have no more problems that couldn't be handled.

Now not only did I soon begin to give a course of the type Jane Addams suggested, but from time to time I brung over Sioux from B.B.W.W. to show them slum kids what real Indians looked like and if they was women (usually the case, for the warriors couldn't teach much that Miss Addams would approve of), why, they might demonstrate their type of sewing, decoration with beads, and all, and show how they chewed a hide to make it soft, the way they braided hair, and so on. Most of my class was girls, for boys would of been interested only if Sioux men showed the use of weapons, something I doubt Miss Addams and her ladies understood, but then Hull House was mainly a female affair, speaking of which, after I was there awhile, I begun to get an uneasy feeling which I'll get to later.

At last not only was I doing something with my life I could be proud of, but also I had that closer connection with Amanda that I had yearned for, and it might not seem much, us just being at first teachers in the same place, but it turned out to be the right way to start towards something more, and I mean not only personally but by way of profession, for though giving music lessons to poor children was a mighty fine occupation, as was my own, I kept after Amanda on the subject of that book she had wanted to write about Indians, whether just about Sioux women or an account of Sitting Bull's death, or what seemed best to me, combining the two, and I admit at the back of my mind was including a good bit of my own story with it, though how that might be done I never had no idea, being as you know barely literate, not to mention I hadn't ever so far told her more than bits and pieces with respect to my childhood with the Cheyenne.

My time at Hull House was of a morning, for I hadn't asked nor was offered any pay, so stayed on with the Wild West, continuing to draw the wage, which come in handy now, as seeing Amanda all the time I took more care of my appearance, getting shaved daily by a barber, which cost me twenty-five cents but he also kept my hair and mustache trimmed, the former having taken on more gray at the sideburns and receding some at the temples, which concerned me a little but the barber assured me I looked the more distinguished for it, and then combed my hair down with pimp oil, adding to the stink of the bay rum he had earlier doused my face with, but if that's what it took to look like a gent, I would endure it, along with acquiring a striped blazer, a pair of white flannel pants, and a summertime straw skimmer to replace the winter derby.

I dressed more sober for Hull House, and of course around the Wild West you couldn't look like a cake-eater from the East, so the fashionable outfit was for my off-time, the fairly rare occasions when I got any, given my two employments. And when I did find a few free hours, it had to coincide with Amanda's for it to be of value to me.

I'll go into that subject further in a minute, but first I don't want to forget that matter that led to my reconnection with Amanda. I had promptly reported back to Annie Oakley that Rain in the Face denied killing either Custer brother.

"Do you believe him?" she asked. "Or was he just saying that?"

"I don't know," I says. "I don't think he'd admit it if he did, but maybe he really didn't. He feels sorry for Mrs. Custer, anyhow." It wasn't exactly sorrow, but that seemed the best thing to call it for the purpose at hand. "He asked me if I could get him a picture of her."

I don't know exactly what Annie thought of the request, for she just looked quizzical. "Well, I don't personally own one, Jack," she says, "and maybe when we get back east I could ask her about it, but I don't know as I really want to."

I never saw Rain in the Face again nor went near Sitting Bull's cabin, but then I didn't see much more of Annie or Cody himself except during the show. I spent all my other time either frequenting Amanda or waiting to do so. What I wanted especially was to get her over to the Fair, and don't mean just the Midway but also the White City with its display of the wonders of the end of the nineteenth century, and not all of them was machines and industrial and farm products: there was that enormous Palace of Fine Arts full of paintings, and concerts of fine music by the brass band of none other than John Philip Sousa, but she never had a good word to say about it, so on the first occasion we "walked out," as they put it at that time when you was courting a girl, which I doubted Amanda had any idea I was doing, we had tea at the Palmer House, the fanciest hotel in Chicago and one they could hold up against any I seen anyplace in the world, for in fact it was constructed as a collection of the best features from other countries, from its French front to its Italian staircases and mirrors, Egyptian chandeliers, the interiors reproducing those of the German Kaiser's palace, and the English rooms for smoking cigars and playing billiards.

Now the way I decided to handle the matter of acting so as not to embarrass her was to copy what Amanda done as to putting cream and sugar in the tea, and so on, and generally I got by using this means, along with being helped by dumb luck at such times as when the waiter wanted to take the order for us both from only me, which later in life I learned was the polite style, with the lady telling the man what she wanted and him telling the help, but independent as Amanda was, she ignored that system and told the waiter what she required, so I did likewise, because it was the same.

Another time I was favored by fortune is when I dropped my spoon but only started to bend down to fetch it off the floor when I realized I better wipe it off before using it again, but not dirty the expensive linen napkin they give you there, so was reaching for the bandanna I carried up my sleeve when a passing waiter, not our own, beat me to the spoon, and did not hand it back but supplied a fresh one. That's the kind of service they had at the Palmer House. Imagine how much silverware they run through in the course of a day.

Along with the tea they brung an assortment of little cakes and miniature sandwiches with I guess some of the same fillings they used in England, which I couldn't identify when over there, either, most of it being air so far as substance went, but it was real grand in that hotel, and had I been able for long to take my eyes off Amanda I would of studied more of the fancy furnishings, which was a real marvel in a city also known for its stockyards. I mentioned dropping that utensil, well, the thick carpet looked so clean I probably wouldn't even of had to wipe that spoon off except for the principle of the thing.

At first, facing her like that across a table of white linen, gleaming silver, and china cups so thin as almost to be transparent, I wished I had fortified myself with whiskey before coming to drink tea, for the foregoing, including the crystal vase of fresh flowers, was as a setting of which Amanda was the jewel. She was wearing frosty blue today, a couple shades paler in hue than her eyes. In the summertime then women wore more than nowadays in the dead of winter: it was really a production, along with the wealth of hair carried on their heads, plus a hat.

Anyway, on setting down there in that place where I didn't belong, with a lady I didn't deserve to know except maybe as her servant, I got a feeling of panic: any minute, the hotel detectives would show up and give me the bum's rush for disgracing the Palmer House by just walking onto its premises.

But one of Amanda's abilities, once you got to know her personally, and vice versa, was to actually show an interest in what you told her. I admit this surprised me, though I did remember its beginnings back in the short time we was together after Sitting Bull's murder, at which time I guess I didn't believe it.

Now I expect you been thinking throughout this story of mine, wasn't there one single person of all them I run across who wanted to hear about the remarkable historical events I had participated in or at least witnessed? True, oftentimes for one reason or another I never tried to get into that subject, and I have showed you some examples, particularly with regard to the Little Bighorn, but also with my failure to keep Wild Bill Hickok alive when his bodyguard, and then that matter of the Earp–Clanton shootout at Tombstone, when I never wanted to testify for either side. But the way I found many people to be who was fond of their own reminiscences was not to encourage those of another person, considering it not information but only competition, and in my case, from a nobody.

Well, wonder of wonders, Amanda turned out different when I finally got to know her after all them years of slight acquaintance, and it started that day at the Palmer House. In trying to talk her into writing the book, I got into my boyhood with the Cheyenne, and for the first time she asked me how that come about, and I begun to tell her, much as I have related it here on this machine, for she was real interested, to the degree of asking for details when I left them out, and as I guess you know by now I ain't tongue-tied once I get going and know somebody's listening, even if it's only on faith, as right here.

I sure didn't get it all told on that one occasion, but continued at her request during many similar hours we spent together over that summer and into the autumn, and at some point Amanda decided to write her book based on my experiences, not a biographical account but a summing up of the history of the West during my lifetime as I witnessed it, and she had her own point of view on the subject, which was more condemnatory of the whites than I would of been, for while I certainly agreed that much of it was fairly rotten, I couldn't help being impressed by what happened since Chris Columbus had the guts to cross the Atlantic in that eggshell boat and find a whole new world for the Europeans to corrupt, if you want to put it that way, but also to build some remarkable things and establish principles that if ever carried out in full really might offer a better life for many, in fact had already done so.

But you tell as much to anybody who is so bothered by the bad stuff they don't want to consider the good, why, you might not get far, for that is their nature, and such was Amanda, who thought most of the people in charge of everything done a bad job with the exception of the women what operated Hull House.

Which is to say she never approved of much done by men including even George Washington and Tom Jefferson, what kept black slaves, the last-named supposedly even being intimate with the females thereof. I didn't know how much of this was true, reluctant as I was and am to think ill of the Founding Fathers, and I never heard any of it even from Lavender, my friend who died at the Greasy Grass, and he should of knowed, being colored. But she believed it and never even was that complimentary about Abe Lincoln, who had been Lavender's hero, Amanda claiming that his freeing of the slaves had been more politics than moral commitment.

But I don't want to sound as if I'm knocking or making fun of her. It was just I thought it a pity she didn't get more enjoyment and take a little time off from the cares of the world to have some fun, ride the Ferris wheel with its panoramic view of Chicago without thinking of all the people out there too poor to buy a ticket: the ride took only twenty minutes, going around twice.

The other thing bothered me was in a different area, but one I considered fundamental, given the character of my attachment to her. Though treating me fine and being partial in memory to Sitting Bull, Amanda as I said generally took a dim view of the male sex. Now combining this and what I had noticed around Hull House, that the unmarried ladies there was so self-sufficient amongst themselves, with the Misses Addams and Starr being such close companions for many years, it begun to occur to me that I hadn't ever heard Amanda speak of any male person in her life but her father, who she condemned.

If I was barking up the wrong tree, my admiration for her would not be diminished, but the nature of it would definitely be altered. After all, I admired Old Lodge Skins and Sitting Bull and Bat Masterson for that matter, and Bill Cody in my own way, along with friends of the opposite sex like Allie Earp and Annie Oakley. If between me and Amanda there was only the barriers of upbringing and culture and class, the situation was not totally impossible, for we was Americans. But if we was separated by basic inclination, then any hope I had of future intimacy was useless.

Which even so didn't affect the telling her my life's story so she would write that book. The tape machine hadn't yet been invented at the time, and only Tom Edison had the equipment to record a human voice (an example of which was on display in the Fair's Electricity Building), so Amanda presumably depended on her memory, assisted by the jottings she begun to make after a while, in a little leatherbound notebook with a cunningly attached pencil on a silk ribbon.

She listened patiently to everything I said, but perked up and took notes when I got to subjects which took her special interest, which wasn't weapons and hunting or horses or food, or even them stories us children was told from Cheyenne tradition by Old Lodge Skins, including my favorite about the great hero Little Man. I don't mean Amanda nodded off when I deal with such topics, but she seldom wrote anything down, and in fact the same was true even of the real dramatic events like the big battles, culminating in the biggest of all at the Greasy Grass, except she did ask more than I first mentioned about the women mutilating the soldiers' bodies, but I still never went into it as thoroughly as I could of, as I haven't here, for it turns my stomach even at this late date. All I can say is Indians expected the same to be done to them when they lost, which is sure savage but I guess fair in its own fashion.

So here she was, showing her usual partiality to subjects pertaining to females, which, given as she was one and preparing to write a book from that point of view, was not unbalanced. But it did add to that feeling of mine that like some of the others at Hull House, she could make her way through life without the help of a man, to put it politely. And when she did show an interest in a male matter, it could be called that only with a twist: I refer to the *heemanehs*, born as men but finding while growing up they preferred to do girls' things instead of training to be warriors, was allowed to do so, wear dresses and do women's work and even get married though usually as only one of several wives one man would have, the others being females.

Amanda was more fascinated with this subject than I wanted her to be, for it wasn't all that important in Cheyenne life. *Heemanehs* wasn't that common, and in fact I only ever knowed one, Little Horse, and he seemed so natural you got used to him in no time and nobody beat him up or even insulted him as I knowed happened to white Percies as far back as during that short time I went to school when adopted by the Pendrakes. Amanda being so taken with this minor theme, while regarding as ho-hum all I had to tell her about war, increased my feeling as to her personal constitution, if I can call it that, and once again it looked like I was heading into a melancholy phase concerning her, as I had often in the past, except that this time it was likely to be permanent.

I won't keep you in suspense, but I will give you another surprise, knowing what you do about me by now, which of course she did not, for as it happened I neglected, for reasons of delicacy, modesty, or what have you, to include in my story any mention of my Indian wives or, for that matter, Olga, the Swedish woman I had previously married but who got captured by the Cheyenne as I described way back. I have always had a habit never to tell a woman I liked about any other I was associated with in the past, and I still think I have acted right in so doing, for the only means by which not to provoke jealousy is to slander them you once thought enough of to take up with, and that I won't do.

Anyway, to get to the point, while my suspicions of Amanda was nearing a disappointing conclusion, for her own part she had gotten the idea, believe it or not, that I might be a *heemaneh!* Or the white version thereof, for she never seen me wearing a dress.

Lucky we was walking in the park at the time and not at tea in the Palmer House when I found that out, else I might of dropped my china cup. I can't even remember clearly what she said to give me the idea, but I got it correctly, as she proceeded to admit when I said she had gotten it wrong.

"But *never* have you mentioned a woman," she said, more annoyed than apologetic for her error.

I also was irked a little, for I still figured *she* was the odd one and what bothered her was to find out I was not, maybe to the degree that I might still, after all these weeks, make an unwelcome advance. So I adds, with some heat, "Don't worry, the last thing in the world I'll do is get fresh with you."

Amanda stopped there on the path and says in what I can only call indignation, "Why not?"

"You ain't never mentioned a man!" says I. "You don't care for the whole tribe, it's plain to see."

She stared at me for a time, still standing there, and a young couple passed, holding hands, smiling about us. Then she asked, "Do you really want to hear about my private life?" Funny, that's all she had to say to make me realize I was as wrong about her as she had been about me.

"No," I says, "nor tell you about mine," and found it possible to grin, and neither one of us ever told the other more than a few hints of our previous connections, which policy I can recommend.

Well, we're coming to a new phase of my existence at this point, and if I live long enough I hope to tell you about it, for it was as remarkable as anything else I ever done though real different from all. I guess you could say it begun with my finally now being able to talk Amanda into going to the Fair and sharing some of my pleasures such as the Ferris wheel and the Venetian gondolas, eat German sausage and drink French cider, see Hagenbeck's tiger ride the velocipede, and it wasn't just the Midway I cared for, but the exhibitions and sights of the White City, interested as I was, now more than ever, in self-improvement. Of course Amanda never needed that. She already knowed a lot about pictures and statues before visiting the Palace of Fine Arts and in fact didn't think much of quite a few of them on display which I thought as fine as they could be, the paintings looking real only prettier, and telling a story you could understand right away, like a mother trying to cheer up a sulky little kid with an apple, but Amanda said them vague kind of pictures I told her about seeing in Paris was better than the glossy. Fond as I was of her, I believed she was a snob about cultural matters, for you take the concerts of John Philip Sousa, where the highest-browed kinds of orchestral music was played, but also real heartwarming tunes like "Old Folks at Home," which could bring water to my eyes, but Amanda never cared for at all, and it was the last straw for her when Sousa's bunch did "Tarara-Boom-De-Ay" on the same program with the works of some of them Germans.

Neither did she think much of Frank Butler's poetry which I showed her examples of that I was greatly partial to, and I didn't fail to notice her disdainful sniff when I pointed out the amazing coincidence of both me and Custer shedding tears at performances of *East Lynne*.

I suspected, from hints she dropped, that at least one of the men in her earlier life, probably at New York, might of been some kind of sissy connected with culture, but never knowed in detail, for we both kept to that agreement about our pasts.

There was a place at the Columbian Exposition that did hold special interest for Amanda, and that was the Woman's Building, commemorating the contributions of the fair sex to civilization and largely the creation of the leading lady in Chicago at that time, Mrs. Potter Palmer, wife of the fellow who owned the Palmer House hotel, who she got to pay for a good deal of the costs of putting it up according to the plans of a female architect, and maybe it was for that reason Amanda liked the design better than most of the other buildings, being what she called Italian rather than neoclassical, which I gather meant not as cold as the designs of men, or anyhow that's my interpretation.

I want to make it clear that Amanda, though real biased on the women's question to the point where I might call her slanted, still liked men well enough personally. This might be hard to understand, for it sure was for me in those days, and that probably was why Mrs. Palmer who was real forceful on the matter of female rights in general and was an ally of Jane Addams in helping working-class women, found it needful from time to time to announce she still thought that "in presiding over a happy home, a woman is fulfilling her highest function," and she always made it clear she wasn't no anarchist, in case it wasn't already apparent in somebody whose husband not only owned the fancy hotel but also their home on Lake Shore Drive, which was so enormous and luxurious it was called the Palmer Palace. When entertaining, Mrs. P. was said to wear a collar sporting seven diamonds and two thousand pearls.

Now to show you the difference between me and Amanda in our reactions, she condemned Mrs. Palmer for doing so little for others, whereas to my mind it was remarkable, being so rich and powerful, that Palmer's wife done anything at all.

Not that me and Amanda got into quarrels on these matters: we just each expressed our opinion, then listened to the other's, me because I was crazy about her, her at first probably on account of she believed I had saved her life, but then she gradually developed something more, though for a long time I couldn't believe it possible she could ever care for me except as the acquaintance I had always been.

Well, just one more incident occurring at the Fair.

The different states of the U.S.A. had each its own building boasting of its achievements and products, with the host, Illinois, naturally having the largest, though California weren't far behind, while Texas was a surprise at being only of average size. The states' area was behind the Fine Arts Palace at the north end of the exposition grounds, and the day me and Amanda had been looking at them paintings that I thought was swell and she didn't, we took a back exit and come out on 57th Street, right across which was the buildings of several states and beyond them a big comfort station, for which I was in need, having swallowed too much of Dr. Welch's grape juice, which I was possibly overdoing due to having gone teetotal as to stronger drink now I had the Hull House connection, where I didn't want to smell of it, as it was frowned on.

However, I considered it impolite to let on to Amanda that I had to take a leak, figuring the most graceful way was to stroll near the facility, and then take notice of it as if by chance. So we headed in that direction.

Now as it happened the Kansas Building was right where you turned to go along the walk to the comfort station, and I was just fixing to ask Amanda if she wanted to visit the display celebrating her native state, hoping she would decline at least at this moment, hearing the call of nature as I did, when I seen somebody I recognized just going in the Kansas door, or rather holding it for the lady with him to use first.

I tell you I forgot my need.

Amanda now and again held my arm when we walked nowadays, and this seemed to indicate warm feelings towards me, for she sure wouldn't of done it to be conventional. She was doing so right now.

"Say," I says, "will you look there at Kansas? We got to look in there. Suppose they have something about Dodge?"

Now, though I was distracted at this moment, I still remember what Amanda said. "I'll meet you inside." She dropped my arm and pointed up the path to the comfort station. "I have to take a pee first."

I had never even heard a sporting woman refer in such a literal fashion to a bodily function. But my shock wasn't as important as my realization of how close we had become if she could speak so freely.

However, I was not diverted long from the purpose at hand. I just had to see if it was who I thought it was, even before relieving myself, even before thinking further on the intimacy between me and Amanda, so I says okay and she went off and I entered the building.

Kansas did have displays based on the history of cattle camps like Dodge, Abilene, Wichita, and the rest, and its agricultural accomplishments with wheat and all, in celebration of which there was a big life-sized replica of the Liberty Bell made of stalks of grain all glued together, the kind of thing I thought real cunning but I doubted Amanda would.

I mention the bell because the man I was looking for had stopped in front of it with his lady. He was a tall, lean, mustachioed fellow in his mid-forties who hadn't changed much during the dozen years since I last seen him though he wasn't dressed in that dead black coat of the old days but a gray suit and a softer hat.

I got close enough to see him plain without him noticing me in particular. It was Wyatt Earp, sure enough, and while I had actually seen her only a few times in Tombstone and usually at a distance, the woman with him was likely Josie Marcus, who Allie always referred to as Sadie, still, though no Amanda, quite a looker, with her dark hair and eyes and, having put on a pound or two over the years, an even more curvaceous figure of the kind set off by the wasp-waist style of them days.

I'll admit I was amazed to see them still together, and not only because of the way Wyatt had treated his women in the past, but Josie herself supposedly come from a well-to-do family to have a career on the stage performing in places like Tombstone, which was only slightly above a harlot's level in society, and she had been Johnny Behan's kept woman before Wyatt took her off him. So when she was young she had been sowing her wild oats, but why had she stayed with Wyatt, who if I knowed him hadn't never, like most of his breed, made a killing except literally? Of all the celebrity Westerners I was ever acquainted with, only Buffalo Bill Cody made a success at business, but he hadn't ever been a gunfighter. Maybe young Henry Ford might of had some theory regarding Jewish women, of which Josie was supposed to be one, but I didn't have none for her and Wyatt as a pair except that they was in love.

That a woman could know Wyatt Earp for a dozen years and still put up with him give me hope for myself, because I was a much nicer fellow.

But now I was certain of his identity, I was in a quandary. Should I speak to him or not? And if I wasn't going to do so, why had I followed him in here, despite that pressing need to relieve myself? Some kind of instinct had took over. Pard would get a scent in the wind and stiffen his tail, a raised black stripe appearing along his spine, meaning, I figured, something like I SMELL A RAT.

I expect there might of been something of that in my reaction to Wyatt, but if so, why then stalk him unless I wanted to chew the fat about the good old days? The trouble was, I never considered them good at the time, insofar as they concerned him. Except for buffaloing me not once but twice — and being hit over the head with a .45 barrel you feel it for a week after — he barely spoke to me. I mean, I was on close terms with Wild Bill, Bat, Cody, the Prince of Wales, to name a few distinguished people who did not consider my friendship beneath them, but unless he was cracking my skull Wyatt Earp had always looked right through me.

Why, if I stepped up to him now, he likely not only wouldn't recall me by sight, he wouldn't even recognize the name. For ten years I had been associated with the premier attraction on earth, meeting the leaders of the world, and now was a respected member of the staff of Hull House, but more important than any of these was my friendship with a lady I esteemed above all others. Yet that bastard wouldn't even be civil to me!

I'm making fun of myself here. It was so long ago, I can look back with a certain evenhandedness, seeing at least some of my own failings. Wyatt had had reason both times he buffaloed me. I mean, he never just up and done it without no cause, and as for the rest I personally had against him, well, a man has a right to make such friends as he wishes — and Doc Holliday was supposed to of saved his life, which was more than I'd probably of done, because *I always thought him a son of a bitch and still did.*

Frankly, I never give him the chance to greet or snub me. Instead I did a rotten, sneaky thing. I had a mean streak in me at that time, which I hope I've outlived but probably haven't if riled.

The Fair had its own police force called the Columbian Guard, officers of which was all over the place in their smart gray uniforms and capes with a yellow lining, for in addition to the pocket-picking and purse-snatching such as happened to Jane Addams, the authorities was on the alert against any sign the visitors to the Exposition might form an uprising and overthrow the very civilization celebrated by the Fair, led by labor-union rabble-rousers or even foreign-born bomb-throwers, like them at the Haymarket Square seven years earlier, who really had killed a lot of people.

What I done now, and I ain't altogether proud of it, was take quick leave of the Kansas Building and find, not far outside, for there was thousands patrolling the grounds, a pair of them caped Columbian Guards.

I steps up, and mind you I was dressed respectable, so they was obliged to believe me, and I says, confidential-like so as not to alarm the passersby, "You fellows better get some reinforcements before you tackle this job, but you oughta know there's a dangerous anarchist inside Kansas at this minute. He's carrying a concealed firearm." This was likely to be the actual case: in later years I heard that Wyatt, then working as a boxing referee, got arrested for wearing a pistol in the ring, his excuse being he had enemies everywhere. "I think," I went on, "he's got a bomb as well. I heard him tell the woman with him he wants to blow up that Liberty Bell made of grain."

I gave Wyatt's description and that of Josie, who I said looked like Little Egypt from the "Street in Cairo," and them guards begun to blow their whistles to summon help.

I didn't wait there but went up the walk towards the comfort stations, meeting Amanda en route.

"The Kansas Building's just got a lot of stuff about the cattle business," I told her. "I doubt you'd be interested."

"Someone told me the horse that survived the Little Bighorn is displayed there in a stuffed form," Amanda says, wrinkling her newly powdered nose in disapproval.

Due to my spite against Wyatt Earp, I had forgot entirely about old Comanche. Well, neither him nor me could do each other any good by now.

"Yeah," I says, "who wants to see that?" Then I excused myself and finally went where I probably should of gone in the first place, and afterwards we left the Fair by the nearby exit. I never heard what happened with Wyatt at that time, and I expect I ought to be ashamed of what I done, but for some reason, though I know it was wrong, and reflects badly on my character, I ain't.

23

Doing Well

I N T H E D A Y S F O L L O W I N G T H A T S I G H T I N G O F WYATT
Earp, I brooded a good deal on the situation which I was apparently
stuck with lifelong, namely, being naturally attracted to a lady superior to me in most every department.

But you might well ask why I never done more to improve myself, beginning with trying to use better English. Well, to be fair to me, I did and
though I would talk better for a while, it didn't stick for long at a time. I
remember that German friend of mine back at the Major's school, Klaus
Kappelhaus, told me he knowed how to talk better in his adopted language than you would think if you heard him only late in the day when
he was tired. . . . Which reminds me of how tired I am at this minute, after talking so long into this machine since my last rest, way back when
telling of our second trip to Europe, but I got so much to relate and so
little time.

So I did improve my speech by picking up words and grammar from
Amanda, along with the other ladies on the staff at Hull House, and I
even tried some of Buffalo Bill's rhetorical flourishes, which I admit impressed me all the more for him having no more education than me, but
Amanda generally caught these right away and warned me against them.

I already mentioned acquiring an up-to-date city wardrobe and learning how to act like I belonged there when in respectable restaurants, tea-
rooms, and the like. Books still scared me, for even in the smallest of
them there was so much printed all at once, so I was working my way up
to them by starting with newspapers, which I had seldom read previously, and I didn't take to them much now so far as content went, but I

realized certain sacrifices was necessary if I was ever to be worthy of Amanda's friendship.

However, I was also convinced I'd basically stay a sow's ear no matter how much effort was expended towards achieving another result, and that accounted for what looked like a permanent despair on my part. It seemed pretty clear that my use to Amanda would be at an end once she had exhausted what I had to offer for that book she was writing. Which by the way, if you think by now she wasn't ever going to, for I believe that is the case with many who prepare for such a job for a long time, you are wrong.

She had already wrote several chapters by this point and read them aloud to me from her manuscript while we sat side by side on a park bench, and it was the truest commentary I ever heard from a white person on Indians, and not only because of all the information I had furnished her with but what she added by way of interpretation, not to mention how it was wrote, which even exceeded my high expectations. Every once in a while I would ask her to repeat a certain passage just for the grace and authority of her language. She wasn't given to writing pretty but rather true, and there was a beauty in that.

Unfortunately, the finer I considered her achievement, the more discouraged I was about myself, for apart from the Indian lore I could impart, what else was left?

Well, maybe a sense of fun, which apparently had been missing hitherto in Amanda's life. I actually got her to go with me to the building at the Fair called Manufactures and Liberal Arts, a name itself which made her snicker for some reason, and look at a knight on horseback modeled in California prunes, a chocolate statue of Venus de Milo, and a recognizable map of the U.S.A. at a distance, which when you got close turned out to be an arrangement of pickles. The last-named made Amanda laugh out loud, something she was lately doing more and more, I guess as a result of knowing me better. I had had this effect on many people, always with the exception of Wyatt Earp.

"Amanda," I said at this point, "you want to go down to the Casino and ride the moving sidewalk?" The former was the building where you would wait for the excursion boats on Lake Michigan, and then go out on the pier to board them by means of the latter, which according to the Wild West cowboys lived up to its name, a sidewalk that was one big conveyor belt, operated by electricity.

"And take a cruise?" she asked with a little knowing grin, being aware of my feeling about boats larger than a gondola on an enclosed waterway without waves.

"Why, sure," I says. "If you really want to, I'm game. Or we could just go on board the *Santa Maria*. I know you don't think much of Columbus, but if you see that dinky little ship of his, you'll have to admit he done a remarkable job in getting here at all."

As I say, we didn't ever argue with bad personal feeling, like the other person was a fool or scoundrel, but nevertheless always held to our own positions, hers being that the mischief resulting from Columbus coming to the New World probably outweighed the good, whereas mine held that somebody was sure to of done it sooner or later with the same results, for such was the natural itch of mankind to go to wild places and tame them, and of all the examples of such throughout the world, America was by far the best result even if not yet perfect.

But Amanda was in a funny mood today, and I couldn't get her going. "I expect you're right, Jack," says she, winking her blue eye, "ole Chris was better than most."

"Are you making fun of me?"

"Of course," she says, bumping me with her hip real saucily, which some old biddy seen and scowled at as we strolled out of Manufactures and Liberal Arts onto the lakeshore walk.

"You're getting mighty fresh, as well," I noted.

"Someone has to," said she.

Lake Michigan, as I have pointed out, might as well of been an ocean when you looked at it from the shore. You couldn't see across it in any direction, and it got real rough in a wind, of which Chicago was seldom without. I looked at today's whitecaps and said, "I guess when he closes here Cody will want to go back to Europe." I didn't know any such fact, as I hadn't talked to him on the subject, but was saying so now for effect.

"And you'll be going along," Amanda said rather than asked.

I scraped my foot a little. "I don't know about that."

"Jack," said she, "I've seen you at moments when you could have been killed, and you had more confidence than you've ever shown with me."

"You're right about that, Amanda." I was amazed she understood. "It's probably because I seen a lot of dying and know what to expect. I ain't, uh, haven't ever been able to figure you out."

"You don't know whether I like you or not," said she.

"By golly, you're right again!" I says loud enough so we was stared at again by passersby.

"Well, I do," said Amanda. "I like you, Jack. I like you a whole lot. I should have told you that before."

I had quite an elated feeling. "Oh, that's all right, Amanda, I realize a lady ain't supposed to speak first —" I stopped, on account of she just had. "That is, I mean —"

"You ought to know by now that I care little about what others, usually men, present company excepted, ordain that women should do. At quite a young age I was married for a short time to that sort of person."

"I'll be damned," I said before I could catch myself.

A gust of wind come off the lake at that point, threatening her hat, which she had to grab, but she was smiling at me.

"Amanda," I says, "and if this is insulting to you, feel free to —"

"Jack, will you stop pussyfootin' around?"

She was making fun of me again, but I never minded. In fact I thought it was nice. "Well, what I wanted to ask you is if you would want to get married, again. I mean, to me."

But now I had gotten it out, I flinched inwardly at how crude I sounded. I hadn't even said I cared for her. So when she answered as she did, I wasn't surprised.

"No," said she.

"Well, at least I got the nerve to say it." And at that, my own skimmer straw was seized by a sudden violent blast of wind and sent on a whirling flight that ended out in Lake Michigan, where the hat bit into the water with the brim, like the blade of a circular saw, which meant it sunk as quick as my hopes just had.

But when my eyes come back to Amanda, she was still smiling sweetly. "I didn't say," said she, "that I wouldn't live with you."

Now I was real shocked. "Don't talk like that, Amanda. It ain't decent."

She snorted in derision. "Jack," she said, "you used to tend bar in a whorehouse!"

"Yeah," I says, "but they was whores."

"I played piano in another," Amanda said, "and didn't work upstairs, but maybe I was corrupted all the same."

"No!" I says. "That couldn't be true."

"Not the least interesting thing about you," Amanda noted, "is that while you tend toward cynicism in most other areas of human behavior, you are mawkishly sentimental about women."

"I thought it was you who was always sticking up for them," I said, "not wanting them mistreated. Your Ma, way back in Dodge, told me you even believed women should vote."

She wrinkled her brow to pretend to be irked. "Jack, are you sassing me?"

"Oh, no, Amanda, now don't you —" At that point I realized she asked that with her tongue in her cheek, and I stopped, but didn't have nothing better to say than, "Well . . ."

Amanda was laughing, which made her somewhat less beautiful, her features being more elegant in repose, but also made her less distant. I had begun over these weeks to slowly replace my worship of her with genuine enjoyment of her company, but had not understood that till now.

"It's true," I says, "Wild Bill Hickok never lasted long after he finally got married, whereas I heard in Tombstone that none of the Earps ever actually married any of the women they lived with, and Virgil and Allie sure seemed happy, and if the same principle applied to Wyatt and Josie, they are still together after a dozen years."

"Jack," Amanda says now, "are you talking to yourself? You're mumbling."

"Sorry, I guess I was. Say, maybe we ought to get something to eat instead. What's your pleasure, the Swedish Restaurant, the Polish Café, the Japanese Tea House, or the Clambake? Unless you don't want to be seen with a man without a hat."

"Jack, you got a yella streak where your spine oughta be," says Amanda, imitating me further, which made it hard to stay serious.

"You gonna keep that up when we're living together?" I said it lightheartedly, but the idea still shocked me, I admit.

"Probably," she said, "if it works now."

"Oh, it works," I says, "but you oughta be ashamed of yourself."

"For what?" She was laughing while hanging onto her hat again with one hand, the other fastened tight to me.

"Corrupting my morals," I says.

You can see Amanda was a real modern woman, advanced beyond her time.

I read in a newspaper that all politics is local, and maybe all discovery comes down to that point as well. Whatever Columbus means to others, pro or con, I'll always be grateful for the favor he done me: Amanda.

Well, I'm going to tell you about what became of me and her during the best period of my life, what happened with her book, what kind of work I done next and where, for the Fair ended in October of '93 and while I was technically speaking a middle-aged man, I had lived not quite half my life at that point, so there's lots left to relate of what still for some time was my competent years, with quite a bit happening, in the world at my disposal, as the nineteenth century turned into the twentieth: for example, Tom Edison begun to make moving pictures to be shown in theaters rather than just peep machines, gold was discovered in the Klondike, and Colonel Teddy Roosevelt's Rough Riders fought in a battle at Santiago de Cuba, not on horseback as you might think but on foot, and took a hill with the name of Kettle and not San Juan. Who would straighten you out on such details but me?

I had some kind of connection with them events and more, and as usual you might hear a somewhat different version from me than from them with axes to grind. All I ever tell is what I seen and heard for myself.

Right now, though, I got to take a nap. If I ever wake up, you sure will hear the rest of my story.

Printed in the United States
27629LVS00001BA/175-177